CU00917988

THE VULCAN
AND THE STRAITS

Jox McNabb Thrillers
Book Four

Patrick Larsimont

SAPERE
BOOKS

THE VULCAN
AND THE STRAITS

Patrick Loriral.

Published by Sapere Books.

24 Trafalgar Road, Ilkley, LS29 8HH

saperebooks.com

Copyright © Patrick Larsimont, 2024

Patrick Larsimont has asserted his right to be identified as the
author of this work.
All rights reserved.

No part of this publication may be reproduced, stored in any
retrieval system, or transmitted, in any form, or by any means,
electronic, mechanical, photocopying, recording, or otherwise,
without the prior written permission of the publishers.
This book is a work of fiction. Names, characters, businesses,
organisations, places and events, other than those clearly in the
public domain, are either the product of the author's
imagination, or are used fictitiously.
Any resemblances to actual persons, living or dead, events or
locales are purely coincidental.

ISBN: 978-0-85495-261-8

For my beloved parents-in-law, June and Peter Neale.
Reunited again.
Peter served all over the world as RAF ground crew after the war.
His older brother John was a Spitfire pilot serving in Burma during the
war.
Per Ardua Ad Astra.

PROLOGUE

London, 1991

'I'm sorry this isn't much of a date.' Doctor Melanie McNabb turned to her boyfriend, Luc. 'Looking through a bunch of old photographs is hardly me showing you London's high life. You'll think me very dull and end up mocking me in the mess. I know what you soldiers are like.'

'I'm delighted you think you know me so well,' replied Captain Luc de Ghellinck, sitting on the sofa beside her in her Fulham flat. 'There's nothing boring about this, *pas du tout*, on a wet and dreary afternoon in rainy London. I have a fine bottle of wine, the company of a beautiful woman, and together we're looking at evidence that our lives have been intertwined long before we ever met. What could possibly be dull about that?'

Melanie and Luc had met a few months ago at her uncle David Pritchard's funeral — a decorated war veteran who had served with Melanie's grandfather, Jeremy 'Jox' McNabb. Their romance had progressed since then. They were now at the point of declaring they were 'exclusive', and Melanie would soon meet Luc's parents. His father, *Chevalier* Olivier de Ghellinck had been her grandfather's great friend and wartime comrade.

'Ooh, you *are* a silver-tongued rascal. Nancy warned me that I'd have to watch out for you.' Nancy Wake had been Pritchard's 'special friend', and she'd described Luc and Melanie's first meeting at the funeral as a *coup de foudre*, a lightning strike. Nancy knew about such things; during the war she had been a Special Operations Executive agent, codenamed the 'White Mouse' by the Germans, and considered the deadliest SOE agent in the whole of occupied France.

'Nancy is indeed a wise woman, and I would never disagree with such a *fameuse* resistance fighter, but everything I ever learnt about being a gentleman was from my father,' said Luc. 'During the war he was just known as Ghillie and has always said it was his great friend and mentor, Jox McNabb, who taught him everything he knew.'

'My Grandpa Bang-Bang,' Melanie replied, referring to her childhood nickname for Jox.

Luc smiled and took a sip of his wine. 'Your Grandpa Bang-Bang.' He reached into the ridged metal cannister on the coffee table before them. It was filled with a mass of curling black and white photographs. The shabby tin of pressed metal had a clasped lid, and to the casual observer was fairly unimpressive. However, they both knew that it was an *Afrika Korps* gasmask tube, complete with the palm tree and swastika logo on the lid. It had come a very long way from Tunisia and languished for many years in Jox's home in the gamekeeper's lodge on the Dundonald Estate in Perthshire. He'd used it as a handy place to keep snapshots and half-remembered memories, some treasured, others too painful to recall. It had been part of Melanie's childhood for as long as she could remember.

'Here they are together.' Luc held up a fading snapshot of two airmen, bare headed in the evening sun, wearing shorts and standing in front of the dark silhouette of a Spitfire Mark IX in the livery of a night fighter. Melanie peered at it, then looked on the back. It said '333, The Black Pigs, Malta '43.' She flipped it over. 'What are they doing with their fingers?'

Luc took the picture and looked closely too. '*La hur du sanglier*,' he replied. 'The boar's head, you see, for the Black

Pigs. The emblem is on the aircraft. See, their fingers are like the boar's tusks.' He curled his forefingers and held them to his face and suddenly squealed like a pig.

Melanie jumped at the loud noise and they both dissolved into giggles. 'You're a man of many talents,' she said.

Luc looked again at the photograph and passed it to her. 'My father's aircraft bore his sister's name, *Véronique*.' He took another sip of his wine. 'My father fought his war in his sister's name, whilst she stayed in Belgium with her children, working with the resistance and not yet knowing if she was a widow or not. I joined my regiment, *Les Chasseurs Ardennais*, the same regiment my aunt's husband fought in before he died in the war, to honour her.' He pointed to the picture. 'This photo dates to when my father and his great friend Axel Fisken had just transferred from the Treble Ones to join Jox as his flight leaders. It was a great honour for them.'

'They both seem so young, and yet they had the weight of the world on their shoulders,' Melanie replied, 'but somehow they still seem to be enjoying themselves.'

'I often think it's *incroyable* that they lived through so much at such a young age. I'm not sure I could have handled it.'

'I'm not sure they always did. My grandfather had terrible nightmares all of my life. I've no doubt it would have been diagnosed as post-traumatic stress disorder now.'

'My father was the same. My mother always said that's why they had separate beds. He flailed around too much.'

Melanie peered again at the snap. 'You do look like your father.' Luc had the same pale eyes, slim face and long aristocratic nose as *Chevalier* Olivier de Ghellinck.

He took her hand. 'And you look like your grandfather, although may I say, rather prettier.' He leant across and kissed her, then reached for another snapshot, this time in colour. It showed a young blonde girl wearing a blue spotted swimsuit, red-faced and looking rather hot. 'Is this you?' he asked, turning it over to see it was annotated with 'Sandbanks, Dorset, Summer 1976'.

'It is, but I was rather hot and grumpy. I would've been about twelve. Britain was going through the longest heatwave on record and Grandpa Bang-Bang had spent the last ten minutes covering me in sun lotion.'

'That seems reasonable; your shoulders are already freckled and do look a little red.'

'That's my peely-wally, milk-bottle-white Scottish skin he was so keen to protect.'

'Hardly seems a reason to be in such a bad mood with him.'

She smiled wistfully. 'No, that wasn't it. In my annoying twelve-year-old way I'd asked him a question he didn't want to answer. He was a man of many secrets, my grandfather. There were things he didn't want to talk about, things he didn't want to remember.'

'My father's like that, only opening up to my mother and old comrades. What had you asked him?'

'I asked him why he never talked about the war. Whenever I posed him a question like that, he'd look up into the sky, but never answer. This time was different though.'

'Different, how?'

'This time he answered. It had a profound effect on me, and I might even say it changed the direction of my life.'

'Wow, if you're comfortable, please tell me.'

'Well, we had an ice-cream and he said he'd take me somewhere that might explain why he didn't like talking about the war. We would need to get dressed and that I should be on my best behaviour. I remember agreeing, but starting to feel perhaps I shouldn't have asked. He warned me, "It's a solemn place, my darling, with a very sad story attached." I said something like, "That's all right, Grandpa, I can handle it." He looked so forlorn when he replied, "Yes, my darling, but can your old Grandpa Bang-Bang handle it?"

'We drove along the tree-lined avenues of Bournemouth in Grandpa's open-topped Triumph Spitfire. Seagulls and wood pigeons were overhead, and it felt like we were racing against them. Grandpa had bought the car a few years earlier, choosing the colour because he said it was RAF blue. He'd even had *Marguerite* lettered on her bonnet.' Luc smiled but didn't interrupt, aware that *Marguerite* was the name Jox had always had inscribed on his planes. 'I loved that car and liked to trail my fingers in the cool airstream, with my grandfather's white silk scarf wrapped around my neck. I thought I was the epitome of glamour.

'Grandpa had put on his RAF tie and jacket, even though it was quite warm. He'd insisted I put on my white flannel trousers, despite everyone in the sunny streets of Bournemouth being in shorts and T-shirts. Grandpa never did much like the fashion of the seventies, hating the long hair, calling it scruffy. I guess for a professional soldier, it all seemed rather slovenly and unkempt. In his world, things should always be done properly, especially if old comrades-in-arms were involved.

'We pulled into the car park of Bournemouth North Cemetery and Crematorium. It wasn't very busy, as I suppose few people would choose to visit their dearly departed in such scorching weather. The cemetery's trees were brown-leaved and rustled in the warm breeze. Large patches of yellowed grass had grown around abandoned graves, the stalks dry and parched, trembling in the shimmering heat. I remember the paths between the different sections of the cemetery were brown and dusty on my toes in my bright red flip-flops. Grandpa was holding my hand. He seemed to know where he was going, and I just followed without paying too much attention.

'We came to a weathered wooden panel with details of the Second World War graves that were located within the cemetery grounds. Grandpa explained that there were seventy-five buried in a section maintained by the Commonwealth War Graves Commission. This area was green, precisely mown and surrounded by a rectangular yew hedge.

'He pointed out the towering Cross of Sacrifice made of carved stone and bearing a bronze sword. He began searching amongst the rows of pale sandstone, each carved with either a winged eagle, a maple leaf or a fern crest. There were some flowers and shrubs planted at the feet of the stones, but the vegetation was dry and struggling under the drought conditions.

'He stopped at the third row, off to the left, seemed confused for a moment, then found what he was looking for. I was watching him, beginning to feel a deep sense of dread. I'd noticed that all these people had died on the same date. "What happened on the 23rd of May, 1943, Grandpa?" I asked, my voice quavering.

'He let out a mighty sigh, like he was in physical pain. "There was a terrible air raid on Bournemouth. It was a beautiful day, just like today. It was the week after the famous Dambuster raids, and the newspapers were full of the story. I was due to meet some friends for lunch."

'I had already worked out that something terrible must have happened for his story to end up here. He began rubbing his damp eyes with those scarred hands of his. "Twenty-six Focke-Wulf 190 fighter-bombers came from the sea, each carrying a single bomb. I think one was shot down, and another crashed, but twenty-four dropped their loads on the town in a terrifying high-speed attack. Afterwards, they flew over the crowded streets and parks, machine-gunning the crowds, then headed back across the Channel before our own fighters could react. Over a hundred civilians were killed, plus twenty-two airmen, including Brits, Canadians, Australians and Americans. Two of them were my great friends."

"'Who?" I asked, terrified of the answer.

'He raised his hand and pointed. "You know how I sometimes talk about my great friend Moose from Canada? Well, this is the grave of one of the best and most faithful men I've ever known. His name was Maurice 'Moose' Grant, and he's buried here beside his wife, Stephanie. They were killed by the bomb that hit the Metropole Hotel, as they waited for me to join them for a celebration lunch."

'I looked where he was pointing. Two gravestones were side by side, a little separated from the rest. I remember, they were inscribed with Moose's name, and that of his wife, who had been a codebreaker at Bletchley Park.

'Grandpa had tears in his eyes, something that I rarely saw, and it frightened me. I hated to see him so upset. I'd seen a picture of Moose up at the house in Scotland. He'd always looked so big and strong, like an invincible giant.

'Grandpa put his hand on the headstone. "My old pal Moose was a big Canuck. Steadfast and strong, right from the very earliest days of our training together. I loved him like a brother. But that's not the saddest part of this story, my darling." I could tell he was trying hard to control his emotions. "You remember, I said we were meeting up for a celebratory lunch?"

'I nodded, terrified about what he would reveal.

"'Moose had shared something he wasn't supposed to. Stephanie was pregnant. Their baby was due in November. He was desperate to tell me that if the child was a boy, he would name him Jeremy Argyll Easton Grant." Grandpa was watching my face very closely. "If they had a girl, she would be Melanie Alexandra Florence Grant, named after Stephanie's grandmother."

'I blurted out, "But those are my names, Grandpa!"

"'Yes, they are my darling," he replied, taking my hand. "You're named after that unborn baby who died with her parents. Years later, when your mother was pregnant with you, I begged her to name you after that lost child. As a tribute to a life never lived." He gave a heartbroken smile. "It's such a sad story, but hopefully now you understand why I don't like talking about the war."

'I remember looking down at his scarred old hands, noticing for the first time two raised lumps between his thumb and forefinger. "What happened to your hands, Grandpa?"

"'There are many more sad stories that I'll tell you one day. Far too many, and whilst yes, there were thrills and spills, underneath there was nothing but tragedy. I still struggle to keep that pain from my mind." He knelt before me. "Now, this is really important for you to understand. Your generation and the ones that come after, will soon start to forget the sacrifices my generation made for your tomorrows. Please, promise me, my darling, that you'll never forget what Grandpa Bang-Bang and his pals, so many brave men and women, did for this country and many others."

'I looked at my grandfather. I searched his wrinkled face for any clue to the torment I knew these memories brought back. I squeezed his hands and said as solemnly as I could manage, "Yes, Grandpa, I promise, for the rest of my life."'

Melanie turned to Luc as she finished her story. 'You know, I kept that promise, dedicating my work and career as a historian to remembering what they all did for us.'

'What an incredible story,' said Luc with tears in his own eyes.

Melanie squeezed his hand. 'Anyway, that's enough reminiscing. We have a dinner reservation and you promised to take me somewhere nice.'

'*Ah oui*, and again my father's recommendation. *L'Escargot* is the oldest French restaurant in London. It's in Soho. During the war it's where de Gaulle and the Free French did all their plotting and scheming, over plates of garlic and parsley *Escargots à la Bourguignonne*. He and your grandfather enjoyed them many times when together in town.' He laughed. 'They would always have dinner there, then end up in the RAF Club on Piccadilly or the Royal Anglo-Belgian Club on Belgrave Square.'

'Snails! I really can't imagine my Grandpa Bang-Bang eating snails. He only ever liked the plainest of foods.'

'No, no, *vraiment*, he was really quite the fan,' said Luc. 'The two of them were even members of *L'Escargot*'s snail club. My father said as they aged, the club's motto, "Slow and sure," rather suited them.'

'Okay, then,' laughed Melanie. 'Anything Grandpa Bang-Bang can do, I can do too. Let's go have some *escargot*s.'

CHAPTER ONE

11th November, 1942

The coast of North Africa should have been in sight by now. What Flight Lieutenant Jox McNabb saw before him certainly wasn't what he'd been expecting. Instead of sun-blasted shores, he was flying in leaden clouds, squally rain lashing against the canopy of his Spitfire. The flight from Gibraltar had been bumpy and even his cast-iron gut was struggling. He gasped oxygen from his mask, hoping to settle his nausea.

What Jox and the Treble Ones were embarking upon tonight was Operation Torch, the Allied invasion of French North Africa, which had begun a few days earlier. This was the first large-scale deployment of US ground troops in the North African theatre, with air and seaborne assaults in support. The main thrust from British and Commonwealth forces was coming from Libya and Egypt in the east, but here in the north, the three-pronged American-led attack targeted Casablanca in Morocco, Oran in Algeria and Algiers, near the border with Tunisia.

Jox was still recovering from his experience in the parched desert sands of Libya. It was his Belgian squadron mate, Olivier 'Ghillie' de Ghellinck, who'd somehow managed to find him in the featureless expanse of rock and sand, plucking him from danger in the midst of the Second Battle of El Alamein. He had been suffering from exposure and dehydration but was now deemed fit enough to re-join his squadron in Gibraltar.

Jox tapped the compass on his dashboard, checking his heading was still good. He looked for signs of the squadron, wiping the condensation from the inside of the Perspex canopy with his glove. What a peasouper.

His return to the squadron was welcomed by the boys, many of whom had given him up for lost. Squadron Leader Tony 'Bolshie' Bartley, in particular, had feared he'd lost both of his flight commanders, since Jox's great friend, David 'Pritch' Pritchard had been sent home for rest and recovery. Pritch was washed out by the desert war, not to mention the nasty bout of 'Pharaoh's Revenge' he'd picked up in the bars and fleshpots of Alexandria.

If Jox's own bout of 'Malta Dog', picked up during the siege, was anything to go by, he didn't envy his friend's predicament. A quiet spell at a training wing as an instructor would do Pritch the world of good. It was somehow reassuring to think of his pal out of harm's way. He'd miss him, as in the close-knit family of the wartime RAF, old friends are rare and precious.

Whilst Jox was in hospital, the squadron's sections had been shuffled around. Ferdinand 'Jimmy' Baraldi had replaced Pritch to lead A Flight and Jox would lead B, which included the long-time Treble Ones like his aristocratic desert rescuer Ghillie de Ghellinck, the deadly Norwegian Axel Fisken, Australian pilot Shane 'Kanga' Reeves and Ralph Campbell, who Jox had been at school with.

As the formation approached the coastline of Algeria, Jox exhaled with relief. The bumpy three-hour flight from The Rock had taken longer than anticipated due to a strong headwind and the unfamiliar drag of the Vokes filters. The squadron had been issued new Spitfire Mark IXs, replacing the worn-out Mark Vs they'd been flying in the harsh desert conditions. The replacement aircraft had been tropicalised with

Vokes Aerovee filters, designed to protect their Merlin 60 engines from the Sahara's abrasive sands.

Jox hoped that, given the time of day and the poor weather conditions, they wouldn't make contact with the enemy. On this dark, wet and windy morning, the Treble Ones' part in Operation Torch wasn't starting particularly well.

'WAGON aircraft, this is WAGON Leader,' said Squadron Leader Bartley. 'Report fuel status.'

Replies from the sixteen aircraft confirmed what had been feared, they were running short. They were due to patrol over seaborne units coming into the Bay of Algiers, then land at Maison Blanche airfield, in the suburb of Dar El Beïda in eastern Algeria. Getting there was proving a challenge.

'WAGON Green Leader, WAGON Blue Leader, can your flights make it?' Bartley asked his flight commanders.

'We can only try,' replied Jox. 'Not looking too good, I'm pretty much on fumes.'

'Aye, I'm in the same boat,' confirmed Baraldi, his west of Scotland accent distinct on the R/T. 'I cannae see a damned thing. My eyes are playing up. At this rate I could miss the whole of Africa. We need to get over land pronto, I don't fancy ending up in the drink —' Baraldi's chatter was interrupted by an urgent voice.

'Blue Three here. My engine's just died, I'm going in. I'll do my best to slow my glide but I'm losing altitude fast. Turning south, trying to reach landfall…' Blue Three was Barry 'Gusty' Gale in Baraldi's flight, an Australian pilot.

'That's a tough break, Blue Three,' said Bartley. 'Blue Four from WAGON Leader, follow your mate down and take note of his final location. You should be all right, Gusty, there's plenty of friendlies down there. Just hope the trigger-happy sods don't start taking potshots at you.'

'All right, mate, gotcha,' replied Gusty.

Jox searched the grey tiers of cloud stacked high above him. He looked down to where it had cleared a little. Minute vessels dotted the slate-coloured water. He scanned the turbulent skies for his flight, spotting several in a loose double 'finger-four' formation, as they bumped through swirling thermals. Lower and to the rear, was a single Spit in a shallow descent on a tangent away from the formation. He was pursued by a second, which Jox identified by its squadron and aircraft identifiers, JU-V. His own bore JU-X, plus the name *Marguerite* scrawled on the fuselage alongside a rough drawing of an arm holding a Scottish claymore. The former was in homage to a little French girl he'd been unable to save during the Battle of France, the latter to honour his Scottish heritage.

Instinctively, Jox reached for the pocket of his flight blouse and gave the hard lump within a squeeze. It was the real Marguerite's porcelain doll's arm, a peculiar talisman that had seen him through thick and thin. Despite being battered and cracked, he found the cool, hard porcelain reassuring against his chest.

'Oh damn, I'm out too,' blurted Kanga Reeves. 'Sorry, boys, this cobber's going to get his feet wet before reaching Algeria.' It sounded like he was looking forward to it. Reeves was a real 'water baby', a keen surfer and sailor, who had mystified the crofters in the north of Scotland by swimming with the grey seals even during the peak of the October storms.

'Damn it,' said Jox. 'Roger, Yellow One. This is Green Leader. Listen, Shane, you know the drill. Make sure the canopy is well back before you decide whether to brolly-hop or ditch. You've still got enough height, but watch out, that water looks choppy. Plenty of traffic down there, so your chute should be visible. Our Navy pals will be along in a jiffy. Good luck, mate.'

'No worries, Jox. Should have worn my swimmers. Right, cheerio cobbers, one way or another I'll see you on the other side.' Reeves was already a few thousand feet below them when the aircraft barrel-rolled and, once inverted, fell away. Jox lost sight of the plane against the dark sea, but when the chute popped, it was stark against the water. Reeves was a strong swimmer, so if anyone stood a chance in the drink it was him.

'Damn,' fumed Bartley over the R/T. 'I can't have the whole bloody squadron drop out of the sky. Come on, boys, tighten up, we can make it. Longers, you stick with me,' he added to his wingman, Sergeant George Longbottom.

The skies were lightening from the east, providing a scant source of optimism. Appearing through the thinning clouds was an impressive panorama of massed ships, some moored, others moving across the vast harbour of Algiers. It was unlikely that any downed pilot would be missed, as long as he made it down safely. Naval vessels of all sizes churned the choppy water, leaving frothy wakes like slug trails across a garden patio.

After several tense minutes they droned over the coastline. The city was bathed in smoke rising from several fires and signs of recent battle were everywhere. Algiers' elegant squares and boulevards were debris-strewn, fire-streaked and bomb-cratered. The hulks of destroyed armour and burnt-out fortifications were scattered across the landscape.

'Shouldn't be far,' said Bartley with a degree of wishful thinking. 'There's the airfield up ahead. Right, chaps, get down anywhere you can. It doesn't have to be pretty.'

Jox searched the horizon and spotted the straight lines of concrete runways alongside a row of corrugated iron hangars. Their sheets were perforated with ragged holes, evidence of heavy fighting before the airfield fell. Burnt-out vehicles and the charred remains of aircraft were everywhere, with extensive cratering and traces of recently extinguished fires.

'Jox, Ralph here,' said a quavering Scot's accent. 'Sorry, I mean, Green Leader, this is Green Four. My engine just died. I can see the aerodrome but I'm not sure I can make it.' It was Ralph Campbell. 'Christ, Jox, I'm too low to bale out and the ground's coming up fast. Might make the fence, but that runway is full of junk and it's going to be a rough landing.'

Jox pulled out of his own approach and swung back around the aerodrome, intent on finding Campbell and coaching him down. He spotted Campbell's cruciform silhouette low on the horizon.

'Keep calm, Ralph, you know what to do. Full flaps, just short of stall and keep the nose up.' Campbell was wobbling and still several hundred yards from the fence. 'Take it nice and slow.'

The aircraft glided over the fence line, it's front wheels just clearing the top. The fixed rear wheel on the tail assembly clipped it and became tangled in a coil of barbed wire. It unwound like a giant spring, slowing the aircraft's momentum and pitching it onto its nose. Propeller blades ground into the concrete runway, gouging like a giant cat's claws. The kite tipped forward, then was jerked backwards as if tethered, a convincing impression of an arresting cable on an aircraft carrier.

The Spit came to a halt in a crumpled heap, miraculously still in one piece. If it hadn't run dry, this is when fire was likely, which explained why Campbell vacated his cockpit, jumping out like a scalded cat. Unlike the said cat who always lands on its feet, Campbell collapsed onto the concrete after tumbling off the wing. Jox feared he was hurt, but he struggled to his feet and limped away as fast as he could manage.

Jox exhaled a whistle of relief. Now it was his turn to make it onto the hard deck. He swung low over Maison Blanche a second time, lining up as best he could between the hazards littering the field. His fuel-starved engine coughed as he touched down, the last fumes in the tank exhausted. Using his momentum, he taxied towards the battered metal hangars, parking alongside Bartley's aircraft, identifiable by the JU-B on the fuselage.

He pulled up short and braked. Unclipping his straps, he struggled to his feet and stood on the seat. Head and shoulders out of the cockpit, he found Bartley huddled on the concrete, beneath the wing of his aircraft. His head was bowed with elbows on his knees. In a sweaty pile between his feet lay his goggles, leather flying helmet, flight gloves and Mae West. His face looked utterly dejected, shoulders heaving, overcome by his emotions.

Jox ran over to offer what comfort he could. There would certainly be hell to pay. The squadron had lost three brand new aircraft, with not a shot fired. This was a far from auspicious start for the Treble Ones' campaign in North Africa. The failure was weighing heavily on Bartley's shoulders and by the look of things, he wasn't coping well. Jox put a comforting hand on Bartley's shoulder until his sobs subsided.

Bartley heaved a sigh and looked up, red-eyed and embarrassed. 'Right, I suppose for better or worse we ought to get this shit show going.'

CHAPTER TWO

'What a dump,' said Bolshie Bartley, the following afternoon, confirming his nickname. 'Have you seen the state of the bogs? I know this place took a pasting, but it looks like the Vichy French never looked after it. Maison Blanche is supposed to be Algiers' main aerodrome, but it's completely dilapidated. Can you imagine if we let Croydon get into this state?'

Jox looked up from his newspaper. He knew very well what state the war had left Croydon in. Several Treble One ground crew were killed there during the terrible raid of the 15th of August, at the height of the Battle of Britain.

'Good job we're moving on,' said Bartley, rubbing raw eyes with his knuckles.

Jox was trying to decipher what the newspaper was saying but only had his schoolboy French to work with. He hadn't figured out yet if it was a Vichy or Free French rag, but there were certainly a lot of pictures of plump French generals raising and lowering flags. He was surprised to see illustrations of heroic, bare-breasted Marianne figures, complete with doves, flags and rifles with long pointed bayonets. As a Muslim country, he'd expected Algeria to have frowned on that sort of thing. Perhaps this was the celebrated French *joie de vivre* he'd heard so much about.

'So, what's the gen?' Jox asked. 'New orders come through?'

'Nothing specific,' replied Bartley. 'But the Vichy forces are collapsing faster than expected. The Yanks have only encountered a few pockets of determined resistance and despite the weather, Casablanca, the main Atlantic naval base, has already been captured. Oran surrendered quickly and here in Algiers things weren't as tough as anticipated either. The commander of the Vichy French forces, Admiral François Darlan, switched sides and has ordered his troops to cooperate. Our American friends are rather pleased their first large scale operation has gone so well. They've appointed Darlan as High Commissioner of France for North and West Africa. That's him in your paper with the tall hat and all that gold braid.'

Jox flicked back to a thin-faced man with grey hair and a hat covered with scrambled egg.

'Apparently, we're letting the French get on with it and will be relocating closer to the Tunisian border, where Jerry can be found,' said Bartley. 'They'll be tougher to crack, with plenty of veteran air units equipped with those bloody Focke-Wulf 190s and the latest Bf 109 *Gustav* variants. Good job we're in new Mark IXs, the bad news is we've already lost three of them.'

'We should count ourselves lucky, it could have been worse,' replied Jox. 'We might have had another Morlaix disaster on our hands.' Jox was thinking of the American squadron he'd been leading after Dieppe. When blown off course, they'd run out of fuel, and all had been lost. He'd only escaped because he'd turned back early with engine problems.

'Ah, sorry, Jox,' replied Bartley, pulling a face. 'Didn't mean to rub salt in the wound. Apologies, old boy.'

'No offence taken,' said Jox. 'I just think we're lucky that all three pilots made it back, more or less all right. Ralph has knackered his ankle, but it'll heal. Kanga got picked up by the US Navy and arrived back last night well-lubricated. Gusty's not back yet, but he spoke to Jimmy Baraldi on the blower and he's on his way. He's unhurt but pancaked in the mountains west of here. Got picked up by Vichy troops, spent a couple of hours as their prisoner and then they promptly surrendered to him after orders came through from Admiral what's-his-name. He's on his way, no damage done. Well, except for three kites, of course.'

'Don't go on so,' groaned Bartley. 'I've already had an earful from Sheep Gilroy up at Wing, not to mention the engineering officer.' Bartley grinned. 'At least, we're getting out of here.' He launched himself onto an under-stuffed Ottoman sofa with a black and red Persian pattern. Under his weight, the pillows sighed, releasing a plume of sour dust. He groaned. 'I hope this blasted sofa hasn't got fleas,' he said. 'God, I hate this place.'

'Be careful what you wish for, there's no guarantee conditions will be any better near the front. They'll probably be worse.'

'That's a cheerful thought.' Bartley looked around the scruffy lounge currently serving as a reading room and bar. 'Got a gasper?'

'Sorry, chum, don't smoke,' replied Jox. 'Can't stand the smell. I've seen too many things burn. It stinks in here anyway.'

'Heavens forbid,' replied Bartley. 'Damned things are the only thing keeping me on an even keel. That and a good bellyful of gut-rot red. D'you think it's too early for a snifter?'

Jox glanced at his watch. It was only nine in the morning. 'Yes, damn it, Bolshie, it's too early for a drink. You had a skinful last night and by every right should be green at the gills, but you're being far too chipper.' Bartley had always been a drinker, a man for a party and a *bon viveur*. Lately he'd been leaning rather too heavily on the bottle. Sure, yesterday had been rough, but today was no different. The squadron needed their CO in shape; after all, there was only so much a restorative whiff of oxygen could fix.

Jox needed to escape the stink of the *Gauloises* cigarette Bartley had managed to find. He was puffing hungrily, filling the already evil-smelling room with a toxic Gallic fug. 'Right, I'm off to give my kite the once over. Bolshie, you better get your act together. We're wheels up in half an hour.'

No. 111 Squadron's move to the front wasn't long in the making. They transferred to Bône, three hundred miles east of Algiers.

As Jox had feared, conditions at Bône were worse than Maison Blanche. The airfield was within easy reach of several Axis airfields and the threat of attack was constant. With no radar, nor any form of early warning system, they never knew when the enemy were coming. This was a former *Luftwaffe* airfield, only just captured a few nights ago by the British 1st Parachute Brigade. Ever since, they'd been grimly defending it against heavy counterattacks.

The entire region was hotly contested, and squadron operations would be over hostile territory, across the border in Tunisia, where multiple threats abounded. Bône itself was located a hundred and twenty miles from the edge of the Axis bridgehead, with the nearest other Allied airfield being at Souk-el-Arba, sixty miles away. In contrast, the *Luftwaffe* had several all-weather airfields within ten miles of the front.

After a miserable arrival, weather conditions continued to deteriorate. Rather than the African sunshine that many had expected, the men were cold and wet, resorting to chopping up furniture and the remains of the *Luftwaffe*'s dispersal huts to cook and keep warm in the thin canvas tents provided. Heavy rain, sleet and sometimes even snow came lashing down from the mountains ringing the airfield, creating a perfect pocket for the worst of the storms. The airfield soon became waterlogged and turned to a sea of red mud.

After a patrol over the border, at midday on the 17th of November, the Treble Ones returned to the red mud of Bône to find it under attack by a mixed force of enemy fighter bombers, dive bombers and a strong fighter escort.

Frustration at their continued discomfort was the perfect incentive to unleash fury on an unsuspecting enemy focussed on their attack. A fully recovered Ralph Campbell was flying as Jox's wing man, and the pair were first to strike. They selected a clumsy-looking Ju 88 as their target; Jox's instinct was to always go for the bombers. Fortunately, they no longer used the line astern head-on attacks like they did during the Battle of Britain. He'd seen far too many of his comrades killed in catastrophic collisions to believe that was a reasonable tactic and preferred to use stealth instead.

Jox approached the *Schnellbomber* from the rear, keeping well-hidden beneath its fat tail. Manoeuvring carefully, he fired a burst along the fast-bomber's fuselage, surprised at the pleasure he felt when he saw solid strikes across the large black cross and the letters P1+LK. The aircraft yawed towards the portside, trailing a line of oily smoke. Jox skidded sideways and dropped, allowing Campbell, sitting on his shoulder, to get a clear shot at the raider.

Campbell fired and his projectiles shattered the aircraft's panelled cockpit, making the whole aircraft tip forward, plunging near vertically towards the red earth. The bulky bomber struck the ground with a tremendous boom, scattering burning aviation fuel in a wide arc across the mud and sodden grass. As their Spits pulled away, Jox was relieved to see at least two parachutes escape the plunging wreck.

The grey, cloudy airspace above Bône was a swirling melee of aircraft, feathery contrails and patches of low cloud acting like theatre curtains for the unfolding drama. Amongst the confusion, there were snatched glimpses of friend or foe, the snarling sound of complaining engines, with rattling gunfire and booming explosions. The squadron's many accents called and screamed, encouraged and warned one another as they pursued and evaded opponents.

Already in the drizzling rain, Bône airfield received a second shower, this time a golden, tinkling deluge of shell casings fizzing and sizzling in the red mud.

The squadron emerged from the fray, victorious but not unscathed. For a score of three Ju 88s claimed, including the one shared between Jox and Campbell, were added a Bf 109 and two more damaged Ju 88s. For the Treble Ones, their first fatality in North Africa was Sergeant Nigel Steevenson, a soft-spoken lad from Lancashire, and a recent graduate of No. 4 British Flying Training School in Mesa, Arizona. Nigel was only twenty years old.

Jox and Campbell were amongst the last to land on the litter-strewn field. The CO landed before them and described the loss of Sergeant Steevenson. 'I'd only just landed and was climbing out the kite. Most of the Jerries had buggered off, those that still could. The rest were burning wrecks across the airfield. Earlier, I'd seen Sergeant Steevenson attacking a Ju 88, as Axel's Number Two. He got clobbered by the rear gunner of the brute. Axel dodged the return fire, but young Nigel ran straight into it. His aircraft was hit but he flew on unaffected. I saw him circle the field and come in. After a bumpy landing, his Spit skidded to a halt, but he didn't turn off the engine. The propeller was spinning furiously and the engine began to overheat, getting ragged and starting to smell. His canopy was shut tight, even as flames vented through the exhaust stubs on the Spit's nose. That went on for too long, by which time ground crew had run over to see if he was all right.'

Bartley bit his lip and shook his head. 'We struggled to get the hatch open, but it was too late. The poor blighter was dead, a ragged hole in the temple of his flight helmet and another bloody great one out the top of his head. I just don't know how he managed it, landing perfectly, with a bullet through his brain. It's the damnedest thing I've ever seen. His ground crew were terribly upset. Poor sod, now I've got to write a letter to his parents and say how he died a hero. God, I hate this job!'

Jox didn't envy him the task.

Over the next few days, the squadron's luck began to change. The weather improved and the air defences for the airfield were enhanced dramatically. Paratroopers that had liberated the nearby port city of Bône, also known as Annaba, had been tasked with the job. They'd salvaged AA guns from sunken ships in the harbour, redeploying them around the airfield. The tough paras were relishing the opportunity to have a go at the Jerry raiders that had been harassing them for days.

Completely by accident, Bartley had also come to hear of some redundant French Tunisian radar operators, who until recently had worked at a nearby civilian aerodrome. To keep abreast of the country's liberation, they'd been tracking air traffic movements and were swiftly engaged to continue to do so. They were keen to get involved, and a telephone line was run between their civilian Radio Direction Finding (RDF) facility and the airfield, providing at least some advance warning of incoming raids.

Bône aerodrome was soon operating as an effective airfield despite trying conditions and the constant threat of attack. Switching to the offensive, the Treble Ones were tasked with providing air cover for Convoy MW13 steaming from Alexandria to Malta, consisting of just four merchant ships with a heavy escort of navy cruisers, HMS *Cleopatra*, *Orion*, *Arethusa* and *Dido*, plus a further seven destroyers. The number was an indication of the convoy's importance.

Malta-based Spitfires would provide air cover for the final stretch, but No. 111 Squadron were tasked with their initial protection alongside some Bristol Beaufighters which had a similar range. For Operation Stone Age, the RAF would provide continuous air cover, hopefully allowing the convoy to proceed unimpeded. Each squadron would relay the next despite the harsh weather conditions out to sea.

At dawn on the 20th, four Beaufighters handed over to the Treble Ones, arriving after the long flight from Bône. The squadron patrolled the surging seas until relieved by No. 126 and No. 185 Squadrons out of Malta. The Treble Ones emerged unscathed from this their first major operation, but three Maltese Spitfires were not so fortunate. American Pilot Officer Gardner Kelly of No. 126 Squadron was pulled lifeless from the water and his Kiwi squadron mate Sergeant Henry Roberts was seen clambering into his dinghy, but the rescue launch never found him. Similarly, Flying Officer Park of No. 185 Squadron, an Aussie, baled after engine problems, but was drowned by the time he was reached. Their nationalities were a telling indication of the multinational effort involved in defending the island fortress.

With improvements in the weather, No. 111 Squadron's logistical tail finally caught up with it. Administrative HQ staff, ground crews and support personnel arrived, along with replacement sergeant-pilots, enthusiastic, but intimidated by the grizzled veterans.

An exception amongst them was a confident young American introducing himself as William Huntington the

Third, better known as Billy Three Names. He said he was a 'Maryland Huntington' and was surprised no one had any idea what that meant. Elegant and groomed, he was a well-heeled young man who saw war as a glorious adventure. Charming and gregarious, he was immediately popular and a lively addition to a squadron hungry for divertissement. He also seemed to have an endless supply of Vat 69 Scotch whisky and cartons of Camel cigarettes. He told tales of his escapades with Ivy League heiresses and the Bright Young Things of London, and how pre-war, he'd raced Bentleys at Brooklands and mastered the Cresta Run in Switzerland. He'd even had a brief period fighting for the Republicans in Spain. Apparently, he'd joined for romantic reasons, losing his ardour when promptly dumped by the *senorita* in question.

Bolshie Bartley was particularly taken by Billy Three Names. They shared similar backgrounds and, as it turned out, several girlfriends. The pair got roaring drunk, compared and contrasted past amours and then discussed their respective Rolex timepieces. The CO's was a gift from the studio when he was the stunt pilot on *The First of the Few*, whilst Billy's was a graduation present from his father, William Huntington the Second.

For Jox, it was the return of Tim 'Doc' Ridgway, the squadron's intelligence officer that was most appreciated. His wit and insight on the progress of the war had been missed and as a part-qualified medical doctor, he was also helpful tackling the many ailments that dogged aircrew through general wear and tear.

Operations from Bône continued despite the constant attention of enemy raiders. The British paratroopers manning the airfield's Bofors guns had by now perfected their skills and began to take a regular toll on the marauders. The airfield was littered with downed aircraft, some friendly, but mostly Axis. It was now a vast scrapyard of burnt-out wrecks. At one end of the runway were the remains of a Wellington that had crashed just short of sanctuary. It now lay as a sentinel indicating the correct approach to take, languishing like a whale's skeleton washed up on a beach.

Jox and Jimmy Baraldi were sitting in the fly-specked shack that doubled as the squadron's dispersal hut. Operations were over for the day, and they were enjoying some American coffee. Baraldi had firm opinions on the beverage, and had already declared it as rubbish, and yet after years in wartime Britain, they were both very grateful for it.

'So, there you are, chaps,' said Bartley, banging the screen door of the hut. 'The 3rd Parachute Battalion pongos want to celebrate bagging their latest brace of Jerry dive-bombers. They've been running some competition with their Yank counterparts, the US Rangers, and are rather pleased to be in the lead. Anyway, they've got hold of a cow — or at least I hope it's a cow and not some passing dromedary. They've invited us for Sunday lunch, roast beef with all the trimmings. They're promising Yorkshire puddings, but alas no horseradish, so mustard will have to do. Should be a treat. Terribly resourceful chaps these paratroopers. Airborne initiative they call it. I'd be surprised if they don't have a well-stocked bar too.'

'You feeling all right, Skipper?' asked Baraldi. 'Look a bit peely-wally.' Bartley was sweating despite the chill in the air.

'I'm all right. Spot of tummy trouble. Nothing like 'Pharaoh's Revenge', but perhaps the local variant,' he replied. 'Nothing a drink won't cure. Come on, let's gather up the lads.'

The party was held in a clearing amongst the citrus groves beyond the airfield. The rows of stubby, dark-leaved trees were heavy with fruit. Jox was surprised, but then recalled there had always been oranges available at Christmas before the war.

The paratroopers were big men in grubby camouflage uniforms covered in straps. They were all immaculately shaved, some with resplendent moustaches. They wore a maroon beret with a winged cap badge, the only shiny thing about them.

The men were in a boisterous mood, good natured at the prospect of a feed. They joshed and laughed, clinking cans of American beer which the paratroopers relished stabbing into with their Fairbairn-Sykes daggers. Jox was introduced to a pair of burly captains, each with three olive pips on his shoulder. Grant MacNeish was an Irishman with an enormous ginger moustache growing horizontally from under his nose. It bristled like porcupine quills when he spoke, pale eyes glistening with humour and a touch of madness that promised untold violence.

'A fine evening, Flight Lieutenant,' he rumbled. 'The name's MacNeish. I'm told you're a McNabb. In which case, there's a fair chance our ancestors crossed swords a while back.'

'I wouldn't know about that,' spluttered Jox. 'I'm certainly glad we're on the same side now, your fellows are absolutely terrifying.'

'So, they are,' replied the burly Irishman. 'A fine mess of lads to do your fighting with.' He smiled a shark's grin. 'You're the fellow with the claymore drawn on his aircraft, are you not? I've seen it, with the name "Marguerite". That'll be your wife then?'

Jox frowned. 'No, it's the name of a little girl I failed to save in France. It's there to remind me what I'm fighting for, so I never lose focus.'

'Focus, is it? Well, that's grand. You see, I've an interest in swords. I carry my grandfather's blade into battle. Been through the Afghan, Crimea, Indian Mutiny, Boer War, and of course the last war. Sort of a family charm and I'm proud to carry it now.' MacNeish held up a heavy sword, basket hilted, with grubby lanyards and a stained grip. It was clearly well-used and was certainly no ceremonial weapon. 'I can tell you, there's a few Jerries who had the shock of their lives when my Maeve started shrieking like a banshee.'

'Shrieking?' asked Jox.

'Aye,' said MacNeish, pulling the blade from its scabbard with a scraping sound. He began spinning the blade through the air and it began to whistle.

'Take it easy, Grant, you'll do yourself a mischief,' said MacNeish's companion. 'I'm fairly sure fighter pilots need both their ears and nose. Put that thing away, you're in civilised company now.'

The other fellow introduced himself as Captain Dougal Preston. He held out a hand the size of a ham hock. Raptor-nosed with wind-burnt features, he had a ready smile and a gap between his teeth. 'Come on, let's get away from this maniac and get something to eat.'

The roasting oxen was enormous, rotating slowly on what appeared to be the antenna of a downed enemy bomber. The aroma was delicious, especially to men used to iron rations, with melting fat dripping and sizzling onto the hot coals. Jox found the sight a little unsettling, as he'd seen more than his fair share of men in burning aircraft. Even the motion of the rotating carcass reminded him of a dying bomber when cannon shells found their mark, the aircraft rotating off its axis as it began to fall.

'You'll be wanting a drink,' said Preston, in his deep baritone voice. They crossed to a barrel cut in half and filled with water to keep the beer cool. Preston had his sleeves rolled up past sizeable biceps and fished out fresh drinks. 'There you go, wet your whistle.'

'They're an impressive band of men, Captain. Not the sort you'd want to tangle with down some dark alleyway,' Jox remarked.

'Call me Dougie. Aye, they're a fair bunch of scrappers, but by the look of the fruit salad on your tunic, you've seen some action yourself. The George Cross, DFC and Bar, and what's that, an MC? That's pretty unusual for a flyboy, what's the story there?'

'Malta,' replied Jox, a little embarrassed.

'Been there too? You certainly get about, don't you?'

'You could say that. The advantage of flying for a living, I suppose.'

'Nah, that's not for me,' replied Preston. 'Like to keep my feet firmly on the ground.'

'But surely you're airborne?'

'Not through choice. Gives me the jitters, jumping out of a perfectly good aeroplane. The truth is, I'm not terribly keen on being in someone else's hands. If the pilot gets taken out, that's me done for too, so on balance, I'd prefer to be airlanded than airborne.'

'What's the difference?'

'We're developing our capabilities, and our troopers are trained for both. Airborne means we land with parachutes, airlanded means we arrive as a cohesive unit in gliders. That's the way forward for me.' Preston grinned. 'D'you know, our opposite numbers, the *Fallschirmjäger*, are actually part of the *Luftwaffe*, so get the pick of Germany's best fighting men. Isn't it amusing to think the Nazi's best infantrymen are actually airmen? I'm sure we'll face them some time. That'll be a different ballgame to the Frogs we faced here.' He glanced over at MacNeish who was swinging his sword again, now terrifying Ralph Campbell. 'Don't worry about Grant. He's a bloodthirsty bampot, but a sound fellow in a scrap. Saved my bacon when we jumped on Bône.' Preston grinned. 'Took command of my company, wiping out a Spandau nest after I'd got my bell rung.'

'What d'you mean?'

'I was leading my company when I got dinged. Went out like a light. Grant scooped me up and tucked me somewhere safe until I came around. He then cracked on and took out a machine gun nest that was causing havoc, swinging that bloody chopper like a whirling dervish. Lopped a few heads off, I'm told.'

'What happened to you?

Preston looked sheepish and took off his beret. In the middle of his forehead was a purple bruise. 'I don't usually wear a helmet, but since they'd just been issued, I thought I'd better set an example. Bloody thing was so uncomfortable, rattling about when I ran, but it's a good job I did, or I'd be pushing up daisies now. I was looking down when I got hit, taking most of the zing out, but still got smacked hard and went down.' He rumbled with laughter. 'The men call me Captain Cyclops, the cheeky wee devils. Ma always said I didn't have much in there to damage anyway.' He laughed again, patting Jox on the shoulder. 'Come on, laddie, let's get some scran. You must be hungry and I'm starving.'

CHAPTER THREE

The next morning there were more than a few sore heads around. Unfortunately, the enemy were no respecter of hangovers, and the Treble Ones were jolted from their slumber by the clanging air-raid alarm and the sound of Bofors guns banging away at targets. The men sprinted to their parked aircraft, sweaty and blowing by the time they climbed aboard and got strapped in. Many sucked hungrily at the oxygen in their masks, desperate to blow away the cobwebs. Within moments, bombs were exploding across the airfield and the continuous AA fire did little to soothe pounding headaches. Paratroopers, it appeared, were better at recovery than the bedraggled pilots of No. 111 Squadron.

Bartley's stomach had taken a turn overnight and he was signed off Ops by Doctor Mear, the squadron medical officer. The amount he'd consumed the previous night wasn't discussed, but Jox and Baraldi exchanged glances before heading for their respective Spits in the parking stands. In the rush of imminent action, their concerns dropped away as they focussed on more pressing things like the enemy and staying alive.

First to get off the ground were B Flight, with Ghillie de Ghellinck, Ralph Campbell and French-Canadian pilot Ernest 'Moules' Mouland flying with Jox in Green Section, and Kanga Reeves, Axel Fisken, Billy Three Names Huntington and a replacement sergeant in Yellow.

'Jox, my flight is right behind you,' said Baraldi over the R/T. 'We'll be with you in a couple of minutes.'

The Ops room near the tower interrupted. 'WAGON Green Leader, this is SKELETON control. Head for Vector 220, over the Lake of Fetzara, southeast of your current position. Should be easy to find, with all this rain it'll be full and surrounded by water meadows. Intercept and destroy the raiders retreating over the water.'

Jox and his men opened up their throttles and began the pursuit.

'WAGON Flight Leader from Blue One,' said Baraldi. 'Enemy formation at twelve o'clock below. About eight miles out.'

'Righto, I see them,' said Jox, easing his flight starboard, so as to achieve a better sun-up position. 'WAGON B Flight. Let's get into the game.'

The retreating Messerschmitt Bf 109s and Ju 88s hadn't seen them yet.

There was a sudden cry from the rearmost flight. 'B Flight, break port, break port, killer Shrikes coming at you from above.' It was the voice of Mack Gilmour in Baraldi's flight. It appeared the stalkers had been seen and were being stalked in turn.

'Keep turning, keep turning,' beseeched Baraldi.

Jox grunted under the strain of the G-force, but managed to croak, 'Tell me when to stop.' He hoped the rest of the flight were keeping up. His breath rasped in his throat, and he felt himself greying out.

'Keep turning, Jox. Four on your tail,' said Baraldi. 'Mack, get your Red Section stuck in, those boys need your help.'

'Can't help right now,' replied Mack. 'Mixing it up with some Snappers who have just turned to face us.'

'Right then, it's down to us, Blue Section. Come on, we're the flipping cavalry.'

'I've been hit, I've been hit,' cried a shrill voice which Jox didn't recognise. Must be one of the new sergeant pilots, but he didn't know which one. 'I'm baling out, lost stick control, temperature's going through the roof.'

'Keep calm,' said Jox. 'You know the drill. Make sure you've got your dinghy handy. You can drown just as well in a lake as in the sea. Good luck, mate.'

'Keep turning, B Flight, keep turning. You're pulling away from them now,' insisted Baraldi. 'Hold on, boys, we're coming.'

The moisture-laden air above the red lake was a mass of vapour trails, with fleeting glimpses of twisting fighters flashing between the low-hanging cloud. Enemy Ju 88s still carrying partial bombloads, jettisoned their munitions trying to lighten themselves and get away from the dogged pursuers. Huge, coffee-coloured plumes of water exploded from the shallows, loaded with earth and mud which splattered the parachute canopy of the hapless new sergeant drifting through it. He was lucky not to be struck by something more substantial or deadly. Sergeant Longbottom, the CO's wingman, reported seeing him hit the water and then the orange lozenge-shaped dinghy floating on the muddy surface.

Jox pitched over to take a look, seeing how the explosions had terrified teeming masses of waterfowl living on the Lake of Fetzara. He was no ornithology expert, but could make out numerous nests on denuded, fallen trees and along the grassy shoreline. There were flocks of pink-hued, long-legged flamingos, with smaller white egrets and the more familiar form of ducks of various kinds. Quite apart from the vast number killed by the shock and splinters from the detonations, the noise and disturbance sent a dense flurry of panicked birds into the air, all taking off at once, creating the very worst form of bird strike threat. Jox knew the terror of hitting a Canada goose on a night flight to Clydebank in Scotland in 1941 and had seen the devastation that the ragged vees of bulky birds had wrought on the squadron. Here the threat was ten if not a hundredfold.

For the dozen or so Ju 88 *Schnellbombers* flying fast and low across the lake, the impact of bird strikes was like cannon fire. At least three of the forty-five-foot-long aircraft with their seventy-feet wing spans were immediately in trouble. Two trailed flaring engines, with smashed canopies and fuselages. They tipped immediately towards the turbid waters, before somersaulting into it, tail over cockpit and moving very fast. One lay on its back like a dead albatross and began to sink, the other disintegrating into component parts as it hit the water. A third struggled for height, straining every rivet to escape the draw of the lake's waters, just managing to limp homewards. Less stricken companions scattered like terrified mackerel under the avian onslaught. That's when the Treble Ones struck.

At no little danger from bird strikes themselves, Jox's flight hammered into the panicked Ju 88s. Baraldi's flight joined the fray, as did their pursuing FW 190 Shrikes.

Heading home in ragged ones and twos, the remnants of the squadron returned to find the aerodrome under fresh attack. Some of the planes were damaged, others out of ammunition or low on fuel, and several needed to land urgently. To do so, they had to navigate through a second wave of retreating enemy bombers, plus their fighter escort, all the while negotiating a heavily cratered and bomb-damaged airfield. That's not to mention the attention of vengeful AA gunners, some of whom still had work to do on their aircraft recognition.

Jox was one of the first to bump down, quickly turning to find a hardened shelter to park JU-X, before running to the squadron dispersal hut. Rather confused, he couldn't find it. He scanned the shattered airfield, trying to make sense of the chaos of smouldering buildings, clanging fire trucks and faithful ambulances treating the wounded.

Jox asked a corporal with his arm in a spotted sling, 'Where's the CO?' His mind racing with concern, Jox feared the worst, but the man pointed in the direction of trenches, beneath a tattered RAF ensign flapping stubbornly over some parked lorries. Jox ran over to find Doc Ridgway bunkered down with the majority of the Treble Ones' admin staff, sheltering like moles with their tin helmets on.

'Nice weather for ducks,' said Ridgway, trying but failing to be funny.

'You all right?' asked Jox. 'Our hut's been flattened. Anyone hurt?'

'No, I think we're all right. I got everyone into these holes despite vehement protests. Good job I did too.'

'Where's Bartley? He didn't take off with us because of a gyppy tummy. He about?'

'He was just a minute ago. When that last lot of Jerries came over, he got rather hot under the collar and said he was fed up being bombed like a blooming pongo. Ran off towards those lorries.'

Jox looked to where Ridgway was indicating and saw a figure sheltering beneath a tractor. 'I'll go take a look. You stay here and watch our people. The rest of the chaps will be making their way back in dribs and drabs. You're not going to believe how well we did, but I promise you, the chaps won't be exaggerating. Those bloody birds on that lake took out more Jerries than we ever did, but we did well too. Took some

41

losses, but nothing like the Germans. I'll get my report to you but want to make sure the CO's all right first.'

Jox sprinted to the cluster of parked vehicles. Bartley's face peeked out from between the outsized tyres of the tractor. As Jox approached, he saw to his horror that the tractor was attached to a fuel bowser. Bartley sheltered between the robust wheels, but was oblivious to the many thousands of gallons of volatile aviation fuel just feet away.

'For heaven's sake, Bolshie, you're under a flipping petrol bowser, the whole bloody lot could go up at any second!'

Bartley's handsome face, grimy with mud and oil, looked shocked. Jox held out his hand and Bartley reached out and grasped it.

'I'm a bit of a silly sod, aren't I?' he said, embarrassed.

'I won't disagree. Let's find somewhere to hide where we won't risk getting blown to kingdom come. Plenty of room with Doc and his mob. Come on, it's getting hairy out here.'

As the pair ran for shelter, a tattered-looking Spitfire was landing. Approaching too fast, it bounced several times on bloated rubber wheels, then slewed off the runway, coming straight towards them. The faster they ran, the more it seemed to chase after them. There was a sudden bang as a tyre burst, and the careening fighter spun violently, colliding with the bowser they'd been beside just moments earlier.

The spinning propeller screamed as its blades carved into the metal side of the fuel tank. Flames from the Spitfire's exhaust stubs flared in reaction to the sudden resistance, all that was needed to ignite the volatile liquid that was gushing from the disembowelled tanker. Locked in a deadly embrace, they were engulfed in a fiery ball which mushroomed skywards. The resulting shock wave was enough to bowl both Bartley and Jox off their feet, their clothing and the backs of their heads singed by the liquid heat that pulsed over them.

Inside the fighter's cockpit, the stricken pilot was beating against the canopy with his fists. It didn't take long for his struggles to cease and for his goggled, helmeted head to drop back, mouth frozen in a silent scream. Jox rushed towards the conflagration and, with his flight gauntlets and flying boots still on, tried desperately to get at the cockpit, but it was far too hot. He fell back, frustrated; all he could do now was stand in silence beside a morose Bartley, as the fire burned. The fire crew arrived but it was already too late.

Mesmerised by the flames, Jox was transported back to Montrose, where in similar circumstances, he'd tried to save his friend, George Milne. George had been the first of his friends to perish in the flames that had claimed so many since. A wave of sadness hit Jox like a body blow. Tears streaked down his smoke-blackened face and when he pulled off his singed gloves, his scarred hands were painful mementos of that first fire.

'Who is it?' asked a distraught Bartley.

Jox scanned the fuselage but the paintwork and identifying letters had already been taken by the ferocity of the fire. It was turning to a mottled oxidised colour, hissing and steaming as it was splashed by the fire hoses.

The rescue crew worked at the warped cockpit canopy with a crowbar. With a final groan, they managed to pull it back, releasing a nauseating cloud of burnt fabric, hair and something akin to charred pork. Covering his nose with his flight glove, Jox peered into the cockpit. The body was leaning back on the remains of the seat, its head tilted and throat exposed, as if waiting in a dentist's chair. The face was unrecognisable, jaw open mid-scream, and in the recess of the mouth, golden molars glittered.

'I can't tell,' he said. 'There's not much left.'

The body had been reduced to skeletal remains, the fingerless white bones of the right arm extended like that of a scarecrow, the left folded across the body as if clutching at his heart.

'That's Billy Three Names,' said Bartley in a hollow voice. 'Look at the wrist, that's his watch.'

On the left wrist was a blue-faced stainless-steel watch smeared with soot. Jox looked at it and detected a tiny movement — the second hand was still ticking. He wiped the face of the watch, surprised at how hot it felt, blistering the pad of his thumb.

'That's Billy's Rolex Oyster Perpetual all right. We had a bragging contest the other night over drinks, arguing who's was best. Looks like his is rather fine, if somewhat charred.' Bartley exhaled. 'What a bloody shame, such a fine fellow, could have become one of us. We shared many friends and a couple of girlfriends, as it happens. Barely got his feet under the table, poor chap.'

Jox and the CO caught up again later that evening, after what had proven to be a very long day. Bartley was sitting at a battered table in the reconstituted mess, just a canvas tent put up in the lee of its wrecked predecessor, a timber hut crushed during the day's raids. He was amusing himself by balancing on the back legs of his wooden bistro chair. The scarred card table before him was covered in a stained green baize. What little comfort there was in the tent came from a pot-bellied wood stove with a tarnished silver chimney that snaked through the slanted canvas roof.

Bartley was three sheets to the wind, having found additional warmth from a half empty bottle of VAT 69 that was on the table beside a few glass tumblers. 'Here, Jox,' he said, sloshing a measure into a glass and shoving it across the baize. His chair fell forward with a clatter, and he giggled. 'Join me in a dram to the immortal memory of Billy Three Names. A fine fellow we barely got to know, but a fine fellow nonetheless.'

Jox raised his glass, swallowed and enjoyed the throat burn then the fire in his belly, the warmth of his homeland. '*Slàinte Mhath!* To Billy … what was it … Huntington the Third.'

'Here, take this,' said a slurring Bartley. He reached into his tunic pocket and retrieved a blue-faced watch, placing it on the table. 'It's Billy's.'

'What … why should I have it?' spluttered Jox. 'Surely, he's got parents it should go to.'

'No chance, look at the state of it. Remarkable that it still works, charred to buggery. It'll polish up but will always be marked by the fire. Really doesn't take much imagination to figure out what happened.' Bartley sighed. 'I've written the letter to Mr and Mrs Huntington the Second, filled with grand sentiments like "It is with my sincerest regrets to report … your son has died in the finest traditions of the squadron…" Blah, blah, blah. You see, I can't then send them his cremated watch as a keepsake. Better for them to imagine him "Gone in a blaze of glory, here one instant gone the next, he now flies amongst the stars." *And so the story goes…*' he sang tunelessly.

He fixed Jox with bleary eyes. 'Seriously though, I've put some thought into it, you did more than anyone trying to get him out of there. Christ, you've been burnt before and for a chap to go into the fire a second time, well it beggars belief.' He gave a tired smile. 'Not to mention saving my sorry arse from under that bloody tractor. I've a good mind to put you up for another medal, but frankly you won't do better than the George Cross you've already got. Least I can do is let you have his watch.' He chuckled mirthlessly. 'Not as if he's on the clock anymore.'

Bartley splashed another shot of whisky into his glass. 'Don't feel bad, I've already liberated the bottles of VAT 69 from his footlocker and distributed the Camels amongst the boys. One for all and all for one. Since you don't smoke, nor drink terribly much, I'm sure he'd appreciate you having his watch. Wear it in memory of Billy Huntington the Third of the Maryland Huntingtons. He died a worthy Treble One, didn't he? Come on, bottoms up!'

Jox sighed and gave the back of the watch a wipe with his sleeve. The silver metal was engraved with 'W.I.S.H. III'. He strapped it on. 'What were Billy's middle names?'

'No idea, why?'

'The watch says, "W.I.S.H. III". Wish ill, not exactly a great omen, is it?'

46

CHAPTER FOUR

'Hurry up and wait' is a common expression in the British Army. So too is, 'Settle in and you'll be moving soon'. In the RAF, things were no different.

As December roared into North Africa like a rather damp squib, No. 111 Squadron was on the move again, crossing the border into hotly contested Tunisia. Their destination was a military airfield near the city of Souk-el-Arba, liberated just a few weeks earlier by paratroopers of the British 1st Parachute Brigade on the 16th of November 1942. The Treble Ones arrived on the 5th of December, to join the already resident No. 225 Squadron, who were there providing reconnaissance missions in support of the British First Army in the mountains. Unusually for a single RAF squadron, one of the unit's two flights were equipped with North American Mustangs, the other with Hawker Hurricanes.

The airfield was on a low oval-shaped plateau, ringed by round-shouldered hills usually planted with extensive fields of cereal crops. There were very few trees, so visibility was good for miles, providing useful advance warning of the attacks the airfield was routinely subject to. Evidence of that was clear on the pockmarked landscape, littered with bomb craters and wreckage, an all-too familiar vista for the jaded Treble Ones. The only substantial structure left on the airfield was an old farmhouse, painted the colour of bone. Clustered around were canvas tents housing the pilots, maintenance crews and No. 225 Squadron's assorted staff. The Treble Ones and other arriving squadrons were there to build up the beleaguered airfield's defensive capabilities, and their accommodation was even rougher and dispersed across the field.

The commanding officer of No. 225 was Squadron Leader Edward Millington, a tall, thin and rather stiff fellow with aristocratic pretensions. He advised Bartley and Jox that his squadron had been through a rough time, losing several pilots, two gone that day alone. 'My chaps aren't really fighter pilots, having been trained for reconnaissance. Can't tell you how pleased I am that you're here. Please don't be fooled by these innocent-looking skies, I can assure you Souk-el-Arba is rife with danger. There's every chance you'll run into those damned FW 190s, in my view a vastly superior aircraft to anything we've got. I hope your Mark IXs can fare better than we have.' He looked rather dejected. 'And it's not just that Jerry has better planes, they're flown by the *Luftwaffe*'s most battle-hardened pilots, veterans of the Eastern Front, Malta and the Western Desert. They've all been rushed to Tunisia to hold back our recent landings.'

With a bravado that neither of them felt, Bartley replied that he had plenty of experienced aces of his own. Millington's sour reaction to this flippant response was embarrassing for Jox, as it implied criticism, a reproach No. 225 Squadron certainly didn't deserve. After Bartley's posturing, the Treble Ones would unnecessarily have to prove their worth.

Souk-el-Arba was an unremarkable agricultural city located at tactically significant crossroads between several towns and Tunis, the country's capital, which was only eighty miles away. Being mid-winter, the fields around the aerodrome were still in stubble. There was little sign of mechanised farming or ploughing, but that may well have been because of the recent active warfare in the environs.

Every morning though, long lines of women would appear on the purple-hued fields, wrapped in voluminous robes against the biting wind. They could be seen bending and squatting, and at first it was feared this was some sort of communal toilet until it was realised the local women were actually harvesting the stamens of the purple *Crocus sativus*, from which precious saffron is derived. The spice, worth more than its weight in gold, was in the form of delicate golden strands, which when added to dishes provide a subtle aromatic and honey-like flavour exported worldwide for centuries.

It took a while to get used to the local culture and ways, but for Doc Ridgway it was a great delight to be in this ancient and historic land, abounding with the architecture of previous civilisations, including the vast Roman city of Bulla Regia close by.

As the squadron settled in and the supporting infrastructure formed, the Treble Ones were tasked with a fresh variety of missions. These ranged from fighter sweeps and reconnaissance flights over enemy positions, to escort duties for the light bombers operating in support of the Allied advance, often bogged down by stubborn enemy resistance with atrocious fighting conditions on the ground. They were sometimes tasked with providing a ground-attack role, but that became rarer as specialised fighter-bombers began to arrive.

Chief amongst them were American units belonging to the Twelfth Air Force, and soon the airfield was feeling rather crowded. A novelty was the extraordinary-looking Lockheed P-38 Lightnings of the 82nd Fighter Group, the P being for 'Pursuit'. They were in fact heavy fighters, weighing in at some 12,800 pounds compared to a fully loaded Mark IX at just 8,575 pounds. Twin-enginned but with a single-seat, they had distinctive double-boom tail assemblies and a central nacelle holding the cockpit. The aircraft's nose armament was four fifty-calibre Browning machine guns clustered around a central 20mm Hispano cannon capable of such a prodigious weight of fire it was known as the 'watering can'.

These fearsome and somewhat peculiar-looking beasts were painted the colour of the desert sand but some had colourful spinners and noses. When viewed from the ground, they looked like flying squares but parked on the deck were all propellers and nose, usually emblazoned with paintings of native American chieftains or voluptuous, scantily clad women. Amongst them was a 'Chief Whooping', a 'California Cutie' and even a 'Miss Margarita' — a Latina lovely in a tiny bathing suit, holding a cocktail glass. Their gum-chewing pilots were loud, flamboyant and brimming with self-confidence, promising, 'The planes are kinda funny-looking, but mean and fast, and it's our fighting that does the talking.'

This attitude seemed fairly representative of the gung-ho attitude of the Northwest African Strategic Air Force, which had unified command of US Army Air Force and Royal Air Force units operating in North Africa. They were under the overall command of Major General James Doolittle, the famous aviator who planned and led the 'Doolittle Raid', the United States' first retaliation against Japan after the attack on Pearl Harbor, Hawaii on the 7th of December 1941. He was now tasked with bringing that same vigour and sense of daring to the lacklustre performance of air operations in the North African theatre thus far.

Somewhat counter to his name, Doolittle intended to 'grab the Twelfth Air Force by the scruff of its neck and shake it into action'. Apparently, the general wanted to find evidence of USAAF and RAF collaboration, and some tangible examples of what they might learn from one another. He wanted to see 'team spirit' and was keen to hear the Treble Ones offer a point of view.

Because of the long-range capabilities of their Spitfire Mark IXs, the squadron was often paired up with the 82nd Fighter Group's Lightnings. It was early December when they went on a joint patrol northwest of Tunis, over the recently liberated airfield at Youks-les-Bains, just within the Algerian border. A few days earlier, at this same location, an unescorted squadron of twelve Bristol Blenheim bombers were jumped by a fighter beehive of over sixty Bf 109s and FW 190s. One solitary aircraft made it home and with each crew accounting for three men, that represented losses of over thirty airmen and the destruction of an entire fighting squadron. The tragedy was an affront to Doolittle's pride, a slight for which he demanded swift and savage retribution.

This part of Tunisia was familiar territory for Jox. Earlier in the war, he'd led a flight of seven Spits over here, flying the aircraft unarmed to save weight to deliver the precious aircraft to besieged Malta. They'd set off from the now sunken aircraft carrier HMS *Eagle* and it was a memory that twinged painfully. Chasing the dark thoughts away, Jox remembered instead that east of here, they'd sighted a U-boat on the surface charging its batteries. They'd given those *Kriegsmarine* matelots sunbathing on the sleek hull quite a fright. Though unarmed, they'd swooped low, causing the panicked men to pile down the hatches before the U-boat crash-dived beneath the shimmering waves.

It was dangerous territory, heavily contested and well within range of Pantelleria's several aggressive *Luftwaffe* and *Regia Aeronautica* units. The weather conditions had improved in recent weeks, but cloud cover remained extensive, with layers of low thick grey nimbostratus, and only the occasional gap to provide a glimpse of what lay below. Since both No. 111 and the 96th Pursuit Squadrons were equipped with pressurised cockpits, they were cruising above the clouds and flying under the wide blue arc of the African sky.

Capable of speeds of four hundred miles per hour, the 96th Pursuit Squadron's Lightnings still chose to fly in tight formation. They were below the Treble Ones, who instead flew in a looser series of tiered formations. Jox recognised the American formation as similar to the wing tip to wing tip manoeuvring that was all the rage at air shows before the war. In the RAF they'd long since been superseded when their deadly ineffectiveness had been learnt the hard way during the battles of France and Britain. British fighters now used the 'finger-four' formation, blatantly stolen from their wily Teutonic opponents. This was a point that had been made several times to the leadership of the 82nd Fighter Group. The belief persisted that given the Lightning's speed, range and firepower, and its poor manoeuvrability compared to the Spit, and for that matter the latest Bf 109s and FW 190s, faith remained in formation flying to provide a mutually protective defence.

Over the previous few years, Jox had flown with some excellent, highly experienced American aviators, not least over Dieppe and Morlaix. Nevertheless, for Bartley and his veteran flight commanders, Jox and Baraldi, the lack of combat experience amongst Doolittle's Twelfth Air Force was painfully obvious. All three had the ominous presentiment of an impending 'I told you so' moment.

Trying to make the clumped formation of heavy fighters less obvious in the sky, Bartley, commanding the 'beehive', instructed the Yanks to descend below the cloud base. Here, the Lightnings were hidden from above and had good visibility of what lay below. The Treble Ones were positioned higher and flitting in and out of the dispersed clouds.

Jox and Bartley were flying as wingmen and were the closest pair to the Lightnings, below and to their portside. They spotted a pair of Bf 109s at the same time, nipping down through a gap in the cloud cover and then pulling back up again, a manoeuvre akin to twitching a fishing fly above a pool of basking trout. The Lightning pilots flew on oblivious, which in retrospect was probably a good thing.

Sensing a trap, Bartley said to Jox, 'WAGON Leader to Green One, go take a quick look at what those jokers are up to, I don't like the look of it.' To the rest of the squadron he said, 'All WAGON aircraft, hold your positions but stand by for imminent action.' He then clicked over to the frequency used by the P-38s, 'WAGON Leader to SWALLOW Leader. Maintain your formation, altitude and current heading.'

'Roger that, WAGON Leader,' drawled William 'Dixie' Sloan, a Virginian who was leading the 96th Pursuit Squadron of the 82nd Fighter Group's P-38s. He had a reputation for being a bit of a hothead, a maverick with an aggressive style of flying.

Jox carefully lifted his nose through the cloud, poking just above it to see what was about. A formation of some twenty enemy fighters were circling to hold their position, poised to pounce on any aircraft foolish enough to venture through the cloud cover. He instantly dropped back down, hoping he hadn't been seen.

'Green One to WAGON Leader. There's a nasty nest of Snappers up there, just waiting for someone daft enough to poke his head through. I think we should sit tight. They may get impatient, throw away their height advantage and come looking for trouble.'

'Good idea, Green One, you hold back with your section. Ghillie, Moules and Ralph, you stick with Jox. I'll take the rest of the boys and see if we can't wiggle enticingly enough to get Fritz to come down and have a pop. Don't wait too long before clobbering them, and for God's sake, don't bloody miss.'

After several agonising minutes, Jerry's patience ran out and Jox saw the same two 'bait' Bf 109s drop through the cloud and begin stalking the still oblivious Yanks. So intent were they on the easy pickings before them, that 'greed' overcame 'guile', and they forgot the most basic of precautions. The four Spitfires Mark IXs of Green Section dropped from the clouds and before the *Gustavs* knew that the tables had been turned, both were blown from the sky. De Ghellinck and Mouland, both veteran pilots, added a score apiece to their tallies.

Up ahead, the P-38 Lightnings were still holding their tight, very smart formation, flying on completely unaware of the brutal contest that had occurred in their wake. They'd been seconds away from destruction but had no clue. There would need to be a firm and frank conversation if the 82nd Fighter Group were to learn 'the facts of life', and if they were to have any chances of survival.

The return flight was uneventful, the Lightnings landing first and in good order. That in itself wasn't necessarily a straightforward task, given the aircraft's reputation for instability when landing or taking-off. With yoked flight controls, not unlike half of a car steering wheel, the P-38 was known to sometimes lock up when in a dive. Its unconventional configuration could also mean that if one of its two engines cut out on approach, there was a tendency for the other to overcompensate, resulting in the aircraft flipping, with disastrous consequences.

As the smaller Spitfires landed in pairs, Jox saw a shiny aircraft parked alongside olive dun-coloured bombers on the other side of the new Perforated Steel Planking runway installed by American engineers. This had been built to allow large US bombers to land at the ever-expanding 'Engle Field', the new name for Souk-el-Arba aerodrome to suit Anglo-Saxon tongues. More and more aircraft were arriving from the United States, transiting through the UK, coming unpainted and shiny in the glare of the albeit rather rare African sun. It appeared that some genius had figured out that painting an aircraft took time, cost money and added significant weight, with no discernible benefit when flying at high altitude. Bombers were therefore going into battle 'naked', not unlike the semi-clad lovelies painted on their fuselages.

Remembering the aircraft recognition charts he been boning up on, Jox identified the shiny aircraft as a Martin B-26 Marauder, a twin-enginned American bomber. As he taxied his Spit to a stop, the nearest flagpole to the B-26 carried a blue flag that he didn't recognise. It had a row of three white stars, the outer ones larger and the central one with a solid red dot like on the Japanese flag, and a pair of golden wings. Whatever it was, it was flamboyant and rather out of place on the bleak Tunisian plain.

Once his feet were back on the ground, Jox asked the nearest ground crewman, an armourer with a snake of linked .303 rounds around his neck, 'What's that flag all about?'

'Sorry, sir, no idea,' the plumber replied. 'Something to do with the Yanks.'

Jox was still looking when he was distracted by the roar of an approaching jeep. At the wheel was Ridgway, with Bartley beside him and Baraldi in the back. 'Hop in,' said Bartley.

Jox repeated his question. Ridgway grinned, shading his eyes as he looked up at the flag. 'That, my friend, is the flag of a USAAF Major General. Major General James Doolittle is in residence, and, gentlemen, he would like to have a word.'

Doolittle was a short, intense man with a receding hairline, dark eyes and a chin with a pronounced cleft. He was wearing a brown leather flying jacket over an Army Air Corps uniform with a tie and numerous decorations for valour.

'You must be Bartley, McNabb and Baraldi,' he growled. 'Thanks for making the time.'

They didn't exactly have much choice in the matter, but he was decent to extend the courtesy.

The general saw Jox glance at his decorations. 'I have you beat with this one, McNabb. One up on the George Cross, I believe.' He pointed to a pale blue rectangle with five white stars. He'd obviously been reading their personnel files. His Medal of Honor was awarded for the Doolittle raid on Japan, America's first retaliation after the attack on Pearl Harbor. 'This award is the greatest honour my country could bestow upon me. It is my life's mission to repay that trust and I count on my men to achieve that. Can I depend on you?'

'Yes, sir,' replied the well-trained Americans in the room. The Brits were perhaps a little uncomfortable with the theatrics, coming from a world ruled by the 'stiff upper lip'. Only orators like Winston Churchill could really get away with being so bombastic.

The meeting was held in the largest room of Engle Field's old farmhouse, what had once been the stables. They'd been cleaned and spruced up, but the smell of horses lingered. Between the stalls, Jox recognised Squadron Leader Millington of No. 225 Squadron and Lieutenant Colonel William

Covington, CO of the 82nd Fighter Group. With them was Dixie Sloan of the 96th Pursuit Squadron, just returned from the patrol over Youks-les-Bains. Space was tight, but the press of bodies meant at least it was warm.

'I understand your patrol over to Hammamet was uneventful,' said Doolittle. 'Major Sloan tells me it was a cake walk, a joyride across the country and back.'

Jox and Baraldi exchanged glances. Bartley cleared his throat. The general arched an eyebrow. 'Something on your mind, Squadron Leader? I expect my subordinates to speak up. Don't appreciate candy-assing around and got no time for that British reserve. I have even less patience for animosity between Yanks and Limeys, so come on, spit it out.'

'Well, the thing is, sir, we very nearly did get jumped,' said Bartley.

'What the hell are you talking about?' snorted Sloan. 'We didn't see a thing.'

'That's exactly the point, you didn't see a damned thing, but that doesn't mean there wasn't anything there,' replied Bartley. 'You were so keen on keeping your boys all tight and tidy in that pretty formation of yours. The fact of the matter is you're damned lucky McNabb here spotted two Snappers nipping through the clouds for a sneaky peek before popping back up to where their pals were waiting. That's why I kept your lot under the cloud base whilst I sent Jox up to investigate.'

'Why the hell didn't you tell me?' demanded Sloan.

'Are you saying that if I had, you wouldn't have gone charging up after them?'

'That's enough!' said Doolittle. 'McNabb, I think you better tell us what happened. Don't leave anything out and don't worry about bruising egos.' He glanced at Bartley and Sloan, adding gruffly, 'You two, keep it zipped.' He turned to Jox. 'Go on, son, I won't bite, well, not unless I get really riled up.'

Jox was never a great fan of being in the spotlight and began self-consciously. 'I followed the Snappers back into the clouds, being careful not to get seen…'

'Speak up, son, I want them all to hear.'

'Yes … sir,' stammered Jox. 'I saw the pair of Bf 109s join up with a holding circle of what must have been two dozen Snappers and Shrikes. They were obviously waiting to swoop down onto anything that broke through the cloud cover. I dropped back and advised Bartley, suggesting we sit tight to see if they might grow impatient and come looking for us. That way we could turn the tables on them. As I suspected, they lost patience and sent the two scouts to look for us.' Jox smiled. 'I led my section after them and two of my men took them out.'

'That's absolute horseshit!' exclaimed Sloan.

'Can you prove what you're claiming, McNabb?' asked the general.

'Yes, of course, sir. Our Mark IXs are fitted with gun cameras. It's a perk of having the latest kit. The Air Ministry are always keen for footage to use for propaganda purposes. I'm sure the film is being processed as we speak.'

'Ahem, perhaps I can take care of that, sir,' said Ridgway. 'I'm Ridgway, the intelligence officer for Souk-el-Arba, I'm sorry, I mean Engle Field. I'm also the Treble Ones' adjutant.'

'Better get hold of the rolls from Ghillie and Moules' guns, Doc. They did most of the shooting,' said Jox. 'That's Flying Officer de Ghellinck and Warrant Officer Mouland, sir. They rarely miss.'

Doolittle snorted. 'Mouland and de Ghellinck? Don't sound very British.'

'They're not sir, one's French-Canadian and the other's Belgian,' replied Jox. 'It's never been about nationality for us, we fly and fight with a common intent, to simply beat the enemy. It's fundamental to our squadron camaraderie. I don't care that they're not Scottish. I've flown with Ghillie since the Blitz and Moules since Dieppe. They're both first-class pilots.'

'I admire the loyalty to your comrades, McNabb. Most admirable,' said Doolittle. 'Dieppe, huh? That was quite a show. Biggest since the Battle of Britain, sorry we missed that.'

'You didn't, sir,' replied Jox. 'There were plenty of Americans flying with us that day. Several Eagle Squadrons were there, whilst technically still part of the RCAF. There were also a few USAAF P-51 Mustang squadrons, brought fresh in for the show, getting blooded that day. I had the honour of leading the Eagles of No. 133 Squadron on one sortie.'

'Good Lord, that's the kind of cooperation I want to see in this command,' cried Doolittle, clapping Jox on the shoulder. 'Say, any chance of a cup of coffee around here? I'm getting mighty dry with all this jawing.'

There was complete silence as the flickering footage projected onto the white-washed stable wall came to an end. The grainy images had clearly shown a formation of P-38 Lightnings being stalked by the dark cruciform shapes of two Bf 109 *Gustav* fighters. Each in turn was seen to be torn apart by focussed cones of fire, with great chunks being gouged from their fuselages before disintegrating. The views were from two gun cameras, each of which confirmed the actions of either aircraft. There was no doubting the veracity of the kills.

'Major Sloan, I believe you owe Squadron Leader Bartley an apology,' said Colonel Covington.

The Virginian stiffened, but like the Southern officer and gentleman that he was, he graciously followed orders. 'Please accept my unreserved apologies, Squadron Leader Bartley. It appears I have misspoken. We clearly have a lot to learn, and I do hope you can forgive me, sir.'

'It's all right, Dixie,' replied Bartley. 'There was never any intention of embarrassing you. We just wanted to demonstrate there's a world of hurt out there and we need to watch each other's backs. We Brits have been at it for rather too long, but I've no doubt you'll save my arse someday too.'

Sloan smiled and they shook hands.

'Let's have a drink over it,' said Bartley, visibly brightening.

'Hell, son, I like a drink as much as the next man,' replied Doolittle. 'But we've got work to do. If what McNabb is saying is correct, we need a heap of sharpening up.' He glanced around the room. 'Are you gentlemen familiar with the term FUBAR?' Some of the Americans laughed nervously, the Brits exchanging puzzled looks. 'It's a term which is becoming common amongst the fighting soldiers in North Africa when describing the progress of the war. To save the blushes of those offended by colourful language, I'll spell it out: Fouled Up Beyond All Recognition, and I can assure you a more piquant word is most often used.'

With a dangerous glint in his eye, the general went on. 'This is an unacceptable state of affairs. To simply believe things are just as they are is intolerable. There's been a mite too much horsing around and it's time to get serious. Our offensive is bogged down, and in the air, we are simply not being effective. I'm hearing reports that logistically things are in a mess, in terms of aircraft serviceability, scrapped missions and objectives not being met. Most squadrons are short of aircraft and struggling to fulfil their allocated tasks. Let's be clear, gentlemen, this will not do.' He scanned the room. 'So, what are we going to do about it?'

'May I make a suggestion, sir?' said Jox.

Bartley and Covington both looked at him, frowning.

'During the Blitz, when our squadron was re-trained into a night-fighter role, and then again before Dieppe, we really benefited from dogfight training. The most experienced provided the aggressor role to challenge the others. These experts were tasked with stalking the squadron just as the enemy would. I certainly honed my skills by getting bested over and over by the squadron's veterans. I was taught a hell of a lot that I'm sure has saved my life. I won't soon forget George Brotchie screaming at me on the R/T, "Bang-bang-bang, you're dead, McNabb. Drop out of formation and head for the showers."' Jox shook his head with a sad smile. 'Most of them are gone now, but I'll not forget what they taught me. Maybe that's what we need to instil in the men new to the desert, tangling with wily old Jerry for the first time?'

'My men have been practising dogfighting and aerobatics for weeks, even months,' said Covington. 'Is there really anything you think you could teach us?'

'Frankly, I do, sir,' replied Jox. 'Many of your pilots, and, in fact, the entire new crop of RAF replacements trained in the wide-open spaces of the American Midwest need guidance. They've arrived with basic gaps in their navigation skills. Here, most of the roads, such as they are, have evolved from animal trails, often meandering across the landscape, not the dead straight American roads running from one compass point to another. The sole exceptions being the vestiges of ancient Roman roads, or more recent additions near metropolitan areas built by the French or Italian colonialists. In my view, this simple fact explains why so many mission rendezvous are being missed, and targets or friendly troops not located, and aircraft simply running out of fuel. In other words, they just plain get lost. The level of attrition is even worse than I saw in Malta, and that's saying something.'

'I'm afraid Jox is right, sir,' added Bartley. 'As fighter pilots, the very nature of our mission is changing. These days we rarely intercept fellow fighters. Most of our work is ground-strafing and dropping bombs in support of troop advances. As more bombers come on board and we take the fight to the enemy, the fighters' role will no doubt evolve to a more defensive one, escorting and clearing the airspace ahead of bomber streams. That's when the Lightnings with their range, speed and firepower will flourish, but first they'll need to adapt their tactics to survive.'

The audience of American officers were listening intently.

'I know the skies haven't been very bright recently, but as we approach the deserts, they'll doubtless clear and we'll need to adapt how we fight,' said Jox. 'In the Western Desert, we learnt to spot a threat coming from the brightness, apparently out of nowhere. Pinpricks in the vast sky rapidly developed into threats, with the old adage "beware the Hun in the sun" never more apt. He almost always has height advantage too.'

Jox wondered if he was overstepping the mark, but Doolittle was nodding at everything he said. 'I'm afraid the Vee formation you're using, whilst very smart, is now completely obsolete. We've learnt that the hard way. The future is Jerry's "finger-four" formation with all aircraft well-spaced and working in pairs, a leader and a wingman. Sections are based on multiples thereof and in the Treble Ones we work with four separate sections of four. I lead one flight of eight, Baraldi the other and we both report to Bartley. Everyone has a good sightline and anyone who spots a threat tells the section or patrol leader, who acknowledges, then decides what action to take.

'The key decision is when to call the "break" with all aircraft dispersing in separate predetermined directions. The desired effect is to force the attacker to descend at speed from on high, hopefully overshooting, and to then be engaged on a more level playing field with the advantage of numbers. This of course assumes Jerry is cooperating and frankly, he rarely does, but with a few hard learnt lessons we can perhaps mitigate against the advantages he always seems to have.'

The room was filled with an uneasy silence.

'And where would you start, McNabb?' asked General Doolittle.

Jox looked at Bartley, who nodded his encouragement. 'Sailor Malan's "Ten Rules for Air Fighting" is as good a place as any. During the Battle of Britain, they were drilled remorselessly into us.'

Baraldi and Bartley both nodded.

'Refresh my memory, son,' said Doolittle, who was surely no stranger to the edicts.

Jox parroted, 'One: wait until you see the whites of his eyes. Two: fire short bursts of one to two seconds only, making sure your sights are definitely ON. Three: when shooting, think of nothing else. Brace your body; both hands on the stick and concentrate on your ring sight. Four: keep a sharp lookout and always be on it, never in a daze. Five: a height advantage gives you the initiative, but even without it, you should always turn and face the attack. Six: make your decisions promptly. It's better to be quick, even with poor tactics. Seven: never fly straight and level for more than thirty seconds. Eight: when attacking, leave a proportion of your formation as a top guard. Nine: always be guided by the words INITIATIVE,

AGGRESSION, AIR DISCIPLINE and TEAMWORK. They are the crux of Air Fighting. Finally, ten: get into a fight quickly, punch hard, then get out." There, that's it, sir.'

'Well, well, it appears you've got yourself a new job, Mister McNabb,' said the General. 'Any problems with that?'

Jox looked to Bartley again, who nodded. 'No, sir, no problem at all.'

'Okay then, let's get organised. You'll liaise with Colonel Covington. I want you to select a cadre of your best air fighters and start training my boys. Paint the spinners of the "aggressor" aircraft a different colour, so we know who's who. What colour would you choose?'

'Why, yellow, of course, sir. If we're going to pretend to be Jerries, we might as well look like them. Everything else should remain in standard RAF livery.'

'That's fine. As soon as you think they're ready, I want some American boys to join the "aggressor squadron". Let's make a big deal of them making the grade, getting them all painted up when joining. Actually, I don't much like that name, how about "Pirates"? Kinda captures the spirit. Yes, McNabb's Pirates has a certain ring. Can I count on you to get it done?'

'Yes, sir,' came the resounding answer around the room.

'Good, I'll be keeping an eye on your progress. As soon as we see the programme is working, I want it rolled out across the Twelfth Air Force. By God, my men are gonna be the meanest gunslingers in the skies, or I'll want to know why. You got that, boys?'

'Yes, sir,' came the thundering reply.

As the meeting broke up, General Doolittle called Bartley and Jox over to him. 'Good job, gentlemen. I hope I can count on you to be tactful as you proceed. It won't be easy for these guys to accept they've a lot to learn. It is that very confidence and self-assuredness that means the American aviator can achieve anything he sets his mind to. My own raid on Tokyo I believe demonstrates that. We need your knowledge and skill but can't have it erode that innate self-confidence. It won't be easy, but get it done.' He stared at Jox for a moment. 'You're an impressive young fellow, Mister McNabb. Hard to believe you've seen so much action.' He turned to Bartley. 'Say, Squadron Leader, how will you cope if McNabb takes your best to set up his unit?'

'We'll manage, sir,' Bartley replied. 'We have more pilots than serviceable aircraft anyway. The men recruited to the Pirates will still be available to the squadron, when and if Jerry turns up, and ultimately, we'll benefit from their training both as trainees and instructors.'

'Okay, keep me posted. McNabb, choose carefully. Only the best are to be amongst the Pirates. Come to think of it, Squadron Leader Bartley, don't you think we ought to bump young McNabb up to Acting Squadron Leader?'

'Why, yes, sir. I would certainly say he deserves it.'

'I'll have a word with Sheep Gilroy of No. 324 Wing. Your squadron is in his mob, right?'

'That's right, sir,' replied Bartley. 'We're scattered across the country and acting independently, though.'

'Yeah, we've got to tackle that, too. We need cohesion and cooperation, not this chaos. Fighting in a piecemeal manner is a recipe for disaster. Carry on, good day gentlemen.'

Jox and Bartley came smartly to attention as the general left.

'Well, that qualifies as something to celebrate,' said Bartley. 'Also sorts out a headache I've had for a while.'

'Really, what's that?' asked Jox.

'Admin have been chasing me saying you're overdue a break from operations. Technically you're tour has expired, but now if you're working as an instructor, that kills two birds with one stone.'

'How's that?'

'Well, I don't actually lose you, as you're still here, but you're also technically out of frontline combat. So, perfect,' said Bartley. 'And, to top it all, you've just been promoted and will be getting your own squadron too. It's about bloody time.'

CHAPTER FIVE

The Spitfire Mark IXs were parked in a row, freshly painted with pollen-yellow spinners, the same as seen on countless Snappers and Shrikes. The paint was official *Luftwaffe* pigment found in storage sheds on the newly renamed Engle Field and was an appropriate way to differentiate Jox's Pirates from their erstwhile squadron mates.

Having the aircraft so dangerously close to one another for the photo opportunity, was making Jox eye the horizon nervously. They were a hell of a target for any raider brazen enough to have a go. He certainly hoped the paratroopers at the Bofors defending the airfield had their eyes open for trouble.

'Come on, take your shot and let's get this over with,' Jox said to the *Stars and Stripes* magazine's photographer. He glanced at the Spits, resplendent in tropical sand and olive camouflage, each fitted with a jaw-like Vokes air filter under the propeller. Usually, these were painted sky blue or tan, but these were black, and some wag had added a skull and cross bones motif. Jox's aircraft, JU-X, even had 'Jox's Pirates' added below the crossed bones. *A fine bunch of Pirates*, he thought, smiling for the camera. The shutter clicked as his motley crew jostled around him.

He'd chosen based on experience, can-do and self-reliance, trying his best to emulate the qualities found amongst the *Luftwaffe*'s *Experten*, airmen who often worked alone or in hunting pairs. His Black Section would be Axel Fisken and Ghillie de Ghellinck, both skilled killers he could count on.

Each had proven their worth over Dieppe and Libya respectively.

Ensuring that he didn't just opt for his own people, he'd asked Mouland to join them, knowing the Canadian WO2 was also very experienced. Yellow Section was led by Reeves, another Treble One stalwart, now recovered from his impromptu dip in the Mediterranean. He was backed by the American Tom 'Monty' Montague Falls, another newcomer, but whose nationality was 'politically helpful'. He was a very experienced pilot from Chicago, who'd served with RCAF from early in the war. He was an eccentric character, a skilled musician, performer and raconteur. Constantly smoking a pipe, of them all he was best described as a pirate, possessing a long black moustache, a certain swagger and an outspoken manner.

For Jox, his permanent cloud of smoke, severe black moustache and eagle beak nose, made him the spitting image of another character he'd met earlier in the war. King Zog the First, the exiled king of the Albanians had taken a shine to Jox and his friend Moose during the London Blitz. Jox still wore the crimson ribbon of an Albanian Order of Merit, which he wasn't entirely sure he deserved.

Monty Falls spoke fluent English, French and German, and was already playing up to the role of being a *Luftwaffe Experte*, shouting, '*Achtung!*' and '*Gott in Himmel*' whenever the feeling grabbed him.

Completing Yellow Section were the 'fair dinkum mates from Down Under', Barry 'Gusty' Gale and his sidekick, Kiwi Jim Waring. Both were Dieppe veterans, dependable and resourceful with the 'can do' attitude typical of pilots from the Dominions.

It was only once he'd made his final selection that de Ghellinck pointed out that Jox was actually the only Brit amongst the Pirates. That hadn't been deliberate, but an unexpected side effect of such a multi-national crew was the realisation that something as simple as the words 'Bang-bang-bang' were proving problematic. This was particularly important as this was how the trainees would know they'd been bounced and defeated during exercises. The thrice repeated word was something of a mantra with Jox, who had unashamedly stolen it from his own dogfighting tutor, the late, great George 'Wee Brotch' Brotchie.

The issue was that, in Norwegian, Fisken said 'Bung-bung-bung', the Francophone pair in Black Section said 'Pan-pan-pan' — pronounced 'Pong-pong-pong' — whilst the Aussie and Kiwi in Yellow Section did say 'Bang-bang-bang' but each delivered in their own particular accent. Topping things off, the forceful American refused to use anything other than 'Pow-pow-pow'. It may have seemed like a small thing but it would require careful explanation to Yank pilots who came from right across the United Sates and already had a bewildering array of accents to contend with.

At the pre-flight briefing it was explained the exercise would consist of two halves: first a straightforward interception by the Pirates against the 96th Pursuit Squadron, as they were held in a 'cab rank' which was a fairly typical starting scenario for the squadron's missions.

The second operation would see half of Sloan's Lightnings tasked with protecting the other half, taking on the role of bombers. The 'active half' of the 96th would provide close escort and were there to defend against any Pirates getting through. The objective of the first scenario was to survive, the second to protect the bombers at all costs.

Jox was at pains to point out that, 'You are no longer wolves but sheepdogs, there to protect your flock. If they go down, you have failed. Learn the lesson, gentlemen, as it is most likely the future of the Lightning force in the European theatre of operations. The bombers must get through and it's your job to make that happen.'

The vector points of a circuit over the Tunisian mountains were provided and beyond that there were no hard and fast rules. 'However,' Jox said, 'there is *one* thing. An important consideration. *Do not* live fire in *any* situation on *any* friendlies. Your aircraft will be armed as there is always the possibility you could run into unexpected real bogeys. This is unlikely as we'll be well behind our frontlines.' He stood, hands on hips, in what he hoped was a martial pose. 'Mark my words, I have the full authority of Colonel Covington, and Major General Doolittle for that matter, to deal with any idiot that fires on a friendly aircraft, especially one of my Pirates. All your aircraft and ours are fitted with gun cameras, so the evidence will be clear. The procedure is that the film is switched on before engaging and you say the words loud and clear over the R/T. Now, do I need to remind you what those words are?'

The room remained silent.

'I want to hear them.'

'Bang-bang-bang,' replied the room.

'And again.'

'Bang-bang-bang.'

'There, couldn't be simpler,' said Jox, the grin on his face showing greater confidence than he was actually feeling. He was very aware that any one of these men was quite capable of filling his Spits full of holes. 'Right, let's get this show going. Carry on.'

Whilst the P-38 Lightnings got themselves organised, taxiing and taking off, Jox gathered up the Pirates for a final briefing. 'Gents, I want this done correctly. We're here to teach these fellows some humility and that they've got a good deal to learn. Hopefully by doing so, we keep them alive.' His eyes narrowed. 'On the ground, we make a show of being supportive allies, but up there I want you to chop them to pieces.' He gave a wolfish grin which they returned with nodding heads. 'Moules, I want you as my wingman. Axel and Ghillie, you two will climb and come out of the sun. The minute you hear my "bang-bangs" on the R/T, you swoop and "take out" as many as you can. Make sure it's all on film and you're audible on the radio. Engle Field Ops room will be recording every transmission.'

He paused, allowing them to absorb what he was saying. 'Once we hit them, they'll scatter.' He glanced at the Australian surfer, noting that his uniform was looking a bit tight. 'Kanga, I want your section to appear from the east, moving fast but making yourself rather obvious. You're there to be seen and offer a tempting target, one I hope they'll go haring after.'

'Righto, got you, mate,' said the big Aussie.

'Monty, at the rear, I want your best bluster and acting skills over the R/T. If any of them are sneaky and listening to our frequency, let's mess with them.' He smiled. 'During the Battle of Britain, Jerry was on our airwaves all the time, so two can play that game.' Jox put a hand on Monty Falls' shoulder. 'I want you shouting in German to your whole "*Staffel*". Then switch languages to your best Southside Chicago and give orders to the 96th's Lightnings. Lay it on thick and be as creative as I know you can be. Your job is to create confusion and distraction.'

Falls stroked his black moustache with his forefinger, one side at a time. He was relishing his part in the drama of the forthcoming mission. 'I'll give it my best shot,' he purred. 'Going to be a hell of a lot of fun.'

'Moules, our job is to stalk the P-38s.' The Canuck looked up. 'I want to get behind their formation. Won't be easy, but my plan is to get beneath them and hold our position in the blind spot under their bellies. I want camera footage proving we were there, then we simulate belly shots and get out.' He pointed at de Ghellinck and Fisken. 'By then, our "Huns in the sun" are attacking and providing further distraction.' The pair nodded. 'Finally, once Black Section have "taken out" a few, it'll be Yellow Section's turn to follow the "survivors" home to Engle Field. I want you to hit them as they land. Not exactly playing by the Marquess of Queensberry's rules, but Jerry's no gent either.'

'*Qu'est ce que c'est le Queensberry?*' asked Mouland.

De Ghellinck explained who Queensberry was in rapid French.

'And again, in English for us blokes from the Dominions?' said Gusty Gale.

'Oh, it doesn't matter,' grinned Jox. 'Let's just say we're not following the rules of cricket, so you take the "body line". All right, Gusty?'

Gale grinned wickedly. 'You got it, cobber.'

'Listen, we're here to show the Yanks that war is a dirty, thoroughly ungentlemanly business. A hard lesson they need to learn.' Jox glanced at the charred blue Rolex on his wrist. It was half an hour since the Lightnings had left. Jox knew the P-38's cockpit was notoriously chilly, so by now, hands and feet would be numb, attention dulled, and reactions slowed. Just in time for the fun and games to begin.

The airwaves crackled with a guttural voice. '*Kommt nah heran, meine Kinder.* Come close, my children. *Schiessen Sie nicht zu früh.* Don't shoot too soon.' Falls was in fine form, streaking across the azure Tunisian skies with just a faint scattering of high cloud. There was nowhere for the Pirates to hide. 'Come on, Mack, watch your back!' he added. 'Jox's *Experten* are all over you. Break left, break left!'

Jox looked towards the sun. Barely discernible were two little crosses just off to the side of the glaringly bright globe. Fisken and de Ghellinck were in position. He and Mouland were on an opposing course, hugging the rocky terrain, blending in with the sparse vegetation as they crept nearer the rearmost four P-38 in a double diamond formation. The Lightnings were fast, powered by liquid-cooled 12-cylinder Allison V-1710 engines with turbo-superchargers, but were flying too close together, intent on holding their places in the formation.

Compared to his own Merlin 60 engine, the P-38s were unusually quiet for fighters, muffled by their turbo-superchargers. They were powerful but not manoeuvrable enough for dogfighting. In a straight line they could outrun the Mark IXs, but this wasn't a sprint race, it was a deadly game of cat and mouse.

The big, box-like American fighters bounced in each other's turbulence, visibly rattled by Falls' chatter. '*Führen Sie sie direkt in ihr Feuer.* Lead them straight into your fire.' The Teutonic consonants sounded harsh across the airwaves. '*Die Amerikaner halten immer zusammen, ein größeres Ziel für Ihre Waffen.* The Americans always stick together, a bigger target for your guns.'

The Lightnings began to climb, whilst Mouland and Jox slid their Spits into position beneath the rearmost pair. They held the precarious attack stance, bouncing in the hot wake of the paired Allisons. Mouland was under the back P-38, Jox the one ahead and to the portside.

Jox licked his lips then took a breath. He swallowed, trying to find some moisture in his mouth. Despite his mask, he could smell engine oil, glycol and petroleum fumes. He clicked his throat mike twice, the signal agreed with Mouland to switch R/T frequency to that used by the Yanks. He recognised Dixie Sloan's drawl in his earpieces. 'Keep it tight, boys. Don't get distracted by that pig Latin. Y'all know it's just ol' Jox up to his tricks. Keep your eyes open.'

Sloan was wilier than Jox had given him credit for. He smiled and exhaled, a final moment of calm before the storm began. He started his gun camera rolling then glanced back at Mouland, who was looking straight at him. He raised a gloved hand in the shape of a pistol and mimed shooting upwards. Jox nodded and lifted the nose of his Spitfire, seeing the reflector sight projected onto the forward canopy slowly creeping towards the shiny horizontal tail bar of the P-38 directly above him. He was close enough to see the red stiletto of the swimsuit-clad lady painted on the aircraft's nose.

'Bang-bang-bang, you're dead Yank.'

A beat later, Mouland parroted, '*Pong-pong-pong, toi aussi, Oncle Sam.*'

The Lightnings scattered like mackerel under plunging gannets. One aircraft shot directly across Jox's flight line, eye-wateringly close to a collision. Playing these pirate shenanigans wasn't without its dangers, he thought, jostling with the controls.

Fisken and de Ghellinck were now falling from the sun, their own distinctive accents crying 'Bung-bung-bung,' and 'Pong-pong-pong' respectively. If they'd been live firing, it would have been a massacre.

In the meantime, Jox and Mouland were making their escape, a pair of swift Lightnings in pursuit. 'Two on my tail,' said Mouland, never one for idle chitchat.

'Draw them in,' said Jox. 'And keep turning hard to starboard. They can't hold a turn like us.'

Mouland's aircraft was jinking across the sky, his Merlin growling like an angry hornet. He executed a long, looping dive, the leading edge of his portside wing trailing white condensation which drew part of a circle across the sky. The pair of them were balletic in their synchronised precision with burbling pursuers struggling to follow suit. Mouland entered the first half of a Split S manoeuvre and the P-38s' engines backfired as they tried to keep up. He half-rolled the Spit with his cockpit inverted whilst his vision reddened as blood rushed to his head.

'I'm going to climb and get behind them,' said Jox. He jerked the stick towards his chest and climbed steeply. The pursuers continued after Mouland as Jox reached the top of his near vertical climb. He allowed the aircraft to stall, hanging in the sky like a mottled crucifix, before falling back on itself and beginning a tremendous dive.

He reached Mouland and his two P-38s, cutting between them. 'Jink left and I'll nail the bastard behind you,' he cried. 'Bang-bang-bang, Lightning Two, you're dead,' he said.

Seconds later, an American voice responded. 'Pow-pow-pow, Spitfire, you're dead too, buddy.' These Lightnings weren't entirely defenceless.

'Right, Moules, that's us. Let's go. Exercise over. Well done, that P-38 jockey.' Jox banked his aircraft and was followed by the French-Canadian, who added, '*C'est la vie.*'

The pair were on their way back to Engle Field when more 'Bang-bang-bangs' were heard on the R/T. Reeves and his boys were making a nuisance of themselves amongst the P-38s returning to roost. The airwaves were filled with angry expletives, frustrated Yanks making accusations of cheating. All the while, Falls roared with laughter.

'God damn it, that was a dirty trick. Picking us off like that when we were heading home.'

'Season's greetings to you too, Dixie. All's fair in love and war,' replied a grinning Jox. 'Your chaps need to learn they can't relax until they're back on the ground. It's one of Jerry's favourite tactics. Many of their multiple aces made a speciality of following our chaps home and taking them out when most vulnerable. They even gave it a name, *Fernnachtjagd*, long-distance night hunting, but as we've just demonstrated, it's just as possible in daylight,'

Sloan wasn't happy. 'All right, Jox, but you're a sneaky… What is it you Limeys say? Sneaky little sod.' He managed a resigned smile. 'Okay, I guess it's better for my guys to be humiliated by you than in a real gunfight. Come on, put us out of our misery, how many did y'all get?'

Jox flicked through the sheets he'd just been handed by Ridgway. His sweaty hair was standing on end from his flying helmet. He wiped his forehead before answering. The papers were the results of the exercise, expressed in dispassionate, objective terms, Ridgway's speciality as a graduate of the Intelligence College at RAF Medmenham. Photographic reconnaissance and interpretation were a speciality, and he gave Jox a quick wink. 'Thanks for getting the rolls processed so quickly, Doc,' he said. 'Let's see, according to the footage…'

'Yeah, thanks a lot, Doc, I appreciate it too,' interrupted Sloan. 'I suspect I'll be eating my words in a second. Come on, spit it out, McNabb.'

'According to this, the 96th Pursuit Squadron would have lost eight aircraft during your recent engagement.'

'Eight! That's half my goldarned squadron!' said Sloan, open-mouthed.

'That's not the worst of it. You were one of them.'

'Aww shit, how am I ever going to live that down?'

'I've got what you need for that.'

Sloan looked up, hopefully.

'Your lot did put up a fight and managed to down one of our Pirates.'

'One? Those are terrible odds.'

'That's right, aircraft PT410 with the lettering JU-X.'

'Wait a minute, that's you!'

'That's right, old boy. I'm not infallible. Been shot down more than a few times. Half a dozen if memory serves.' Jox smiled. 'Let me assure you, I won't be counting this as one.'

'Who got you?' asked Sloan.

'It was you,' cried Jox. 'But only after I took a nice photo of your tummy. You got me just after you were actually 'downed', but I'll not quibble. No damage done.' Jox laughed again. 'It appears our squadrons are now leaderless. Under usual circumstances, I'd suggest lunch or a celebratory drink, but we've got work to do.' He clapped the American on the shoulder. 'We go back to scratch, for the next exercise in an hour. Tell your boys this morning was a warm-up. Protecting the "bombers" is where things start to count.' He handed the clipboard to Sloan. 'Here, tell your chaps who'd have bought it if this was for real. I'd start by saying you're one of them. Hammer home this is no game.' He paused. 'I couldn't be more serious, Dixie.'

'I got you, Jox, and thanks for making my job a whole lot harder.' Sloan flicked through the typed sheets. He stopped. 'No, really, thanks a lot. What your guys did today, may well save our lives tomorrow.'

The afternoon's exercise was undertaken with a seriousness that might have been lacking that morning. What Sloan had shared made harrowing reading. The Yanks didn't fall for Monty Falls' tricks a second time, although he managed to confuse some, drawing away some 'sheepdogs' with ribald exclamations. Mimicking the Boston accent, he said, 'Got me that fell-ah right in the piss-ah. He's bangin' a fast uey, come on boys, get aft-ah him.'

Two P-38s lurched away in pursuit of Falls' Spit as he sped past. It was like triggering the chase instinct of lurchers. Unfortunately, in doing so they opened the 'hatch' for several Pirates to get at the 'bombers', the P-38s playing that role. There were fewer 'kills' than in the morning, but it was still a sobering exercise.

The cycle of training continued for weeks, with Jox's 'phony war' extending to other US fighter squadrons, whilst a very real one raged over beleaguered Tunisia. Rommel's forces were counterattacking and the troops on the ground were reeling. Allied fighters were struggling against the experience and aircraft superiority of the *Luftwaffe,* and it was only the Allies' numerical advantage, the abundant supplies in terms of fuel, war materiel and manpower which evened things up. The butcher's bill was proving eye-watering.

Losses amongst the Twelfth Air Force's P-38 Lightnings were appalling. The heavy toll on the 14th Fighter Group squadrons meant the 82nd Fighter Group, including Dixie Sloan's 92nd Pursuit Squadron, were fully activated, and their training curtailed. Jox and his 'Pirate Squadron' continued to train the airmen of the Twelfth Air Force, but on a more ad-hoc basis and only once operational commitments were met.

For units serving in the Twelfth Air Force, aircraft serviceability and airfield working conditions continued to be challenging. As December dragged on, only an estimated quarter of aircraft were serviceable. There were shortages of spares because of logistical foul-ups, and ground crews were struggling with the harsh conditions and constant airfield-hopping of squadrons keeping up with the battlefront.

'Where are the goldarned air force?' became a common complaint, a familiar refrain to Jox and veteran Treble Ones who'd heard similar reproaches over Dunkirk and St Valery. It was no less painful this time around. Whenever leave away from the front was possible, disgruntled ground troops took to taking out their frustration on innocent airmen. The number of barfights over that Christmas period increased, with military police kept busy. Frustrations over the progress of the North African campaign and the grim fighting conditions saw the troops increasingly fighting each other as much as the enemy.

With the year drawing to a close, the Pirates were reintegrated into the squadron. Their aircraft kept their differentiated livery in case they were called to restart the programme, but otherwise the Treble Ones were complete again. Their comrades were delighted at the return of the 'prodigal sons' and *bon-vivant* Bartley saw it as an opportunity for several boozy parties in the lead up to Christmas and Hogmanay. It had always been a favourite time of year for Jox, but even he thought the CO was rather overdoing it.

During the Battle of Britain, every squadron had a drinking culture to steel themselves for the next day. Bartley and the gentlemen flyers of No. 92 Squadron partied rather harder than most. Now though, it appeared Bartley was not so much filled with *joie de vivre* but rather drinking for Dutch courage. In the squadron diary, Jox saw a melancholy note Bartley had scribbled, *What a thoroughly miserable month in the run-up to*

Christmas. God, I hate this dump. I've seen too bloody much, and Jerry can keep it for all I care.

Jox was getting worried; Bartley wasn't himself, drinking every night and getting rather too merry even for the time of year. It was beginning to affect squadron morale and also its reputation. There were stories circulating and complaints made by an American unit advancing under fire which had called for air support.

No. 111 Squadron were rostered on call but were missing in action. Bartley had discovered that a nearby farm had a vineyard, and there were rumours of a vast barrel of Tunisian red wine. Led by their intrepid squadron leader, the Treble Ones were 'liberating' the said wine when they should have been in action. Investigating officers discovered that when the call came through, the squadron was already 'well in its cups', racing to drain the barrel before the authorities caught up with them. Even if they'd wanted to, and some were 'fighting drunk' enough to consider it, they would have been of little use.

Disciplinary actions were underway, but Bartley simply found the proceedings hilarious in his 'devil may care' belief that this was what the Treble Ones stood for. Jox and the other veterans were starting to find the situation embarrassing, affecting the squadron's standing amongst their colleagues, allies and friends.

Things came to a head once Jox and the Pirates were fully operational with the squadron again. It was Christmas Eve, a day that would end as one of reckless triumph, but also anguish with a profound effect on several lives and careers.

The day began innocuously enough, the squadron tasked with coming to the aid of a beleaguered column of British infantry on the road to Medjez el Bab. They were being harassed by Stuka Ju 87 dive-bombers. With air superiority and control of the skies, the Stukas' pinpoint accuracy was devastating and terrifying for besieged infantry huddled in what little shelter there was in the exposed desert. Streaking to their rescue like knights of old, the Treble Ones hit the swirling mass of inverted gull-winged Stukas like the wrath of a vengeful God, offended by their actions on this day of all days.

Stukas have sturdy wheels on spatted undercarriages, which project forward like the talons of a fish-eagle. Each aircraft can carry a single 550-pound (250 kg) bomb between its legs, plus a further two 110-pound (50 kg) under each wing. They are clumsy flyers at the best of times but more so when weighed down with armaments, making them easy prey for the fast and agile Spitfire Mark IXs. The blood-curdling wail of the Stukas wing-mounted air sirens were known as Jericho Trumpets and had petrified troops and refugees across Europe, but now only served as a Valkyrie's lament heralding the Stukas' doom.

Bartley led from the front, blinded by a desire to get at the 'easy meat'. There was never any doubting his courage, just his judgement and recklessness. Jox's fighter pilot instincts scoured the auburn-streaked skies, searching amongst the dust plumes raised by the dive-bombers for their inevitable escort of fighters. They would be positioned to swoop in textbook style, the classic 'Huns in the sun' if there'd been any sun.

The Stukas scattered like sheep panicked by dogs. Bartley was right amongst them, laughing demonically, his wingman Sergeant George 'Longers' Longbottom tight on his shoulder. The pair ripped through the Ju 87s with savage abandon, several falling and trailing smoke, cross-hatching the lower reaches just above the scrubby desert. Drifting through were the parachutes of several Jerry airmen who'd taken to their silks. The lucky ones made it to the ground in one piece but would then be at the mercy of the infantrymen they'd just been strafing. It was likely they'd spend a rough half hour before being handed over to the MPs, battered and bruised. It was the season of goodwill but there seemed to be little compassion to spare.

Jox gave instructions for his flight to turn and climb into the watery brightness of the sun. He glanced sideways through the tinted lenses of his goggles and detected movement like sandflies around a naked bulb. The fighter escort were up there, and on their way down.

'WAGON Squadron, Green Leader here,' Jox spoke into his mask. 'Bandits in the sun, stand by for trade.' He glanced down at the section led by Bartley and Longbottom, mixing it up with the Stukas. 'Watch your back, WAGON Leader. They'll be on you in a sec.'

'Roger, Green Leader,' said the excited voice of Bartley. 'Not going to be of much use, no ammo left. You and your boys take care of them. I can see that there are some heavies on the horizon, trying to sneak past us and get to the pongos on the ground. They're Ju 88s.' Jox could hear the rasp of Bartley's breath. 'They won't know we're out of ammo, but we'll give them a damned good fright. Keep the vultures off our backs, there's a good chap. Tally-ho, tally-ho, Red Section. Green and Yellow Sections providing top cover.'

Jox sighed. Bartley's orders put his men at a tactical disadvantage, climbing blind into the sun, but they had no choice. He was fortunate and the sight of eight Spitfires manoeuvring aggressively towards them, their element of surprise clearly lost, was enough to dissuade the lurking Bf 109s from attacking, opting instead for easier quarry elsewhere.

Below and behind Jox's flight, the open desert suddenly erupted in a flurry of fiery explosions. Huge flowers created from red sand, viewed from altitude, were like ephemeral

Christmas poinsettias before they began to drift, dissipating onto the pock-marked ground. For a moment, Jox wondered what the hell was going on, but then he saw Bartley's fighters had panicked the Axis bombers into jettisoning their bombs prematurely. Despite their strength in numbers and the defensive screen of onboard gunners, the bomber crews like their fellow fighters, had little appetite for conflict at Christmas.

As the dust settled, a garbled flurry of voices were on the R/T. Jox recognised an agitated Bartley, followed by the sight of a smoking aircraft tracing a curving parabola towards the ground. A moment before it flashed into a bright explosion, a figure fell away from the fuselage. Jox feared the falling man had been caught by the blast but was relieved when the white half orb of a parachute deployed, rapidly filling with dust-laden air. He exhaled with relief, grateful the unknown airman had successfully joined the Caterpillar Club, his life saved by those distant Indian silkworms. Jox was a fully paid-up member of the club; in fact, he probably qualified for a bulk discount.

By the time Jox and his section completed the patrol over the ragged column of infantrymen, then handed over to No. 225 Squadron's Mustangs, the best part of an hour had passed. Circling overhead, they'd been a protective 'big brother in the sky' for the shell-shocked troops on the ground, who emerged blinking from cover after the aerial assault of the Stukas. Jox's flight swooped low to provide encouragement but also to make sure they knew there were RAF aircraft overhead. The weary infantrymen waved berets and helmets in appreciation of their deliverance from the Stukas' wrath. When ground-to-air coordination worked, it was wonderous to behold, and Jox felt a surge of pride that he hadn't felt since the beginning of the North African campaign.

Back at Engle Field, Jox parked up and ran through his routine checks and debriefs with his ground crew. Overseeing things was WO2 Seamus Black, known as Blackie, a Dubliner that Jox had known since before the Battle of Britain. Jox was as frustrated as any pilot by the recent poor aircraft serviceability but appreciated the tough conditions the crews were working under. It was reassuring to know that the tough and uncompromising Irishman was now in charge. The ever-resourceful Seamus would soon have the Treble Ones' riggers, fitters, electricians and plumbers firing on all cylinders or there'd be hell to pay.

Entering the dispersal tent, Jox searched for Bartley, curious to discover who had brolly-hopped over the desert. He hoped it wasn't Bartley but could find no sign of him. Instead, he found Baraldi looking hot and bothered, sweat-stained in his flight clothes. His face was red, and he was gulping thirstily at a canteen of water. He upended it over his head, a cascade of water splashing over his sweat-beaded forehead. He exhaled like the blowhole of a dolphin, scattering water across the floorboards.

'Bloody hell, Jimmy,' said Jox. 'Bit hot under the collar?'

'Too right,' Baraldi replied. 'That was a hot half hour, I can tell you.'

'Why? What's going on?'

'That bleeding "Charge of the Light Brigade" bullshit, with that idiot Bolshie haring off after those Ju 88s, even though he knew we were out of ammo. Brave, but bloody daft. Thanks, by the way, for being the sensible one and keeping those vultures off our backs. Good to know I can depend on someone up there, rather than a bampot like bloody Bartley!'

Jox glanced around and was relieved the tent was empty. 'All right, Jimmy, tell me what's got you so riled up.'

'I just told you,' he replied, temper barely under control. 'We never should have gone after those heavies. Sure, they panicked and dropped their loads, but why were we stooging about amongst them? Their gunners had a field day. Peppered most of us and we're damned lucky we only lost the one.' His face was showing the strain. 'Longers stuck with Bolshie until he got nailed. Thankfully, he baled out before the whole bloody lot blew up.' Baraldi was shaking, what he'd witnessed still before his eyes. 'Bolshie knows it's his fault and as soon as he landed, he was off trying to find Longers. They're close and Bolshie will never forgive himself if he's hurt. I can tell you, Jox, I'm glad you're back in the fold.'

'Okay, Jimmy, we'll take care of it. Let's see if we can't find a cool beer somewhere. I'm sure the Yanks will have some, they always do. Come on, mate, let's cool you down before you blow a gasket.'

CHAPTER SIX

It was dark by the time Bartley reappeared. He was three sheets to the wind and clutching a bottle of American bourbon into which he'd clearly made some serious inroads.

'All right, calm down,' he slurred as his men gathered around, keen for news of Sergeant Longbottom. 'Longers is fine. Wounded, but in good shape, all things considered.' He giggled. 'Actually, we've had a little Christmas drink together.' He caught Jox's eye. 'Would you believe our Longbottom has actually been hit in the arse?' He started laughing. 'I dare say it's uncomfortable, but what are the chances of that?'

Bartley clearly thought it was hilarious, chuckling until he was overcome by the hiccups. He took a swig. 'Awfully decent of those Yank doctors to give me this for Chrimbo. Nice drop, actually. Fancy a pull?'

Jox shook his head. Bartley was drunk again, and in front of the men.

'They're grateful we scared off those Ju 88s this afternoon,' Bartley continued. 'Apparently, their ambulances were sheltering with the British column when the Stukas had a go. They were worried the Ju 88s would attack next.' He grinned. 'One good turn deserves another, eh? The season of goodwill and all that rot. Promised to take good care of old Longers. He may well have copped a Blighty wound for Christmas. He was dosed up when I left but wishes one and all a happy Christmas and is sorry that he's missing the party. He was smiling, but that was probably the drugs. So come on boys, for old Longers let's get this soirée going!'

And the party was certainly a merry one, the stillness of the Tunisian night fractured by raucous laughter, chatter and lustily sung carols. The noise attracted the other units on Engle Field, the news spreading that the Brits were having a 'knees-up'. Things became high-spirited, verging on riotous, since the Treble Ones were confident they'd done well and, despite the lucky escape, felt they deserved to let their hair down.

Tired from the day's exertions, after just a few drinks Jox was nodding off at the bar. Never the biggest of drinkers, he peered at the charred face of his recently inherited watch, seeing it was past midnight. The party was going strong and there was little prospect of it ending any time soon. 'I'm sorry, chaps, I'm knackered,' he finally said. 'Can barely keep my eyes open.'

Standing at a trestle table covered in scavenged food and bottles of varying origins, Bartley had his arm around Monty Falls' neck. The pair were arguing over something or other, neither listening to what the other was saying.

'Wait, Monty, wait, hold that thought,' said the CO. 'I've got something to say.'

The gathering settled down with the few hecklers being hushed up. Bartley waved his cigarette to quieten them further, peering myopically through the smoke-filled interior of the tent. 'Gentlemen, we did well today but things could have turned out differently.' He was breathing heavily and rocking slightly. 'I know some of you believe I may have been rather cavalier and I'm sorry for that. You see, the reason I'm always so confident when flying with you lads is that I know you've got my back. Mixing it up with Jerry's heavies today, giving them a fright, even with empty guns, was only possible because our Jox here and his valiant boys had our backs.'

He staggered as he raised his glass, splashing in Jox's direction. 'So, there we have it, to Jox McNabb, who always has my back. On this Christmas Day, as ever, he's the backbone of our squadron.' He looked momentarily confused. 'I, for one, bloody well know it. So, here's to Jox, my friend and yours.'

There was a chorus of cheers as the assembled men raised their bottles and glasses and began to sing a rather racy song.

Bloody hell, this is all getting a bit much, thought Jox. He raised his hands in surrender, then waved to say his goodbyes. Making his way to the exit, he passed Baraldi, who leant towards him. 'See you in the morning. Merry Christmas, Jox. Don't worry, I'll keep an eye on him.'

Jox nodded his thanks, then spotted his roommate, Ralph Campbell leaning on one of the tent poles.

'Take it easy, Ralph, you'll bring the whole bloody lot down.'

His former schoolmate smiled crookedly. He'd never been terribly good with alcohol. It was him vomiting on the house mistress's prize Paisley carpet that had gotten Jox expelled in the first place. Ultimately, that was the reason he was a pilot in His Majesty's Royal Air Force, so perhaps he should be grateful. Tonight 'all the King's men' weren't really putting on much of a show.

The pair shared a room, or rather a sectioned-off portion of a communal dormitory tent. At least it had a warm stove, reasonably comfortable cot beds and wooden floorboards laid on Marston Mats of perforated steel planking to keep out the damp. It did, however, creak noisily when walked upon.

'Don't make a racket when you come in and don't forget we've got Ops tomorrow.'

Campbell nodded drunkenly and Jox saw the futility of getting the Treble Ones to rein it in, especially since the CO was chief dilettante amongst them.

Moments later, Jox was on his cot, pulling off his socks. He heard the laughter of his comrades and a piano banging out Christmas carols. It reminded him of Pritchard, who always took a turn on 'the old Joanna'. He had the long fingers of a pianist, unlike Jox's own scarred and rather stubby efforts. He cracked his knuckles and wondered how Pritchard was doing, far from here, and safe from all this mayhem. He missed him and smiled at the idea that the old fox would be chasing women at some Christmas party, right about now.

It was Monty Falls playing. Actually, he was rather better than Pritchard, being a gifted pianist who'd given concerts in Canada and America. He was playing one of Pritchard's favourites, 'Roll Out the Barrel'. Jox leant back and closed his eyes. He sighed, drifting off to the sound of his squadron mates massacring a wartime classic.

The next morning, Campbell was sprawled fully clothed on his cot, snoring peacefully when Jox got up. Jox got dressed and went over to the latrine tents, grandly called the 'bathhouse', hoping there might still be some hot water for a shave. He'd long since learnt that feeling clean and fresh did wonders for one's mental attitude. It also set a good example to your subordinates. Never a terribly hirsute fellow, unlike Monty Falls and the other moustachioed members of the squadron, he didn't have much to shave but somehow the ceremony was soothing and felt significant.

He was finishing up when Jimmy Baraldi came out of the shower, a khaki towel wrapped around his waist. He was older than Jox, almost thirty, and a little paunchy. He was another hairy fellow, clean-shaven but with a thatch of dark hair on his head and fur over his chest, stomach and even his shoulders. Jox had no idea there was so much fuzz hidden under his uniform, but perhaps that was down to Baraldi's Sicilian heritage.

Baraldi waddled up to the mirror and peered red-eyed at his reflection. He held open his eyelids, peering intently at each eye. He covered one, then the other, comparing the vision in each, blinking several times, then rubbed them with his knuckle. He sighed and began lathering up a soap dish with a badger tail brush on an ivory handle. He spread the foam onto his face in a circular motion, then looked up.

'Hello, Jox. You feeling all right? Wise man to have escaped when you did.'

'Morning, Jimmy. I needed the kip,' replied Jox. 'Thankfully Ralph's not too much of a snorer. Trouble with your eyes? They look a bit red, or is that the booze or the sleepless night?'

'They've been bothering me a bit. Scratchy all the time and sometimes weepy. I get a touch of double vision and fuzziness occasionally. It's weird, looking at you now, I can see you, but your face looks a bit squished. It gets worse at night, so maybe it's because I'm tired.'

'Sounds a bit odd. Better get it checked out by the M.O. He'll sort you out.'

'I'll have a word with Doc Ridgway too, he's always good for medical advice.'

'Righto. Fancy taking a walk over to see how the maintenance boys have managed overnight? There's a new crew chief in charge and you ought to meet him. I've worked with Blackie before, he's one of the best. He's got the bit between his teeth trying to get our aircraft availability figures up. Afterwards, we can swing by the Yanks' mess tent and see if there's some breakfast we can scrounge. They must owe us, after last night's bar bill.'

'Sure, capital idea,' replied Baraldi, his razor poised over the blue five o'clock shadow on his cheek. 'I'll be there in a bit.'

Jox finished his ablutions, then took a stroll between the accommodation tents while he waited for Baraldi. Unfamiliar songbirds were twittering, and the sky was tinged orange from Saharan dust high in the atmosphere. The tangerine glow was pretty and somehow felt seasonal, but Jox knew the same grit played havoc with aircraft engines. The air was still and warming up nicely, a nice change from the rest of the month's rain which had pounded relentlessly. A few grasshoppers leapt from the grass with curious-looking flycatchers in pursuit. From the tents came the sounds of waking men, coughing, groaning and invariably farting.

By the time Jox reached the maintenance sheds, Baraldi had caught up with him.

WO2 Seamus Black saw Jox approaching and grinned. There was mischief in his eyes and a grimy forage cap perched on jet-black hair as greasy as it was long. No shortage of reasons then as to why he was called Blackie. 'So, Acting Squadron Leader Jeremy McNabb, is it, sir? Should I be saluting you or shaking hands, your honour?' He'd clearly already made up his mind and held out a grubby paw. It was a test, which Jox knew well. If he took the maintenance crew chief's hand, it would be filthy, but by doing so he was paying his respects, showing he valued the effort that the ground crews had put in through Christmas to get his aircraft airworthy. Jox gripped it without hesitation, knowing he would wipe it later on his socks, a habit from school from when he'd worn knee-high woollen socks and shorts, even during the bleakest of Scottish winters. It was a hard habit to break.

Black's Irish brogue was like soothing music to his ears, reassuring Jox that the squadron's aircraft were in the best of greasy hands. His dark eyes glistened with pride as they shook hands. Jox had seen this reaction before, but never fully understood it. How could he possibly refuse the hand of a man so vital for his own job? The snobberies and associated petty humiliations that infused the British military system still baffled him.

'Blackie, let me introduce Flight Lieutenant Jimmy Baraldi. He leads A Flight, now that Pritch has gone off home for a spell.'

'My great pleasure, sir, and a Happy Christmas to you. To be sure, it's an honour to meet you.' Black held out his grimy hand once again. Quick as a flash, Baraldi grabbed it, pumping it enthusiastically. He'd been in the service long enough to know the old tricks.

'No, it's my honour, Mister Black. Season's greeting to you and your crew,' Baraldi replied, using the appropriate terminology for an officer addressing a warrant officer.

'How are things shaping up, Blackie? Things running smoothly?' asked Jox.

'Well, sir, maybe not exactly smoothly, but these young slackers certainly know there's been a change of regime, shall we say.' Black had left the Treble Ones to earn the warrant officer shields on his overalls. He'd served at RAF Duxford, and more recently at Port Said in Egypt, whilst Jox and Baraldi had seen action at Dieppe and the North African desert. He'd only recently re-joined the Treble Ones, part of the move to get things kick-started in the stalling North African campaign. 'We're getting there, Jox, but for today…' Black reached for a sheet of paper from his overall pocket. 'We've got, let me see, eleven Marks IXs ship-shape and ready to roll. A few needed some patching up after that tangle with the Ju 88s. We did lose one though and two more will need working on as they're still unserviceable.'

'Very impressive, Mister Black,' said Baraldi. The hangar was a hive of industry despite the early hour. 'The other week, we only managed to get six kites up.'

Black nodded, steely-eyed but appreciating the compliment. 'You call me Blackie, sir. We're all friends here, ain't that right, Jox?'

'We are, Blackie,' replied Jox.

The stocky warrant officer grinned, appeared to perk up and put on a show, pretending to dust the crests on his forearms. He strutted about, dark-haired locks bobbing comically. 'Look at us, Jox, fine pair of swells we've become. Who'd have thought, eh?'

'We've certainly come a long way,' Jox replied. 'Quite the journey and we've got hard miles ahead.' He looked around the hangar, inhaling the odours of oil, metal dust from the rivet guns, soldering irons and aviation fuel, combining in a surprising balm for the senses.

'Well, sirs, you can count on Blackie and his boys.'

After a cadged breakfast, Jox returned to the Treble Ones' dispersal tent. Activity was starting up right across the airfield. The deep throb of a multiple-enginned American bomber echoed across the PSP runway, the sound cut by the high-pitched burbling of a P-38 Lightning taking off. Its undercarriage whirred as it retracted and the box-shaped fighter banked away, the winter sun flaring through the clear cockpit and off the aluminium fuselage. The fluidity of its movement was reminiscent of flowing quicksilver, as it was joined by a wingman, and the pair raced northwards.

It was still early enough for the local women to be working on the purple-tinged crocus fields, shrouded forms advancing in lines across the landscape like an army of beetles. On the surrounding hillsides stunted olive trees held onto the hazy moisture of the low cloud. They were islands of green against the terraced rocky backdrop. On the far horizon, the vast, ancient Roman city of Bulla Regia loomed.

Last night Doc Ridgway had spoken of a trip to take a look at the ruins, a sort of Christmas treat. He said the ruins were spectacular and not to be missed. Jox had agreed to tag along. It would provide a bit of variety and culture to the mind-numbing routine of daily missions. Speaking of which, they needed to get cracking to make the morning's pre-flight briefing. He found Bartley seated at a table, head in his hands and sobbing.

'Come on, Bolshie, the hangover can't be that bad,' said Baraldi, instantly realising the quip was ill-timed.

Bartley raised his head, red-eyed with tears streaming down his face.

'What on earth's the matter?' asked Jox, grabbing a seat beside him and laying a comforting hand on the CO's shoulder.

Bartley tried to compose himself, wiping away tears with the cuff of his flight jacket. Jox handed him the tartan handkerchief from his pocket, which he accepted, blowing his nose before speaking.

'Longers died during the night.'

'Oh my God, I thought the doctors said he'd be all right.'

'They were wrong,' Bartley replied flatly. 'I got the call half an hour ago. He lapsed into a coma overnight. Apparently, an infection took hold and spread like wildfire. They couldn't do anything. They tried giving him some new penicillin drug from

America, but the infection was too strong. It was septicaemia or in other words, blood poisoning.' He lowered his head and began weeping again. 'I can't believe Longers is gone. We were just joking over the chances of a Longbottom getting shot in the arse, but I never imagined it might actually kill him. Christ, neither did he. While I was partying, my wingman was dying all on his own.'

Other Treble Ones began filing into the dispersal tent for the morning's briefing. It was immediately clear something was up, by the state of their leader and those huddled around him. Jox worried about the impact on morale.

'No way you could have known, Bolshie,' said Baraldi. 'Don't be so hard on yourself.'

'Damn it, I should have known better,' Bartley replied, his voice cracking. 'I'm supposed to be the flipping CO. It's my fault it happened in the first place. All that man ever did was follow me faithfully, no questions asked. Now he's dead and that's on me.' He stared dead-eyed at something only he could see. 'I might just as well have shot him myself.'

The next morning the CO insisted he would lead the men despite being in no fit state. He wanted Jox as his replacement wingman. Jox only agreed because Bartley emphatically declared that no one else would be lost on his watch, an unrealistic expectation from a man clearly on the edge.

Jox pulled on his flying helmet, his oxygen mask flapping with cables and pipe trailing. Bartley was beside him.

'I'm so tired this Christmas,' Bartley said. 'I never thought I could ever be this tired. I'm not sure I can keep this up.' He then proceeded to fly like a man possessed, everywhere all at once, utterly fearless and unpredictable. He took unreasonable and unnecessary chances, unsettling to his fellow Treble Ones and making him every bit as dangerous as the enemy.

The squadron's mission was scrapped almost as soon as they were airborne. They were called back to defend Engle Field against yet another raiding party of Bf 109s and Ju 88s, targeting the airfield on Boxing Day. Bartley took this as a personal affront, outraged at being attacked on this day of 'brotherly love'. He raged at the enemy's 'boorish behaviour', reacting like a maniac, suicidally brave and utterly determined to take down his opposite number. He found their *Staffel* leader from the black arrowhead on his aircraft's dun-coloured fuselage. With Jox struggling to keep up, Bartley pursued him across the tiger-striped skies. His opponent was skilled and experienced, the victory tallies on his tail testament to that, and he would surely prove no easy victim.

Bartley threw his Spit into manoeuvres that shouldn't have been possible. He used logic-defying recklessness to unsettle his measured opponent, who soon realised he was surely dealing with a madman. As he gained on his opponent, the CO's guns hungrily sought the jinking enemy ace. Every ounce of Bartley's rage poured into his cannon fire until he finally managed to blast through his victim's fuselage. Aiming by instinct, he split the elusive Bf 109 like a well-hit bird at a pheasant shoot. Bartley skidded his Spit, fishtailing before he fired again, this time at the enemy's wingman, his *Rottenflieger*, who swiftly caught fire as Bartley watched his latest victim fall. Tactically, this was a basic mistake, exposing himself to a pursuant, but Jox was watching his back during his entire *fugue de folie*.

They circled the airfield, risking the defending AA fire, but Bartley insisted on counting the Treble Ones in. He was gabbling away on the R/T, manic and excitable, the joy of his victories short-lived. They watched in horror as the squadron landed on the bomb-damaged runway. One after the next, four precious Spitfire Mark IXs touched down, skidded and suddenly tumbled into grinding heaps. It appeared the torn PSP metal planking was shredding the tyres as they landed, tipping the aircraft over with catastrophic results.

By the time Bartley landed, he was seething. He stormed straight to his locker and grabbed a bottle of VAT 69. He polished off at least half before speaking. He then seized the dispersal telephone and called the Ops room, first berating the air controller, of equal rank, then made irate follow-up calls to the American base commander and airfield's group captain, CO of the entire RAF component. His words were to the effect of, 'I don't bloody well care who you are, I refuse to take further responsibility for pilots if they are forced to operate from a bloody death trap of a field which you are incapable of protecting. We can't even land without writing off aircraft which groundcrews have sweated through the night to get airworthy. They worked through Christmas to achieve that, and where I wonder were you? I've had it with you lot, take your war and shove it where the sun doesn't shine.'

He then proceeded to get drunker, only calming down once sluggish with the drink. By the time the bottle was empty, he was slurring, 'I don't mind the flying, Jox, the hunting or even the killing. It's everything else. If they can't do their bloody jobs, why the hell should I? I've done enough, that's it.'

Bartley was having a nervous breakdown. Every man has a limit and he'd reached his. He'd lived at the razor's edge for too long, longer even than Jox, and now he was done. All reserves of courage, leadership and resilience had simply run out.

Jox and Baraldi were determined to protect him. They needed somewhere he could sleep it off, out of harm's way and where he could do no more damage. There would surely be fall-out, but that could be dealt with tomorrow, hopefully when tempers had cooled, and Bartley could string together a coherent sentence in his defence.

Where could they stash him? They needed someone trustworthy to watch over him, someone who wouldn't ask too many questions. That could only be Black. He had access to sheds and hangars and was known for going on legendary benders himself. Jox dragooned Baraldi, Fisken and de Ghellinck into helping him, the four of them carrying the comatose CO under a blanket to disguise his identity. Four officers carrying a fifth, and the CO at that, might have been daunting to any senior NCO, but Black didn't bat an eyelid. He immediately agreed to help.

'I don't know Squadron Leader Bartley,' said the wily Dubliner. 'But if you boys vouch for him, that's good enough for me. We've all over-celebrated in our time. I'll watch over him like one of my own.'

'You're a lifesaver, Blackie,' Jox said. 'We just need to straighten things out. He's always been a drinker but losing his wingman has tipped him over the edge. Seeing four of our Spits getting written off certainly didn't help.'

Black's eyes narrowed. 'Four Spits? You bleeding eejuts have crashed four of my aircraft? After me boys spent all night fixing them?'

'Well, we didn't prang them,' spluttered Jox. 'The airfield got bombed because it was inadequately defended whilst we were up there fighting the blighters off. We tried to land, and half of us crashed because of the ragged PSP. Don't even know the fate of the pilots, just that the Spits were trashed.'

'If that's the case, people will be looking for me,' said Black. 'I can't stay with him; you'll need to find someone else to watch him.'

Jox knew the answer before he asked. 'Ghillie, Axel, will you do it?' They exchanged glances and nodded. 'Thanks chaps. In the meantime, Jimmy and I'll think of some kind of plan. We just need somewhere quiet where we won't be overheard.'

'Actually, Jox, we're due to meet Doc in ten minutes,' said Baraldi. 'I know there's a lot on, but we did promise to visit that Roman city he's always banging on about. He really could help, he's a handy chap in a crisis, medically trained and always offers a useful perspective. And he's our spy after all, so we can trust him to keep schtum on delicate matters. It'll be a change of air for us and might offer some perspective. We'll agree a plan for when Bolshie's sober, but it'll take a while for that to happen.'

The road to Bulla Regia was dusty, their jeep raising a red plume that was visible for miles and an enticing bait for any lurking *Jabos*.

Ridgway was driving, Jox scouring the heavens for any threats. Baraldi was splayed across the back seat, relaxed and rather enjoying the ride. This part of Tunisia was quite desert-like, empty save for military traffic. Earlier they'd been held up by a convoy of 'Deuce and a Half' trucks, loaded with supplies and escorted by a phalanx of American Military Police on bulky motorcycles with Perspex windshields.

'What were the Romans doing all the way over here?' asked Baraldi. He had to shout over the noise of the engine.

'They weren't actually from Rome,' replied Ridgway. 'All this was conquered territory after the Punic Wars. You'll know the story of Hannibal threatening Rome after coming through Spain and France?'

'The chap with the elephants?' asked Baraldi. 'Didn't know they came from here.'

'The capital of the Phoenician empire at war with Rome was a place called Carthage, near Tunis, but yes, from around here. Where'd you think they got the elephants?'

'Elephants?' said Jox. 'I haven't seen any elephants, just camels and little donkeys.'

'Well, maybe they weren't actually from here, probably further south, but they were African elephants sent north. I've often wondered how they managed to control them rather than using more docile Asian ones. Have you ever considered how hard it would be for tropical creatures to survive the freezing Alps?'

'Can't say I have, but it's pretty cold around here,' said Jox. 'They must have acclimatised, like we've had to.'

Baraldi suddenly laughed. 'Well, they're certainly thicker skinned than us.'

'I suppose so,' replied Ridgway. 'But d'you know, the epidermis of…'

They both laughed at him.

'For God's sake, Doc,' cried Jox. 'Don't give us a lecture on the skin of an elephant.' He shook his head, smiling. 'How do you keep all that information in your head? Do us a favour and keep it simple. We're air jockeys that just point the damned things and shoot when told to. Nothing too complicated, all right?'

'All right, I'll stick to the historical facts. That's what we're here for anyway, to get some culture and lift our minds from the humdrum of global warfare,' said Ridgway. 'I apologise for the digression, but I must say you're both rather grumpy today.'

'We have our reasons,' replied Jox. 'I'm sorry, I don't mean to take it out on you. We'll fill you in once we get there. I can barely think with that racket. Take it easy with that gearbox, you're not stirring soup.'

Ridgway grinned. 'One of you air jockeys should have driven so I could stick to more cerebral matters.'

The track eventually led to a straighter Roman road made of sandstone slabs, the chiselled rock flat and smooth as any runway. Centuries of oxen carts had worn grooves into the surface and Ridgway was doing a terrible job of avoiding the ruts.

'Take it easy, Doc,' cried Baraldi. 'We want to get to this city of wonder in one piece.'

Up ahead, a row of stone columns stood like the teeth of a broken comb, some at shoulder height, others taller. Each was ridged like a celery stick and must have been part of a significant building or temple. It appeared they'd reached Bulla Regia.

'So, where were we?' asked Ridgway. 'Ah yes, the Punic Wars raged between Rome and Carthage for some forty years. It was a devastating conflict for the domination of the Mediterranean, one side emerging triumphant the other utterly destroyed.'

'What do you mean?' asked Baraldi, gazing at the peaceful countryside.

'They hated each other so much that according to legend, when Carthage fell, the Roman legions were ordered to plough salt into the soil, so crops could never grow again to feed a rival empire.'

'Is that why everything is so bleak around here?' asked Baraldi.

'I doubt it,' replied Ridgway. 'Actually, the region has the reputation for being rather bountiful: wheat, grain, saffron, grapes and olives. Empires have fought for it for centuries. We're not the first foreigners to pass through, I doubt we'll be the last. In a funny sort of way, you could argue we're now fighting the descendants of those Romans and their Germanic vassals, who came here back then.' He'd slowed to negotiate a narrow street. 'When Mussolini took over, he reorganised his armies along Roman lines and, in the process, confused the hell out of his generals. We saw the result in Libya and the Western Desert. This particular patch of North Africa was left to the Vichy French, but they threw in the towel fairly quickly, so I'm sure Jerry will want it back and we can expect a counterattack. Assuming we cope with that, my bet would be we'll be having a crack at Sicily before we start climbing the boot of Italy.'

'Is that where we're heading?' asked Jox.

'Not officially,' said Ridgway, tapping his nose. 'But logic tells us it's most likely.'

'Well, if what I saw in Malta was anything to go by, it'll be no picnic.'

'I think you're right. Let's not forget the Italians are defending their homeland for the first time. It puts backbone into the fight. Look what happened during the Battle of Britain when we were up against the wall. But who am I telling? You two are glorious members of the Few.' His eyes glistened mischievously.

Ridgway pulled into a square and parked beside a dried-up fountain. Where water had once flowed, there was a black and white mosaic of fish partially covered in red dust. The fountain's central feature was a towering cascade of dolphins carved from sandstone.

'This is one of the oldest villas in the city,' said Ridgway. 'It's known as *La Maison de la Pêche*, the Fisherman's House. The mosaics inside are apparently exquisite. All around this square there are temples dedicated to the trades and virtues: hunting, fertility, agriculture, winemaking, metalworking, the lot.'

They mounted the steps of the nearest temple and filed through arched porticos leading to a colonnaded courtyard, shaded by pillars open to the sky. The space was filled with tinkling laughter and the chatter of local women. Stone flagstones were covered in hessian matting on which were piled mounds of wilted, ochre-coloured flower stamens. The cool breeze through the courtyard carried a heady aroma. Clustered at the edges of the mats were scores of women of all ages, squatting as they tossed flower parts into the air, separating out the clumps that had stuck together. Dry stamens floated like yellow snowflakes scenting the air. The airmen had stumbled upon the next stage of processing for the saffron picked every morning around the aerodrome.

'What's above ground at Bulla Regia is impressive,' said Ridgway. 'But the subterranean chambers are said to be the city's glory. It gets very hot in the summer and the ancients wisely built most of the city underground. Whilst it's sunny and cool, these ladies are drying their crop. It'll be returned to the cellars for storage and then go to the next stage of processing.'

The instant the trio were seen the chatter stopped. Faces were veiled immediately, bare feet and legs covered. The trio were watched by dozens of suspicious eyes. The anxiety, like the spice in the air, was palpable. Jox held up his hands, a gesture he hoped indicated they meant no harm. A thick-set, older woman spoke in a rasping whisper, her kohl-ringed eyes fearful, the rest of her features hidden by layers of material.

'*Shukran lak sayidi alkarim*,' she said. Behind her, younger companions melted away into various doorways giving onto the square. Soldiery had passed through here for centuries and the women were understandably fearful of what to expect from these latest invaders. Their leader bowed her head and backed away, abandoning the precious piles of saffron to the bewildered airmen. It was depressing to think they had created such fear.

Baraldi picked up a strand and tasted it.

'Don't do that,' said Jox. 'We can't just help ourselves. That's exactly the behaviour we're here to liberate them from.' Jox felt nauseous. 'Come on, chaps, this smell is making me queasy. I don't like this situation either. We can explore later, but we need to have that chat regarding our great and glorious leader.'

The men retreated to some underground chambers, the floors and walls covered with mosaics depicting muscular gladiators fighting wild animals. The tableau background had red flames and a volcano erupting. Ridgway explained this temple was dedicated to Vulcan, the god of fire and war. This was a holding area for the nearby amphitheatre, a place for ancient warriors to contemplate impending contests in the arena. The walls were intended to inspire greatness in the ring. Earlier, Jox had seen the amphitheatre, noticing how it rose steeply around a simple sand circle where men and beasts had shed blood. The horrors that happened here made him shudder.

In the dark recesses above their heads, nocturnal bats squeaked, their teeming movement creating a living ceiling, sensed rather than seen. At ground level, from the other end of the long, dark chamber came animated chatter. A troop of Barbary macaques had been alarmed by the intrusion to their daytime refuge from the heat.

Jox was familiar with these monkeys. He'd gotten rather too close to some in Gibraltar. He wasn't a fan, particularly after spotting the dominant male baring impressive fangs, as the troop scattered to hidden parts of the underground cellars. With a grunt of outrage, he made a show of urinating, then sauntered off on all fours.

'God, I hate monkeys,' said Jox. 'They give me the heebie-jeebies.'

'I rather like them,' said Ridgway. 'Like miniature humans.'

'That's what gives me the creeps,' replied Jox. He took a breath, smelling animal mustiness, from either the macaques or the bats, but probably both. It was a potent mix.

Twin rays of sunlight filtered through two apertures near the ceiling. Positioned to illuminate the delicate mosaics they were the sole light source. There was the slightest of tremors and dust particles fell through the light, illuminated like fireflies.

Baraldi swore, placing a hand on the damp wall to steady himself. 'What was that? Can't see a damned thing. Someone help me before I fall flat on my face.'

Ridgway took his outstretched hand and guided him to somewhere to sit.

'I'm no damned good in the dark. Eyesight seems to be getting worse,' sighed Baraldi. 'Yeah, I know, Doc, it's been worrying me. I've got an appointment with the M.O. Maybe you can take a quick look once we're out in the light again.'

'We'll get to that,' said Jox. 'Come on, chaps, we can't put it off much longer. What are we going to do about Bolshie? After what we saw today, I think he's at the end of his tether. We can't keep tidying up after his drunken outbursts. There's already too much collateral damage.' He glanced at Ridgway, whose head was cocked, looking quizzical. 'Sorry, Doc, you're not up to speed. Bolshie was knocked for six by losing Longers yesterday. This morning, he flew like a man possessed, putting us all at risk. When we got back, the field was under attack, and several kites were lost trying to land. That flipped a switch, and he was furious from the moment we were wheels down.' Jox shook his head. 'Of course, the first thing he did was reach for his favourite medication and got blotto. He then proceeded to berate several senior officers. He's not known as "Bolshie" for nothing, but that sort of thing doesn't go down well. Now, he's refusing to fly, saying he won't put his men at risk.'

'I was afraid something like this was coming,' said Ridgway. 'Things have escalated quicker than I expected. I know Doc Mear spoke to Bartley before Christmas, saying he needed a break. Bartley's response was to take the squadron on another bender. The M.O. is really worried and passed the message up the medical chain of command. From what you're saying, things have come to a head. No one's doubting the CO's courage and track record but having a go at senior officers like that is sure to set the vultures circling.'

'So, what are we going to do?' asked Jox.

'He may have already pushed things too far,' said Ridgway. 'He's got a reputation for being belligerent and disrespectful anyway. The Yanks are sensitive to that, especially from the Brits. The fact that he drinks every night, becoming rowdy and difficult is well known.'

'I think the question is two-fold,' said Baraldi. 'First, how do we get Bartley to step down with a minimum of fuss? And second, how do we limit the damage to his longer-term career prospects? Remember, he's pre-war RAF and doesn't have anything else.'

'There's no doubting his distinguished career, we don't want that tarnished,' said Jox. 'He's just exhausted. Reserves run dry.

He'll recover, he just needs a chance. We can't afford to lose men with Bartley's front-line experience.'

'That's all well and good,' said Ridgway. 'But the way he's mouthing off he's making enemies. Our advance in Tunisia is bogged down, stagnating even, and those in charge don't appreciate having their shortcomings pointed out. We're in a world of politics rather than military tactics now. A brave new world as deadly as any minefield, and one which Bartley is ill-equipped to handle, especially when inebriated, which is too often.'

'Let's first try to keep him sober and more importantly away from people who'll use his words against him,' said Jox. 'Next up, we need to convince Doc Mear to send him home. Bolshie has told me he's not coping, so he might be open to it, but he is stubborn. At least Doc Mear is on board.'

'What's the worst that could end up on his file?' asked Baraldi.

Jox and Ridgway answered at the same time. 'LMF.'

'LMF?'

'Lack of Moral Fibre,' said Jox. 'Your records get stamped with a red "W" for "Waverer". In the RAF, officers lost their commissions and were refused ground jobs. Jox knew this because during the Battle of Britain, his mentor and friend Cameron Glasgow was nearly declared a waverer, when depressed after his twin brother Anthony had been shot down over France. He'd had a breakdown, categorically refusing to fly. Jox recalled the efforts he'd put in to change his mind. Thankfully things had turned out all right, with a footsore Ant making his way home after a trying spell as a POW. Cam was now serving in Malta, where Jox hoped to see him again.

'It depends how vindictive the "forces that be" are,' said Ridgway. 'The LMF designation is intended to stigmatise aircrew who refuse to fly. They're classified as either medically fit, medically unfit on nervous grounds or medically unfit for other reasons. According to the regulations, pilots in the first two categories are deemed to be "proven to be lacking in moral fibre" unless subject to "exceptional flying stress". The question is, who and what defines that stress. If Bolshie is classified as LMF, he loses his flying badge, so can't even get an aviation job on civvy street. Flying is his life; it would be disastrous.'

His hand still resting on the damp wall, it was Baraldi who first felt the vibrations. Light to start with, they came from deep underground. The bats were the first to react, exploding into frantic movement and noise, all taking to their wings at once, blocking out what little light there was and plunging the men into an inky darkness. Panicked, the bats hurtled in every direction and for the trio, it was like being in the middle of a hurricane, pelted by dozens of songbird-sized creatures, all squeaking, flapping and scratching. The men could only ball themselves and fall to the grimy floor, where the thumping and crashing felt even stronger.

'It's a raid!' cried Jox, trying to make himself heard over the vortex of noise and movement. 'Jerry's bombing the city.'

'Those bastards!' raged Ridgway. 'Why on earth would they do that?'

Masonry began to fall, and the air filled with choking dust. The ground was jolting so violently they were thrown to the ground.

As the chamber rattled, entire sections of the precious mosaics crashed down. Jox tried to stand but was flung into a puddle of brackish water, welling up from some underground source, smelling strongly of sewage and earth.

The reverberations were unlike anything he'd experienced. As a pilot he'd been in several aircraft with failing engines, feeling the misfiring torque and the shudders going through the fuselage as they tore themselves apart. He'd lived through heavy bombing in Malta and the awesome artillery barrages in the Western Desert, but this was different. Manmade explosions have a uniformity of intensity, but these tremors were random. Here the power surged and waned like an ocean wave, or perhaps what he imagined it would be like in the centre of an avalanche or landslide. His arms outstretched in the darkness, Jox found his companions and they huddled in a pathetic knot of humanity, as forces beyond their comprehension raged around them.

It stopped as suddenly as it had started and was followed by an unexpected stillness. Rising from the darkness came screeches and screams from within the catacombs of Bulla Regia. Lying in a foot of filthy water, their stunned senses were now assaulted by the noise.

Jox felt one of the others shivering, from shock or the dunking in the subterranean water. Ridgway started to rummage through Baraldi's pockets to find some matches. He was the only smoker amongst them but was mute and trembling. Ridgway struck a match.

The brightness flared like a lance to their eyes. It revealed the trio, sodden and dust-smeared, eyes reflecting the tiny flame. In its fleeting halo, Jox saw that Ridgway had a cut to his scalp, a trickle of blood snaking down his face. Baraldi was clutching his left arm like a wounded bird, blinking at the flame, desperate for the warmth it promised.

'What a sorry bunch we make,' said Jox. 'Is everyone all right?' No one answered, but no one complained. 'Let the match die out, Doc, and let's see if we can find another source of light. It may take a while for our night vision to kick in, so take it easy for a moment and hopefully the light can show us a way out.'

There was movement in the darkness, then the sound of scrambling. Jox's heart was in his mouth as Ridgway struck another match. The sudden flash revealed the snarling face of a monkey, teeth bared, and hackles raised. Behind it was another, smaller, and with an infant on its back. They were pitch black and wet, caked with mud, the female's snout bubbling with blood. Jox jerked back, sending the male into attack mode. Within the brief illumination, man and monkey grappled in a blur of limbs, snarls and snapping teeth. Jox felt a sharp pain in the fleshy part of his right hand, a tug and tremor, then release. The bloody thing had bitten him and Jox roared at the top of his lungs, terrifying the creature and its companions.

Baraldi shrieked with fear as the monkeys scrambled away. 'What's happening, what the hell's happening?' he cried, blundering like a blind man. 'I can't see a damn thing.'

'It's all right, Jimmy,' said Jox. 'Calm down, I've been bitten by a bloody monkey.'

'Everyone, quieten down,' ordered Ridgway. 'Raised voices will only spook them. If we keep calm, they may even show us a way out. They've got sharper survival instincts than us, seeing and smelling far better.'

They hushed their laboured breathing, hearing dripping water and the plaintive keening of the infant monkey. There was some scrambling as its parents climbed up the sloped scree towards a pinprick of light near the ceiling.

'There, up there,' said Ridgway, pointing. 'We need more height. This water is getting deeper.'

It was past their knees now, and they were chilled to the bone. The chamber was filling, and they needed to find a way out. The silence after the commotion was interrupted by a scraping sound, metal against gravel. A bolt of light shone through. It was followed by a flurry of activity beside the newly opened aperture. The animals screeched and in a streak of muddy fur, scrambled through the opening, accompanied by shrieks both human and monkey in origin. After several exclamations and more scraping, the intensity of light increased. Rubble rolled down the slope and fine choking dust made them cough. The silhouette of a head peered down from above.

A voice spoke in French and Ridgway replied.

'What's he saying?' asked Baraldi, staring blankly but with frantic, grasping hands.

'I've asked for a rope,' Ridgway said. 'Maybe we can haul ourselves out of here before the water gets too high.'

There was silence at the hole, the sole source of light. The beam was like a searchlight during the Blitz or perhaps an usherette's torch through the smoky fug of the flicks on a Saturday night.

There was more scraping at the hole and light flooded in. Jox glanced at Baraldi, looking frail and dazed. Ridgway looked determined but frightful as blood from the gash in his scalp had soaked into his tunic jacket.

'You all right there, Doc?' he asked.

'Looks worse than it is,' Ridgway replied. 'The scalp always bleeds.' He touched the wound with his fingers and gave a sharp intake of breath. 'Stings like a…'

There were more voices from above. A flaming torch was flung through the gap, sliding down the mound of loose scree, followed by the thump of a hemp rope with several knots tied along its length.

Jox moved quickly to save the spluttering torch from the water's edge, lifting it to cast an orb of light over them and causing more bats to panic because of the light.

A husky voice called down. Jox lifted the torch and saw an old man. He couldn't understand what he was saying, but his gesticulations were clear — he wanted them to get moving and quickly.

The bite on his hand was hurting, so Jox put the torch on the ground, then anchored the rope with his foot, urging the others upwards. They set off, one after another, as fresh vibrations began thumping through the ground, not as powerfully as before but increasing in frequency. Gravel and larger debris began rolling down the slope, slowing their progress.

'Come on, we need to get out of here,' urged Jox.

It was hard going but the airmen were fit and strong and determined to escape the fetid chamber that had so nearly become their tomb. Nothing was going to stop them.

CHAPTER SEVEN

Jox was the last to climb out of the underground chamber. The sun was blindingly bright when he surfaced, and his eyes took a while to adjust to the glare, let alone absorb his surroundings. Blinking and bewildered, he was met with a disaster of biblical proportions. Bulla Regia was no longer regal nor magnificent anymore.

Where earlier there had been elegant avenues, columned temples and impressive dwellings, there was now just rubble and dishevelled people milling around like ants from a kicked nest. Most were civilians, but some were Vichy gendarmes and others were Scottish soldiers, sightseers like them, identifiable by their floppy Tam o' Shanters. There were also a large number of American military policemen, active in directing relief traffic, coordinating rescue work and providing first aid to the wounded. On their helmets were the letters MP and a white band that stood out. Their uniform consisted of tan-coloured blousons with a black armband, knee-high gaiters and pistols at their belts.

The MPs had rushed here from a nearby US Army encampment, some of whom they'd encountered earlier on the road. Their powerful motorcycles meant they could get to the scene rapidly and many were now parked, tall Perspex windshields emblazoned with MILITARY POLICE and their rear paniers bulging with blankets, water and first-aid equipment. Most of the men were large and intimidating as military policemen usually are, but it struck Jox how gentle these rough men were, when tending the cowed and bedraggled survivors.

Jox was trying to make sense of the destruction around him. He searched for reference points from when they'd first entered the underground chambers. He was struggling to do so. Even the steep, sloping circle of the amphitheatre was reduced to half its original height. Whatever the Germans had intended, they had certainly wrought devastation to this noble ancient city, but Jox still couldn't fathom out why.

He caught Ridgway's eye. His friend was pale, eyebrows now hidden under a bulky bandage wrapped around his head. Humpty Dumpty from the nursery rhyme came to mind but Jox hoped it wouldn't take 'all the King's horses and all the King's men' to put his friend back together again. Ridgway had a murderous scowl on his face, unusual for the mild-mannered doctor. He was clearly seething at the sacrilege of the destruction of such a priceless archaeological site.

'How could they do this?' Ridgway spat out. 'There is no reason to bomb ancient ruins, monuments of such historical significance. It's sheer vandalism and barbarity. Mark my words, these are the people we are fighting, bloody barbarians!'

A tall bespectacled MP had moved on to Baraldi. He was winding a bandage around his arm and fitted it into a sling. The old man they'd met earlier, instrumental in getting them out, was standing beside them. He patted Jimmy Baraldi's shoulder with a gentle hand as dark and weathered as worn leather.

'*À vôtre bonne santé, soldat*,' he said in a rasping voice, wishing him good health. Baraldi gave a weak smile.

The old man wobbled over to Ridgway and they spoke briefly in French.

'What's he saying?' asked Jox, his schoolboy French failing to keep up.

'He says it wasn't the Germans who did this, it was the ancient gods playing with our lives. I'm not sure what he means.'

'Odd thing to say.'

'I'll ask.' Ridgway carried on the conversation with the old man, who put his palm over his heart, then pointed heavenwards as he replied.

'He says the ancient Roman gods are playing. Vulcan, Poseidon, and the rest,' Ridgway told Jox and Baraldi.

'I don't get it,' said Jox, surveying the devastation. 'How on earth can the gods be responsible for this?'

'I don't know,' replied Ridgway. 'Maybe the old chap's taken a knock to the head, but he was certainly *compos mentis* enough to get us out of that hole.'

The old man held his weathered hands out and seized Ridgway's within them. He began to shake from side to side, mimicking things falling and tumbling, as he spoke more urgently.

Ridgway looked at him, stunned. His hand went to his mouth, and he gazed around as if seeing through fresh eyes. 'My God, now it makes sense. This was no Jerry raid, it was a bloody earthquake. He says Vulcan was playing with us, showing us mortals that we are nothing compared to the ancient gods and the powers at their disposal. I knew this area was prone to seismic activity, but since these ruins have been here for centuries, I thought nothing of it. We've been through an earthquake of epic proportions. It's a bloody miracle we're alive. If this old boy is right, then Vulcan has been merciful.'

'I'd say,' piped up Baraldi, who had just got up on unsteady feet. He gestured with his good arm towards a row of shrouded bodies on the ground. Beside them were a wailing coterie of mourners.

'God, haven't these people suffered enough, because of our damned wars? On top of that, now this,' said a deflated Jox. 'They don't deserve this. Makes me sick to my stomach.'

'I'll tell you what's going to make you even sicker, old chum,' said Baraldi. 'Don't know if the ancient gods have really got it in for us, but they've certainly done a number on the jeep. Seen the state of it? Someone at the MT depot is not going to be happy.'

Their borrowed vehicle had been crushed by the central feature of the water fountain they'd parked beside. The whole weight of the gambolling stone dolphins had squashed the jeep.

'Listen, Jox, I'm not one to pile mischief onto misery,' said Ridgway. 'But that bite looks nasty. Medical protocol is that animal bites need to be treated within twenty-four hours. I'm afraid some nasty jabs are coming your way.'

'Jabs? What for?' asked Jox, as Ridgway examined the wound. It was red and inflamed, with two deep puncture marks in the fleshy part of his hand between thumb and forefinger.

'Rabies, I'm afraid. Quite common in North Africa. Less so in monkeys but we can't take any chances, especially due to their close proximity to bats, which are known carriers. This is serious and we need to get you treatment pronto. If a rabies infection gets established, there's no effective treatment and the disease is fatal. You'll need to start a series of shots to prevent any potential infection from taking hold.'

Not liking the sound of that, Jox asked, 'What is the treatment?'

'I'm no specialist but you should expect injections near the wound and then a course of further jabs into your abdomen over a fourteen-day period.'

'In my stomach! How many bloody jabs?'

'I'm not sure but I'd say four or five doses of immune globulin, but it could well be more. The key is to get your treatment started. If the virus has time to get to the brain, you're pretty much done for.'

'For Christ's sake, what are the symptoms?'

Ridgway considered the question. 'As the disease progresses, the patient becomes restless and agitated; insomnia, delirium and hallucinations are common, as is a fear of water. Typically, the acute phase ends after about ten days and once clinical signs appear it's too late. We need to get you treatment.'

Jox gave an unexpected high-pitched laugh.

'What could possibly be funny?' asked Ridgway.

'I knew there was a reason I've always hated monkeys.' Jox's bravado was a front, however, for the cold flush of fear surging through his body. In moments of stress, he always reached for his talisman, the porcelain doll's arm in his chest pocket. He rubbed it furiously with the pad of his thumb, the friction bringing some comfort, but it felt somehow strange. He looked down to see that the doll's arm had broken into two pieces during their scramble from the pit. He fished them out of his pocket, a tiny hand in the palm of his, swelling now from the bite. He would get it fixed, as he had before, but somehow this time the fracture felt symbolic. He forced emotion from his voice. 'Come on then, better have a word with the "snowdrops" and see if we can get a lift to Doctor Mear at Engle Field. He'll have what's needed.'

'Let me speak to that medic,' said Ridgway. He walked over to the tall MP in the white helmet from which he derived his nickname. 'You there, soldier, what's your name?'

'O'Connor, sir, Corporal Stephen O'Connor,' the man replied, standing at attention, as you'd expect from a military policeman, even a medic.

'Relax, O'Connor. I'm Flying Officer Ridgway. I'm also a doctor. My friends and I are from Engle Field. We're here visiting Bulla Regia and got caught, well, in all this. Our vehicle's been flattened, and we need a lift back to our airbase. We've got a medical emergency. My friend, the squadron leader here, has been bitten by a monkey and there's a chance he's contracted rabies.'

The medic's eyes narrowed. 'Ah … yes, sir. This whole city is pretty much a medical emergency but let me see what I can do. Please follow me, we're gonna need to speak to my first sergeant, in charge of the detachment.'

O'Connor's NCO was a bulky fellow in an immaculate uniform which contrasted markedly with the squalor and chaos of the surroundings. He was in his mid-thirties, a little old for his rank, but had the look of a seasoned career non-commissioned officer.

He was slouching against his bulky motorcycle as they approached him. He watched them with an arched eyebrow, tapping his truncheon with his right hand into the palm of his left.

'What-cha got there, Oh-Connah?' he asked. 'Couple of Limeys been dragged through a hedge, huh?'

Jox recognised the accent of New Jersey, having met several "Joisy Boys" in the Eagle Squadrons. Jox had always admired exemplary NCOs like Mouland but he didn't like the look or the attitude of this one. Not exactly in the best of moods, after surviving an earthquake and suffering a monkey bite, having to deal with a Yankee martinet was going to seriously try his patience.

'Is that the usual way for an American military policeman to address a superior officer?' asked Jox, straightening to his not particularly lofty height.

The first sergeant looked uneasy and stood straighter. He was considerably taller than Jox. 'Ah … yes, sir … I…'

Of the three airmen, only Jox still had his forage cap on. 'I believe its customary to salute in these circumstances, Sergeant.'

'Sir, yes, sir,' stammered the first sergeant, saluting.

'Please report.'

'First Sergeant Patrick Atkinson, sir. Convoy escort detachment leader, 793rd Military Police Battalion, based at Souk-el-Arba, Tunisia, sir.'

'It's a pleasure to meet you, Sergeant. May I call you, Patrick?'

'Err … Pat, sir. My name is Pat Atkinson,' he replied hesitantly.

'Now, that's much better. My name is Squadron Leader Jeremy McNabb of No. 111 Squadron. My friends call me Jox. I am in need of your assistance. My friend here, Flying Officer Ridgway, is a medical doctor and has advised me that since I've just been bitten by a wild animal, there's a chance that I may have contracted rabies. I therefore need to get to specialist medical care as a matter of urgency. Our base at Engle Field is some miles away and our transport is well, out of service, and so I hope you can be of assistance.'

First Sergeant Atkinson stared at him. 'Let me see what I can do to get you back to your airfield. Everything here is FUBAR, but I'll get you to the medical treatment you need. O'Connor, your bike parked around here?'

'Yes, Sergeant,' replied the soft-spoken medic, shoving his spectacles up his nose.

'Good, I got mine too,' replied Atkinson. 'You go find Corporal Schwarz and get him to come over. We got ourselves an urgent mission to get the squadron leader to the doctor. Tell Joe it's important, as in a capital I.M.P. You got me?'

'Yes, Sergeant,' said O'Connor, saluting the officers before scuttling off to his task.

The return to Engle Field might have been exhilarating if Jox hadn't been preoccupied with dark reflections on what he'd witnessed. He was worried about what awaited him at the airfield, they'd been away far longer than expected and who knew what Bartley might have been up to. The prospect of rabies treatment didn't exactly fill him with joy either.

His hand was hurting, and he was struggling to hang onto Atkinson from the pillion seat of the policeman's roaring Harley-Davidson WLA. It felt awkward being so close to the burly sergeant, and he was finding the man's cologne stomach-churning.

Atkinson seemed determined to give Jox the thrill of his life whether he wanted it or not. Jox could only grip with one arm and at every pothole or burst of acceleration, risked toppling off the back of the bike. He was grateful for the goggles and helmet he'd been lent, but still managed to swallow what felt like half of the Tunisian desert.

Adding insult to injury, every fibre of his body felt stiff and sore from the subconscious stress clenching during the earthquake. He suffered through every bump and swing of the road, with Atkinson up front in dark sunglasses, constantly turning and asking if he was all right, his concern hardly matched by his driving.

It took less than half the time to get back as on the way out, but Jox and his companions were exhausted and monosyllabic by the time they arrived. They thanked the Yank snowdrops, wanting nothing more but to get to bed. Jox had important tasks though, first to get urgent medical attention and then to see whether Bartley had kept out of trouble during their absence.

A few days later, Jox was still in the infirmary. He'd been ordered off Ops by Doc Mear, as had Jimmy Baraldi. As soon as Mear had heard of the trio's misadventures, he leapt into action, particularly alarmed by Jox's potential exposure to the rabies virus.

He secured the required vaccines from a nearby Royal Army Veterinary Corps unit that held stocks to protect Army dog-handlers and their working dogs. These were used to patrol sensitive military sites and, in this region, regularly got infected in fights with feral packs of dogs roaming Tunisia's countryside, occasionally transferring the virus to their handlers.

The jabs began straight away. The first few were quite painful, around the site of the bite on his hand. His whole arm was now swollen, rather mottled and a fearsome scarlet colour. Mear assured him this didn't mean the virus had taken hold, simply that the wound was infected, which was hardly surprising considering the unsanitary conditions when received. Subsequent exposure to filthy water, potential contaminants, not to mention bat guano, hardly helped.

Great, thought Jox. *Now I run the risk of sepsis, gangrene or even tetanus. God, I hate bloody monkeys.* Unsurprisingly, Doc Mear's broadening prognosis brought with it even more injections.

The specific treatment for potential rabies infection began with Immunoglobulin administered around the bite site. These were more painful than the subsequent shots of the vaccine itself which he began receiving with depressing regularity. He was relieved to discover vaccines were no longer administered to the abdomen, as Ridgway had predicted, but rather into the bicep above the wound site. The intention was to ensure that any virus in the bloodstream was prevented from travelling up nerve tissues to the spine and brain. Doctor Mear explained that the virus, when spreading, could quickly damage nerve tissues, leading to headaches, confusion, anxiety, coma, acute behavioural changes and overt aggression. It was now just a question of watching and waiting.

Jox was kept apart from other patients, a Yank sergeant with a nasty ingrown toenail and an RAF armourer who'd broken a leg falling off a heavy bomber's wing. He was told it was to minimise cross-contamination, but the net effect was being treated like a leper.

The only person who didn't seem worried about his diagnosis was a Canadian nurse called Lucy McMahon, who would sit by his bed. She had sparkling blue eyes, artificially enhanced blonde hair and the straightest, whitest teeth Jox had ever seen. Nurse Lucy was a ray of sunshine for the patients in the infirmary, chirpy and chatty, her feminine company the best medicine for 'her boys'. She was nonetheless a no-nonsense nursing sister, who handled them with the right balance of authority, charm and flirtation, ensuring they all behaved.

To pass the time, she played cards with Jox and introduced him to Marble Solitaire, which he could play on his own. It consisted of a circular wooden board with thirty-three nooks drilled into it in a cross-shape within a circular holding groove. The game started with thirty-two marbles in the nooks, the objective to eliminate all but one marble in the centre, by jumping marbles over others as long as there was any empty space for it. 'Taken' marbles were placed in the groove until the end of the game and packed away in a leather pouch with a drawstring.

At school, Jox had never been terribly good at mathematics, but there was something about the spatial dynamics and strategy of sequences involved that appealed to the fighter pilot in him. It felt akin to lining up a deflection shot or anticipating an opponent's next move, with the game really beginning to intrigue him, but he couldn't put his finger on why. He spent long hours between rounds of inoculations resetting the marbles on the board and playing game after game. He'd just finished one, managing to get down to a solitary marble and was feeling rather pleased with himself when Nurse Lucy came in with a syringe on a tray, a ball of cotton wool and some antiseptic alcohol.

'Time for your next shot, Squadron Leader,' she said. 'I know it's not much fun, but you must be getting used to it by now.' She flashed one of her smiles. 'Sharp scratch, there you are, all done. You sit tight now.' She checked the watch pinned to her pristine white uniform. 'My instructions are to wait with you for fifteen minutes to make sure you don't have an adverse reaction to this latest dosage. The rabies vaccine can occasionally trigger allergic reactions, but since you've already had a few doses now, we should be all right.' She began fussing with his bedding and then filled a glass with water, handing it to him.

He drank gratefully and she smiled.

'Well, that's a good sign,' she said. 'Hydrophobia is a key symptom of infection, so that's encouraging. Tightness around the throat? Any headaches? Anxiety?'

He shook his head.

'You seem in a good mood, if a little monosyllabic,' she said. 'Something on your mind?'

'No, I'm fine, Lucy. Just keen to get back to Ops.' He grinned. 'Although, I am rather enjoying this game you let me have. It's completely absorbing.'

'Good, I'm glad you like it. I picked the board up in the souk. It's an ancient Arab boardgame apparently. Keep it, my present to you.'

'Thanks very much, I'm grateful. It may prove to be just the thing to keep my mind occupied when waiting to be called out on shouts. It's usually too tense to concentrate on cards or read, but this could be the ticket. I'm going to tell all my boys.'

'Happy to be of service.' She suddenly looked a little embarrassed. 'Listen, I hope you don't mind, but I'm due to be stepping out with an American chap once my shift is over. You don't mind if I make myself a little presentable while we wait?'

'No, not at all,' replied Jox, quite intrigued to see what mysterious process women go through to get ready for a romantic assignation. He wasn't terribly worldly on such matters. 'Who's the lucky chap, then?'

Lucy smiled, picking up her purse and taking out a compact mirror. 'His name is Steve. He's rather lovely. Actually, he's one of the Yank policemen that brought you in. He's ever so softspoken but was still bold enough to ask me out. I rather like that; he's been nothing but a gentleman.'

'Glad to hear it,' replied Jox. 'That's young O'Connor, isn't it? He certainly did me a good turn. Quite the dark horse, there's more to him than meets the eye. Hidden depths, eh?'

'You've no idea,' she said. 'He's quite a tiger as it happens.' She swiftly applied her makeup, finishing off with a bright scarlet lipstick.

The final look was a remarkable transformation from an already pretty young woman to a Hollywood starlet.

'What do you think, Squadron Leader?' she asked. 'Not too much?'

'No, not at all, you look lovely,' replied Jox.

Jox felt rather jealous of O'Connor but wished him well. Nurse Lucy too for that matter, as she was clearly smitten by the young policeman, given the effort she was putting in. It was heart-warming to see something sweet and normal in the midst of all the gratuitous violence and carnage of war.

When Ridgway and Baraldi came to visit, neither were exactly the picture of health. The ordeal at Bulla Regia had taken its toll. Ridgway was still pale, a fresh bandage around his head. He complained the stitches were too tight and giving him headaches. Baraldi had a yellow tinge to his face in addition to his damaged left arm. He had contracted some illness from the dank waters of the catacombs and was jaundiced. He was blinking repeatedly.

'Those bloody mosquitoes,' said Baraldi. 'Got eaten alive in that hole. Doc Mear says I've got Dengue fever. The little cousin of malaria apparently, so on top of everything else I've got the shakes, a fever and my face is the colour of saffron risotto. Never even saw the little bastards devouring us.'

All three had tell-tale red blotches confirming they'd indeed been feasted upon.

'Why haven't Doc and I come down with it?' asked Jox.

'Not everyone develops symptoms,' replied Ridgway. 'In any case, you're so chock-full of antivirals, you probably wouldn't anyway. I guess I'm lucky I don't react to mozzie bites like some.' Baraldi looked fed up, scratching furiously at an angry red spot by his ear.

'What a sorry bunch we make,' said Jox wearily. 'Hardly the "pride of the fleet".'

'Speak for yourself, I'm Cock o' the North, can't you tell?' said Baraldi, showing his sense of humour hadn't completely deserted him. 'What I wonder is why every damned thing in that blasted hole had to bite?'

'Speaking of the "pride of the fleet",' said Jox, 'how are things with Bartley? I'm completely out of touch. It's like being sentenced to solitary confinement. Most of the nurses seem to think I'm going to bite them given half the chance.'

Ridgway took a deep breath, and it was obvious his news wasn't going to be good. 'After drying out, supervised by Axel and Ghillie, Bartley managed to keep on the straight and narrow for a grand total of twelve hours. Then he hooked up with Monty Falls who was in the mess playing the piano and having a singsong with young Dennis Moss. Falls, Mossy and Bolshie went on a bender, which I guess was what tipped him over again.'

'What do you mean?' Jox asked.

'Their piss-up was fairly harmless in itself, but the next day during a fighter sweep over the mountains at Djebel Mansour, we lost Mossy. The squadron were supporting the 1st Parachute Brigade and the French Foreign Legion, and afterwards no one could find any sign of him. He disappeared somewhere over the mountains. Officially, he's Missing in Action, believed lost. Maybe they'll find him, but there are a lot of mountains to get lost in.' Ridgway winced before continuing. 'Then the flawed logic in Bolshie's head told him Mossy's death was his fault too.' Shaking his head, he added, 'He's been pretty much blotto ever since. True to belligerent form, he's refusing to fly, which is probably just as well. He's making an absolute nuisance of himself, offending every senior officer on the airfield.'

'That's not good,' Jox said.

'To top things off, Doc Mear has let me know that he's been asked for Bartley's medical records by the station commander, with a view to supporting a LMF rating,' said Ridgway. 'Seems like Bartley's on a mission to self-destruct.'

'That's exactly what he's doing,' said Jox. 'The man's unravelling, his mind turned by the demands of rank and the pressure of responsibility. And that's not even considering the enormous emotional cost of continuously losing comrades. I can truly empathise, but what I can't accept is that while he's self-destructing, none of us are doing a damned thing to help. We owe him too much for that.' Jox fell silent, staring into the middle distance. 'What's the one thing that could halt or interrupt the process of LMF classification, once underway?' asked Jox, in a flat voice.

'I don't really know,' said Ridgway. 'I suppose if he was charged with something even more heinous, something that superseded the "Waverer" rating. It would need to be serious. Gosh, the list is long but hardly bears contemplating.'

'Try me,' said a grim-faced Jox.

'Well, ah … there's treason for a start, mutiny, espionage, theft, fraud. I would guess rape, violence, homosexuality, dealing in the black market, basically anything that brings dishonour to being an officer and gentleman, or the service into disrepute. None of which are exactly palatable solutions, are they? Why do you ask?'

'I'm not sure yet, but I think I may have an idea,' replied Jox.

CHAPTER EIGHT

The crumpled man at the bar was no longer the dashing playboy he'd once been. Bartley was hollow-eyed and sallow-skinned, staring at the bottom of his glass. He barely looked up when Jox took the stool beside him, a solitary island of misery in the sea of alcohol-fuelled bonhomie in the mess.

The room was low-ceilinged, windowless and was once just a lockup at Souk-el-Arba airport. The Americans had done a great job of making it feel homely with bits of enemy aircraft mounted on the walls like hunting trophies, some tattered flags and a large poster of Betty Grable's famous legs. In the corner stood a battered piano while a record player on the bar blared out big band numbers with a lot of brass. De Ghellinck and Fisken were having a beer. Jox waved and they nodded back.

'Aren't you a picture?' said Jox.

Bartley barely acknowledged him. 'So, they've let you out?' he replied, draining his glass. He refilled it from a bottle in front of him. 'Want a drink?'

'No, thanks. Doc says it might interfere with the medication.'

'All the more reason in my book,' Bartley replied, wiping what he'd spilt with his sleeve. 'I'm glad you're all right, Jox. I was told there was a chance you'd be stark raving mad by now.'

Jox laughed, but it dissolved into a wheezing cough. The fug of cigarettes in the bar was thick. 'No such luck, but the evening's still young,' he spluttered.

They sat side by side, a mute pocket amidst the chatter and laughter. Officers of the many services and nations on the airfield were doing their best to ignore the two grim-faced Limeys at the bar.

'I'm not the only one who might end up in a straightjacket,' said Jox. 'What the bloody hell are you playing at, Bolshie? This has got to stop. They're going to get you, you know?'

Bartley looked blindly at Jox. 'I know, but I can't change that. It's a train crash I can see coming, almost in slow motion, but I can't stop myself. What comes just has to come.'

'But you'll be left with nothing. Not your name, not your career, not even your reputation. You've got to stop drinking, it's the root of all this chaos.'

Bartley peered at the amber whisky in his glass. 'I've run out of Billy Three Names' VAT 69. This is Yankee bourbon. Not bad as it happens, a bit sweet.' He giggled. 'I've become quite the aficionado. Not a patch on Irish whiskey, but beggars can't be choosers. I'm sorry, of course you're a Jock, but when talking whiskey, it has to be Irish.' He found the wordplay hilarious, dissolving into puerile laughter. He wiped some tears from his eyes. 'I'm Irish, of course, on my father's side. Yes, the great Sir Charles Bartley, barrister and judge. I wonder what he'd make of his washout of a son. What about Patricia? My sister's a big cheese at Bletchley Park, decrypting all manner of hush-hush stuff.' He frowned. 'Doesn't your pal Moose's wife work there? Lovely redhead, Stephanie or something?'

'Yes, why d'you ask?' said Jox, struggling to follow Bartley's meanderings.

'Fluent in German, isn't she?' Bartley tapped his nose with a forefinger. 'That's why our Patricia recruited her for the German Diplomatic Section. Very clever, those ladies.'

'In which case, perhaps we shouldn't be talking about them,' hissed Jox.

'I wouldn't worry, no one listens to me. I'm just a washed-out drunk who was once a half-decent fighter pilot.'

'Come on now.'

'Rather clever, my family,' Bartley added. 'My baby brother, Chris, he's a swot. Training to be a doctor at Trinity College, Oxford. Me, I'm the dumbo of the family. All I have is a talent for getting my men killed and then going doolally. Come to think of it, our Patricia had a bit of a breakdown before the war, so maybe it does run in the family. We Bartleys are brilliant but have fragile minds.'

'You're being silly. Come on, Bolshie, get a grip.'

'All rather academic,' said Bartley with a shrug and a resigned smile. 'I know they're after me, but I'm not going to give them the bloody satisfaction…'

This was not going as Jox had hoped. He wasn't getting through to Bartley and now the man was threatening to do God knows what to himself. Jox chewed his lip, realising he needed to turn to his rather more drastic Plan B. He glanced around the room; it was full enough for his purposes. There were enough witnesses once things started. He leant forward and with sudden steel in his voice said, 'Look at me, Bolshie.'

In his booze-addled state, Bartley looked up. He was unshaven, with dark bags under his eyes. The handsome, if sometimes rather vain, Bartley of old had completely disappeared.

Jox reached into his tunic. 'Here, take these, put them in your pocket and don't lose them. In the future, every now and then, take them out and remember this moment.' Jox handed Bartley a leather pouch containing several hard lumps. Bartley looked confused and went to untie the drawstring. 'No, keep them for later,' said Jox. 'In your pocket, now, go on.' Jox took a deep breath and squared his shoulders. 'I'm doing this for you.'

In front of Bartley's increasingly confused eyes, Jox popped an Alka-Seltzer tablet that Nurse McMahon had let him have earlier into his mouth. It began to fizz with his saliva, tasting disgusting on his tongue. Then, at the top of his lungs, Jox screamed, 'You stupid bastard! You're a bloody disgrace to that uniform.'

Bartley jumped like a scalded cat. 'Steady on, you can't speak to me like that! I'm your commanding officer…'

'My CO!' roared Jox, white foam boiling from his mouth. 'You stole my squadron and now you're driving it into the ground! You pathetic drunkard.' He swung at Bartley with his uninjured hand, landing a glancing blow across his chin.

Bartley tried to swing back but missed entirely. His face had blanched, and he was backing away from Jox, wide-eyed and terrified at the sight of the frothing maniac before him. Jox reached out for Bartley's tie, hanging loose at his neck. He jerked Bartley towards him like a ragdoll on a string. Neither was terribly tall, both flailing clumsily, one inebriated, the other demented with rage.

Jox had learnt the move playing rugby, but his technique had been perfected under the tutelage of the Glasgow twins. The 'Glasgow Kiss' was a great way for a wee guy to cause maximum damage, as long as he was quick and hard-headed. Jox was both, and the move had served him well in the past and would doubtless do so again.

The hollow wet sound of Jox's forehead connecting with Bartley's now not-so-handsome nose was audible over The Andrews Sisters' latest hit. As 'Don't Sit Under the Apple Tree' played, Bartley's glass shattered with a bang. The USAAF captain that was sitting beside him jumped back with an angry, 'Hey watch it, buddy.' He'd been covered by an arching spray of Kentucky Bourbon.

Jox had hold of Bartley's tie and pulled at it for a second crack. There was blood gushing from Bartley's ruined nose, his head lolling, either punch-drunk or drunk-drunk, but probably both. They connected with an odd 'pock' sound. Bartley's eyes rolled back into his head, and he went down like a bag of dropped cement. He was out for the count and lying in a groaning heap on the sticky wet floor. To protect his injured hand, Jox used his feet to strike further blows on the inert body of his commanding officer. Wet globules of foam sprayed from his mouth, landing on Bartley's crumpled and soiled uniform.

In the heartbeat it took for the occupants of the bar to register what was happening, Jox had landed several blows. His arms were suddenly pinned behind his back, and he was forced to the floor, down amongst the stinking stale beer and cigarette ash.

Enough of the crowd in the bar knew what he'd been sent to the infirmary for to keep well away from his snapping mouth. Two burly fellows sat on him to make sure he stayed down. Others lifted Bartley, who flopped like a drunk-tank alcoholic. Droplets of scarlet blood splattered the floor amongst the globules of Alka-Seltzer foam. A burgundy nape of it had already seeped down Bartley's shirt and jacket.

Jox's last recollection was of spotting the round spectacles of Axel Fisken glinting just before his fist crunched into the side of his temple. 'Stay down, Jox,' he said. 'Quick, Ghillie, help me, he's stronger than a berserker. The strength of a mad man.'

When he came to, Jox couldn't move. His mouth was dry, and he had a raging thirst. He struggled to sit up, but to no avail. His arms were crossed over his stomach and he was pinioned to what was evidently a hospital bed. When he tried to move his arms, there was a sharp jolt from his wounded hand, reminding him in an instant what had happened the previous night and the gravity of what he'd done.

He could see no one, just the familiar surroundings of the infirmary, but all the other beds were empty. He closed his eyes, a pulsing headache raging between his temples.

As he caught his breath, Jox heard a familiar voice. 'So, you're awake, eh?' said Nurse Lucy. 'You've got me into all kinds of trouble, Squadron Leader.'

'If that's the case, I'm sorry, Lucy,' croaked Jox. 'Please forgive me. I wonder, could I have some water? I'm parched.' He looked down at his strapped arms and asked, 'What the devil are these things? I'm trussed up like a chicken.'

'More like a raving lunatic,' she said with mock severity, but was betrayed by her trademark smile. 'I told them there was nothing wrong with you. It's all in your notes: "Completely lucid, no signs of stiffness in the neck, no manic or paranoid behaviour and no symptoms of hydrophobia." Like I told them, whatever set you off, it certainly wasn't rabies. I don't know what you're up to, Squadron Leader, but I'm not carrying the can for you, being blamed for a misdiagnosis.'

'No, it wasn't rabies,' said Jox. 'I'm perfectly calm, but parched. Please let me out of this contraption. You've got nothing to fear from me.'

'I know that, Jox,' she replied. 'You've just asked for a glass of water, so you aren't hydrophobic. I don't know what shenanigans you're up to, but as far as I'm concerned, they're not medical in origin. Unless they're somehow linked to that cut on your forehead, or black eye, but I'm pretty sure they happened after you went "Looney Tunes" in the officers' bar.' She looked at him, deciding what to do. 'I'm not going to loosen that straightjacket, that's up to the doctors, but I'll get you some water and a straw. That all right?'

'I'd be grateful. Thank you.'

'Never mind that,' said Lucy. 'You better start working on an explanation for your behaviour. There's a ton of trouble heading your way, and you better have some answers.'

He drank greedily from the straw, as she held the glass close. 'Take it easy. There's plenty more. If you want, I'll get you some soup once you've spoken to the doctors. How about that?'

'The doctors?'

'Yes, Doctor Mear and that friend of yours, Ridgway. They've been quite insistent they want to see you together. He's a doctor, too, isn't he? Certainly talks like one.'

'Is Squadron Leader Bartley in the infirmary?'

'He was, but he left yesterday on a flight to Algiers. I'm told he's heading back to Blighty. Doctor Mear told me the diagnosis is of "nervous exhaustion" and after all the trouble with you, the group captain has signed it off. Squadron Leader Bartley wasn't given much of a choice in the matter. Doc Mear says he's got over three hundred and fifty combat missions under his belt, so he deserves a rest.' Lucy fussed with Jox's bedding and pillows but left the restraints in place. 'You certainly made a mess of him, but he seemed strangely grateful.'

'Wait a minute, he left yesterday? But, how…?'

'You've been out for the count for almost three days. We've kept you sedated, to observe if your symptoms had taken a turn for the worse. We couldn't have you raging but, thankfully, nothing materialised, so you've been allowed to wake up and re-join the living.' She had a strange look on her face. 'Squadron Leader Bartley did ask me to pass on a message. He said to say, "Thanks for my marbles, I promise I won't lose them again." Does that make any sense?'

'Yes, it does,' said Jox, grinning. 'Could I ask you to fetch the doctors now? This get-up is getting bloody uncomfortable, and I've got a hell of an itch on my bite wound.'

Ridgway and Mear were quick to arrive. They came with Axel Fisken, who was anxious to check he hadn't damaged Jox too much. They all looked apprehensive, not quite believing Jox wouldn't kick off again.

'Relax, chaps, nothing to fear.' They remained unconvinced as Jox looked from face to face. 'Can I count on you to keep anything we discus confidential? It's important.'

The doctors nodded, he was safe because of physician-patient confidentiality, and Jox knew he could trust Fisken. They'd saved each other's lives, so there was no loyalty to prove.

'I understand Bartley has been sent home, and more importantly, he agreed to go. I'm assuming the threat of an LMF rating has disappeared, and the wolves are now after me.'

'I'm not sure I'd put it that way, but you will need to provide some explanations,' said Ridgway. 'From a medical standpoint, Doc Mear assures me there is no link between your attack and what was suspected as rabies, but clearly isn't. What on earth were you thinking?'

'Actually, it was something you said, Doc. When I asked what would supersede Bartley's Lacking Moral Fibre rating, your answer was that it would need to be very serious, like mutiny or violence. That got me thinking. What if a fellow officer and subordinate were to cause that mutiny and violence on the superior, wouldn't that subvert the process?'

'Yes, but the guilty officer, i.e. you, would then face very serious charges. Mutiny and violence are court-martial offences, and they'll throw the book at you,' Ridgway said.

'Not if the offender was deemed to be acting violently and out of character because of an infection of say, the rabies virus, known to bring on paranoia, aggression and manic behaviour. It would require someone who'd been bitten by a suspected rabid animal and confirmation by two trusted medical practitioners. Wouldn't that be the case?'

Jox could see the penny drop. Both doctors looked uncomfortable, but he knew they were onside.

Fisken was chuckling. '*Ja*, very clever, Jox. That is the strength of the berserker, no?'

'I was meaning to ask you. Why did you hit me so hard?' said Jox.

'You were very convincing,' replied Fisken. 'I've seen wolves mad with rabies and what they can do to the reindeer herds. You had the same wild eyes and the, how do you say, frothing mouth.'

'So, how about it, Doc? Are you with us?' Jox asked Mear. 'We were all struggling with how to extricate Bolshie from the mess he was in. I was led to believe you wanted to help us. The only way out I could see was to create an even bigger mess than the one he was already in. Sure, I expect repercussions, but the main thing is to get Bolshie out of harm's way. I don't expect to get out of this scot-free, but with your support, I may yet walk away with a career.'

Mear looked at him with a grave expression. 'You were willing to sacrifice yourself for the sake of Bartley?'

Jox smiled and shrugged, in spite of the restraints.

'John 15:13,' said Mear. 'There is no greater love than to lay down one's life for one's friends.'

'Yeah, something like that,' replied Jox. 'To be honest, I'm probably more in the camp of "*Dulce et decorum est pro patria mori*," but Bolshie needed a way out and I could do that. Any of the Treble Ones would have done the same.'

Mear glanced at Ridgway and Fisken, who both nodded.

Jox never felt prouder, but it was time to face the music.

'You seem remarkably recovered from your ordeal,' said Wing Commander George Gilroy, Commanding Officer of No. 324 Wing, in his lilting Perthshire accent. He was responsible for four squadrons of Spitfires, including the Treble Ones, plus a squadron of twin engine Bristol Beaufighters. 'The medical officer tells me it's practically a miracle. So, McNabb, what do you have to say for yourself?'

He sat behind his desk smoking a pipe, the sweet-smelling smoke obscuring his features. His hair was curly and rust coloured, and was the origin of his nickname 'Sheep'. Gilroy was a tough, uncompromising CO who wouldn't give Jox an easy ride. With over twenty kills, and wounded in action three times, he took no prisoners.

He looked at Jox with unnerving intensity. 'I'm told you were bitten by a *monkey* in the middle of a bloody *earthquake*. Good Lord, man, you really do attract trouble. Makes one wonder if we're being taken for fools in all this palaver. Care to enlighten me?'

Jox stood ramrod straight, sweating under Gilroy's gaze. He already felt embarrassed to be standing in front of the wing commander in his baggy shorts and crumpled battle blouse. 'I've no excuse for my behaviour, sir, I wasn't feeling myself.'

'Hmm, yes, I've read your files.' Gilroy jabbed the stem of his pipe in Jox's direction. 'You've got form in this area, haven't you? Fisticuffs with a senior officer isn't new to you.

Not exactly the behaviour of an officer and gentleman. I see you've no shortage of detractors but also have some powerful friends.' Gilroy crossed his arms and rapped his fingers on his bicep. 'Passing through East Africa with No. 325 Wing, I met a scar-faced fellow who wasn't a fan. The name Drummond ring a bell?'

Jox bristled at the mention of his name. Drummond was the nearest he had to a nemesis. Following lecherous intentions he'd had on Jox's fiancée, Alice, it had in fact come down to 'fisticuffs', albeit in the middle of an air raid. At the time, Jox was very fortunate to escape without serious censure, thanks to the support and influence of, yes, some powerful friends. Drummond later sought revenge by trying to implicate Jox and his men in a tobacco smuggling racket he was involved with in Malta. The scheme backfired, and Drummond was reprimanded, demoted and exiled to the deepest reaches of Africa. It was just Jox's luck that this particular bad penny should turn up when he was least wanted.

'Rather an unpleasant sort of fellow that Drummond, full of bile and recriminations,' said Gilroy. He puffed and exhaled. 'In your defence, there are no shortage of chaps willing to come forward and say nice things. Very commendable, McNabb, up to a point.' He began scraping out the bowl of his pipe with a penknife. 'Even old Bolshie Bartley has written to me, singing your praises. Now why would he do that after getting duffed up by you? How the devil do you account for that?' Gilroy's tone changed like a bright blade whipped out from a hidden sheath. 'Cut the crap, laddie, and start explaining yourself.'

Jox swallowed and felt a trickle of sweat down the back of his collar. He was still feeling a bit wobbly after all the drugs he'd been given whilst out for the count, but this was no time to pass out. 'Th-they were going to send Bartley down,' he stuttered. 'I couldn't let that happen. He was lost but none of them could see it. I had to find another way.'

'What? By throwing yourself to the wolves in the process?'

'If that's what was required, sir. Better me than him.'

'Yes, well, Bartley is, or rather was, one of our best, but has become a right pain in my arse recently,' said Gilroy. 'A liability to the squadron. He managed to upset just about every senior Yank he spoke to. Got to be some sort of record. Simply had to go.'

'I don't disagree, sir,' replied Jox, pushing the limits of what might be considered insubordination. 'But the man has done so much for the service, serving Fighter Command faithfully. I couldn't watch him written off as LMF. That's the very last thing he has, he's just tired and, to my mind, the service owes him an opportunity to recover, rather than simply drumming him out in disgrace.'

'You're skating on thin ice, McNabb,' said Gilroy curtly. 'As it happens, I agree with you. I wasn't consulted when some overzealous types fell over themselves to appease the Yanks. I'm rather cross, but that's my problem not yours. What kind of shepherd would I be if I allowed the politico wolves to come after my flock, even a bad-tempered, ill-disciplined old goat like Bolshie Bartley? In my book, that's what you did, albeit in such a hare-brained manner you've caused no end of bother. So, what exactly are we going to do about this?'

'Well, I…'

'That was a rhetorical question, McNabb,' said Gilroy, the blade glinting once again. 'I'm going to tell you what's going to happen.' He took a deep breath. 'There's no question of you continuing with the Treble Ones. We can't be seen to condone violence in any form between a subordinate and senior. We're fortunate that you are both technically squadron leaders, albeit one still "acting". At least you're brother officers of the same rank. The impact on the squadron's morale of your squabbling will be bad enough.' He sighed. 'I've no option but to bring in someone new. I have a South African chap, Johannes Le Roux, in mind. He's a veteran of the Desert Air Force and should be able to pull them together.'

Jox took a sharp intake of breath. 'What about Jimmy Baraldi? He's more than qualified to take over and is popular with the men.'

'Jimmy's out of the picture too,' replied Gilroy. 'I'll leave it to him to explain. It's a tough break, but there it is.' He began repacking his pipe whilst Jox waited. 'So, it appears I have two separate doctors, one the airfield M.O., the other the squadron's I.O. and adjutant, both swearing blind that you were not responsible for your actions since you were infected by some mysterious virus. A virus, which, it appears, a few days later, you seem to be miraculously free from. I won't ask too many questions, as clearly, it's not my field of expertise, but I'm no fool.

'In any case, I've received orders, since as I said, you have powerful friends, McNabb. I got a telephone call from General Doolittle who said, and I quote, "I ain't going to have a pirate punished for behaving like a pirate. McNabb's done the wrong thing for the right reasons. We must ensure the displeasure of the service is clear but I ain't going to ground a warrior of his calibre because of an excess of fighting spirit." Now, what the devil am I supposed to do with that?' His pale eyes bored into Jox. 'Export the problem, that's what I'm going to do. Group Captain Thompson in Malta says he wants you, and as far as I'm concerned, he can bloody well have you.'

Gilroy smiled unexpectedly. 'I wish you good luck, McNabb. I feel sure our paths will cross again, hopefully in better circumstances. You've a fine career ahead of you, if you don't self-sabotage with capers like this. Now, off you go. Say your goodbyes to your Treble Ones. I'm afraid you're no longer one.' He smiled a little sadly. 'Don't worry, it comes to us all as we make our way up the slippery pole. I still miss my old Edinburgh boys of 603 and that'll never change.'

After shaking Gilroy's hand, Jox was out in the open for the first time in many days. It was a fine morning, the sky was clear, and the sodden landscape was steaming, drying out under the unfamiliar rays of bright sunshine. Jox's attention turned to a pair of Spitfires coming in to land. He recognised them as Treble Ones from the JU prefix on the fuselages.

Jox watched Ralph Campbell clamber from his cockpit, undoing the straps of his yellow life jacket and removing his leather helmet. In the meantime, ground crew lifted the tail of the aircraft and swivelled it around to face towards the landing strip, ready for a quick take-off. Wooden chocks were placed under the spatted wheels and various panels on the aircraft were opened for immediate post-flight servicing.

The ground crews had bare torsos and were already sweating as they worked in the sunshine. Campbell looked like a seasoned veteran now, as he searched for his wingman, who'd also just landed. Jox recognised him as Mouland, the squadron's French-Canadian senior NCO. As they walked together towards Jox, a tangled-haired fitter released the catches of Campbell's engine cowling to check the oil and coolant status. Campbell raised his arm in greeting, his words lost to the sudden 'pop-pop-pop' of flak bursting overhead.

'Incoming raid!' screamed the fitter, sliding from the wing before sprinting away as fast as he could.

Someone with a cockney accent shouted, 'Oi, come on, sir, there's a shelter over 'ere.'

Campbell and Mouland ran after him, Mouland with a resounding, '*Merde!*'

They sprinted towards a mound of red earth amidst the scrubland by the runway. Jox hared after the swift fitter, his bare knees getting scratched as he ran through the thorny desert vegetation. He scrambled down some steep steps into the dank darkness of the air-raid shelter. His first reaction on entering was to shudder, recalling the ordeal of being trapped underground at Bulla Regia. He never thought he'd be in that situation again so soon.

'Dive bombers,' said an American voice in the darkness. 'God-darn-it, they ain't supposed to have any of those left.'

Outside, the drone of engines had changed pitch, as the terrifying 'Jericho trumpets' of Stuka 87s began wailing, heralding their vertiginous dives delivering deadly ordnance with pinpoint accuracy. Jox had been on the receiving end in France in May 1940. He reached for the comfort of the broken doll's arm in his tunic pocket. The raiders up there were devastating when operating with air superiority, but the question was, why the devil did they still have air superiority? Engle Field was crawling with fighters. Surely someone should have been on 'readiness' as a rapid reaction force. Between the pulsing booms of detonations, it sounded like at least the flak gunners were shooting back, but someone's head would surely roll for the failure of the fighter response. It was a stark realisation when Jox remembered it was no longer his responsibility.

As his eyes adjusted to the gloom, Jox could see that the shelter's walls and low roof were a deep red, pretty much like everything else in this part of the Tunisian front. The stone was cool and soft, leaving a reddish coating on the palm of his damp hand. The shelter was little more than an arched tunnel with exits at either end, the headroom not much higher than six foot, a problem for some of the taller men but not for diminutive Jox.

On either side, men were packed like sardines, backs against the walls, or squatting down the middle on the dusty floor. As he pushed in deeper, some of the men shuffled along at the sight of an officer, making room for him to sit by the opposite stairway. He recognised many of the faces. Some stared wide-eyed at the ceiling, flinching at every thump and vibration as a sprinkling of fine dust settled on heads and shoulders. There were a few pilots amongst them, but most were ground personnel, the real craftsmen and technicians who kept the airfield armed and flying. Down here, mastery of the deflection shot or knowing how to manoeuvre to get one's guns to bear was of little use.

The tempo of the flak quickened. The men up top didn't have the option of seeking shelter, their job was to man the guns, defend the exposed airfield and their cowering comrades and brothers. Jox wondered if the Bofors were still manned by paratroopers, like the jovial, hulking Preston or mad-eyed MacNeish who he'd met a few weeks ago. He'd once heard a quote from somewhere: 'people sleep peaceably in their beds at night only because rough men stand ready to do violence on their behalf.' He, for one, was grateful for such men, and despite being no stranger to violence himself, realised how privileged he was as a solo combatant, in control of his own powerful machine with the freedom of the open skies. Not everyone was so fortunate; their task was to sit tight, keep firing, and doggedly take the worse of the onslaught.

A bomb landed nearby, louder than the others. The impact hunched the shoulders and pulsed against the eardrums of the men in the shelter. The impact on those up above didn't bear imagining.

'There's more coming,' said a voice in the darkness.

The barrage grew more thunderous, and a high-pitched voice recited, '*Hail Mary, full of grace. The Lord is with thee. Blessed art thou amongst women, and blessed is the fruit of thy womb, Jesus.*'

Beside him, a dusty figure turned to Jox and buried his head in his shoulder. Jox didn't know who it was, and took a while to recognise Ralph Campbell. Jox did what he could to soothe him, stroking his damp hair like perhaps a mother would. This was not a role that Jox was familiar with, having for all intents and purposes grown up motherless, but he was glad to help the terrified youngster. He rocked him back and forward until he stilled, continuing until Campbell fell into a disturbed sleep.

The barrage eased and Jox looked around the stuffy shelter. He could now hear snatches of whispered conversations, voices that he knew well. These were the Treble Ones, the closest thing to a family he'd ever had. War had taken many already and yet their replacements were now just as dear to him. Sitting amongst them, he could feel the ghostly presence of their predecessors. Faces like his early mentor, Mike 'Wheelie' Ferriss, the talented Basil 'Bubbles' Broughton who he'd seen grow from boy to ace, that dear old rascal Morgan 'Mogs' Chalmers and the ball-breaking George 'Wee Brotch' Brotchie, friends and leaders, all gone now, but not erased from his memory.

The squadron still had familiar faces from the Battle of Britain, but they were few and far between. Reeves was in the corner joking with fellow Australian Gusty Gale and his New Zealander pal Jim Waring. Sharing a cigarette in the fug of the shelter were Jox's most trusted flight lieutenants, de Ghellinck and Fisken. Fisken caught his eye, formed a pistol with his maimed hand, and fired a pretend shot at him in jest, as he had many times before.

Jox would miss them. He had never imagined having to leave. How would he manage without his band of brothers? The furnace of war would undoubtedly demand more human fuel, and some would go to the fire. It was something he'd come to accept, but he bitterly regretted not being able to lead them anymore.

CHAPTER NINE

It was suddenly quiet, apart from the persistent ringing in Jox's ears. Through jagged holes punched in the shelter's iron door, dust floated in the sunbeams like sparks.

Outside there were occasional crumps of explosions, punctuating the crackling flames that consumed precious war materiel across the airfield. Released from the airless shelter, Jox climbed the steps to discover the toll from the raid. Beyond the doorway, a meadow of prickly thistle, wild rosemary and sedge grass had been reduced to a wasteland, as if a forest fire had passed through. The blast-proof pens where Campbell and Mouland had carefully parked their aircraft had failed in their purpose, both suffering direct hits. Instead, they'd acted like firepits, containing the burning Spitfires, black oily smoke rising from each conflagration. The fuel tanks perforated by steel fragments had spilt petroleum onto the metal planking, now burning to add to the shimmering heat haze rising through the pall of dust hanging over the airfield.

Beyond the cratered runway, a Bofors gun position had also been hit. The circle of sandbags exploded out like the petals of some terrible flower, the stamens the twisted metal of the guns, the pollen the remains of the paratroopers manning them. There wasn't much left, and the medics' urgency was not to save lives but to remove body parts to avoid traumatising the stunned survivors. A red blanket over a carried stretcher caught Jox's eye, the movement highlighted by blackened appendages flopping like wet cow hides. They weren't of recognisable human form, simply boneless, blasted vestiges of what might once have been limbs. Standing behind the stretcher-bearers, Jox recognised Ridgway, his face black with soot, hair singed on one side.

'You all right, Doc?' cried Jox.

'I'm fine,' Ridgway replied uncertainly. 'B-balance's a bit off from the pressure in my ears. Can't hear too well … got caught in a blast. Look at the state of those poor sods.'

'Nothing we can do for them,' said Jox, pulling Ridgway towards him. 'I'll take you to the infirmary, get someone to have a look. You may be concussed.'

Ridgway nodded, dazed.

The scene in the infirmary was one of chaos. The wounded and burnt filled the wards, consulting rooms, offices and even the corridor. What last week had been clean, calm and orderly now teemed with injured men and the smell of sweat, charred flesh and the coppery stench of blood.

Nurse Lucy McMahon was one of a dozen nurses and orderlies trying to cope with the sudden influx. With them was the airfield's harassed M.O., Doctor Mear, triaging the most urgent cases and making the tough calls when someone was too far gone. Lucy's blonde hair hung limp, her whites splattered and smeared, and even her trademark smile was missing.

She quickly assessed Ridgway as non-urgent, but since she knew the pair, kindly said, 'You two can rest in the nurses' wardroom. It's empty since everyone's on duty. No guarantee it'll stay that way at the rate the injured are coming in.'

'Nurse, some help,' called Mear from across the room. He was struggling with a flailing airman on a stretcher. Ridgway and Jox ran to offer their assistance. The injured man was in a dreadful state, an explosion had terribly damaged his head and face. His matted fair hair had melted into a suppurating mass, his eyes were swollen shut and his cheeks blistered with pockets of yellow-filled liquid. What little clothing he still had on was shredded with just the vestiges of a sergeant's triple chevrons.

'I think it may be Scott, one of the squadron's replacements,' said Ridgway through clenched teeth. 'He joined last week; I don't think he's even been out on an Op yet.'

'Please, I can't bear it. Something for the pain, I beg you,' gasped the young man through ruined lips.

The medic in Ridgway kicked in. He knew his way around the infirmary and swiftly returned with a syringe and ampoules of morphia to ease the sergeant's suffering.

'Gently there, lad,' said Ridgway, breaking off the tip of an ampoule with remarkably steady hands, proceeding to fill the glass syringe. 'Won't take a minute and it will help with the pain.'

Mear nodded his gratitude and moved on to the next patient with no time for niceties. For a brief moment, Ridgway looked a little lost before catching the eye of Nurse Lucy, who flashed an encouraging smile. She crossed over, retrieving a gold-tipped cylinder of lipstick from her apron. She turned it with practised ease and lettered a capital M on Scott's blistered forehead, then she was gone too, her attention already on the next patient.

The lad on the stretcher mumbled, 'Thirsty, water.'

'I'll get some,' said Ridgway. 'Try to keep him calm, Jox. Talk to him.'

'What's your name, son?' asked Jox, assuming he was younger than him, but there was no way of knowing.

'Scott … Michael Scott,' he croaked. 'I'm awfully thirsty.' Jox caught the accent of Morningside, a genteel neighbourhood in his adopted hometown of Edinburgh.

'It won't be long.'

Ridgway returned with two enamel mugs brimming with tepid water. 'Here, boys.'

Jox drank greedily, despite the taste of grit.

Ridgway lifted the boy's head as gently as he could manage, so he might drink too. Most of it ran down his blistered neck, but he licked his lips gratefully. He moaned and began to mumble words which only made sense to him.

His swollen eyelids trembled, as his sticky face attracted a buzzing fly. Jox waved it away and was reminded of Ravi, the Sikh soldier he'd lain beside in the desert, waiting for that brave boy to die. His torment was made immeasurably worse by the flying vermin. There were less of them here, thought Jox, but he still spotted a large bluebottle starting to feed on Scott's ruined flesh. He waved his hand again, the movement making the lad stir.

'I see stars above you…'

'What's he saying?' asked Ridgway.

'Something about stars,' replied Jox, wondering who Scott might be thinking of. Perhaps someone waiting for him back in Auld Reekie, someone who would find him unrecognisable if he even survived.

'I just flew,' said the boy, becoming agitated.

Several other wounded soldiers turned, attracted by the commotion.

'He's gone,' said Ridgway with terrible finality. Scott had expired with a long bubbling exhalation. Perhaps he'd gone to that moon to be with that special someone waiting in Morningside.

Jox slumped and felt the loss of this unknown boy harder than he'd expected. He was desperately tired. Maybe it wasn't so terrible that he was moving on. He would regret not seeing through the mission in Tunisia, but was exhausted, perhaps on the edge of cracking as Bartley had done. He'd been down this particular precipice before, and had no problem being the coward and backing away. He wasn't too proud to be 'the one who fights and runs away, to live and fight another day'.

He looked at Ridgway, who'd covered Scott's ravaged face with a handkerchief. 'I'm done for too, Doc,' said Jox, clumsily introducing the topic.

'What do you mean?' asked Ridgway.

'I'm being transferred from the Treble Ones.'

Ridgway looked as crestfallen as Jox felt.

'It was bound to happen eventually,' said Jox. 'Couldn't get away scot-free, now, could I? I'm being sent to Malta for reassignment. My days as a Treble One are over.'

Ridgway sighed. 'We're going to miss you. Hell, how am I going to manage? The Treble Ones without Jox McNabb is inconceivable.'

'Don't be daft, there's plenty of bigger shoes than mine who have passed through. Too many to name, gone but not forgotten. It's strange, but back in that shelter as we were getting bombed to bits, I could see their faces, I really could. They were right there with us.' Jox sighed. 'Come on, let's go to that nurses' room. You could do with a sit down.'

'I should be helping,' protested Ridgway. 'I could be useful.'

'We're getting in the way. You've done what you can, and the squadron doesn't need to lose another officer. I'm serious, you look done in.'

They found the room and settled on the bare pine floorboards. All the furniture had been pushed to one side to make room. Despite the emptiness, it was nicely decorated, with curtains and pictures that weren't the usual Ministry of Information exhortations to do something or other to help the war effort. Rather, some art deco renderings had been chosen, of exotic destinations previously served by the French civilian airline based here before the war. Posters selling the delights of *Le Caire*, *Le Liban*, Jerusalem and Tripoli, added colour to the room. There were even some wildflowers in a vase. That normality was surprisingly soothing.

On the windowsill was a portable gas stove with which Jox got a brew going, having found a stash of teabags in an *Afrika Korps* gasmask canister complete with palm tree and swastika logo on the clasped lid. By the time it was ready, Ridgway was slumped in a corner, dozing with his head on his knees, the calm after the storm having had a soporific effect.

'Here, grab a hold of this,' said Jox, waking him. 'It'll see you right. There's nothing like a nice cuppa to perk things up. Pity we haven't got a spot of Navy rum. Still, here you are, bottoms up.'

'No, no rum, thanks,' replied Ridgway. 'My head hurts enough as it is. The last thing I need is a headache on a headache.' He reached for the proffered cup, his hand trembling. He had to hold it with both, to avoid spilling it. 'When are you off?' he asked between sips, his voice strengthening with each swallow.

'As soon as it can be arranged. I'm a bit of an embarrassment, apparently, bad for squadron morale.'

'I don't know how they figure that, you practically *are* squadron morale as far as I'm concerned. You terrified the Yanks in the bar, though. They're calling you "Mad Dog McNabb, the wolf of Engle Field".'

'Christ, I hope that doesn't stick.'

'I rather suspect it might, Mad Dog. Who'll be taking over with you and Bartley out of the picture? Jimmy?'

'Well, no, apparently not. Gilroy was rather mysterious. There's a South African chap taking over. Le Roux, I think he said he was called.'

'Wonder what's wrong with Jimmy?' said Ridgway. 'He's not been himself since we got caught up in that earthquake. Can't imagine he's very happy about that.'

There was a knock at the wardroom door. It opened cautiously and the man himself was standing there.

'There you are, chaps,' Baraldi said, relief evident on his face. 'We were getting worried you'd been blown to smithereens. Padre Radford has been compiling the casualty list and was loathe to add you without evidence.'

'We're fine,' said Jox. 'Doc here got his bell well and truly rung during the raid, so I brought him to the infirmary. I'm afraid we do have one loss to report. Young chap called Michael Scott. I didn't know him, but Doc tells me he's a replacement. He didn't make it.'

Baraldi frowned. 'Scott? I think he's one of mine. Gosh, he didn't last very long. I better let the padre know.'

'Replacements never seem to,' replied Jox.

That was something that had often puzzled him. Old hands like him and Baraldi had started in exactly the same way but had somehow managed to survive the relentless attrition and had seemingly beaten the odds. When replacements arrived, even the recent, better trained ones from America, the odds seemed catastrophically stacked against them. How Jox had survived this long was beyond him. Why had he, when so many others hadn't?

'What's up with you, Jimmy?' asked Jox. 'It's no surprise I'm getting the chop, but Gilroy told me you've had it too. What on earth's happened?'

Baraldi smiled sadly and blinked repeatedly. 'Nothing much stays secret around here.' He took a deep breath. 'Yes, I've been grounded. "No longer certified for air operations" is the official terminology. You know I've been having trouble with my eyes. You saw the state I got in when we were stuck in that hole during the earthquake. Christ, there's certainly nothing in the training manual about that. Anyway, gets worse in the dark, but even in good light, it's far from ideal for a fighter pilot.' He looked embarrassed and covered his right eye with his hand. 'Looking at your face, Jox, your features are squished together. You look slimmer than in the other eye.' He snorted. 'Found out I have diabetes. The legacy of eating too much *gelato*, I thought, but Doc Mear tells me it's probably hereditary. I hope it doesn't bugger up my golf handicap. Now, that would really be a blow.'

'Diabetic retinopathy,' said Ridgway. 'I know you mentioned blurry eyes, but never expected that. You're fit and reasonably slim, and I've not seen any sudden significant weight loss or persistent thirst.'

'I do get thirsty, but we all do,' replied Baraldi. 'We're near enough in the desert, despite this rain. It's the needing to pee the whole time that's the main symptom for me. Sorry, if I'm havering, boys. This news has rather thrown me. I could do with a cup of tea, mind.'

'Could someone please explain?' said a mystified Jox.

'Diabetic retinopathy is an eye disease that develops when high blood sugar levels damage the vessels in the retina of diabetics,' replied Ridgway.

Baraldi smiled. 'In layman's terms, it means my body can't get rid of the excess sugar in my blood. That in turn causes problems when it gets into places where it shouldn't and builds up. In my case, my eyes.'

'That's right,' said Ridgway. 'It's a progressive eye disease that can lead to blurred vision or even irreversible vision loss, but now there is a diagnosis, treatment can slow the progression.'

'It can be fixed, right?' asked Jox.

'Afraid not,' replied Baraldi. 'Hopefully they can stop it getting worse, but I'm done for as a flyer, wings well and truly clipped.'

'Here I was worried that Bartley was grounded,' replied Jox. 'And it's happening to you too. I'm so sorry.'

Baraldi snorted. 'Don't worry, Jox. Flying was never my life. I've got an ice-cream empire to run. Flying was only ever a busman's holiday. I'll be all right, I just need to find a role until the war's done.'

The rear cabin of the USAAF Douglas C-47 Skytrain was dark and noisy. The throb of twin Pratt & Whitney engines had a soporific effect on the passengers during the night flight to Valletta.

Jox was still awake, his mind racing and keeping sleep at bay. Beside him, Baraldi was wobble-necking and would undoubtedly feel it when he awoke. With them 'in the rear with the gear' were a pair of Italian-American Army officers. They'd introduced themselves as Major Giuseppe Paolino and Captain Giovanni Lomasso. 'Call me Glen,' said Lomasso, initially friendly, but less so when his companion scowled. They were from New York City. Paolino was squat, dark and bull-necked with a gravelly voice, whilst Lomasso was tall, heavy-set with a high intelligent forehead. They had been uncommunicative and were both now asleep.

Baraldi had chosen not to reveal his Sicilian roots, simply introducing himself as Jimmy. He whispered to Jox that he'd worked out the pair were in the OSS, the Office of Strategic Services, the American equivalent to Britain's Secret Intelligence Service. It was a murky world that Jox didn't much like, the only 'secret squirrels' he knew being Ridgway on a squadron level, and his old chum, Sandy Bullough, who was now a rather senior operator in those dark arts. Plotting intrigues and dastardly deeds were outside Jox's area of interest and well beyond his pay grade.

The Americans had no idea Baraldi was fluent in Sicilian and Italian. He was fascinated with them and strained to hear what they were discussing. After listening, Baraldi sank into a filthy mood. Jox assumed it was the prospect of long-term medical care slowly dawning on him. He had asked if he was nervous about the treatment, and he replied it wasn't that.

'Did you see their hands?' he asked, drawing a symbol on the back of his with a finger. Jox shook his head. 'Both of those chaps have a star-shaped tattoo between the thumb and forefinger of their right hand. In Sicilian they're called *stidda* and signify membership to a clan, not like a Scottish clan, but a mafia clan. I don't know exactly what that means, but I don't think it's good,' he added sourly.

Jox knew these shady mobs had played a part in forcing Baraldi's own family to flee their native island after a disastrous earthquake. They'd built a life on the west coast of Scotland, grateful to have escaped the island's insidious darkness.

Whatever these chaps were involved in, it was likely to be underhand, given the covert nature of their employers, the OSS. Jox couldn't help wondering what these Americans would be up to in Malta, but then chided himself. It wasn't any of his business. Subterfuge was a game for others, he was happy to be a simple, straight-shooting aviator.

He turned his mind to his departure from Engle Field. The exuberant Americans flying their box-shaped Lightnings had become allies and firm friends. As too had the burly paratroopers he'd come to so admire and the base's medical team who'd gone beyond their duty of care through the various 'complications' of his medical predicaments. Saying goodbye to Black and his ground crews had been tough. He hoped to see them again but felt the familiar anxiety of leaving old comrades to uncertain futures.

Amongst the Treble Ones, only Black, Reeves, de Ghellinck and Fisken remained from the days of the Battle of Britain. Those dark times when the country faced its greatest peril seemed like a lifetime ago, but it was actually only three years. That realisation made him long for the familiar faces that he missed, and he was glad that in Malta at least he would find some.

On the plus side, he'd see Group Captain John 'Tommy' Thompson and Cameron Glasgow, but on the minus side he'd finally need to confront Julianna Vella and Billy 'Cocky' Cochrane. He'd ignominiously fled when he discovered their relationship. Before he'd left Malta previously, he and Julianna had an 'understanding'. She'd brought laughter and light back into his life after the dark days of losing Alice. Gradually, she'd shown him there was a future, a new reason to fight and dream of a better tomorrow. Back then Cochrane had been a trusted friend and comrade, which had made the betrayal doubly painful.

Times had been hard on the besieged island, and yet with Julianna in his world, they'd been bearable, passionate, joyous and even something to be treasured. When he'd returned to Malta after Dieppe and Morlaix, he'd arrived full of hope, expectations and some trepidations. The island had suffered terribly in his absence but at least the siege had eased off. That's when he'd discovered that his betrothed and one of his best friends had betrayed him. At the time, he'd felt incapable of dealing with it, choosing denial and flight, getting back to the war to escape the reality. Now, there was no way of moving forward without a confrontation and he needed to face them for better or worse.

Jox rubbed his eyes and wondered what time it was. Landing couldn't be far off. He peered at Huntington's charred Rolex on his wrist. The reflective radium on the dials still worked but it was difficult to see through the heat-clouded fascia. It was close to six in the morning, and the island would be awakening.

Kidney-shaped Malta, with the arrowhead of Gozo to the northwest, was the size of the Isle of Wight. From the air, it was brown and yellow and looked dry, arid and rocky. It also had the dubious honour of being the most bombed spot on earth.

The others were stirring. Baraldi looked tired and rubbed itchy eyes. Lomasso nodded to Jox, whilst his superior gazed out of one of the square-cut windows in the fuselage. The navigator made his way from the front, saying they'd be down in twenty minutes. His announcement triggered a wave of nostalgia within Jox. How many times had he landed on the island, cursing it for a godforsaken rock? Yet somehow it had become a rare, albeit blood-soaked, gem in the Mediterranean Sea.

They landed with a bump, the wireless operator then swinging back the side door as soon as the aircraft was parked at its stand. RAF Luqa in the centre of the island was also where Jox first landed in Malta. He'd delivered a flight of desperately needed Spitfires, arriving unarmed to save weight and fuel, then immediately found himself in the middle of a furious air raid. He and Cameron Glasgow had swiftly armed and refuelled and taken their chances against the raiders rather than staying on the ground like sitting ducks. Their decision created no end of commotion, but things ended well considering that inauspicious beginning. He was looking forward to seeing Glasgow, his partner in crime on that and so many other fateful days.

A cool breeze wafted through the door carrying the unmistakable fragrance of the island, salty air infused with wildflowers, rosemary and other fragrant herbs. The sun was already warming the island's vegetation and cicadas were singing in the long grass alongside the taxiways. They were chased by long-tailed lizards which inhabited the dry-stone walls that criss-crossed the island, a very real hazard to crash-landing pilots as he'd learnt to his chagrin. Mind you, it was just such a crash that had first introduced him to Julianna. Try as he might, everything about Malta led back to her. He sighed and followed Baraldi out of the aircraft.

There on the tarmac, Jox recognised Glasgow immediately. Not much taller than Jox, he was broader, had thinning dark hair and pale eyes. He cut quite a menacing figure, bareheaded and squinting in the sun's glare. Back home in Dundee, where he and his brother Anthony were from, they'd had the fish-belly complexion of Scotsmen brought up in the tall dark tenements by the jute factories on the river Tay. Here and now, he was the colour of mahogany and every bit as hard.

Cameron Glasgow was already a seasoned Treble One NCO when Jox joined the squadron at RAF Northolt, straight from flight school at RAF Montrose. It was the Glasgow twins who'd made a fighter pilot out of him. Ant Glasgow was now worn-out after his sojourn as a prisoner of war and his long, weary walk home. He'd briefly re-joined the squadron, participating in the Dieppe raid but had soon recognised he was past active frontline service. He and Badger Robertson, the squadron's long-serving adjutant, were now instructors at Montrose, still managing to scare future generations of would-be pilots into shape.

Cam Glasgow had come out to Malta with Jox the first time but had been ordered to remain as Tommy Thompson's, their previous commanding officer, right-hand man. Thompson was now responsible for all fighter stations on the island, a big job, and he needed someone he could depend upon. Glasgow had been commissioned and was now a flight lieutenant. It was a long-running joke that Ant would now have to salute his twin brother, should the pair see each other again.

Glasgow's stern face cracked with pleasure as he saw Jox. He strode over, but then stopped in his tracks and executed a smart salute, before grabbing his young friend in a bear hug. Jox was surprised at how emotional he felt on seeing his mentor again.

'You're a sight for sore eyes,' roared Glasgow. 'I hear you've been getting yerself into all kinds of bother without old Cam keeping you on the straight and narrow.' He held his arm around Jox's shoulder. 'I was very sorry to hear they took the squadron from you. I'd always fancied the idea of the Treble Ones led by my wee laddie.' He patted Jox's chest with surprising tenderness. 'Don't worry, son, me and Tommy will sort you out. There's no shortage of demand for fine young fellows like yerself and we're in no risk of running out of war any time soon.' He glared at Baraldi hovering in the background. 'Speaking of fine young fellows, who the devil's this?'

Baraldi's smile withered under the intensity of Glasgow's gaze.

'He's with me,' said Jox. 'This is my good friend, Jimmy Baraldi. You play nice now, he's the same rank as you, a Scotsman and a Treble One to boot.'

'Is he now?' replied Glasgow, eyeing Baraldi with fresh interest.

'Jimmy, I'd like you to meet Cameron Glasgow. I wish I could say his bark is worse than his bite, but the truth is he bites too. In fact, as far as I'm concerned, the "Glasgow Kiss" is named after him and his brother, not the city. I'm afraid old Bartley learnt that to his cost, but the less said about that, the better.'

Glasgow chuckled, secretly delighted at his new claim to fame. The pair shook hands.

'Fine by me,' said Glasgow. 'Baraldi? Unusual for a Scotsman. Where you from then, son?'

'Went to school in England, but the family's from Kilmarnock, south of … er … Glasgow,' replied Baraldi. 'But they're originally from Sicily.'

'Ma used to take us to get ices at Baraldi's. Best ice cream I've ever tasted.'

'Yes, that's us!' said Baraldi, delighted to have found common ground. 'My family's business. Ice cream parlours right across the west of Scotland.'

'Aye, that's right, we always went when visiting my ma's brother, Uncle Kenny on the Isle of Arran. Baraldi's ices, eh? That's marvellous, we could do with them in Malta.'

'Well, I know the recipes and I've got time on my hands — it may not be such a bad idea.'

'I'm not following, son,' replied Glasgow, frowning.

'Jimmy's been grounded,' said Jox. 'Trouble with his eyes. He's here to get treatment.'

'You're being polite and far too kind, Jox,' said Baraldi. 'My eyes are knackered. I don't expect I'll be flying again, so I'll need to find something worthwhile to do. In the meantime, my orders are to report to the 90th General Hospital at Mtarfa. Any idea where that is?'

'Och aye, that's just west of Ta Kali airfield. North of Rabat where the officers' mess is, which of course you also know well, don't you, Jox?'

Jox frowned. 'Yes, Cam, but not now. All in good time.'

Glasgow held his gaze. 'Aye, right, sure, fine. Come on then, Jimmy, we'll give you a lift, and then, Jox, I'm taking you to see Tommy, who's keen to catch up.' He placed a hand on Baraldi's shoulder. 'Don't you worry about a new assignment, laddie,' said Glasgow. 'Good job I'm the adjutant to the Group Captain in charge of flying in Malta. I'm sure that together we'll find something suitable once you're medically discharged. Come on, boys.'

There was a commotion amongst the crowd meeting the OSS officers. Photographers scrambled and one dropped his camera, the flashbulb popping like a pistol report when it hit the ground. The group flinched, heads dipping to reveal a diminutive figure in a Group Captain's uniform. Jox recognised the large head, thin face and prominent teeth of Sandy Bullough. The last time they'd seen one another was during the planning phases of the Dieppe raid.

Jox waved to attract his attention and walked towards him. Bullough's steely gaze caught Jox's. There was a beat of recognition, a barely perceptible shake of the head and his friend turned away, pointedly ignoring him.

CHAPTER TEN

The 90th General Military Hospital at Mtarfa had been caring for sick and wounded servicemen since 1915. Built in response to the surge in demand after the Gallipoli campaign, it helped cement Malta's role as the Empire's 'Nurse of the Mediterranean'.

Dropping Jimmy Baraldi outside the hospital's front entrance was an intimidating affair. The building was a huge, sand-coloured edifice built on an incline, several storeys high, and every bit as imposing as the Whitehall buildings Jox had seen in London, but somehow it seemed out of place on the tiny Mediterranean island. Looking up at it, Baraldi looked rather lost, small and forlorn.

'Well, cheerio chaps, I guess that's me,' Baraldi said, blinking in the morning's brightness, then peering at the deep, dark shadow of the towering building.

'Aye, up those steps and present your orders at reception,' said Glasgow encouragingly. 'They should have a record of you. I'm sure you're expected. Any problems, call the number I gave you, and we'll get things sorted. Give Jox and I time to get back to the office if you do call. Take a wee look around, looks like they've got a fine garden. Try to enjoy it and we'll have you back at the fore soon enough.'

'You'll be fine,' added Jox. 'You've faced worse. Enjoy the sun and I'll be in touch.'

Baraldi managed a sad little smile. He gathered up his bag, came to scruffy attention and gave them a half-hearted salute. 'Gentlemen, it's been a pleasure.' He trotted up the steps leading to the hospital entrance. Watching him go, Jox couldn't help thinking it was like turning the last page of a chapter and starting another. It was the same for him too. He smiled as Glasgow gunned the engine. 'Right, lead on, Macduff.'

Glasgow laughed. 'And damned be him that first cries, "Hold! Enough!"'

Jox looked at him, surprised and impressed.

'You didn't expect a chookter from Dundee to know his Shakespeare, did ya? I didn't go to your fancy school, but what kind of Scottish sojer would I be if I didnae recognise *Macbeth*?' As they roared down the track and through the wrought-iron gates, he added, 'Don't you realise I'm an officer and gentleman, the now.'

Jox laughed. It was grand to see Cam Glasgow in such high spirits.

They'd been driving for a while when Jox realised Glasgow was taking no precautions over what might be overhead. It had become second nature for Jox in Tunisia, where it was never obvious if friend or foe might be stalking a vehicle's dust trail across the landscape. During Jox's two previous sojourns in Malta, daytime journeys had always been risky, and he recalled one of Julianna's letters saying the enemy fighter-bombers harassed anything that moved. Farmers couldn't even care for their crops or livestock in the open, and fishermen dared not head to sea since the raiders targeted the smallest of boats.

'You don't seem worried about getting jumped by an opportunist Hun,' said Jox. 'Things have certainly changed on the island.'

'Aye well, they got worse before they got better, but I think we've pretty much established air superiority over the island. The island of Pantelleria between here and Tunisia is still a hornet's nest, and they have plenty more in Sardinia and Sicily, but I'd say we have the upper hand on Malta. Nothing like when we were defending the island in the good old, bad old days. We took a complete pasting. I know it was bad when you were here, but God knows it got worse. Thankfully, the convoys are getting through, and more and more aircraft are crowding the airfields, the Yanks arriving in droves. Feels like we're on the move again, and it is no real secret that once things are sorted in Tunisia, Sicily is next. That'll be our first toehold on occupied Europe.'

'Ridgway, the Treble Ones' current spy, would be horrified to hear you say that openly,' said Jox. 'Loose lips sink ships and all that.'

'Well, I'm not exactly Mata Hari,' replied Glasgow. 'In any case, we've got enough spies on the island already. The place is fair crawling with them.'

'Yeah, I was meaning to ask, I saw Sandy Bullough at the airfield. Was going to say hello, but he completely blanked me.'

'Aye, I saw the Group Captain too,' replied Glasgow. 'Funny to think that wee fellow gave us such a hard time on our kill counts during the Battle of Britain. Now he's wearing the hat covered in scrambled egg at the same rank as Tommy Thompson. How's that even possible?'

'He took on some big jobs organising sizeable operations. Last time I saw him he was briefing the great and the good before the Dieppe raid.'

'Look how well that turned out.'

'To be fair, he did warn them it would be no cakewalk. Made himself quite unpopular with Mountbatten and his Combined Services lot. I expect when he was proven right, it may have done his career in Intelligence a lot of good, away from the newspaper headlines.'

'As I recall, he was never short of an opinion even back then,' said Glasgow.

'He's certainly a colourful character but has always been a good friend to me. That's why it's so strange to be blanked like that. I wonder what he's doing on the island.'

'No idea, no one tells me anything. You can ask Tommy when you see him.'

'Speaking of which,' said Jox. 'Where are you taking me? I thought we were going to see Tommy now. I've not been on the island for a while, but I think you missed the turning at the last crossroad.'

Glasgow grinned. 'No flies on you, eh, laddie? Tommy can wait. I'm taking you to a quiet spot, so we can have a wee chat about something important.' He spun the steering wheel through his hands and took the next turning.

The scenery looked familiar and Jox soon recognised the brooding ruins on the skyline. It was a Hospitaller castle of the Order of St John, looming above the Dingli cliffs, south of Rabat. At the foot of those cliffs was a narrow beach where he and Julianna had swum and made love.

'Why the devil did you bring me here?' Jox asked, a cold edge to his voice.

'Where better to figure out the situation you've been hiding from?'

Glasgow parked and they both got out. The dark yellow stone ruins were covered in climbing thorns and clinging vines, but the cliffs were bathed in sunshine. Below, the azure sea crested in small, even waves washing up on the narrow beach of honey-yellow sand.

Jox remembered how Julianna had told him this was her favourite childhood beach. War had tainted it when the carrier HMS *Illustrious* was struck by a thousand-pound bomb dropped by German dive-bombers in Valletta harbour. The bodies of the sailors committed to the sea had washed ashore in droves, dotted across the wet sand and bumping against the cliff face below the castle. Julianna had said the memories of them together, spending happy times here had erased those terrible images. He had brought joy back to a beauty spot, so dear to her heart. They'd come here often, sometimes with her young brother Elias tagging along.

'You need to face up to the memories some time,' said Glasgow. 'I know it hurts, but you can't keep running away. It does you no credit and frankly it isn't the behaviour of the man I call a friend. You're just like me, you feel things too deeply and simply bury them. Got to face your problems, get them out in the open. Can't just skulk away, licking your wounds and letting them fester. That's not the Jox I know.'

'Sometimes when you're hurt, that's all you can face doing.'

'Away with you,' replied Glasgow. 'You were wronged, there's no denying that, but you have no idea the suffering they went through. After you left, the people here were starving. Everything was falling apart, and nothing worked. You couldn't move an inch without getting bombed or shot at. If that Operation Pedestal convoy hadn't limped in on the day of Santa Maria's feast last year, the people would have given up hope.

'On top of that, that lovely wee laddie, Elias, Julianna's brother, was killed. I'm sorry to say, the bloody Snapper that strafed him on the way to school didn't leave much to bury. His death destroyed the Vella family, and Cochrane too. He was close to the lad, saying he reminded him of his younger brother. I've heard that the grandmother died of a broken heart and now the old man lives alone, refusing to see anyone. In their despair, Cocky and Julianna turned to one another. How could they tell you that? I know it wasn't right, but I can understand how it happened. It's not your fault, but you just weren't here, laddie.'

Jox felt Glasgow's words like body blows. He was having trouble breathing, his eyes filling with tears that he'd held in for a long time.

'I can see you're upset and I understand why, but you've got to see that it's water under the bridge. We all have to move on and live our lives, from where we are now, not where we wanted to be. Life, and certainly war, doesn't give you "do overs".'

'I can't forgive them, Cam,' said Jox. 'I just can't…'

'Yes, you bloody can, and you will. I won't tell you to suck it up like a man, because I think too highly of you. I'm telling you as a friend, one who's seen you through thick and thin. This has got to stop. It's done, it's over, we move on.'

The two friends stood eyeing one another. Above their heads, gulls screamed, and the sea breeze carried the sound of the crashing surf and the iodine smell of seaweed from the waves.

'If it makes things any easier,' said Glasgow. 'You'll not have to face Cochrane, just Julianna. Cocky's been posted to HMS *Indomitable*, leading a flight of Seafires from the carrier. He's stationed off the coast of Tunisia somewhere. I do have to tell you though, they got married. Mrs Julianna Cochrane now runs the bar at the Officers' Mess at the Belle Vue Hotel and lives in the naval married quarters nearby.'

This new information was another slap in the face. There was no turning back from that. The Belle Vue was where he and Julianna had gotten betrothed, if not actually officially engaged. It was also where he'd caught Julianna and Cochrane in each other's arms when he'd returned unannounced to the island. It had stung then, and still stung now. He couldn't help that.

Perhaps the hurt stemmed from something deeper? Was he still mourning the heart-crushing loss of Alice during the Blitz?

'You're right,' he whispered. 'But it hurts. You're gonna need to give me a minute.'

'Take your time, son.'

Jox turned his back to the beach and walked towards the castle ruins. He had to step carefully to avoid tripping over the tangled thorns that had grown up the worn stairs to a dark, open doorway. As he walked, volleys of leaping grasshoppers were set off until he stepped into the musty darkness of a high, vaulted hallway. He felt a twinge of fear, the legacy of that hole at Bulla Regia. He wondered if dark spaces would forever trigger such fears, memories of facing the wrath of Vulcan and Poseidon. *Yet more baggage*, he thought bitterly. Everyone had baggage, but why did he have more than most?

He entered what had once been the banqueting hall of the castle. It now smelt vaguely of urine, damp earth and the roots that grew through fissures in the rock. The whole place looked unstable, with stone supports which had once held mighty beams projecting out from damp stone walls. They were redundant now but still bore carved shields with heraldic symbols of the Hospitallers and the other military orders they'd cared for during the waxing and waning campaigns of the Crusades.

Malta was a staging post for centuries of invasions. The Hospitallers' mission was to care for fellow warriors of Christ and pilgrims desperate to reach the Holy Land. War had always defined this little island, long before the British ever arrived. Doubtless it would continue to do so long after they were

168

gone. That thought somehow put his woes into perspective, miniscule in the grand scheme of things.

He needed air. Steps leading up from the hall took him to a balustraded balcony overlooking the sea. He and Julianna had enjoyed the magnificent view, and it was where they'd first kissed. Now, as then, a cool, fragrant breeze came off the water, a mix of perfumes from the island's wild herbs and those of the sea. The crickets chirped noisily in the long grass growing alongside the scarred walls of the castle.

Over the centuries, assorted soldiery had doubtless visited, carving their names, initials, units and symbols into the soft sandstone. Some were recent, others ancient. Some with bawdy or lewd words, others pious and God-fearing, from men across the ages, perhaps recovering from wounds or preparing to embark on deadly missions of war. All were keen to leave their mark on this world, something tangible and solid that would endure after they were gone.

Jox spotted the same initials as his, carved above the words '2nd Light Horse', so an Aussie cavalryman from 1915. He wondered if that cobber had made it back from the murderous cliffs of Gallipoli. Elsewhere, from just last year, during the siege, a Bombardier Harris had proclaimed 'Fuck the War' for all to see.

Higher than the jumble of most names and numbers, were some crude lettering more ancient in origin. Carved under a large square-sided cross was lettering that spelt out 'Finn o' Struan', followed by a smaller eight-pointed Maltese Cross. This fellow Finn was presumably from Struan, which sounded rather Scottish, and by the shape of the cross was a Templar. He must have used his longsword to carve the rock higher than all others. Doc Ridgway had once explained that Templar knights were warrior monks, pious, poor and forswearing women in their devotion to their faith. This particular fellow was keen to make his mark, a sort of medieval 'Kilroy was here'. He'd seen those words daubed everywhere in Tunisia; in fact, wherever American servicemen had passed. Doubtless, they would end up here too.

Jox suddenly felt compelled to also leave his mark. To somehow show that he'd been here during momentous times. He searched the undergrowth and found an iron fencing post rusted with disuse. He had to tug to pull it up and it wasn't long enough to reach beyond Finn of Struan's scratchings but still got him clear of most.

What should he carve? He considered the shape of the George Cross that both he and Malta had been awarded, but reasoned it was too plain amongst the fancier ones already on the walls. He settled for an RAF roundel and his Treble One identifier letters JU-X. Every iteration of 'Marguerite' had borne those letters, with the exception of some early flights with No. 249 'Gold Coast' Squadron here on the island, but that was a technicality. No longer a Treble One, he would no longer have JU-X. That was worth commemorating.

He spent so long carefully carving the shape and letters that Glasgow came looking for him. The Scotsman said nothing and simply leant against the balustrade, his back to the sea, waiting for him to finish. Jox stood back to admire his handiwork and Glasgow asked, 'Are you done?'

'What do you think?'

'Not bad, JU-X is a nice touch. Why the three dates?'

'Those are the three times I've been posted to Malta. I wanted to leave my mark here for posterity like all these other fellows. Right, I think it's time to go.'

'My dear boy,' boomed Tommy Thompson through his walrus moustache when Jox and Glasgow finally arrived at his office. He got up from his desk, scattering papers as he crossed the room to embrace Jox. There was a lot of back thumping from the former Treble One CO and there was no denying the pleasure on his face.

'By God, you've been getting into hot water, haven't you?' he said, a glint in his eye. 'Time Cam and I kept an eye on you again.' He ushered them to some leather sofas by a coffee table, where food, teacups and a teapot awaited. 'I've got tea and sarnies for the weary warriors. You must be hungry after your flight.'

'It's wonderful to see you, sir,' replied Jox. 'A cup of tea would be very welcome.'

Thompson fiddled with the crockery. 'Help me, Cam. I'm all fingers and thumbs.'

'I'm not exactly dainty myself,' replied Glasgow.

Jox smiled at them bickering like an old couple. It was grand to see them, older, but otherwise unchanged.

'Here, let me,' Jox offered. They readily agreed. 'I hope I haven't blotted my copybook too badly,' he added, pouring tea into the cups.

'I can always use another rascal,' replied Thompson, tucking into an egg and cress sandwich. 'Not bad, come on, tuck in before I scoff the lot.'

'You're living well,' said Jox. 'Things have changed on the island. The grub for a start.'

'We're doing all right,' replied Thompson. 'Perks of being in charge, but it won't last long with all these generals circling. Never mind, I've been hearing good things about "Jox's Pirates". The last time I saw General Doolittle, he could talk of little else.'

'He's been a great supporter. It's thanks to him I got bumped up to squadron leader.'

'Squadron leader, eh?' said Thompson with an eggy grin. 'Who'd have thought the sproglet would get this far, eh, Cam?' Glasgow shook his head in mock disbelief. Thompson chuckled then turned pensive. 'I'm glad we're getting some of the old gang together. Far too many lost along the way.' He raised his cup. 'Absent friends, eh, boys?' They followed suit and had a moment of reflection together. 'So, Jox, you must be pretty fed-up at getting pulled out of Tunisia before the job was done?'

'Disappointed, but actually it's leaving the Treble Ones that's more galling. It's daunting to leave the closest thing to a family I've ever had.'

'Comes to us all,' said Thompson. 'You'll always be a Treble One. Cam and I certainly still are.' He got to his feet and went to the papers on his desk. 'I've been reading about our progress. Seems Montgomery and the Eighth Army took Tripoli on the 21st of January, then needed to rest and refit after hard campaigning. That's when old Rommel chose to counterattack in southern Tunisia, on Valentine's Day as it happens, just when our American friends were mooning after absent sweethearts. His panzers smashed into their inexperienced US II Corps, with the 1st Armored Division suffering over fourteen hundred casualties at Kasserine Pass, a two-mile gap in the Atlas Mountains.

'At the same time, General Von Arnim's 5th *Panzerarmee* attacked in the north, and gave our General Anderson a bloody nose, especially with those new Tiger 1 heavy panzers. I've read that over fifty of our tanks were knocked out, plus hundreds of vehicles destroyed and more than a thousand troops captured. Thankfully, Rommel's *Panzerarmee Afrika* had overextended themselves in the south, and had to turn back once the Eighth Army got going again. Rommel's apparently unwell and been sent home, replaced by some Italian chap. The Yanks have a new firecracker in charge, chap called Patton, and things seem to be improving. We have Commonwealth forces attacking the Mareth Line, and the Kiwis are outflanking through the mountains. The Axis's hold on the country is finally slipping.'

'You've got a far better picture than we ever had,' said Jox. 'I saw a lot of action and furious movement but nothing but setbacks on the ground. The weather was utterly appalling, and we even had an earthquake to contend with.'

'Yes, I heard about that,' said Thompson. 'Right, let's get down to business. What are we going to do with you?'

'I'm at your disposal, sir.'

'Look, I've been impressed at how you pulled that "Pirate squadron" of yours together,' Thompson said. 'What I want you to do, is do that for real. Not by simply cherry-picking the best men from other squadrons but by fusing together the odds and sods we've got on the island into a new fighting squadron. There are men here who for one reason or another have been separated from their previous units. Not bad eggs, just chaps that need rounding up and led with a firm hand. I'm told the No. 333 Squadron handle is available, so that's yours. I thought it was nice symmetry, another form of Treble One.'

'I rather like that,' said Jox.

'It's customary for a new squadron CO to pick some chums as a foundation. You can't have Cam, he's too valuable to me, but perhaps there are others that might like to join you?'

'You'll need a competent adjutant and intelligence officer too,' said the ever-practical Glasgow. 'You could start with Jimmy Baraldi? If he's been grounded, he'd make a fine adjutant. An experienced fighter pilot, smart and mature, and a nice chap too. It's important to get it right, remember what a life-saver old Badger was.'

'What are you talking about?' asked Thompson.

'Jox has a chum, a former Treble One as it happens, who's been grounded with vision problems. He flew to Malta with Jox. We dropped him off at the eye clinic at Mtarfa. He's at a loose end once his treatment is complete.'

'He's of Sicilian origin, speaks French and Italian too, so could be useful,' said Jox.

'Sounds ideal. I'll leave you chaps to get things organised. Cam, will you help Jox sort out the paperwork?'

'Of course, sir.'

'Any thoughts on who you might want from the old squadron?' asked Thompson. 'With Bartley gone and the new chap in his place, there's every chance he'll want his own people too. Good time to get your bids in. I'm told he's South African and a Desert Air Force veteran, so is bound to have plenty of chums in theatre. So, who else d'you want?'

'Let me think … how many is a reasonable request?'

'I'd say no more than four,' replied Glasgow.

'Right, as flight commanders, I'd like Axel Fisken and Ghillie de Ghellinck. I'm not sure if you remember them, sir, they've been with us since we trained as night fighters during the Blitz.'

'Could be handy, after Dieppe and the success of Operation Torch, more operations will be launched at night.'

'They're both top men,' said Glasgow. 'I know them well. Chalk and cheese, but sound Jerry killers.' Coming from Glasgow that was high praise indeed.

'I remember Ghillie joining during the Battle of Britain,' said Thompson. 'French, isn't he?'

'Belgian.'

'All the same,' said Thompson.

'I rather think they'd disagree. Fisken's Norwegian and they're both proud patriots.

'Takes all kinds,' said Thompson. 'We've got chaps from all over.' He sighed. 'I don't suppose there's many left who remember me from when I commanded the Treble Ones.'

'Some still knocking around, but mostly with other squadrons. We're getting a bit long in the tooth to be in a single unit. As far as I know Pritch, Moose, Miro Mansfeld, Pete Simpson and Tom Wallace are all alive and kicking.'

'And your final two?' asked Glasgow.

'I'll go for Kanga Reeves and Ralph Campbell,' replied Jox. 'You'll remember Reeves, big Aussie who's always in the water given half the chance. Ralph is newer, joined us before Dieppe but is solid. Actually, I went to school with him and feel sort of responsible for his joining the service. Apparently, he was following my example.'

'That's settled,' said Thompson. 'Get the ball rolling and I'll sign whatever needs signed. Cam will get you situated, accommodation, aircraft and ground crew. He'll let you have the files on the chaps we want knocked into shape. They're all veterans, so will need careful handling, some more than others.'

Jox looked up, recognising words that could cover a multitude of sins. Especially, since Glasgow began chuckling.

The Bakelite telephone on Thompson's desk started ringing. 'Damn and blast,' he said. 'Can't turn the bloody ringer down. Scares the life out of me every time.' He went to his desk. 'Hello, Thompson here.' He listened to the voice in the receiver. 'Yes, of course.' He nodded. 'He's right here. Yes, I suppose he could. What? Now? I can get him a car, but it'll take half an hour to get to Lascaris. He'll need a driver who knows where it is.' He laughed at the response. 'Good to talk to you too. Feels like a lifetime. What was that? He's to ask for Flying Officer Hook and bring some identification. I'll tell him. Main entrance at St James Ditch, righto, he's on his way. Yes, thank you. All the best.' Thompson cradled the receiver. 'That's a fly in the ointment.' He looked at Jox. 'You keep strange bedfellows, my boy. Just back and you get summoned by the biggest spy on the island.'

'Who's that?'

'Weaselly little fellow who used to be the Treble Ones' spy, what was his name? Bullough, that's it. A group captain now with fingers in all kinds of pies. Wants to see you.' Jox and Glasgow exchanged glances. 'That's put "the best laid schemes of mice and men" on hold until we know what he wants,' said Thompson. 'It'll be hush-hush, so let us know what you can. In the meantime, Cam will crack on with the paperwork.'

'Where does Sandy want me?'

'The Lascaris War Rooms in Valletta. Only the most secret headquarters on the whole island, a complex of tunnels housing the Ops rooms that coordinate the defence of Malta and operations in the Med. There's a chance you'll see some bigwigs.' Thompson jotted something on a slip of paper. 'Here's the address, take some I.D. and ask for Flying Officer Hook. Better get a move on, sounds in a hurry. Cam will sort out transport.' Glasgow nodded and left the room. Thompson put a meaty hand on Jox's shoulder. 'Look, I know Bullough's a pal, but he's involved in shifty business. Be careful and watch what you agree to.'

CHAPTER ELEVEN

'Ever heard of the "Trout memo"?'

Jox raised his eyes from the map of the central Mediterranean on the wall in front of him. The heeled boot of Italy was about to kick the axe-head shape of Sicily. To the west, Tunisia looked like a long-nosed, fat-faced spectator cheering. Scattered between them were islands, including Malta, Pantelleria and tiny Linosa and Lampedusa. To the north, Sardinia was a parallelogram, and above that the teardrop shape of Corsica. They were seated at a table in the centre of a room lined with cubby holes, all vacant, and with a concrete ceiling and floor. It was warm and oppressive, and Jox felt a bit uneasy at being underground again. It didn't help that Bullough was asking random questions about fly-fishing.

Earlier, after having his papers scrutinised by a tough-looking Royal Marine, he'd asked for Flying Officer Hook. He was surprised when a slim young man with a fringe of blond hair appeared, handsome to the point of prettiness. His salute may have been just a flick of his hair before offering a handshake.

'Sorry about the clammy palms, a bit sweaty down there. Haven't fixed the ventilation yet. Nice to meet you, Jox. I hope you don't mind me calling you Jox? Sandy's told me so much about you. I'm Dorian, by the way, his right-hand man.'

Hook led him down corridors into the subterranean complex. They passed several officers from different services, speaking in hushed tones. There was a lot of scrambled egg on show, but it was too dark to recognise anyone, and it was ill-advised to peer too closely.

Bullough was waiting for them in the sweaty boxroom.

'My dear boy, I'm so sorry about the dramatics at the airfield. Our American friends like to be centre of attention, especially twitchy OSS types, suspicious of everything and everyone. They don't look like much but represent some powerful people in the States and hopefully Sicily too. It's on a need-to-know basis, and frankly you don't need to know.' He smiled and stood up. 'Let me take a good look at you. Still a handsome rogue, I see,' he said in his high-pitched South African accent.

Jox caught a tut from Hook behind him.

It was good to see Sandy Bullough. They'd come a long way together since flight school. Bullough had been sacked quite early on, despite his connections, but had found his niche in Military Intelligence. He'd flourished professionally, but it was taking its toll. He was pale, perhaps due to this subterranean existence, his dark hair was thinning, and he'd lost weight, making his outsized teeth more prominent than ever.

'Sorry, you said something about trout?' Jox prompted.

'The Trout memo was published before the war, then circulated to our Intelligence services. It came from the Director of Naval Intelligence, Rear-Admiral John Godfrey, a keen fly-fisherman, but I suspect may have been penned by Ian, a friend of mine. The crux of it is that to dupe the enemy in a war requires the stealth of a fisherman. He patiently casts all day, frequently changing position and using an array of flies. If he frightens the fish, he lets the water rest, but otherwise is constantly trying to lure fish onto his fly.

'The memo lists some fifty imaginative ways the enemy, like the trout, might be fooled. Some suggestions are more hare-brained than others, some simplistic and others rather ghoulish. All have been tried to one extent or another in our battles with the Abwehr, the Gestapo and other Axis Intelligence services.' Bullough pressed his fingers together into a peak in front of his face. He smiled conspiratorially. 'Logic tells us that after Tunisia we'll go for Sicily next. We know that, Jerry knows that, but we must somehow convince him otherwise.

'There are several schemes on the go. One rather grim idea is using the cadaver of some poor sod, dressed in a uniform, then dumped off the coast of Spain chained to a "Top Secret" briefcase full of plans to invade Greece and Sardinia, rather than *La Bella Sicilia*. Seems a bit far-fetched to me, but Ian has his fellows beavering away on what he's calling Operation Mincemeat.

'Our American colleagues are putting their faith in new friends amongst the Sicilian underworld to disseminate similar information. I have my doubts on how effective that'll be. By definition, they're Sicily-based and to me therefore will reinforce rather than subvert expectations we're coming that way. Personally, I think they're uncontrollable too, acting only in their own interests. Look at how long Mussolini has tried to control them.'

'Sandy, what's all this got to do with me?'

Bullough raised his hands in mock surrender. 'For my part, I've been tasked with adding to the mix, getting the enemy to believe we intend to invade Sardinia rather than Sicily. I call the project, Operation Tinned Fish. I had the kernel of an idea but was struggling to know how to make it happen.' He paused, a feline smile crossing his face. 'That's when I suddenly see my dear friend Jox McNabb, and everything became clear.'

'Me? What the devil has this got to do with me? I'm just a fighter pilot.'

'You're much more than that. You and Alice did a sterling job getting under the skin of that Lord Chamberlain fellow,

Mehmet Ali. The pair of you were invaluable in that spot of bother during the Blitz.'

'You know very well it was Alice that had the talent for your intrigues. I could barely keep up when you two got going.'

'That's not true, but she did have the mind of a great agent. I do miss her so. I still grieve for your loss, my friend.' He squeezed the bridge of his nose. 'Now listen, you really can help, but let me first explain the theory of how deceptions work. To succeed, they must work on two levels, one that feeds into something the enemy wishes or already believes. Let's call that the "Wish factor". Once accepted, it becomes something the chain of command can agree to. I call that the "Yes factor". It's particularly important in military hierarchies like those favoured by our enemies. Once a big cheese says yes, everyone falls into line.'

Bullough nodded to Hook, who got to his feet and pinned a photograph onto the map. It showed two men in uniform, both moustachioed and saluting. One was tiny compared to the other, something accentuated by a voluminous cape he was wearing.

'Recognise these chaps?' Jox shook his head. 'The short one is barely five foot tall and is Victor Emmanuel III, the King of Italy. Despite Mussolini running things, Italy actually remains a kingdom, so everything is done in the king's name. Victor Emmanuel, for his sins, is also Emperor of Ethiopia and King of the Albanians.' Bullough watched Jox to see when the penny might drop. 'And … since you know another King of the Albanians, that's where you come in. In fact, weren't you decorated by him?'

'Yes, Moose and I got some gongs from King Zog. No idea why. Who's the tall chap?'

'King Albert of Belgium, but that's not relevant,' replied Bullough. 'This photo is only amusing because of their contrasting heights. Come to think of it though, Albert's daughter did marry Victor Emmanuel's son.' He took a breath. 'What *is* relevant is that the Italian king is named after his grandfather, Victor Emmanuel II, King of Sardinia. The current king is therefore very attached to the island. The other thing to know is that Albania is the land of vendettas and blood feuds. Zog has survived many assassination attempts and holds grudges deeply. If he hates one man more than any other it's Victor Emmanuel, the man who stole his throne. They loathe each other and that's where we come in.'

'I'm not following.'

'What if we could convince Zog to support an invasion of Sardinia? It could be positioned as a first step to regaining control of Albania. He would also know it would be deeply insulting to Victor Emmanuel. If Zog were to visit the region, inspecting troops and making speeches regarding Sardinia, news would certainly get back to the Italians and their overmasters. It's also exactly the kind of thing Victor Emmanuel might expect from his sworn enemy. Once believed on high, the chain of command would accept any directives coming from the king. Then, we would have them.'

It had been a whirlwind since he'd arrived. Jox hadn't even unpacked his bags, nor did he even know where he was sleeping that night. As ever, Cam Glasgow came to the rescue with a stiff drink, a reassuring chat and a cot in his room at RAF Luqa's officers' dorm.

'Come on, give me the news, the good and the bad,' said Glasgow. 'There's bound to be a bit of both so get this down your neck first.' He handed Jox a glass, which Jox knew would be the finest Scotch malt whisky available in Malta. Despite his rough beginnings and an unadventurous taste in cuisine, the dour Scotsman had a discerning palate for whisky.

Jox took a sip and felt the warming heat of his homeland slip down his throat and light the fire in his belly. 'So, it appears I've been asked to join what Sandy calls the Ministry of Ungentlemanly Warfare. They're a murky mix of MI6 — the new name for the Secret Intelligence Service — the Special Operations Executive and a few other shady departments. Suffice to say they're a dastardly bunch of so-and-sos whose job it is to dupe the enemy, spreading chaos and confusion in their wake. You won't be surprised to hear that dear old Sandy is chief amongst them along with that sidekick of his, Dorian Hook.' Jox was grateful for the refill. 'They want me to capitalise on the relationship I have, or rather had, with King Zog of Albania and his sisters. Remember, I told you Alice and I once had a wild Christmas with them during the London Blitz? Moose Grant was with us and made quite an impression on the youngest of the princesses. We somehow both ended up receiving Albanian medals and stipends for no reason we ever worked out. Maybe, we just amused the King. Come to think of it, I'm going to need old Moose if we're going to make this work.'

Glasgow laughed. 'Why the devil do things like that never happen to me? Where are my bleeding princesses, medals and pensions? The last time I followed you, I ended up being stuck here for two bloody years.'

'Come off it, Cam. You've not done badly, DFM and Bar, plus the Military Medal for that Bofors business at Marsaxlokk Harbour. Plus, you're an officer now and Tommy's right-hand man. It's a long way to come, and I'll quote you here, "For a wee lad from the ugly side of bonnie Dundee." It's certainly more than enough to put you twin brother's teeth on edge.'

Glasgow chuckled. 'Aye, well there is that. Come on, what does Bullough actually want?'

'Well, at some point I need to go back to Blighty, reconnect with Moose Grant and then the pair of us will launch a charm offensive on King Zog. The intention is to convince him to publicly support some fictitious plans to invade Sardinia. Ideally, if I can bring him back with me, so he can be seen and heard, there's every chance the message will get back to the Italians, specifically their wee King. There's a long-running feud between them.' Glasgow nodded as he sipped his drink. 'The challenge is that old Zog has pretty much fallen out with everyone back in England. When Moose and I met him, he was living the highlife at The Ritz, with most of Albania's gold reserves in the vaults. I'm told he didn't take too well at the suggestion he might donate some of it to the war effort. In any case, he and his rather large family are now living in some grand old pile called Parmoor House in deepest, darkest Buckinghamshire. His nieces are going to school in Ascot and his glamorous sisters are the darlings of the country set.'

'When you off then?' asked Glasgow. 'More to the point, when are you back? Tommy's keen to get No. 333 Squadron up and running, so it's ready before operations begin in earnest against Sicily. That's not likely to be until the summer, mind.'

'That should be fine,' replied Jox. 'This subterfuge needs to happen well before we make any moves on Sicily. That's the whole point, to get the Italians and Germans thinking we're coming for Sardinia instead, so they move troops accordingly.'

'So King Zog is like some sort of Trojan horse?'

'Well, yes, I suppose so.'

Glasgow peered at the bottom of his glass. 'In the Wild West paperbacks, I sometimes read to take my mind off things, the cowboys have chaps they use to tame mustangs. Not breaking them like the others, but rather encouraging the wilful ones to do what's required. They call them horse whisperers.' He grinned. 'That's what you and Moose are, Zog whisperers.'

'I'm not sure Zog will appreciate being likened to a stubborn nag. As I recall, he and the Albanians consider their homeland the land of the eagles, so they'd rather be noble birds of prey.'

'Wouldn't we all?' sniffed Glasgow. 'Ever thought about that? Every air force out there is chock-full of eagles of one sort or other. The Germans, the Italians and look at the Americans with the huge one on their hats. Even our own cap badge has one. I suppose our pilot wings are those of eagles too. You'd have thought someone somewhere could have picked a different bird for a change. What's wrong with a heron, or a magpie, or even a hummingbird?'

'I'm pretty sure they've all been used as aircraft names. The Italians certainly have the CANT Z.506 torpedo floatplane, the *Airone*, that's a heron. Remember we bagged one with that Bofors over the graveyard harbour at Marsaxlokk.' Jox looked at his friend, realising just how weary he looked. 'Cam, you all right?'

'Don't worry about me, I'm havering, just tired.' He sighed. 'Here, I've got those personnel files for you. Better look them over, if we're going to get things up and running during your "wee holiday". I'm not being funny, but you've got to focus on that side of the master plan too. Some of these guys will be a handful.' Glasgow had switched into his adjutant mode. 'I've been in touch with the Treble Ones' new CO. Seems like a nice chap and is amenable to the transfers as he's just received a bunch of replacements. He wants the new lot trained by the veterans before releasing them, so it may take a wee while before the cavalry arrives. I've spoken to Baraldi and he's keen, so I'll work with him while you're away.'

He looked Jox up and down and shook his head. Jox glanced at his typical desert air force uniform of baggy shorts, short-sleeved shirt, long socks and desert boots.

'What is it?'

'If you're going to be hanging out with royalty, you better think about your wardrobe. It's spring back in Blighty, so you'll find it chilly dressed like that. You'll also need a top-notch tropical uniform if you're trotting after King Zog doing his rounds. Make sure you tap Bullough's lot for the budget, they've got deep pockets.' Glasgow lifted a finger, as if remembering something. 'Speaking of which, Bullough was on the blower to Tommy earlier. I think the pair of them have agreed to a couple of things. Don't have the full picture, but I believe that as we gear up the "Treble Threes", they'll be at Bullough's disposal for reconnaissance and escort duties of a clandestine nature. It'll take time to staff up to a full squadron size, so in the meantime smaller, more discreet operations will probably suit. At least, that's what I think they've agreed.'

Glasgow passed his fingers through thinning hair. 'I think it's reasonable to expect night-time missions. I've been told to have your aircraft painted black, so it seems you're back to being a night-fighter again. The good news is that your lads get first dibs on the latest Spitfire Mark IXs delivered to the island. In Malta, we tend to only have single letter squadron identifiers, so you'll be pleased to hear I've bagged you the letter J. You'll be based at RAF Luqa, alongside three resident squadrons. You already know callsign GANER of No. 249, but maybe not GRIFFIN of No. 185 that evolved from the Malta meteorological flight and BOLD of No. 229 from what's left of our old Edinburgh pals of No. 603 once they rotated back home.'

Jox sighed. 'They certainly had a tough time of it. I heard Salvesen was invalided back to Scotland. Would you believe I had a conversation about him with His Majesty the King when I received my last gong. Apparently, they know each other quite well.'

'That doesn't surprise me one bit, the "Fighting Scots" of the 603 were always a posh lot, gentlemen aviators from before the war. You remember their CO, Lord David Douglas-Hamilton, playing his bagpipes as the pilots returned from sorties? I think he made it back in one piece unlike your Salvesen. Lost a lot of good men. Actually, one of them will be joining you.'

'Who's that?'

'It's all in the files,' replied Glasgow. 'You'll recognise the name of at least the first one, Jimmy Waerea, he's a warrant officer now. I've got him pegged for senior squadron NCO.'

'I know Jimmy,' said Jox. 'How's he doing? Christ, the last time I saw him he was in pretty bad shape after that Marsaxlokk business. Nasty wound in the arm.'

'Aye, that's right, actually no it was the left,' said Glasgow. 'It's taken a long time for him to come back from that. They amputated it mid-forearm and he's now got a hook contraption with spring-loaded pins which allow him to use the controls on the left of the cockpit. It's remarkable how he controls the throttle, propeller pitch, supercharger and mixture with it. The only thing that he struggles with a bit is the landing gear handle on the right. He has to hold the control column steady with his artificial arm when pumping with his right. I've seen some shaky landings but to be honest his are better than most. Anyway, he's cleared for combat, and you won't find anyone as determined and pig-headed as him, and that's coming from me.' Glasgow grinned. 'I respect him. He could have easily gone home to New Zealand, invalided out, but refused, saying he owes it to comrades who died here. Amongst the Māori on the island, he's a kind of chief or shaman. He's certainly an impressive fellow, tough as they come and solid as Maltese rock.'

'Look forward to seeing him again,' said Jox. 'How many more have you got?'

'Four.'

'Well, with me and Waerea, that makes a section of six, almost a flight.'

'Aye, I suppose so,' replied Glasgow. 'I'll leave it to you to decide quite how solid.'

'Sounds ominous.'

'I say it as I see it. They're not all like Jimmy Waerea, more's the pity.'

Jox leafed through the blue folders, each carefully labelled by Glasgow with the pilot's name and nickname. First up was Lee 'Jumbo' Johnstone from Torquay in Devon. In the attached photo he was a bulky proposition, fleshy faced with a high forehead and piercing eyes. At six foot four and over fifteen stone, he was one of those pilots like Moose that Jox had always been baffled as to how they managed to squeeze into a Spit's cockpit hardly known for its roominess. Johnstone had played prop forward up to county level and had been a car salesman before the war. Johnstone had just been released from Mtarfa hospital, as it happened. 'Suffering from a broken neck,' Jox read out loud. 'How the devil…?'

'He's fully recovered,' said Glasgow. 'Got shot down a few months ago and crashed near Mġarr, just west of here. Jumbo thought he was unhurt but had actually cracked a vertebra in his rather sizeable, bull-neck. It's still a bit stiff, rather a handicap for a fighter pilot who should have his head on a swivel, but he's been cleared for duty and has even shot down an Italian reconnaissance plane the week before last. He's a man of few words, but determined. I think you'll like him.'

Jox turned to the next couple of files on the pile. He frowned. They'd been duplicated and had the same name on the covers. 'There's a mistake here,' he said, surprised at the error. 'I've got the same file twice.'

'There's no mistake, read on and I'll explain,' replied Glasgow wryly.

Jox opened the first folder to the freckled face of a flight sergeant, his fair hair carefully pomaded into a side parting. He looked pugnacious and had the badly set nose of a boxer. Patrick Kilpatrick was a twenty-two-year-old Ulsterman from Londonderry, a member of the Orange Lodge, who worked as a machinist in a shirt factory before the war.

His name's sake, Padraic Kilpatrick, was also Irish, but from Kinsale, in County Cork of the neutral Irish Republic. He was dark-eyed with dark hair, square-jawed with the stubble of heavy five o'clock shadow. If anything, he looked more Spanish than Irish.

'Is this just a coincidence?' asked Jox.

'Maybe, but there's more to it,' replied Glasgow. 'Those two laddies are known as the 'Fighting Kilpatricks', not because of what they've done to Jerry, but because they keep fighting each other. They've been in and out the clink near on a dozen times.'

'Strewth, really?'

'They're pals when sober but get a drink into them and it's not long before they're at each other's throats, one calling the other a "Fenian Bastard" and the other responding "Fecking Hun".'

'Hun?'

'That's what the Catholics call hardcore Orangemen, who are conservative British unionist and Ulster loyalists.'

'How d'you know so much?'

'Scotland's full of that sectarian bollocks too,' replied Glasgow. 'I don't suppose it affected the hallowed halls where you went to school, but in Dundee it was rife. Gangs were out fighting every weekend. That's part of the reason Ant and I joined up to be "Trenchard Brats" as under-age apprentices, to get away from the trouble and grief.'

'What about these two? They sound like trouble.'

'They're certainly scrappers,' said Glasgow. 'But also, technically excellent pilots. Pat's a great shot and a real whizz at anything to do with weaponry. Paddy is an excellent air mechanic. They're also both aces and deadly, if we can just keep them apart when they've had a drink. I wouldn't recommend them if they weren't good, but they need a firm hand.'

'Fine, but they sound like more trouble than they're worth.'

'The last folder should be Flying Officer Graeme "Spud" Inverarity.'

'So, what's his tale of woe?'

'He flew with the "Fighting Scots" of 603, but after you left. He's one of Douglas-Hamilton's lads, from Forfar in Angus.'

'Why didn't he return to Blighty with them?'

'He couldn't,' replied Glasgow. 'Got shot down over the Straits of Messina six months ago. Evaded capture for days but eventually got nabbed. He was found by the Italians passed out from dehydration and terribly sunburnt, being a baldy wee fella.'

Jox looked at the photograph of Inverarity and saw a round-headed chap with little hair, craggy-looking with a pronounced cleft in his chin. His skin looked dry and leathery, to the point that Jox checked how old he was, surprised to discover he was only twenty-four.

'Spud spent months at PG 98, a POW camp on the slopes of a mountain near the village of San Giuseppe Jato in northwest Sicily. He managed to escape, then nicked a fishing boat and headed west, navigating by the stars. He only had some water and dry biscuits but drifted for eight days before being picked up somewhere between Tunisia and Pantelleria. He was lucky to be found but was scorched to a crisp and has been recovering ever since.' Glasgow chuckled. 'You see, we Scotsmen are not exactly designed for sunshine; I'm not, but I've had to get used to it.' He brushed his palm over the nut-brown knee jutting out from his baggy shorts. 'Not sure Spud ever will. I've never met a man who hates the sun as much as him. Says that's why he looks like a baked potato and is determined to keep out of it. He wears dark sunglasses most of the time and an Italian peaked cap with flaps at the back. Quite a character, ideally suited to be a night fighter, I suppose. Tough wee laddie who's had a hell of a war. They all have.'

CHAPTER TWELVE

'Room!' roared Glasgow as he marched into the pilot's dispersal of newly formed No. 333 Squadron a few days later. 'Commanding officer on parade.' The men lounging about jumped to their feet.

'As you were, gentlemen,' said Jox. 'Thank you, Flight Lieutenant Glasgow.' He nodded to Warrant Officer Jimmy Waerea, the squadron's senior non-commissioned officer. 'Mister Waerea and I will take it from here.'

Glasgow glared one last time, nodded and took a step backwards. He swivelled on his heels and marched away, arms swinging and the metal segs of his parade ground shoes clicking with the cadence of his stride. A man could be promoted beyond being the squadron's senior NCO, but you couldn't erase the discipline that had been hard-baked into him.

Seizing the 'baton', WO1 Waerea stood bolt upright and hissed just as menacingly. 'Section will come to attention. Officer commanding on parade.'

The four other men in the room were in height order. Tallest and by far the largest, was Jumbo Johnstone. Beside him stood ginger-haired Pat Kilpatrick, sporting a cracking black eye, and then dark-haired Paddy Kilpatrick with a cut lip. At the end of the row and shortest was Spud Inverarity, crimson-faced and wearing dark glasses despite being indoors.

'Composite section No. 333 Squadron awaiting your orders, sir,' said Waerea, his prosthetic hand by the seam of his trousers.

'Thank you, Jimmy,' said Jox. 'At ease, gentlemen.'

Jox offered Waerea his hand, his stony features now creased with pleasure. Waerea had dark hair and large eyes, a broad nose typical of the Māori of New Zealand. Jox also knew that under Waerea's uniform was a swirl of tattoos, representing his nation's ocean waves, feathers, and fern fronds. They ran across his right pectoral, over the shoulder and down the arm. Jox recalled seeing them when watching Waerea perform the Māori Haka, a bare-chested, athletic and resplendent figure. He was thinner and less of an imposing physical specimen now, but no less intimidating.

'Good to see you, Jimmy, fully recovered and in good health,' said Jox. 'I'm delighted we're serving together again. The last time we saw each other, I'll admit, I was worried.'

'Yes, sir, I'm glad to be back in more or less one piece,' Waerea replied, raising his prosthetic left arm. The 'fingers' clicked like a crab claw. 'Sorry about that, they sometimes have a mind of their own, but don't worry, I can fly, no problem.'

'If the RAF says you're good to go, that's good enough for me, Jimmy,' said Jox. 'First task for you is to liaise with Flight Lieutenant Glasgow. I know you're good pals and you can see through his bluster. I'll leave it with you to get the details of the engineering officer and ground crews we've been allocated. I want access to our new aircraft as quickly as possible. A new adjutant is lined up to keep things organised, but he won't be joining us for a few weeks. I hope I can count on you to fill in until then.'

'Yes, no problem, sir,' said Waerea.

'I'm not sir to you, Jimmy,' replied Jox. 'We've been through too much for that. I'm glad we're together again.'

Waerea beamed and Jox turned his gaze to the others.

'Now then, gentlemen,' he said. 'I know you're all experienced veterans, but I also know each of you has baggage.

Frankly, I have some too, so in this squadron we start with a blank slate, but know this — I know, and Jimmy knows, and we still chose you.'

Jox eyed Johnstone's cannonball head and cauliflower ears. 'Jumbo, until my flight commanders join us, you'll be second in command. You're senior to Spud, but only just. I'm interested to hear about your rugby union days. Played to a senior level. Is that right?'

'Yes, sir, Exeter Rugby Club. Loose head prop and scrum captain for four years.'

'That tells me you know how to get hard-headed types to pull in the same direction.'

'Well, push actually, sir.'

'Yes, of course,' grinned Jox before turning to the pair of Irishmen. 'Flight Sergeant Pat Kilpatrick, I understand you're a welterweight boxer, but also played wing forward for the City of Londonderry Grand Orange Lodge team?'

Pat Kilpatrick stammered a reply. 'Aye, dead on, sir, Ulster champions 1938, so we were.'

Beside him, Paddy Kilpatrick sniggered.

'You can call me Jox unless there are senior officers about and then it's "sir". Is that clear?' They both nodded. 'I want to hear you say it.'

'Yes, Jox,' they said in unison.

'Right, so Paddy, your file tells me you're pretty sharp at hurling, which I suppose is like our Scottish shinty. I see you also played rugby but for Munster, is that correct?'

'Yes, sir, I mean Jox,' replied Paddy.

'A wing forward too, I see.' The Ulsterman glanced at the Munster man with newfound respect. Jox nodded. 'I'll be giving you specific responsibilities, as we build up the squadron capabilities. Pat, I'm told you're a decent shot and have a sound mechanical mind. You'll be responsible for liaising with the armourers and ensuring our guns are serviced, in top working order and supplied with the best ammo we can get our hands on. We're of no damned use if we can't hurt the enemy. You'll report to Mister Waerea, but the responsibility is yours before the squadron is fully manned.' He could see he had unsettled the troublesome Irishman, who looked perplexed. Jox turned to the second Kilpatrick. 'As for you, Paddy, I understand you're a whizz at engines. Your responsibility will be to liaise with our fitters to ensure our Merlins are purring correctly and that we have sufficient fuel to fulfil the missions we are allocated. Is that clear?'

Both men nodded.

Jox now addressed Johnstone. 'Jumbo, I have an additional responsibility for you. Your task will be to keep these two boneheads to their tasks and away from each other's throats. You have my authority to use the physical prowess you clearly possess to keep them in line. Anything that's allowed in a ruck is fine by me. You'll find me an understanding disciplinarian and a forgiving match referee. All good, Jumbo?'

Johnstone glanced at the two Irishmen, smiled menacingly and nodded. Jox winked and turned to Inverarity, the last in line.

'Spud, if I may call you that?' asked Jox. 'I believe that's what you prefer.'

'Aye, well the family are potato farmers, and by dint of genetics and then spending a wee bit too long in the sun, I know I look like a baked potato, so Spud it is.'

'Well, don't worry, I haven't forgotten about you. Your experience in Malta and more recently in Sicily and the waters thereabouts will be invaluable. You know the conditions on the ground better than any of us. I'm giving you the responsibility of liaising with Flying Officer Hook of MI6, the Secret Intelligence Service. He's an aide to Group Captain Bullough, for whom we appear to be working at least temporarily. He will be our, or rather my, commanding officer. I'm told they have all manner of dastardly deeds lined up for us, so we better get clued up on what they expect.' Jox grinned. 'Right, gents, that's it for now. Don't get too comfortable, as I suspect we'll be seeing some interesting times. None of us are slackers and have done our fair share, but the service wants another pound of flesh.'

The next morning, Sandy Bullough accompanied by his sidekick Hook came bounding into the near empty squadron dispersal hut. The men looked up at the unusual-looking pair.

'Jox,' cried Bullough, his South African accent high-pitched with excitement. 'Gather your chaps. We'll make introductions later, but we've got important news.' The men crowded around. 'Right so, we've intercepted some encrypted signals from the enemy, and have managed to decipher them. Can't tell you how, but suffice to say we have a unique opportunity within a finite window of time.' He took a breath to calm himself. 'An old adversary of ours, *General der Jagdflieger* Adolf Galland has just been appointed *Jafü*, commander of the fighter forces of *Luftflotte Süd*. We have confirmation that he and an escort will leave Cagliari in the south of Sardinia first thing tomorrow morning, for Trapani airfield on the western tip of Sicily.' He grinned at the assembled airmen, nodding his head vigorously. 'The mission is to intercept that escort and take Galland out. He's been a thorn in our side for far too long.'

'Are you suggesting a state-sanctioned assassination?' said Jox horrified. 'Surely, that's not how we operate? Isn't that the sort of thing we're fighting against?'

Bullough frowned. 'Don't be naïve, Jox. Directly or indirectly, Galland is responsible for the death of hundreds, if not thousands of your comrades. He's a legitimate target, and frankly I'm surprised you have such qualms, given your war record and the list of grievances you surely have against the enemy. I'm sorry, I don't mean to ride roughshod over your concerns, but we haven't the time to debate the issue. You work for me now, and I need you to get this done.'

Jox nodded but didn't like it. He could feel another shred of his humanity slipping away. By the end of the war, how much would be left?

'With typical arrogance,' continued Bullough, 'Galland has given himself the callsign "Odysseus One". By the way, do any your men speak German?'

Jox glanced at Johnstone. 'Yes, I think Jumbo does. He was a car salesman before the war, German marques I believe?'

Johnstone grinned. '*Jawohl, natürlich*, I'm told I have a touch of a Bavarian accent.'

'Excellent,' said Bullough. 'My, you're a big fellow. You do have a habit of collecting them, Jox, what with the lovely Pritch and Moose.'

Jox frowned. 'Why Odysseus?'

'Not much of a scholar of the classics, eh?' replied Bullough. 'It's Odysseus in Greek and Ulysses in Latin. He was the legendary King of Ithaca, hero of Homer's *Odyssey*. According to legend, it was on Sicily that Odysseus blinded the Cyclops. In this instance, I suppose, Galland sees himself as Odysseus, so we must be the monstrous cyclops, but let's make sure we're the ones who punch him in the eye.' He winked. 'Your aircraft will be supplied with long-range slipper tanks, and you'll skirt the southern coast of Sicily, staying out to sea to avoid detection. You'll then dog-leg around the western tip of the island to intercept Galland and his escort as they approach Trapani.' He was standing hands on hips trying to look martial. 'You'll need to fly low, at wave height to avoid detection by the monitoring services. Avoid Pantelleria, halfway through your outbound journey. You don't want to tangle with them.'

Jox nodded. He knew all about the aggressive fighters based on the tiny volcanic island. He'd tussled with them during his earlier sojourns in Malta. He had no doubt his men, all Malta veterans, had too.

'According to our info, Galland will leave Cagliari at 0700 hours and is expected at Trapani, west of Monte Erice, two hours later.'

Hook unfolded a map of Sicily and Sardinia over the table of the dispersal. As Bullough spoke, he pointed out the features and landmarks described, punctuating his superior's speech. He spoke for the first time. 'You'll be provided with Galland's R/T frequency, and it should just be a question of zeroing the flight's position. That's where having a German speaker will be useful, to entice a response if you can't find them.'

'Don't think it will be a walk in the park,' interrupted Bullough. 'His escort will be *Experten*, and with over seventy kills, he's no slacker himself. Surprise will be key but that may be challenging as you won't have height advantage. At least, you'll be coming from an unexpected direction. I'll leave the operational considerations to you.' He gave an embarrassed smile. 'Look, Jox, I'm sorry this comes at short notice and out of the blue. I know it's straight out of the gate, but opportunities to chop off Medusa's head don't come along that often.'

Jox looked to Inverarity. 'Spud here will liaise with Dorian and will be his principal contact in all intelligence matters.'

'Spud?' said Bullough. 'You pilots and your nicknames. I dread to think what you call me.' The room laughed. 'Now, I'll not have you lot calling Hooky and I, Beauty and the Beast, however apt it may seem,' he said waspishly. 'You boys play nice. Spud, please ask for anything you need, and Dorian will accommodate you.'

His aide nodded. 'I'm at your disposal, Spud. In all things.'

After less than twenty-four hours preparation, the dark silhouettes of six Spitfire Mark IXs rose from RAF Luqa into the darkness of pre-dawn. At that hour, there was only a scattering of light across the island. The flight, callsign BLACK, gained altitude on a north-westerly heading parallel to the Sicilian coastline some hundred miles away. Etna was a looming presence in the far distance. They expected making good time as the scirocco was blowing, the hot winds from the Sahara providing a useful tailwind over their shoulders. Conversely, Galland's flight might well be delayed by the opposing headwind. Timing and navigation would be key if they were to converge over the blunted western tip of the island.

Jox was paired with Waerea, Johnstone and Inverarity on their portside, the 'Fighting Kilpatricks' starboard and to the rear. After an hour's flight, they dropped their external fuel tanks through the yellowing gloom, the atmosphere loaded with sand particles. They descended to wave height to circuit the threat at Pantelleria. Everything remained mercifully quiet, as mile after mile of rippling Mediterranean passed beneath their elliptical wings. The glassy sea appeared waveless, changing gradually from onyx black, to slate grey, emerald green and eventually turquoise blue.

Approaching the landmass of Sicily, off the town of Marsala, home of the famous wine, Jox decided that rather than follow the original plan of circling the promontory, they would cut cross-country, remaining low over the sparsely populated terrain beyond the town. They reached a ridge, then a plateau stretching away from the escarpment. There were no villages here, just undulating scrubland that rose towards Monte Erice.

'I was a prisoner near here at PG 98,' said Inverarity unexpectedly. 'Bleak bloody place near San Giuseppe Jato.'

'Radio silence,' snapped Jox, hoping the game wasn't up.

The map on his knee indicated the abandoned Doric temple of Segesta was nestled down there between the folds of terrain, peaceful in its mountain solitude. The ancient monument had columns and triangular pediments which glowed in the golden light of dawn. It reminded Jox of the school building at Dollar Academy, modelled by the architect Playfair to resemble a Greek temple. There wasn't a soul around, the only indication of modern life being the railway line heading towards Trapani.

Jox knew the narrow airstrip where Galland was due was on the reverse slopes of Monte Erice. It could only be approached from the west, entailing an uphill landing. Since Jox and his men had no intention of doing that, he planned to use the topography to their advantage. They would gain altitude whilst screened by the mountain, then attack on the dive as the FW 190s were landing and vulnerable. Johnstone was already monitoring their R/T frequency and confirmed they were close.

The Spits climbed up the slope at eye-watering speed, the pilots' skill keeping them from the rocky faces and grasping trees, sleek shadows racing to the top. It would need a very sharp-eyed observer to spot the fleeting spectres flashing past. Near the summit, they cleared a track leading up to the castellated walls of some Norman towers, then crested the treeline. Once past, the spindly trees gave way to serried banks of agave plants, and beyond that a rustling field of green spring maize. A stone wall marked the perimeter of the airfield and Jox spotted the enemy for the first time.

They were the size of gnats, six Focke-Wulf 190s landing in pairs. A mottled grey-green, their colour reminded Jox of freshwater eels he used to catch as a boy. They had the same sinister blunt noses, housing powerful radial engines and deadly cannons and guns.

Which of them was Galland? By reputation he was a fighter pilot's pilot, always looking out for his men, so likely to want them to land first. At this distance, there were no identifying symbols or letters, so Jox just had to choose.

Hurtling towards their targets, Jox said a single word, 'Six'. His men reeled off their choice of target as Jox switched on the twin rocker triggers the Spitfire Mark IXs were equipped with. He'd always rather liked the old brass rotary trigger on the spade stick but could see the point of the new one to pneumatically control weapons. Pressing the upper part fired the cannon, the lower the machine guns. If the raised centre portion of the rocker was pressed a salvo of all armaments fired simultaneously, packing the maximum punch. He watched as the cruciform silhouette of his chosen victim filled the rings projected onto his windscreen. He inhaled, exhaled slowly and whispered, 'Tally-ho, tally-ho. Fire-fire-fire.'

On Jox's portside shoulder, Jimmy Waerea was the first to fire. A 'Butcher Bird' just feet off the ground burst into a ball of flame, dissolving rapidly into a billowing trail of black smoke. Wreckage tumbled onto the dusty runway with momentum that scraped a shower of sparks. Its companions scattered like starlings chased by sparrowhawks.

When Jox fired, his tracers were harsh in the soft morning light. He nodded with satisfaction seeing the strikes register on target, his foe wobbling under the impacts. Despite the accuracy, the enemy pilot managed to bank and climb very skilfully given the damage. Acting purely on instinct, Jox chased after him like a terrier after a rat.

Continuing his climb, the cruciform shape of the FW 190 was silhouetted against the scirocco sky, saffron-coloured light peeking through ragged cannon holes punched into the wings. The German was almost vertical when he ran out of thrust and began falling like a fishing float pulled into the depths by an unseen leviathan. The impact with the ground embedded the aircraft tail first like a flaming cross, the pilot immolated at the centre of the shattered aircraft.

The contest began with six Spitfires versus six Focke-Wulf 190s, the odds narrowing dramatically with two enemy planes taken down by the opening salvoes. These were no ordinary opponents however, Galland alone being a multiple ace. There was no way of knowing whether he was still flying or down on the deck, but Jox could picture him chewing on his trademark cigar. He'd seen photos of *General der Jagdflieger* Adolf 'Dolfo' Galland, moustachioed with slightly deformed features after a flying accident before the war. He was known to be charismatic, popular with his men, a real man's man and a deadly fighter pilot to boot.

A pair of Shrikes climbed skywards, the second pair electing to break low and escape cross-country. They hugged the slopes of Monte Erice and raced towards the sea pursued by the rest of No. 333's flight. Jox and Waerea went after the 'high birds', the others happy going for the low, ignoring that it was poor form in shooting circles to fire at 'non-sporting birds'.

Yard by yard, Jox gained on the rearmost of the climbing pair, as it reached the summit of the dormant volcano, clearing the castellated walls of a watchtower by scant feet. The FW 190s led their pursuers through a series of left-hand turns over the shrubby trees and green fields on the reverse slope. With each rotation of the deadly carousel, the pursuing pair edged closer to a kill shot.

Jox wondered how Waerea was coping with the G-forces on his prosthetic arm. It certainly didn't appear to be hampering him. Jox felt the strain on his own neck and grunted into his mask, trying to counter the centrifugal force of the continuous turn. Sand and debris from the footwells layered the right-hand of the cockpit and canopy, his shoulder dusted with what looked like a bad case of dandruff.

Inching towards the shot, Jox concentrated on the rearmost of the two, foolishly ignoring what the leader might be up to. He fired, then almost immediately felt a series of dull thumps on his fuselage, the aircraft juddering as it was swiped sideways. Waerea was nowhere to be seen, but evidently the enemy leader had somehow managed to get his guns to bear.

Jox barrel-rolled, hoping that would get him out of trouble, catching a fleeting glimpse of his victim losing his canopy lid, followed by the tumbling airman baling from the stricken aircraft. Waerea had obviously been busy, delivering the *coup de grâce*, convincing his opponent to take to his silk, rather than face more of the Māori warrior's withering fire.

The dashboard was alight with warning bulbs, so Jox turned homewards, discretion being the better part of valour now the element of surprise was gone. They'd achieved what they'd intended in the brief, bloody air battle over Monte Erice. Only fate would confirm whether they'd managed to eliminate their intended target. The focus now was to regroup and make it across the almost two hundred miles of land and sea to Engle Field in Tunisia.

By the time Jox crossed the southern coastline of Sicily, Waerea was back with him. He quickly gave Jox's aircraft an all-round inspection, confirming there was damage to his fuselage and ailerons. He could see no visible leaks, and the controls were still responsive, so cabling appeared undamaged. Once over the water, the remaining quartet caught up, excitedly reporting their success. After a comparatively straightforward return flight they were over familiar territory. Jox and his men had made it back in one piece, his own aircraft probably the one in the worst shape. His men had done well.

That evening they were hosted by the Treble Ones, soon joined by other residents of the base once news of Jox's return had spread. In the meantime, Black and his groundcrews performed miracles, patching up the damage, refuelling and rearming the visitors' aircraft so they could be on their way to Malta the next morning.

In the meantime, Monty Falls, the dramatically moustachioed American, appointed himself *maître de cérémonie* in keeping both the Treble Ones and the Treble Threes entertained. Sitting at the piano, surrounded by great plumes of blue smoke from his pipe, he belted out Gershwin showtunes. Before things got too out of hand, Jox had the opportunity to catch up with Fisken, de Ghellinck and Campbell, who confirmed they were all keen to join his new unit. They'd received early clearance from the Treble Ones' new CO, the affable South African Johannes Le Roux, and were able to return to Malta with the Treble Threes. They were even being provided with a trio of Mark IXs which needed ferrying to the island for routine hundred-hour inspections. It certainly helped to have a pal like Black in charge of RAF maintenance on Engle Field.

Earlier in the evening, before word had gone round that Jox McNabb was back from Sicily with his new No. 333 Squadron, he'd found a moment to speak privately with Ridgway, who had a rather serious look on his face.

'I'm sorry to spoil the fun,' Ridgway said. 'I've heard from Group Captain Bullough, and apparently you didn't get Galland. Our monitoring services have intercepted signals stating he is alive and well after our "cowardly" attack but is expressing alarm at our ability to strike so close to Sardinia with impunity. Bullough is disappointed but amused that General Galland has been reprimanded by *Generalfeldmarschall* Kesselring, Commander in Chief, South with responsibility for the Mediterranean region, for risking his life recklessly. He's been banned from further combat flying, so if nothing else, that's another *Luftwaffe* ace taken out of the equation. We've had confirmation that you brought down three aircraft with two of the escort killed. I understand one of them is an old comrade of Galland's from the *Kanalkampf* days, so he'll be feeling the loss.'

'Well, he's certainly lost plenty of *Alte Kameraden* already,' replied Jox. 'Didn't I read somewhere that his brother was killed last year?'

'That's right,' replied Ridgway, always the man with the facts. 'General Galland is one of four brothers, all pilots. The youngest, Paul, was killed in October 1942 over Belgium.'

Pursing his lips in thought, Jox said, 'I'm rather glad we didn't get him. This kind of mission sticks in my craw. I'll confess I rather hoped a warhorse like Galland might make it through the war. To me he's not so different from old Tommy

Thompson. I just couldn't imagine the service without him. I'm sure the *Luftwaffe*'s *Experten* would feel no different.'

Ridgway looked at Jox for a long while, mulling over what he'd said, then he shrugged. It occurred to Jox that sometimes non-combatants were more bloodthirsty than those who actually did the killing.

Ridgway glanced over his shoulder, checking they weren't overheard. 'Sandy has shared some details of Operation Tinned Fish. He's asked me to help out if I can, sort of be a North African liaison until the Treble Ones relocate to Malta. He wants you on the first flight possible to Blighty. I know it's all rather abrupt but once you're back in Malta, he wants a briefing, then onto the first flight to Gib and back to England. He's told Flying Officer Dorian Hook to be your handler and he'll be accompanying you on your travels.'

'Strewth, really?' said Jox. 'Can't you do it? I'd much rather have you, and you're still one of Bullough's boys.'

'I am *not* one of Bullough's boys!' said the Mancunian more forcibly than expected.

'No, I didn't mean like that,' said Jox. 'I just mean you've been trained by him, and by all accounts, you're one of his star pupils. He certainly sang your praises after the Rutter briefing, that became Operation Jubilee.'

'That didn't exactly turn out to be such an intelligence masterstroke, did it?'

'No, it didn't, but at least Bullough was front and centre in expressing his reservations,' said Jox. 'As I recall, he didn't exactly make himself popular with the great and the good of Combined Operations.' Jox grinned. 'Mind you, hasn't done him any harm in the long run. We started together and now he's a group captain and I'm just a squadron leader.'

'What does that make me?' asked Ridgway.

'You're one of his protégés, or should I say prodigies,' replied Jox. 'Certainly won't do you any harm in intelligence circles.'

'Actually, he's asked me to join his staff once the squadron moves to Malta. Wants me to transfer to his department,' said Ridgway, frowning.

'Is that what you want?'

'Tell you the truth, I rather enjoy working at a squadron level, rather than being surrounded by louche intelligence types constantly second-guessing each other. I don't suppose you've found a squadron spy for your new lot, have you?'

'Squadron spy?' exclaimed Jox. 'I haven't even got a damned name for them yet.' He paused, considering the question. 'Would you take us on? It's not as if we have any sort of reputation or anything.'

'I wouldn't worry, you've got plenty of reputation on your own. The Yanks are still calling you Mad Dog McNabb.'

'Strewth, that's the last sort of reputation I need.'

Ridgway laughed. 'Well, in the words of our American cousins, "If you can't do the time, don't do the crime."'

'This isn't going to go away, is it?'

'I suspect not, but seriously, will you have me?'

'Have you? Christ Doc, it would be a privilege to have you as one of us. Hell, we need some smarts and someone who can help build unit cohesion and identity. Who better than the chap who convinced me to visit a deep dark hole just before an earthquake hit?'

Ridgway laughed. 'You're forgetting the monkeys and the bats.'

'I won't forget that bloody monkey in a hurry.' Jox looked down at his scarred hands with the two fresh puncture marks.

'Which reminds me, you'll never guess who I've got lined up to be squadron adjutant.'

Ridgway looked at him blankly.

'Jimmy Baraldi! Just as soon as his eyesight is back on an even keel. He won't be flying, but he'll keep us organised. My old mentor, Cam Glasgow will show him the ropes and he'll soon be firing on all cylinders.' Jox grinned. 'My, this is simply marvellous. It's going to be like having the old mob back together: you, me, Jimmy, Axel, Ghillie, Kanga and Ralph. Added to which my new chaps; Jimmy Waerea as squadron senior NCO, who I've flown with before —' Jox pointed the others out — 'then there's the big chap over there, Jumbo, the little sunburnt chap, Spud, and our two fighting Irishmen, Sergeants Pat and Paddy Kilpatrick.'

'They've got the same name?'

'Yes, it gets complicated,' replied Jox. 'They all did marvellously well on our first mission. We didn't quite achieve what we intended, but now I know they can fly, and importantly fight. Never thought I'd say this, but sitting in that Dakota back to Malta, drummed out of here in disgrace, I wasn't feeling terribly optimistic, but things are looking up.' He glanced at his men gathered around the piano. 'I better get back to them. Things are getting a little rowdy, and I need to make sure our Irishmen don't get out of hand.'

'I don't follow,' said Ridgway.

'Don't worry, you will.' Jox called over to Johnstone, 'Jumbo, you keeping our reprobates under control? I'm counting on you. No argy-bargy, understood?'

'All in hand,' Johnstone replied, wrapping a burly arm around the scrawny necks of his squadron mates. 'We're all good pals here.'

CHAPTER THIRTEEN

Two sour-faced individuals were waiting when Jox and his now nine squadron-mates landed at RAF Luqa. The walk from the blast-proof pens where they'd parked was long and hot, especially carrying parachutes and flight equipment. By the time they reached the dispersal hut, the pilots were parched and sweating, and Jox was desperate for some water.

Glasgow opened the frosted glass door with 'CO 333' lettered in black calligraphy. Oblivious with thirst, Jox stumbled into the room, plainly furnished with a desk, filing cabinets and a trio of chairs, one behind the desk, two in front. The furniture was old and had obviously been around for a while. Jox dumped his gear in a corner and slumped onto one of the chairs.

'Right, this had better be good,' said Jox. 'I'm gasping for water.'

Glasgow and Bullough exchanged glances.

'No, Jox,' rumbled Glasgow. 'This is *your* office. You sit over here. The group captain will sit where you're sitting.' He glanced at Bullough. 'No offence meant, sir.'

'None taken.'

Jox got to his feet and ran his scarred fingers through damp hair. 'All right, gents, you got me, this is all rather new,' he said sheepishly.

'I'll leave you to it,' said Glasgow. 'But after, there's someone else here to see you, Jox.' Jox's eyes narrowed, but Glasgow shook his head. 'Don't worry, laddie.'

'Right then,' said Bullough. 'Operation Tinned Fish is a go. The plan is for you to head to Gibraltar to check in with my friend in Naval Intelligence, Lieutenant Commander Fleming. He'll update you on the progress of his operation and you can tell him what we have in mind. I've asked Dorian to accompany you as your fixer. He's already been in touch with Moose Grant, who's stationed up in Yorkshire with No. 401 RCAF. You mentioned he'll be key in getting to Zog, or at least getting in front of his sisters. I recall you said one of them is rather fond of him. You're meeting Moose in London in a week's time. Before then, I have another job for you. Do any of your chaps happen to fly a Lysander?'

'Not sure, but Jimmy Waerea probably can. He qualified on everything going when he retrained to get clearance to fly with one arm. Nothing much stops that one.'

'Can you check for me?'

'Of course, what's the mission?'

'Nothing complicated. We just need some agents dropped off in south-eastern Sicily. Has to be done tonight as it's the full moon and you'll need it to navigate your way to the drop-off near Ragusa.' Bullough paused. 'Actually, you've met the chaps, the OSS fellows you flew in with to Malta. They're set to start fermenting trouble before we start our operations.'

'The less I know the better,' said Jox. 'My pal Jimmy Baraldi is not a fan. He's of Sicilian heritage and says the *Cosa Nostra* have been the bane of the island's history for decades. Seems like a rather murky world to be dabbling in.'

'Well, you know what they say, "my enemy's enemy is my friend". Our American counterparts are putting a lot of faith in what the Black Hand can achieve.'

'We may live to regret that, or at least the people of Sicily will.'

'Let's cross that bridge when we come to it,' said Bullough. He shook Jox's hand. 'See you in a bit. I'll tell Cam you're free and do get yourself a drink, you look positively flushed.'

'What do you think I've been telling you? Its bloody hot out there!'

Jox downed two glasses of water before there was a knock at the door.

Glasgow came in. 'There's someone here to see you.'

'Who's that?'

'Giovanni Vella, Julianna's grandfather.'

'Who the hell told him I was back on the island?'

'I did. You can't keep running, Jox,' said Glasgow with chilling finality.

Silhouetted in the doorframe of the office, Giovanni Vella was smaller than Jox remembered. He wore a black suit, probably the only one he owned and was leaning on a walking stick.

This man of the land had once pulled Jox from his crashed Spitfire but was now a frail shadow of his former self. Vella removed a tattered straw hat to reveal a lined face, bristling with grey stubble and sad eyes. Jox got to his feet and helped the old man to a seat. Shuffling towards the desk, Vella reached out his hand in a tentative test of friendship. Jox clasped it fondly, feeling the calluses of a lifetime of toil.

'I am embarrassed, Mister Jox,' said Vella in accented English. 'My granddaughter has shamed her family. We grieved, but that's no excuse for what she did. She was promised to you. I gave you my word on it. She has made a liar of me. I cannot forgive this.'

'You've done me no wrong, Mister Vella,' replied Jox. 'I was hurt when I saw them. It was a shock, but you had no part in that. I hold you in the highest esteem.'

'All the more reason to be ashamed. In Malta, a man's word is everything. Without it, he has no honour.'

'I hold no grudges,' said Jox. 'You cannot suffer on my account.'

Vella looked at him, tears brimming from world-weary eyes. 'My family was shattered when that *Ġermaniż baghal* killed our darling boy. It broke my wife's heart, she couldn't bear the pain. She stopped eating, sleeping, and even speaking to her husband of sixty years. She didn't survive. I am alone.' The old man sagged in the chair, a hollowed husk.

'Surely you still have Julianna?' said Jox, fearing the question might fuel the fire.

'No,' Vella replied bitterly. 'I have sent her away. She lives in that hotel where she works, serving drinks to the soldiers. That man, who called himself your friend but betrayed you, has left Malta. She calls herself *Sinjura* Cochrane, so they must have married, but I don't know, I wasn't there.' Tears followed the furrows of his craggy face. 'My farm is abandoned; it is too much on my own. I only have my pigs — without them I would starve, or else go mad.'

'Pigs?' Jox frowned. 'What pigs? I remember your vines, fruit trees and your flock of goats. You had so many.'

'That was before. We have had hungry times since then,' Vella replied. 'We had no fodder for the goats and if we foraged, planes strafed everything. It was impossible to graze the animals or tend the vines or orchards without inviting death. That's how they killed my Elias, just walking to school…' He began to sob.

Desperate to distract him, Jox said, 'Tell me about the pigs. Where have they come from?'

Vella looked up, some light returning to his eyes. 'The Ministry of Food gave me the first one. They were encouraging people to fatten their own pig on household scraps. My first was a white one, an English pig, I think. Hungry all the time, always escaping and getting burnt by the sun. I was lucky the *Germaniż* didn't get her too.' He smiled for the first time. 'I have smaller ones now, black ones originally from Sicily. They are called *Nero dell'Etna*, an ancient breed of these islands. They are hairy and ferocious, like wild boar, but the meat is lean, and they can live rooting for themselves, even on the hottest of days. They are camouflaged from the skies too. I have many now and they are like a family to me.' He gave a hacking laugh. 'Yes, I have become the mad old pig man of Gozo. They are all over Malta now, feeding the people and giving us some hope for the future. It is something we can thank the Sicilians for, after them sending us nothing but death and destruction from their airfields.' He shook his head. 'It will soon be their turn, if all the soldiers and aeroplanes are anything to go by.' He smiled. 'And you are back, Mister Jox, for this thing I think, no?'

Jox shrugged but smiled.

'Now, I follow my darling wife's recipe and make Maltese sausage, *żalżett tal-Malti*, with ground pork from my pigs, salt from the sea, and some crushed peppercorns, coriander seeds, garlic, and wild parsley from the land. The taste reminds me of the old times and makes me smile. I will bring you some, Mister Jox, for the sake of the old days. Maybe then we drink some of my bad wine. I still have some left.' He shook his head. 'The pigs have saved my life. They feed our people and that is good. I am grateful for them.'

'You have me,' replied Jox.

'Maybe for a little while, my boy, but the war will take you away. I am sure of that, but for now, I am happy.' Vella stared at him. 'Do you still have the blade I gave you?'

Jox shifted uneasily in his chair. 'No, I'm sorry, I lost it during a battle in Africa, but it saved my life twice. Once at sea and once on land. I had to give it to a brave young man, who died in the desert. It is buried with him, as required by his people's beliefs. I cherished it but gave it to him for the right reasons.'

'If it was a good reason for you, it is good enough for me,' said Vella. He reached into his jacket pocket. 'Here, you must have mine, I can make myself a new one.'

In the palm of his hand was an exquisitely handcrafted Maltese switchblade, a partner to the one Jox had left with Ravi in the desert. Giovanni Vella was a renowned craftsman of these blades. The handle was burnished dark wood, the butt inlaid with the red cross of Malta and a hilt like a cross. The old man pressed the silver button on the hilt and the weapon bucked with a life of its own. At the base of the silver blade was etched the word MANIAGO and above was the initials GV for Giovanni Vella. It was a knife as elegant as it was deadly. Vella handed it to Jox, who carefully folded the blade before admiring it.

'This gift to you is my honour and I hope it serves you well.'

Jox bowed his head. 'It is not necessary but thank you, Mister Vella. I will treasure it.'

'Is there anything else I can do for you, Mister Jox?'

Jox shook his head, but then had an idea. He reached into the pocket of his tunic; the material was still damp from his earlier flight. He found the two hard lumps he was looking for, one a tiny porcelain doll's hand, the other the larger section of its arm. He laid the two pieces on the desk in front of Vella.

'This is very precious to me,' he said. 'It belonged to a little girl that I couldn't save earlier in the war. It is my talisman and goes everywhere with me. Recently, it was broken. Do you think you could fix it?'

Vella picked up the pieces of delicate porcelain, assessing them like a true craftsman. 'What was the name of the child?' he asked.

'Her name was Marguerite. She died in France, but I think maybe she was from Belgium. Her name is on my aircraft, to remind me always of why I fight.'

'It is a beautiful name,' said Vella sadly. 'Yes, I will fix it. It will be better and stronger than it ever was.'

'I'll be leaving in a few days but will be back. Ideally, I'd like to have it with me when I leave,' said Jox. 'I feel unlucky without it.'

'I will fix it,' repeated the old man. 'I come back not tomorrow, but the next day. Will that be all right?'

It was dusk as the black Lysander Mark III stood waiting like a squatting insect on the parking apron, just a short walk from No. 333 Squadron's dispersal hut.

The aircraft was painted for night missions with subdued identification lettering and a discreet burgundy roundel on the fuselage. It was twice a man's height and loomed above the two Italian-Americans waiting beside it. The shorter man, Major Giuseppe Paolino, looked sulky, but the taller Captain Giovanni Lomasso grinned and waved a greeting. They shook hands with Jox and Waerea, a brief surprised look crossing Paolino's face as he saw Waerea's prosthetic hand. The foursome re-capped the mission briefing which would entail dropping the two OSS officers off in a high mountain meadow near Ragusa in southern Sicily. They were counting on the aircraft's fifty-feet wingspan and large wheels to handle landing on the rough terrain.

The Lysander was an aerodynamically advanced aircraft, equipped with automated wing slats, slotted flaps and a variable incidence tailplane which allowed it to achieve low stalling speeds of only sixty-five miles per hour. The aircraft was highly manoeuvrable, could turn on a sixpence and had high-lift features which enabled remarkably short take-offs and landing capabilities. It was especially appreciated by Special Duties pilots inserting or picking up agents in enemy-occupied territory or occasionally rescuing downed aircrew. The portside of the rear cockpit had a ladder, up which the men clambered, and under the belly it was fitted with a drop-tank to maximise range. It could carry a pilot and up to three passengers — it was a tight squeeze and yet positively roomy compared to the Spitfire which Jox and Waerea were used to. It didn't stop Paolino complaining his feet were going numb and his back was sore, even before the aircraft had crossed the enemy coastline amidst banks of fluffy clouds, illuminated by the silvery moonlight.

Jox had insisted on joining the flight as he was keen to get a glimpse of the eastern side of the island, having seen the western tip during the Galland mission. Waerea was grateful for the company and later confessed he might have struggled to close the heavy hatch with his artificial hand once the agents were dropped off.

The flight was uneventful as they searched for landmarks on their map in the pale moonlight. At the pre-flight briefing, they'd been told that many Sicilian towns were built on hilltops, the legacy of attacks dating back to medieval times. Ragusa was no exception, perched on a limestone hillside rising between deep valleys called Cava San Leonardo and Cava Santa Domenica. Over the mountains to the east was the city of Syracuse and further north the long, straight beach at

Primosole, leading to the strategically important port of Catania and the plains beyond. In the grey distance were the slopes of ever-present Monte Etna, looming, malevolent and massive. Tonight, it was wreathed with black smoke, Vulcan's eye burning a deep orange in the moonlight.

Initially tight-lipped, the OSS men, Lomasso and Paolino, loosened up enough to share that Ragusa was one of the Sicilian cities where Mussolini's Fascists were deeply unpopular after years of oppression and anti-Sicilian racism. This was due to the pitiless anti-mafia campaign in the late twenties led by Cesare Mori, known as the *Prefetto di Ferro*, the 'Iron Prefect'. The regime had been heavy-handed and brutal, alienating swathes of the Sicilian population who came to resent the mainland and were decidedly anti-fascist. These were the sentiments the OSS agents hoped to fan into flames before the Allied landings started.

Jox wondered whether the agents' motivations were driven by the objectives of the Allied forces, the interests of the oppressed people of Sicily, or simply that the 'Black Hand' were keen to be masters of the island once again. He recalled Jimmy Baraldi being very vocal on the matter. From the timbre of the agents' New York accents and their growing excitement at the prospect of arriving, Jox was fairly clear where their true motivations lay. It struck him that their mood was hardly what one might expect of secret agents entering dangerous enemy territory, rather more like exuberant sons of the island returning home.

The Lysander landed in a swirl of dust and flying grass stalks. Waerea swung the big aircraft around, so it faced the right way for an immediate take-off. In the bright moonlight it was conspicuous against the sun-bleached grassland. Shadows of burly men rose up from the vegetation, like wolves breaking from cover. They surrounded the aircraft, its powerful engine unnervingly loud amongst the chirping night birds and insects.

The hatch slid back, and powerful hands reached for the Americans. Jox and Waerea couldn't hear what was being said, but there was a lot of laughter, hugging and back thumping. Paolino disappeared without a word, but Lomasso came up the ladder, his hand on the railing, and shouted into Jox's ear. 'Thanks, fellas, appreciate the ride. See you on the other side.' Jox caught a glimpse of a star-shaped tattoo on his hand, as Lomasso added, '*In bocca al lupo.*'

'What was all that?' asked Jox. 'Something about a wolf?'

'*In bocca al lupo*, in the wolf's mouth,' replied Waerea. 'It's the Sicilian way of wishing you good luck. The usual answer is, *crepi il lupo*, may the wolf die.'

'Into the wolf's mouth sounds appropriate. How do you know all this stuff?'

'You pick it up when you're on these islands long enough. We Māori are also sailors and islanders, so I'm always interested in their ways.'

Once airborne and on a homeward heading, their conversation restarted.

'What d'you make of those OSS jokers?' asked Jox.

'I don't trust the small one, but the big one seems all right. They seem like brave men, heading into danger like that.'

'Didn't see many signs of danger just now,' replied Jox. 'More like a family reunion.'

'That's not for us to worry about.'

'I don't know, seems to me that we'll be getting involved in more of this murky business before all this is said and done. Your experience of these islands will be useful to avoid the traps and pitfalls. How long have you been on Malta?' asked Jox.

'Over two years, sir,' Waerea replied.

'You don't need to call me sir, Jimmy.'

'Yes, I do, you've earnt it.'

'So have you, Jimmy. We're equals in this war.'

The next morning, Giovanni Vella was waiting when Jox arrived at his office. He'd had a decent night's sleep, a welcome shower and enough breakfast to feel human again.

Vella was chatting with Waerea. They knew each other well, having been through the siege of Malta together. Vella was dressed in his more usual farmer's clothing, baggy trousers held up by leather braces, stout boots and an old-fashioned collarless shirt that had seen better days. He took off a sweat-stained flat cap before shaking Jox's hand, then followed him into the office, taking the same seat as the last time they'd spoken.

'Mister Waerea tells me you visited *La Bella Sicilia* last night,' said Vella, passing the rim of his cap through his large hands.

'He shouldn't have done that,' replied Jox, frowning but unworried. 'That's supposed to be secret, but yes, we dropped off some chaps who'll start stirring things up over there. I went along to see the lie of the land. Never thought there'd be so many damned mountains. In the moonlight, everything looks dramatic and the island's so much bigger than Malta… Etna looming malevolently from the top of the island. I never realised Sicily was the largest island in the Med at almost ten thousand square miles.'

'The Sicilians have no idea the terror coming their way,' said the old man. 'I have reasons to hate them, but many are simple farming people.' He sat pensive then suddenly brightened. 'I have repaired your charm. I hope you'll be pleased with what I've done.'

Vella reached into his trouser pocket and pulled out the porcelain wrapped in a rag. He opened it to reveal the pale ceramic doll's arm. The hand was now re-joined to the forearm by a silver bracelet. At the back of the hand, there was what looked like a silver wristwatch with a Maltese Cross. On the upper arm was some lettering, which Jox peered at closely. At the top, 'Marguerite' was written in cursive script, beneath it, 'Elias'.

'I hope you don't think me presumptuous,' said the old man. 'I thought if you fight for Marguerite, perhaps you would fight for poor, brave Elias, too. I want someone to remember him, other than just his grandfather. Will you do that for me, Mister Jox?'

'It would be my honour, Mister Vella,' replied Jox. 'My greatest honour.'

'I've got a name for the squadron,' said Jox to de Ghellinck and Fisken later that morning. They were in the pilots' dispersal hut, de Ghellinck leafing through a magazine, looking at the pictures.

'Pardon?' de Ghellinck replied. 'I wasn't listening.'

'The "Black Pig" Squadron, named for the *Nero dell'Etna* pigs native to Sicily and Malta. They've been here for centuries, are fearsome, self-sufficient, and independent. Qualities that I want to see reflected in the squadron.'

'*Les sangliers noirs*,' said de Ghellinck. 'I like it. In Belgium, we have a regiment, *Les Chasseurs Ardennais*, who have the boar's head as their emblem. "*Résiste et Mords*" is their motto, meaning "resist and bite". In '40, when Rommel was still a panzer division commander, he said of them, "These are not men; they are green wolves." It is a worthy name.'

'What do you think, Axel?' asked Jox.

'A fierce creature, with teeth and strength. Dangerous when cornered. *Ja*, I like it.'

'It's agreed then,' said Jox. 'Maybe we'll steal that motto too. "Resist and bite" seems appropriate for a squadron created from the rubble of Malta. I'll leave it with you to tell the others and get things underway. Over the next few weeks, while I'm away, I want a crest and identity. By the time I'm back, I'd like 'Black Pig' Squadron firing on all cylinders. Please liaise with Cam Glasgow and Jimmy Waerea on the admin and logistics. You both happy with that?' He glanced from one to the other. 'Once Jimmy Baraldi joins as squadron adjutant, we can hand over the organisational stuff to him, but in the meantime, get things underway. You have *carte blanche*.'

'Leave it with us,' replied Fisken, rubbing his two nubbed fingers over his pointed chin. 'So, I am a "black pig" now?' He laughed. '*Ja*, I suppose it'll do. If a bear can be a berserker, why not a wild boar?' He thumped Jox on the shoulder, then mimicked a boar's tusks with his fingers, squealing like a pig.

The men laughed.

'Let's just hope *les Boches* don't make *boudin noirs*, the blood sausage, out of us,' added de Ghellinck.

CHAPTER FOURTEEN

'Lieutenant Commander Fleming will be with you shortly,' said the leading wren sitting behind the vast reception desk at Admiral's Place, Old Naval Hospital in Gibraltar when Jox arrived early the next day. 'He shouldn't be long.'

Jox had passed through Gibraltar many times but had never realised the impressive buildings on the hillside, painted bright flamingo pink, were the headquarters of Naval Intelligence on the Rock, overseeing espionage operations across North Africa and Iberia. Flying Officer Dorian Hook, Jox's 'handler', had advised him of that, and was sitting across a coffee table from him.

Hook's blond hair was swept off his face, as he scanned the reception area, filled with naval officers carrying on with their secret business. Jox had come to realise that Hook was an expert at getting things done, organised and 'facilitated'. All itineraries, meals, accommodation, travel arrangements, security clearances, appointments and briefings had been set up well before Jox had even considered them. He was warming to Bullough's aide, realising he was razor smart and that not all warriors had to look like warriors to be deadly and efficient.

Jox fiddled with the rim of his peaked cap, something he'd fallen out of the habit of wearing. He was seated on a red Moroccan leather sofa, feeling rather warm in this get-up. Fortunately, they weren't left for long, as an elegant naval officer strode towards them. Fleming was tall with pale blue eyes in a long face. He had a lit cigarette in a three-inch holder clamped between his teeth. He snatched it from his mouth before smiling to reveal nicotine-stained teeth.

'Jox, how lovely to meet you,' he said, holding out a manicured hand. 'You don't mind me calling you Jox, do you? Please, call me Ian.'

Fleming was of an equivalent rank to Jox, but a good ten years older. He had the steely self-confidence and careless erudition that many Etonians seem to carry through life. His attention went to Hook, who was clumsily attempting to come to attention, making Fleming grin. 'You must be Sandy's chap, Dorian Hook, am I right?' After shaking hands, Fleming turned back to Jox. 'I've heard so much about you from that dear old fig, Sandy. D'you know, I was feeling genuinely nervous about meeting a bona fide war hero?'

Jox wasn't sure whether he was being teased. He took it as a compliment.

'Come on, chaps,' said Fleming. 'Let's find ourselves a quiet corner in this blancmange of a building and have a little chat.'

Fleming led them down a corridor trailing a plume of cigarette smoke. Jox and Hook followed, struggling to keep up with his long stride. Once they'd found a private nook, Fleming opened a file which he'd been carrying. 'So, Jox, I understand you're new to the world of ungentlemanly warfare. How are you finding it compared to aerial combat? A world where you've clearly excelled, given the fruit salad on your breast.'

'I've seen some action but working with Sandy and Hook is proving an education.'

'I see you have a previous acquaintance with King Zog which offers us an interesting opportunity,' said Fleming. 'As it happens, I met His Majesty and his delightful sisters helping them get out of France in 1940. I don't suppose he'll remember me. I found him to be rather conceited and priggish.' He observed the thin line of smoke curling from his cigarette. 'I've got a little operation on the go, to convince Jerry our next target is Sardinia and the Greek Peloponnesus, but I understand you're hatching something to add to the mix.'

'Yes, Sandy has briefed me on Operation Mincemeat,' replied Jox. 'In turn, we've come up with what he's calling Operation Tinned Fish.'

'All right, let me give you a quick update on Mincemeat, then you can tell me where you're at. I'll show you mine and you'll show me yours, if you will.' Hook sniggered and Fleming looked at the ceiling, organising his thoughts. 'Let's see, well, we've a little operation involving some poor old chap, who I'll call "Just William", getting dropped off quite dead along the coast of Spain dressed as a Royal Marine officer. Not very far from here actually. Early indications are that Jerry and friends are swallowing the bait that William was carrying, but I believe the enemy needs further convincing to seal the bargain. This Tinned Fish idea may be the ticket and more importantly is elegant enough to be believed.' He sat back and drew on his cigarette. 'If I'm honest, Mincemeat is a rather blunt instrument, but the idea of luring the Italian King into believing that his arch-rival, King Zog, is involved with targeting Sardinia, is delicious enough to be swallowed hook, line and sinker. The key will be Zog, and I understand you're the man to get him. Are you up to it?'

Jox smiled nervously. 'Well, I'm here, Ian, so for better or worse, I'll give it a go.'

'That's the spirit,' replied Fleming. 'Now tell me, how exactly do you know Zog?'

'Long story but suffice to say he took a shine to me and a Canadian pal of mine, Moose Grant. This red ribbon on my tunic is an Albanian Order of Merit he bestowed on us both.

I'm still not sure why, but I'm grateful for the monthly stipend it brings.'

'Sounds wonderful, wish I had something that paid me royalties,' mused Fleming, exhaling a plume of smoke above his head. 'You don't want one of these, d'you?' he asked, indicating his cigarette.

'I'm fine thanks, not my cup of tea.'

'Good for you,' he replied. 'Picked up the habit at Eton. Been smoking like a beagle ever since. If anything's going to get me, it'll be these filthy things. Still, each to his vices, eh?' He inhaled again and got back to the point. 'Full disclosure, we have a few other deceptions in course. Operation Barclay is trying to convince the Hun of a parallel invasion through the Greek Islands and Balkans. We've created a false Twelfth Army, using bogus troop movements, radio traffic and recruiting a phalanx of Greek interpreters and bulk-buying Greek maps, hoping it gets back to them and they buy it. Again, it's a bit rough compared to your Zog plan. Hopefully, they'll work together, and Jerry won't know if he's coming or going.'

Fleming fixed Jox with pale eyes. 'Our machinations appear to be gaining some traction, but I see Operation Tinned Fish as the cherry on top. Success will be when and if German High Command are convinced that the weight of our forces are focussed elsewhere than Sicily. We've seen reinforcements arriving in the Balkans and the Italian fleet has already deployed to the Adriatic, which is encouraging. What's needed now is for the Germans to start pulling troops from Sicily to reinforce Sardinia.' Fleming smiled. 'I don't know about you, but I find all this stuff rather exhilarating.'

Jox shrugged. 'Each to his own. To be honest, I'd rather be on my opponent's tail, trying to get my guns to bear. Perhaps

I'm a more straightforward sort of chap; I like to know who my enemy is.'

Fleming shrugged. 'Takes all kinds to win a war, old boy.'

'Yes, I suppose so, live and let live,' replied Jox.

'No, perhaps more to the point, live and let die.'

Walking through Piccadilly, following the cracked pavement along Green Park, was like strolling down memory lane for Jox. Memories of both happy and sad times swirled, and he was struck by how little had changed in this part of London since the Blitz.

Yes, there was bomb damage in the elegant façades of the buildings, but they were discreetly hidden behind painted panelling and tarpaulins. Where there had been craters in the grounds of the royal park, they'd long since been filled, leaving just the stumps and trunks of downed specimen trees piled like whalebones on a beach.

The RAF Club at 128 Piccadilly was undamaged and unchanged. On either side, however, were the bombed-out remains of Hamilton and Down Street Mews, still ravaged from when the Blitz was at its worst. They remained hollowed-out bombsites, strewn with rubble and the debris of lost lives. That state had a depressing familiarity across war-weary London town and even the fun-loving West End hadn't escaped the *Luftwaffe*'s attention. Thankfully, the club, founded in 1917, was untouched, solid, stoic and unchanged. It was a welcoming beacon to officers of the home nations, the Dominions and many colonies, as well as the various Allied air forces the capital was now teeming with.

Jox checked in with a steward at the reception desk, a man of a certain age with a spectacular curly-tipped moustache of Royal Flying Corps vintage. Despite his comparative youth,

Jox's rank and the ribbons on his breast insured that he received prompt attention and secured a good table for three for luncheon. Hook wasn't with him today, as he didn't know the others, and was busy making arrangements for the trip the next day to Parmoor House to see Zog and his entourage.

Jox was meeting his old pals, David 'Pritch' Pritchard and Maurice 'Moose' Grant. Comrades since his earliest days in the RAF, he'd trained with them, fought and bled beside them, survived the Battle of Britain, the skies of Northern France and the deadly raid on Dieppe with them. They'd all been wounded at one time or another, and were scarred, battle-tested veterans, part of Churchill's vaunted Few 'to whom so much was owed by so many'.

Pritchard had been due to be Jox's best man when he was engaged to Alice. Jox had fulfilled that same role for Moose Grant when he married his Stephanie. The two of them were as close to brothers as Jox, an only child, had ever had.

The moustachioed steward led Jox up the impressive staircase dominating the club's reception. It was overlooked by breath-taking stained-glass windows with poignant aviation-inspired themes. He followed down a corridor with a high domed ceiling, the walls covered with a vast collection of squadron insignia, hand-painted in watercolours.

Amongst them, he spotted No. 111 Squadron's crest. He could almost hear the voice of Badger Robertson, his first adjutant, describing to a youthful Jox that it comprised of 'two red swords crossed in saltire, a cross potent quadrat charged with three black Saxon seaxes, fesswise in pale'. None of which had meant much to the novice pilot, but that crest had grown to mean a great deal to him. The confusing jumble of swords and crosses, and the Latin motto *Adstantes* — 'standing by', ready to serve or fight — had become something under which he'd fought, bled, suffered and seen many comrades die over the last three years. It had always been his greatest ambition to lead the squadron and it was a deep regret that he never would.

Trying to cheer himself up on what should be a happy day, he pondered whether the new crest and motto of No. 333 Squadron would ever grace these walls. Perhaps once there were some exploits to their name. Bagging General Galland might have been a good start.

He stepped through the portico into the dining room, the familiar profiles of his friends already in animated conversation. 'Well, well,' he interrupted. 'Who let you two reprobates in here? This club's standards have certainly gone to pot.'

The two squadron leaders leapt to their feet. Pritchard was first to reach him and they embraced with genuine emotion. Grant was grumbling at being ignored and Jox knew what was coming. His big Canuck friend scooped him up into his bulky arms and swung him like a baby. Jox had hoped they'd all grown out of this sort of behaviour, but in truth was secretly glad they hadn't.

'Jox McNabb is in London town!' cried Grant. 'Lock up your daughters.'

'Put me down, Moose,' cried Jox. 'For heaven's sake, we'll get chucked out. We're too senior to be behaving like cadets on the lash.'

Their outburst had attracted the attention of several greying club members, including a dour-looking air marshal.

Not wishing to push their luck, the trio settled down and took their seats as a bemused waiter bustled around them. Jox hastily ordered some beer, hoping that might calm his excitable companions. He was therefore bemused when a pair of waiters returned with a silver ice-bucket on a columned stand containing two bottles of pre-war Veuve Clicquot champagne and flutes. He began to splutter there must be some mistake when the waiter interrupted. 'With the compliments of Air Chief Marshal Sir Hugh Dowding, sir. He has asked me to give you this.' It was a calling card on which some spidery handwriting was scrawled: *It's a pleasure for me to see my fighter-boys grown to such manhood. Enjoy yourselves, dear boys. I'm so very proud of you. All best, 'Stuffy' Dowding.*

Jox showed the card to the others, who glanced to the elder airman's table. As one, they stood and raised their glasses. The gaunt-looking gentleman with a long face and drooping moustache, indicated they should sit and not make a fuss. There was no hint of a smile, explaining the nickname of the man given credit for victory during the Battle of Britain.

To be honoured by a man universally respected by the fighter-pilot community left them subdued, the three friends settling down to lunch and this rare opportunity to catch up. The other two looked well, both with the triple stripes of squadron leaders on their cuffs. Jox had the same on his new uniform, fresh from Hawkes & Co. at Number One Savile Row. It was eye-wateringly expensive but was all bought and paid for by Hook from the seemingly bottomless coffers of MI6.

Pritchard was thinner and paler than Jox remembered, perhaps the legacy of the bad case of 'Pharaoh's Revenge' he'd picked up in Egypt. He'd spent the last six months as an instructor at No. 58 Operational Training Unit at RAF Grangemouth training day fighters. He was currently lobbying for a combat role, keen not to miss the next big show whatever that might be.

Grant looked bulkier, the picture of rude health. Married life was clearly agreeing with him. He'd recently taken command of a new Canadian fighter squadron, No. 411 Squadron RCAF, the 'Grizzly Bears' based at Kenley with the Canadian Wing. He was happy to be back from the wilds of Yorkshire but complained at not seeing enough of Stephanie. 'She's always off on some secret job at Bletchley Park. It's causing havoc with our marital relations. Good job I've got Georgie to keep me distracted. You must come see him, but you're not having him back.'

Jox laughed. It would be good to see the Border Terrier again, but he didn't want to confuse the dog. He'd been a birthday present from Alice, but when she died, had been adopted by Pritchard, then his parents and now the newlyweds. Jox wanted what was best for him. It's not as if he could take him to Malta. Better he stayed with Moose and Steph.

Lunch at the RAF Club started in a civilised manner. After Lord Dowding's champagne, they'd enjoyed a fine Sicilian Marsala as a second aperitif, then moved on to wine with a remarkably good meal considering wartime rationing.

They shared war stories and snippets of news since they'd last been together. Jox explained his tortuous route to command, the others finding his predicaments hilarious, and were not at all sympathetic in the way true friends seldom are. There are no greater critics nor piss-takers than those you've been through hell and high water with, and they will always give it to you straight. Both were envious of his position at the cusp of a new campaign. Pritchard in particular raged at operational inactivity. He had hopes of taking command of a squadron currently converting to Typhoons, the next generation of ground-attack fighter-bombers being developed for an eventual invasion of Western Europe, where significant armoured opposition was anticipated. In the meantime, he was kicking his heels at Grangemouth OTU, impatient for action.

'Be careful what you wish for,' warned Jox.

'I'll take my chances, just get me to the front,' said Pritchard, fairly glassy-eyed, having imbibed no small amount of 'Dutch courage'.

Grant asked Jox, 'You can't be happy missing the end of the Tunisian campaign, eh? Saw the news reels of the victory parade in Tunis. Quite the affair.'

'Missed all that,' replied Jox. 'Did you both see it?'

They nodded.

'Let me see,' said Grant. 'The commentator spoke of all fighting across North Africa having ceased in early May. A quarter of a million Axis troops have been taken prisoner, including much of the vaunted *Afrika Korps*.'

'Good thing we've got them boxed up,' said Pritchard. 'They're hardened veterans, and we don't want to be fighting them again.'

'There's more than enough of them left,' said Jox. 'Those hornets still have plenty of sting. We're getting an upper hand in terms of air superiority, but desperate men become deadlier.' He turned to Grant. 'Tell me about the parade.'

'Apparently it was to mark the first major land campaign victory of the war,' he said. 'I guess the fall of Tunis concludes what was started in Egypt and Libya.'

'Who took part?' asked Jox.

Grant leant back in his seat, burping loudly and unbuttoning his tunic for comfort. Jox checked to see if anyone was looking, but they were the last diners from the lunch service. 'Representatives of the First and Eighth Armies marched with detachments of American and French forces that participated in the campaign,' said Grant. 'Seemed like a lot of French to me: Legionnaires, Free French and colonial troops in some pretty strange uniforms.' He grinned. 'Then the Jocks came on with their wailing bagpipes. I recognised the 51st Highland Division. I know the Treble Ones supported them during El Alamein.'

'A lot of chaps I went to school with are in that division,' said Jox. 'I'd have liked to cheer them on or at least seen the footage to see if I recognised any faces. It'd be reassuring to see who survived the desert meat-grinder.'

'Plenty of other pongos on parade,' continued Grant. 'The Brigade of Guards, immaculate as ever, wearing peaked caps as if they were on parade in Windsor. The Americans were more relaxed in their drill but were also well turned out and superbly equipped. I saw all kinds of vehicles, then heavy armour bringing up the rear. Overhead there were flypasts, twin-engined fighter bombers, Tomahawks and a few Spits. D'you think the Treble Ones might have been there?'

'I wouldn't be surprised,' said Jox wistfully.

'You don't look so happy about that,' said Pritchard, helping himself to more wine.

'Just a bit disappointed to have missed out, after two years of fighting, with all the losses and strain. Hard to believe quite how many men and tons of equipment were lost to get to this point. Tunis was always the glittering prize. I suppose that's down to Goebbels' propaganda threatening he would make it "Tunisgrad". Now that we have it, the next phase can begin, one which may well prove more costly and desperate. We'll be stepping onto the home territory of Europe. I'm not sure anyone understands or is prepared for the level of attrition we'll face in the months and years to come.'

'Christ, man, stop being so morose,' said Pritchard. 'Look on the bright side, the three of us are together. We've had a damned good feed, a skinful and the evening's still young.'

'Sorry, boys,' said Jox, stifling a hiccup. 'Getting a little blue. Go on, tell me more about the parade.'

'The salutes were taken by Generals Eisenhower, Alexander and Giraud plus a bunch of other guys I didn't recognise,' said Moose. 'There was one American fella with six-shooters, riding boots and a shiny helmet. Damnedest outfit I've ever seen.'

'That'll be General Patton,' said Jox. 'He's a real firebreather apparently. I've heard he's the one American general the Germans are really scared of. Actually, I met another chap a bit like that. A US Air Force general called Doolittle. Hell of a fellow, and he was responsible for giving me the bump-up in rank.' Jox raised his right sleeve and smiled as his friends did the same. 'Gosh, who'd have thought the three lads in the back of that lorry in Woking would end up sitting here, in a place like this, with these bleeding stripes on our cuffs. We've come a long way, my boys.'

'That's more like it,' slurred Grant. 'I've got something to lighten the mood.' He raised his glass. 'I've got good news and bad. You fine gents can decide which we drink to first.'

Jox and Pritchard exchanged glances. Grant could be unpredictable with a drink in him.

'Let's go for the bad,' said Jox tentatively.

Grant gave a wine-stained smile. 'Well, gentlemen, tonight I am well and truly in the doghouse, so one of you will have to put me up until Stephanie cools down. She's furious that Jox has asked me to go see Princess Myze of Albania and is refusing to speak to me. That's another fine mess you've got me into, McNabb.'

'What's the good news?' asked Pritchard.

'Ah, for that we'll need more champagne,' said Grant, raising his voice and waving at the infinitely patient waiter.

'What on earth is it?' asked Jox.

Grant beamed from ear to ear and got unsteadily to his feet. He reached a hand to touch each of their shoulders. There were tears in his eyes. 'Well, this is it. I'm not supposed to tell anyone, but I can't keep a secret from my best friends. I'm going to be a father, boys. Old Moose is going to be a daddy. Now, what do you think of that?'

If the afternoon had grown steadily more animated, Grant's announcement turned things positively riotous. At some point, the trio were shown the door from the RAF Club, having been relieved of a good deal of currency but always treated with patience, good humour and respect. They certainly weren't the first aircrew to let off steam at the club. The RAF's non-stop nightly bombing raids and the USAAF's day raids ensured crew losses were ramping up and the strain was taking its toll. There was therefore no shortage of aircrews to whom the bright lights and distractions of the West End beckoned as a release. Not to mention the attention of young ladies that targeted aircrew, especially American ones, but a trio of inebriated senior RAF officers held a certain appeal too.

Pritchard had a reputation as a bit of a lothario, almost equal to Bolshie Bartley, perhaps explaining why they were such good pals. He certainly knew an awful lot on the topic and drunkenly explained to his friends. 'You see, boys, the world's oldest profession is practiced everywhere, but in London there are also legions of munition workers and other women doing humdrum war work, who come to the West End looking for some uncomplicated fun with dashing uniforms.'

As the trio lurched along arm in arm, he explained, 'On the professional side of things, Burlington Gardens is where you'll find the grander and more expensive variety of ladies, with cut-glass accents and noble lineages. Maddox Street in Mayfair is the place for foreign ladies, many of whom are French and utterly intoxicating. Piccadilly Circus is rougher but good natured, with Glasshouse Street marginally better. Old Compton Street in Soho is probably the worst of the lot but caters for those with particular or peculiar tastes. The streets of London can satisfy all tastes and wallets.'

Grant was suddenly outraged at the suggestion he might be interested, given his recent announcement. Jox was uninterested on principle and so Pritchard was momentarily disappointed, but quickly cheered up at the prospect of the many late-night drinking dens available to them.

It would be a long night and would undoubtably get messy.

CHAPTER FIFTEEN

Jox was woken by insistent knocking at his hotel room door. Feeling like death warmed up, he had no choice but to drag himself from his scratcher to answer.

It was Hook, holding up two sets of dress uniforms on coat hangers. One was Jox-sized, the other huge and obviously intended for Grant. 'I was rather worried this would happen. Will you boys never learn? Come on, Squadron Leader, we've got four hours to get you and Moose in a fit state to meet a king. You jump in the shower, and I'll get some coffee sorted.' Hook scanned the room. 'Who's that then?' he asked, spotting a shirtless Pritchard spread-eagled on the sofa.

'Squadron Leader Pritchard to you and don't wake him. He's lousy with a hangover and will only slow us down. See if you can rouse Moose. You'll have your work cut out there.'

The drive from London to Parmoor House, near High Wycombe took two hours through the winding lanes, meadows and hedgerows of England's 'green and pleasant land'. The time on the road was spent by Hook briefing the queasy, semi-somnolent pair on what was expected of them. Given, he'd never actually met any of the Albanian royal family, and both of them had, they ribbed him relentlessly, fuelled no doubt by the alcohol still in their veins. After finally promising they'd take things seriously, they both settled in for a nap as they headed west in the Air Ministry car.

When they awoke, Jox reminded Grant of how the Albanian salute worked, knowing it was a simple way of getting King Zog onside. They practiced crossing their right arms crisply across their chests with their fingers extended like in a naval salute, then placing their right hands on their hearts. It felt rather close to the first half of the Nazi salute, but Jox recalled one of the princesses explaining haughtily, 'That cannot be helped, we had our salute first, the Fascists copied us.'

Hook recapped the intent to secure Zog's support for the ruse of convincing the Axis, King Victor Emmanuel most specifically, that the exiled King of Albania was returning to the Mediterranean, in anticipation of an Allied invasion of Sardinia. It was to be positioned as a first step in the restoration of his kingdom.

The car was met by a delegation of uniformed guards on the gravel drive of Parmoor House. It was a rambling redbrick mansion with several wings, covered in an out-of-control Virginia creeper. Jox recognised the besuited lead official as His Excellency Ilir Krasniqi, the King's royal chamberlain. The last time they'd met, he was a captain of the Albanian Royal Guards, one of King Zog's personal bodyguards. His immediate superiors were killed in an air raid at the Coconut Grove night club during the Blitz, and he'd been promoted into the role. The once athletic soldier had clearly had a comfortable war and had put on weight. It suited, but also aged him, as did the white-flecked beard he now sported. He was flattered they both remembered him, especially when saluting in the appropriate manner.

'You are very welcome, gentlemen,' he said with no trace of an accent. 'It is an honour to see you, Squadron Leader McNabb and Squadron Leader Grant. You both look well and hearty and have achieved great things since we last met. It is most gratifying that His Majesty chose well when honouring you.'

'We could say the same for you, Your Excellency,' replied Jox. 'A captain when we last met and now the royal chamberlain to His Majesty's court.'

Krasniqi smiled. 'God has chosen my path,' he replied. 'I am grateful of His Majesty's good favour and will serve as he chooses.' He shook their hands and then Hook's. 'We spoke on the telephone, Flying Officer Hook.' They mirrored smiles. 'His Majesty is looking forward to your audience, but I have been instructed that my ladies wish to see you first.'

As he spoke, an excited screech came from behind the white damask curtains hanging across some open French doors.

'*Oh, regardez c'est mon éléphant!*' Barrelling through the draping textile came a petite figure, barely five feet tall with dark curly hair and porcelain skin. She flew at Grant, scrambling up his imposing façade like a billy goat on a rock face. She clung tightly as he enveloped her in his arms, roaring with laughter.

'*Ma petite souris,*' he rumbled.

Jox arched an eyebrow at his Canuck pal. He knew Grant and Princess Myze had been close but never realised quite how close. He could very well understand why Stephanie got hot under the collar at the mention of her name.

This princess was followed by two of her sisters, taller and arguably even more beautiful. There was no denying King Zog's siblings were striking and made an impact wherever they went, not least since there were six of them.

'My sister forgets herself,' said Princess Ruhi. Jox remembered her as the most direct and outspoken of the sisters. 'It's not often she sets her sights on something and doesn't get her way.' She smiled in a world-weary manner. 'I suppose we're all rather spoilt.' She drew on a Sobranie Black Russian cigarette in a gold and onyx holder held languidly between elegant fingers with long vermillion nails.

'Come on now, Myze,' said Grant. 'You've gotta calm down. I'm happy to see you too, but you can't carry on so, I'm a married man now.'

Princess Myze dropped back to her feet, looking up at her *éléphant*. 'In our religion a man can have more than one wife,' she said hopefully.

'I don't think my first wife would like that much,' guffawed Grant, embarrassed.

'A princess of Albania can never be a second wife,' chided Princess Ruhi. 'His Majesty would never accept that, even amongst friends. Please stop this foolishness, Myze. Just enjoy seeing Moose again and leave it at that.' She looked at him. 'You are still a handsome fellow and it is good see you, but we must all remember our place in life.' She turned her gaze to Jox. 'It is good to see you too, Jox. I'm sorry we haven't been in touch since poor Alice disappeared. I miss her friendship so very much.'

The youngest of the sisters, Princess Maxhide, was probably the boldest of them. 'Good morning, gentlemen, what a welcome reminder you are of the fun we used to have in London. I do hope you haven't grown dull and old like everyone else around here.' She held her hand out expecting it to be kissed in the continental manner.

Jox had little experience in courtly behaviour but had played these games before with the royal princesses. Maxhide was the haughtiest of them and the one that got most carried away with her passions.

'I do hope not, Your Majesty,' replied Jox. 'The war has left its mark on all of us, but hopefully not to the point of making us dull.'

'I hope not too,' she replied petulantly. 'For the last few years, we've been buried alive out here in this "glorious English countryside". All the men are so earnest and dull, talking of nothing but war, or else their horses, dogs or fox-hunting. There isn't an artist or poet amongst them. Most wouldn't know culture if it bit them on the nose.'

The king's chamberlain cleared his throat. Jox was unsure if that was to stop the tirade, or simply to usher things along. 'Gentlemen, His Majesty the King will gladly receive you now.'

They were shown to a timber-panelled library, with yellowing portraits of the house's original owners' ancestors. Pride of place was given to a large portrait of King Zog the First of the Albanians, in a resplendent if gaudy military uniform, with a peaked cap at a rakish angle and a self-assured look in his eyes. The room reeked of cigarettes as King Zog was a prodigious smoker, consuming over two hundred a day.

He was stouter than Jox remembered, sallow skinned with thinning hair in a side parting. He still had his dapper little moustache and the same piercing dark eyes that he shared with the rest of his family. He was in a baggy civilian suit with a large golden broach on the lapel, a double-headed winged eagle with ruby eyes the size of a child's fingernails. Albania is known as the 'Land of Eagles' and the jewel left little doubt who was their king and leader.

Jox and Grant came smartly to attention, bowing their heads before executing the Albanian salute. Behind them, Hook parroted their manoeuvre, while Ilir Krasniqi looked on approvingly.

The King got to his feet. 'Ah, my returning heroes.' He smiled, genuinely pleased to see them. He shook their hands. 'Come, please sit, gentlemen. Tell me how the war is going. I'm so out of touch in the countryside.' He indicated two chairs, unconcerned that Hook and Krasniqi were left standing.

'Krasniqi, will you arrange for some tea? Our guests must surely be parched after their drive from London.' He nodded to his chamberlain who bustled away to take care of it. 'It's good of you to visit. I can see you have both become important men since I rewarded your valour after the Battle of Britain. Then you were simply brave young men, now you command them.'

'It is an honour to see you again, Your Majesty,' replied Jox. They'd agreed that he would take the lead, Grant nervous he'd say the wrong thing. 'Yes, I'm afraid we've both had full wars. Mine mostly overseas, but Squadron Leader Grant here at home.'

Unknowingly upsetting their plan, Zog addressed Grant directly. 'Ah yes, Squadron Leader Grant, my little sister's favourite. What is it she calls you? Her elephant?' He smiled with yellow teeth. 'But I know of course they call you Moose.'

'That's right, sir … er … I mean Your Majesty,' spluttered Grant.

'Never mind, both will do. We're amongst friends, although I must say if you'd been Albanian and had spurned my sister, we would have had words. Slights to one's family run deep in my country, we have long memories and hold grudges.' He started laughing, but with a chilling glint in his eye. 'I'm only joking, please continue, Moose.'

'Well, sir, it's like Jox says. I've been posted to various Canadian squadrons, protecting the country from raids but occasionally on sweeps over occupied France and the Low Countries. Jox and I served together again during the Dieppe raid in August 1942, but haven't seen that much of each other since.' Grant grinned at his friend. King Zog listened as he crushed a cigarette stub into an overflowing ashtray and lit up another. 'We're currently countering so-called Baedeker raids, which seem to be targeting sites of British cultural or historical significance. I understand they are in response to the effectiveness of the RAF's night-time heavy bomber raids. After Lübeck was flattened, these retaliatory attacks began and have continued ever since.'

'Why Baedeker?' asked Zog. 'Aren't they tourist guides?'

'That's right, sir,' replied Grant. 'Apparently, the targets were chosen by the *Luftwaffe*'s high command according to the number of stars allocated to sites of cultural significance in those pre-war holiday guides.'

'Yes, I read something about that,' replied Zog. 'The newspaper quoted Herr Hitler saying the air war against England must become more aggressive with the greatest impact on civilian life.'

'The enemy's raids on port cities around the coast is also continuing,' Grant said, 'especially those supporting the cross-Atlantic convoys and the anti-U-boat campaign. The intensity petered off for a while when the *Luftwaffe* focused on the invasion of the Soviet Union, but raids have picked up again with this fair weather.' Grant unconsciously flexed his ankle and foot as he spoke and suddenly winced.

'Does your wound still bother you?' asked the King. 'I recall you were injured when we met. You were limping with a stick.'

'I'm flattered you remember, sir,' said Grant. 'It's not too bad. Sometimes it aches and it took me a while to learn how to keep my balance with some missing toes, eh? Can't complain, a lot of folks have suffered worse.'

'I interrupted you, please continue,' said Zog.

'Since the beginning of this year the *Luftwaffe* seem to be reinforced and reenergised. A new offensive is underway with high-altitude bombers alternating with fast hit-and-run fighter-bomber attacks at low-level. We've now got specially adapted

Spitfire Mark IXs with pressurised cockpits so we can get at those high birds. We're also getting better at detecting and reacting to the hit-and-runs, but there have still been several murderous raids that got through. You may have heard of the Bethnal Green Tube disaster in March. A partially finished section of the station was being used as a shelter. A few people panicked and fell in the rush, creating a terrible crush in a stairwell. Almost two hundred people were killed, mainly women and children trampled to death and asphyxiated. The cause was fear. This war has become a psychological terror.'

'It always was,' interrupted Jox. 'It's just that now we know what horrors it can bring and that is understandably frightening. At the start of the war, we didn't know what we didn't know, and were perhaps naïve. Sadly, we now know all too well.'

'I think you're right,' said Zog. 'What of you, McNabb? Where has this conflict taken you? I was so very sorry to learn of the loss of your charming fiancée whom I had the privilege of meeting. My sisters were very fond of her. You have my deepest condolences.'

'Thank you, Your Majesty. After losing Alice, I had to get away and volunteered to serve in Malta. I had some trying times there, but somehow it was cathartic. I was fortunate to make it through more or less unharmed. As Moose says, I was then home for the Dieppe raid, after which my squadron was posted to the Western Desert. I took part in some action during the Second Battle of El Alamein. That was a tough time too, very tough. I was downed in the desert with the battle raging all around me.'

'I know Egypt very well,' replied Zog. 'There is a large Albanian community, and we have family there. In fact, did you know that the King of Egypt, Farouk the First, is actually

Albanian? His sister Fawzia was a princess of Egypt and is now the Queen of Persia which they're now calling Iran. She's the most beautiful woman I've ever met. Even your Cecil Beaton calls her the "Venus of the East". Yes, the desert is very much like our women: beautiful, wild and untamed,' mused Zog. 'But I'm sure it is a harsh place to fight.'

'I did often wonder,' said Jox, 'why we were there at all? In the middle of nowhere, fighting for rocks or sand that no one really wanted. Sure, it was grand for wide views, clear visibility and tactical manoeuvring, except when the sandstorms got going, but in an aircraft, you could see for miles. Sometimes, alone in that endless blue over the eternal flatness of the desert, I imagined it as the baize of a snooker table. The balls were the troops on the ground careering into one another with such force and violence. Different coloured balls disappearing down the holes, but in reality, getting smashed, destroyed and utterly obliterated.'

'Did you return home after that?' asked Zog.

'No, sir. After some rest and refitting, my squadron, the Treble Ones, took part in Operation Torch, the invasion of North Africa, to liberate Morocco, Algeria and after rather a bloody slog, Tunisia. I missed the end of that through injury and was posted to Malta until I was called to come and see you.'

'Ah, and so we come to an elegant segue to the crux of our conversation.'

'Yes, indeed,' replied Jox, clearing his throat. 'It will be no surprise that the next phase of the Allied war effort will have us launching an attack against the European continent. The question is where and when, but hopefully where the enemy least expects it.'

'Ah yes, your talk of liberating homelands kindles hope in the breast of an exiled king,' said Zog. 'Since my arrival in England, I've seen interest in my claim to the Albanian throne and plans for my restoration dwindling. When we arrived with the gold reserves of the Albanian nation, the British government was very interested and keen for me to donate a portion to the war effort. You will understand that with my large family and commitments, I was and am still reluctant to give it away without any prospect of a return.'

As he spoke, Jox realised Zog was speaking of things well beyond the realm of his own experience. He knew nothing of the diplomatic niceties, intricacies and the murky intrigues that the King spoke of. He looked to Hook for help but only got an encouraging nod.

'The prospect of Allied forces invading Sardinia is of great interest to me,' said Zog. 'Not least because it gives me an opportunity to thumb my nose at that odious little usurper, Victor Emmanuel.' Zog was chuckling, rubbing his hands together with mounting excitement. 'If the Allied powers commit to an invasion of Sardinia with a view to restoring that kingdom to my care, I would be prepared to support the initiative, even providing a degree of funding. I would also happily make the displacement to the theatre of battle to demonstrate my support.'

'That would be fantastic, Your Majesty. That's exactly what we were hoping for,' said Jox encouragingly, but then he faltered. 'The only issue I can foresee is that the plan calls for the illusion of an invasion of Sardinia, whereas the actual attack will be against Sicily.'

Zog's face fell. 'I have no interest in Sicily. What I want is the Kingdom of Sardinia, precisely because it is so precious to

King Victor Emmanuel. Why would I want that island of arid volcanic rock instead?'

'I believe we have a problem then,' said Jox. 'I have no authority to make a commitment like that. What I was hoping was to secure your support of this *ruse de guerre* to convince the enemy our objective is Sardinia not Sicily. Your presence in the region would go a long way to getting Axis observers to believe the plans are genuine.'

'So, you want me to parade around North Africa at great risk to myself, pretending to prepare for a triumphant return to Sardinia, a prospect that has no real chance of materialising.'

'Yes, but it would be of great service to the Allied cause and war effort.'

'Be that as it may, I do all the work and get nothing in return.'

Jox fell silent. 'I'm sorry, Your Majesty, that is all that I have.'

Irritated, Zog lit another cigarette and blew a long plume of smoke towards the ceiling. 'No, I cannot leave the country under these circumstances. It is not safe. My family and fortune are all here. I cannot just leave them unsecured to go gallivanting around North Africa, exposing myself to the bullet of any assassin. I have enemies and they have tried to kill me many times.' He sat quietly, smoking intently and glaring at Jox. 'I will not go with you to Africa. Even if you could keep me safe, I would be made to look like a fool, someone duped into supporting an invasion that never comes. Can you imagine what a clown my enemies would make of me? Any chances of regaining my throne after the war would be ruined. In fact, the chance of any throne. I am sorry, I will show my support and will talk publicly from here, but that is as far as I'm willing to go.'

They sat silently in the car for several miles after leaving Parmoor House. Hook was driving. 'Well, that's it then. He won't do it.'

'You were no bloody help,' said Jox from the back. 'You didn't say a word.'

Hook bristled but didn't react. 'There wasn't anything I could usefully add. It was very clear that King Zog ignores those he considers to be lackeys, taking little account of them. I mean, you saw him send his royal chamberlain out to get tea. That would be the equivalent of our King sending the Earl of Clarendon out to get some crumpets. He was clearly enthralled by your stories and impressed to be speaking with two war heroes, so I thought you were best placed to secure his support.'

'Well, it's not all bad,' said Grant, sitting beside Jox. 'He did say he'd talk to the press and would stoke the rumours of an invasion of Sardinia. He just wants to do it remotely.'

'I don't think that'll be enough to convince anyone,' said Jox. 'If Commander Fleming was here, I'm sure he'd say our Operation Tinned Fish is dead in the water.'

'I wouldn't be so sure,' replied Hook. 'Some support from King Zog is better than none. I believe we can still get a fair head of wind behind the rumour and then add it to the overall mix. Leave it with me, that's my bag. You chaps have done what you were asked to and should just enjoy the next few days' leave, before Jox and I head back to the Med. We fly out of RAF Hurn the middle of next week, so you should make the most of the seaside. As agreed, I've got us booked in for a few nights in Bournemouth, but at separate hotels, I'm afraid. The Metropole you requested, Moose, only accepts Canadian servicemen, so I've got Jox and I in the Royal Bath just down the hill towards the beach. Apparently, it's the oldest hotel in town, once owned by the Mayor of Bournemouth, so it should be all right. Moose, your wife is arriving from her parents' house in Canford Magna this evening and will meet you at the hotel. As requested, I've also booked a table for the three of you for Sunday lunch tomorrow at the carvery of the Metropole.'

'You're very welcome to join us,' said Jox, feeling guilty for giving Hook a hard time earlier.

'No, that's fine. I want to get things underway.'

'What, over the weekend?' said Grant. 'I thought weekends were sacrosanct to you Brits, that and those licensing hours that I can never get my head around.'

'Well, you know how it is, we "secret squirrels" never rest, always ferreting away in the shadows,' laughed Hook, running a hand through his blond mane. 'I suggest you take it easy this evening, your bender in London is bound to catch up with you. Enjoy your celebration tomorrow, then maybe walk on the beach to take in the scenery and the curative Dorset air. What could be more peaceful than that?'

CHAPTER SIXTEEN

The Royal Bath Hotel was like a grey battleship moored alongside the road leading to Bournemouth's beach and promenade. Festooned with flags, the huge Victorian edifice was all castellated angles and points, reminding Jox of the mighty vessels he'd convoyed on through Gibraltar and the Mediterranean. Away from the road, the hotel's clifftop gardens had a magnificent view out to sea and were planted with exotic palms reminiscent of those climes.

He'd woken late, unusual as he was normally an early riser, a habit from school and reinforced in the service. Hook was right though, their shenanigans in London had caught up with him and he'd needed the recovery time. Goodness knows how he pulled off the audience with King Zog. Perhaps not exactly pulled off, he mused, his good mood evaporating through failure. He was hungry, but skipped breakfast as Grant had warned the carvery at the Metropole was spectacular, advising he come with an appetite.

The previous evening he'd gone shopping for a baby gift, then had a quiet supper in the hotel's lounge bar. Hook had already gone off to get a head start on arrangements, so Jox chatted with the barman. He discovered that Bournemouth was full of servicemen on leave, different nations allocated different hotels. The Metropole was Canadian, the Central Hotel near the town centre for the Australians and New Zealanders, and the Royal Bath for the home nations personnel. The royal moniker was thanks to one of Queen Victoria's daughters, a regular visitor along with the then Prince of Wales. The great and the good of the late 1800s followed, as demonstrated by an old guestbook that he was proudly shown. Amongst an eclectic list of patrons were signatures including the King of Belgium, David Lloyd George, Benjamin Disraeli and Oscar Wilde. Wilde was such a regular that the hotel restaurant was named 'Oscar's'.

Now, he chose to take a stroll down to the beach as he still had a couple of hours before he was due to meet the others. It was a fine May morning, and the sight of carefree bathers in the surf tempted him to take a dip. The promenade was crowded with holidaymakers, family groups trying to bag a picnic spot. There were many servicemen, obvious from their haircuts, roaming in packs, often accompanied by giggling female companions, some newly acquired, others reunited after long periods apart. Jox was struck by the jumble of accents, noting that the men, mostly bomber crews, stuck together in clutches of seven for Lancasters or Halifax's, fives for Wellingtons and fours for Hampdens. There was safety in numbers, he supposed.

After a quick dip, lying on a borrowed hotel towel, Jox shivered in the sea breeze, the watery spring sunshine slow to warm him after the sea's chilly embrace. He'd enjoyed his swim, but the English Channel was bracing compared to the warmer waters of the Mediterranean in Malta. As he warmed up, he caught the eye of a pretty, dark-haired girl. Her father's dog collar told the tale of a clergyman taking the air with his family after Sunday service. His wife, a brood-hen sort of woman, was clucking after their four teenage daughters. The girl was the eldest and reminded Jox of someone he knew, but he couldn't put his finger on who. As he searched his memory, he probably glanced at her more often than was decorous, at least judging by her father's glare.

It came to him. She was the spitting image of a girl called Pamela he'd been sweet on at school. He smiled at memories of his clumsy attempts at schoolboy flirtation. Thinking the smile was for her, the young lady smiled back coquettishly, despite her parents' disapproval. Dressed for church, she had taken off her shoes for a paddle, dainty feet and ballerina ankles pink from the cold surf.

In contrast, Jox only had on formless woollen bathing trunks borrowed from the hotel. His slim, athletic body bore the scars of war, but they were perhaps less obvious than his 'farmer's' tan of a dark face, neck and throat, arms to the elbows and legs mid-calf to thigh. The rest was distinctly peely-wally but that didn't seem to have put off the demure young lady. In fact, his variegated body was probably the most exposed male flesh she'd seen, judging by the rosy tint to her cheeks. He'd better put on his bathrobe to save the lady's blushes. Her faced dropped when he did, so Jox thought he ought to say something, but didn't know what might get past her fearsome parents. Considering what to say, he was distracted by a discordant sound behind him.

It was an aircraft engine, several in fact. He turned and shielded his eyes against the glare. It was a familiar sound, but not that of the smooth Merlins he was used to, something deeper and rasping, accompanied by a series of burbling coughs. Squinting into the sun, his heart sank with the realisation of their identity. They were the bulky noses and radial snouts of 'Butcher Birds', deadly Focke-Wulf 190s. These were the fighter-bomber variants, each carrying a bloated bomb under its fuselage. There must have been two dozen approaching from over the water like a swarm of hornets buzzing at the prospect of striking at the sleepy seaside town.

Jox had time to scream, 'Get down,' as a duck-egg grey raider fired up the beach. He pounced on the girl and grabbed one of her younger siblings, pulling them both down into the sand. He saw the outrage on their father's face, replaced by sheer panic as he heard, then saw, the howling beast swooping for his family.

Face down in the sand, Jox had a girl's head under each arm. He twisted his face in time to see great gouges of sand flung skywards, cannon fire stitching up the length of the beach. It sped towards the cowering family, but mercifully clattered on past, leaving them covered in wet sand and panting in the fresh stench of cordite. Further up the beach, red rosettes spread in the sand, evidence that not everyone had been so fortunate.

Up the hillside, towards the town centre, came the sound of detonating high explosives, followed by the groan of collapsing masonry. The noise rumbled down the cliff face to reach the beach, where it could be felt through the ground and their supine bodies. Once it subsided, they all ran for the doubtful shelter of the pier. Shocked and numb, their ears were now assaulted by the wail of air-raid sirens and clanging fire trucks. It was followed by the bang-bang-bang of anti-aircraft guns finally engaging with the enemy. *Better late than never*, thought Jox, checking to see if his wards were hurt.

The pale, shaken vicar offered Jox his hand. 'Thank you, my dear sir,' he said. 'My name is Prebendary Fairservice from St Peter's Bournemouth. I thank the good Lord's providence for your protection of my family. I am unsure how much shelter this wooden pier can provide, but my church will certainly serve. It's over there, under that tall steeple. Please join us.'

Jox looked where he indicated, at a pointed structure that dominated the Bournemouth skyline. It looked like a spearhead, shrouded in thick smoke from a building burning beside it. It was Beales, the department store where he'd purchased the gift for Moose and Stephanie yesterday. The thought triggered concerns for their safety. Distracted, he missed Fairservice's continued conversation, aware only that he'd been asked his name.

'Squadron Leader Jeremy McNabb,' he replied. 'I'm glad I could be of assistance and that everyone is all right. I'm sorry, I must rush off, I've friends in town and want to see them safe.'

At that moment more fighter bombers swooped. They followed Bournemouth's elegant avenues, cannon fire spreading carnage and devastation. Snarling overhead, Jox and the family scattered, as booms reverberated off the timbers of the pier. The timpani of crashes was heightened when an aircraft was struck by groundfire, smashing into a cliff-top hotel beyond the pleasure gardens.

The restaurant overlooking the park, on the second floor of Bobby's, Bournemouth's other department store, burned fiercely. Right across the town smoke and flames rose from bombsites, reminding Jox of devastated Dieppe. The Norman town, however, had been evacuated before the raid, in grim contrast to Bournemouth, heaving with visitors and guests just moments earlier. The naïve, happy and innocent throng were utterly unprepared for this or indeed any attack.

Having said his goodbyes, Jox sprinted up the hill as fast as he could. The streets were deserted apart from rescue vehicles and the occasional stunned straggler. The air stank of smoke with cinders floating like soot-filled snowflakes. He was unsure whether to return to the Royal Bath to change into his uniform or continue up the hill in his bathrobe, woollen bathing trunks and plimsoles. He was desperate to find his friends, but dressed like a holidaymaker, he would carry no sway nor authority amongst the rescuers. He turned into the hotel to find the foyer filled with panicked guests, some injured and most grimy from the smoke. He avoided distractions and ran to his room to get dressed.

No more than ten minutes later he was on the streets heading for the Lansdowne Ring and the Metropole. On the way, he passed the rear of Beales department store, which was now a major conflagration, flames reaching over a hundred feet high. He spoke with a fire service shift commander, who told him that a gas main had been severed, endangering civilians and emergency services alike. It was only because of Jox's uniform and an assurance that he was on urgent war duty that he was allowed past and escorted through the perimeter. By the time he reached the other side of the safety cordon, his face was stinging from the heat and his uniform smelt singed.

At the roundabout at the top of the hill, Jox caught his first glimpse of the Metropole. He'd been told hundreds of Canadians were staying there, and it was immediately clear there was bomb damage. One side of the old Victorian hotel looked fairly intact, complete with columns and gables, domes and tall chimney stacks. On the Holdenhurst Road side, however, it was almost completely destroyed. A single bomb had entered a few floors up, boring deep into the building before exploding in contact with the steel infrastructure and the concrete casing of the hotel's main stairwell. The damage was extensive, the death toll heavy.

Jox volunteered to join the rescuers, alongside several RCAF servicemen anxious to find their friends. From the ground floor, he saw bloodied clothing strewn across the debris and feared they might contain body parts. Seagulls wheeled overhead and across the road from the hotel, a body had been flung onto the clock tower. The birds were fighting noisily over the spoils, before a fire crew could get to it.

Within the rubble, the dismembered torso of a large man in a RAF uniform alarmed Jox, fearing it might be Grant. He felt guilty for the relief when the remains were identified as Flight Sergeant William Abbott, a RCAF fitness instructor and renowned bodybuilder.

After hours of sifting through the debris and helping to carry out terribly hurt victims, Jox took a moment to catch his breath. Standing on Holdenhurst Road, his uniform filthy and dusty, he scanned the demolished façade. Where the bomb had entered and exploded, the seven or eight floors above had collapsed to create a yawing trough of rubble and debris. It was like a giant fist had smashed down onto a multi-layered wedding cake. It made Jox think of the fake tiered cake at Stephanie and Grant's wedding, a drawer within containing a modest wartime fruitcake shared out amongst their guests.

As he watched more bodies and bagged body parts being retrieved from the ruins, his heart began to sink. He felt growing dread, fearing the worst. He laboured until it was dark, helping where he could, before receiving the terrible confirmation that the bodies of Moose and Stephanie Grant had been found.

After that, he was numb, and everything was a blur. Eventually, he caught up with Hook at the Royal Bath. The spy's handsome face was covered by a large bandage across his cheek. It had been sliced open by flying glass. Undoubtedly in shock, he was unperturbed by the wound, simply devastated by news of the Grants.

Funerals for the majority of military personnel killed in Bournemouth's 'tip and run' raid of Sunday, 23rd of May 1943 were held at Bournemouth North Cemetery six days later.

After the attack, the Intelligence services revealed that the Germans had specifically targeted the town as one of the RAF Bomber Command's 'dormitory towns'. The enemy's reasoning was that bombers destroyed by flak or the *Luftwaffe*'s fighters over Germany could swiftly be replaced, but aircrew took much longer to recruit and train. It was a meticulously planned raid carried out by specialist dive-bomber pilots, experienced in high-speed attacks. They knew their targets and hit specific hotels, but what made the attack particularly brutal was the high number of civilian casualties, acceptable collateral damage when trying to get at the servicemen. It was perhaps an unsurprising attitude, given the toll Allied bombing campaigns were taking on the Fatherland. The notion of an eye for an eye was acceptable to the belligerent forces but terribly harsh on innocent civilians.

The coffins of the lost were draped with the Union Jack flag and paraded through the town, four to a flatbed trailer pulled by a lorry cab. Proceeding down the hushed, crowd-filled streets at a slow walking pace, each trailer was flanked by a dozen RAF servicemen on either side. They would serve as pallbearers once the cortege reached Bournemouth North Cemetery. As officers, Jox and the heavily bandaged Hook followed behind the trailer bearing Moose and Stephanie Grant. They were accompanied by Pritchard who had dropped everything when Jox contacted him with the news. With the possible exception of Stephanie's parents, Jox and Pritchard were the only ones who knew of the unborn child, also laid to rest.

Stephanie's grief-stricken parents followed in an Air Ministry car, too upset to walk. In the car with them was Georgie the Border Terrier, not understanding what was happening but sensing something was up.

The couple's flag-wrapped, floral-wreathed coffins were carried to their final resting place on the shoulders of grim-faced Canadian airmen. Those carrying Moose struggled with the weight, their more fortunate comrades with the lighter load unaware they carried two lost souls, a mother and child. Jox followed Moose's coffin and Pritchard Stephanie's. Her parents then followed, her mother stoic and quietly weeping, her father stony-faced and walking like an automaton. At the rear, Hook had Georgie on a lead, his bandaged face, like those of many mourners, proof of injuries sustained during the attack.

In the crowded church amongst the officiating clergymen, Jox saw Prebendary Fairservice, who nodded his recognition but there was no time to speak. Outside, many more hundreds of mourners waited, gathered around the burial plots that had been dug on a stretch of grassland, some distance from the church. The graves were marked by white wooden crosses each with a plate detailing the deceased. The forlorn strains of the Last Post were sounded, and a squad of airmen fired a three-volley tribute, as flags were lowered.

Sitting beside Hook and startled by the shots, Georgie began to howl as Pritchard and Jox raised their arms and saluted. A cool sea breeze tugged at their uniforms, chilling the tears slipping unashamedly down their cheeks.

Neither man would forget Moose Grant, their own dear Mighty Moose.

CHAPTER SEVENTEEN

The stitches in Hook's cheek were like bristles on a boar's face, a fact he insisted qualified him as an honorary member of Black Pig squadron. He and Jox had returned to the Mediterranean and were now catching up with the Treble Ones currently stationed at La Marsa airfield by the Lake of Tunis and the ancient city of Carthage.

Since the fall of the capital, the airfield had become the headquarters for the United States Twelfth Air Force and the RAF's No. 324 Fighter Wing. When their transport from Gibraltar landed, it taxied past a gleaming row of Lockheed P-38 Lightnings, the unorthodox twin-booms a magnet to Jox's eyes. It suddenly struck him how much he was looking forward to getting into an aircraft again and putting these last few torrid weeks behind him.

Since the funerals, Jox had gotten to know Hook, realising he was a sound and capable chap, one he'd underestimated. His handsome features were now marred by the scabby scar which pulled up the side of his face in a lopsided smile as if permanently smirking.

They'd left England in a rush. Saying goodbye to Pritchard and Georgie was tough, the former returning to his training squadron, the latter going to Pritchard's parents in Wimbledon. Jox was pleased they'd agreed to look after him, knowing they doted on the little dog and would help fill the hole left by the loss of Moose and Stephanie.

Being a passenger was always frustrating for a pilot, and Hook was a welcome distraction during the long flight south, passing the time that otherwise Jox would have spent brooding over his grief and the failure to convince King Zog. Without Hook, he'd have sunk into an even darker funk and was grateful for his chatter.

At La Marsa, it was clear there'd been a lot of changes with the Treble Ones since he'd left. There were many new faces and battle stories he'd had no part in. He knew they'd been involved with the liberation of Tunis, helping to clear the skies of the *Luftwaffe*. It had taken a heavy toll on the Treble Ones' men and machines, Jox feeling guilty he hadn't carried his share of the burden.

Bartley's replacement as CO, Johannes 'Chris' Le Roux, had already completed his tour, adding four victories to an already impressive score. He'd returned to Blighty to become an air controller and his replacement was a youthful Canadian called George Hill, teasingly called the 'baby-faced killer'. Hill was twenty-four to Jox's twenty-one and was an experienced pilot who'd made his first kill over Dieppe with No. 403 RCAF. They hadn't met before, but there was mutual respect between them. One point in common they had was Moose Grant. In the close-knit RCAF community of the Kenley Canadian Wing, the Canucks were close. When Jox shared the awful news, Hill's face dropped, his boyish features trying so hard to appear mature and authoritative, crumbling away as they mourned.

At a wing level, there had been changes too. No. 324 (Spitfire) Wing was still led by Sheep Gilroy, but he'd been joined by Wing Commander Hugh Dundas, who was supernumerary and was deputy commander for the planned invasion of Sicily. The wing now included Nos 43 (Fighting Cocks), 72 (Swifts), 93 (Escarbuncle), 111 (Treble One) and 243 (Seahorses) squadrons, plus Jox's newly formed No. 333 (Black Pigs) and two other Malta-based squadrons, No. 185

(Red Griffin) and No. 249 (Gold Coast). Jox obviously already knew Gilroy, having felt the sting of his discipline before, but he didn't know Dundas.

He'd heard good things about Dundas, who was a remarkable-looking fellow, six foot four with protruding teeth, a thatch of slicked-back hair, very skinny with bony knees sticking out of his baggy shorts and a Stowe School cravat permanently wound around his scrawny neck. He had impeccable aristocratic pedigree, and an older brother, John, with whom he'd been an early gentlemen aviator with the Royal Auxiliary Air Force. The elder brother had earnt a DFC and a posthumous Bar during the Battle of Britain, managing to shoot down the German ace Helmut Wick, only to be shot down in turn by Wick's wingman.

Dundas was a laidback personality, often appearing rather scruffy, but he was also intelligent, playful, erudite and loyal, all underpinned by an iron will. He'd been wounded twice, once by the enemy, the second time breaking his leg during a rowdy party in the mess.

One of Dundas's close friends was Wing Commander Brian Kingcome, who Jox knew well from Dieppe and the Morlaix disaster. Both had been held partially responsible and censured despite their innocence in what had occurred. Subsequently, they'd emerged with no permanent black marks on their personnel files.

Kingcome was also a recent arrival in Tunisia, earmarked for command of No. 244 Wing. Its previous CO, the diminutive and colourful Wing Commander Ian 'Widge' Gleed, was another personal friend who'd sadly been killed weeks earlier. Gleed was leading an attack on Italian transports over Cap Bon, his flight managing to destroy seven Savoia-Marchetti SM.82 *Marsupiale* aircraft before he and his wingman were jumped by the Messerschmitt Bf 109s of JG 77. Both were shot down, Gleed's clipped-wing Supermarine Spitfire Mark Vb with its distinctive 'Figaro the Cat' cartoon on the fuselage, left burning in the desert. Described as 'one of the Desert Air Force's greatest leaders' and a 'little pocket Hercules', his loss was keenly felt.

When Jox shared the news concerning Moose Grant, it was another blow for Kingcome. Grant had been his second in command at Kenley during Dieppe. 'Good Lord, Jox, at this rate there'll be none of us left,' said a pale Kingcome. 'If even the best go down, what hope is there of making it to the end? Only the brass survive.'

Jox scanned the room, and Kingcome was right, there was certainly a lot of 'scrambled egg' on show. Normally that would have put him on edge, but he knew many of their faces. The RAF was still enough of a close-knit family despite the tidal wave of replacements. Perhaps he wasn't quite as jaded as Kingcome, but there was undoubtedly a sense of last man standing. Irrespective, he didn't want to get dragged into some dark funk, so made his excuses to Kingcome, and sought out the laughter in the room.

Inevitably, it centred around the piano, where Monty Falls was bashing out a honky-tonk tune. He had his glowing pipe clenched between his teeth, below a dapper moustache, with blue smoke swirling around his peaked cap, tipped at a jaunty angle, as he played. All around were squadron mates and USAAF officers, enjoying the music, clapping and swinging in time.

Amongst them, Jox caught the eye of Dixie Sloan, CO of the 96th Pursuit Squadron. The gleaming P-38 Lightnings Jox had seen earlier were probably his. Sloan came over. 'Hey, Jox, welcome back. You sticking around or passing through?'

They shook hands. Sloan was a few drinks down and a little glassy-eyed.

'In transit to Malta,' replied Jox. 'Can I get you another drink?'

'Sure, mighty kind of you, sir. I'll have a beer, but none of your warm British stuff. They got cold American suds behind the bar.'

When Jox returned with glistening bottles of chilled Schlitz, Sloan slurred, 'God damn, that guy playing is good. He's one of yours, ain't he?'

Jox looked over at Falls, who waved with a demonic grin on his face.

'Yes, he was, but is still with the Treble Ones. Monty's a damned fine pilot but an even better actor and musician. He's the fellow who fooled your chaps when we were doing all that Pirate intruder training.'

'Yeah, that's right,' said Sloan, growing respect in his eyes. 'Made quite a fool out of me, that's for sure. He's quite something.'

'Yes, he is,' replied Jox. That's when the penny dropped. He stood staring at Falls, stunned and dumbfounded. Why on earth hadn't he seen it before? Sitting there at the piano, wreathed with tobacco smoke, his hat at the same cocky angle, Falls was the spitting image of King Zog. He always had been, which Jox had often found amusing, but just hadn't made the connection. Zog was Falls' double and vice versa. Only an expert could tell them apart. In one fell swoop, Jox knew Operation Tinned Fish was well and truly back on track.

Where the hell was Hook? He looked furtively around the mess. Doc Ridgway was sitting at a corner table, so Jox stood on tiptoes to see who he was with. Yes, it was Hook, so Jox rushed over, with Sloan calling after him, 'Hey, where you going?'

Jox must have been quite the sight, bursting dramatically on the pair of spies having a quiet drink. They looked at him, startled, Ridgway no doubt recalling Jox's previous 'rabid' behaviour in the mess.

Jox pointed. 'Listen to the music.' Hook lifted his chin, the bristly scar becoming more evident in the light. 'Now, look at the man who's playing.'

Hook turned, bemused but obedient. It took him a second to realise what he was looking at and then he said, 'My God, we've bloody found him.'

Monty Falls thought they were joking when they'd explained what they had in mind. When Jox and Hook clarified it would mean a break from operations and involve touring cities and visiting troops, being wined and dined by the great and the good, he readily agreed to being part of the ruse. It was the sheer audacity of what was being attempted which appealed to him most. Success would depend on his commitment and acting abilities, catnip to an old tomcat like him.

It didn't take long for Hook to pull together a ramped-up programme and within days they were up to four visits, lectures or press jaunts per day. Jox had agreed to stay involved for the first few weeks, mainly because Hook didn't think it was appropriate for someone of his lowly rank to chaperone 'King Zog'. He was also worried his scarred face would attract attention, something he understandably didn't want because of his 'in the background' Secret Service role.

It was agreed Jox would hand over the lead of the 'King Zog Tour' to Wing Commander Dundas, who was up for the job as he was currently supernumerary. He would also provide some senior officer clout and it turned out he was well suited to the task given his aristocratic, diplomatic and journalistic talents.

The constellation of stars that came out to greet King Zog of the Albanians was blinding. Generals of various hues and colours were wheeled out and always accompanied by a phalanx of press. Some had been briefed by Jox and Dundas, but many hadn't, all playing their part for the cameras. The more flamboyant amongst them were always keen to host royalty and never missed an opportunity to raise their profile with the 'folks back home'.

Masters of publicity and public relations like General Bernard Montgomery, Lieutenant General George Patton and Lieutenant General Mark Clark played the game masterfully, and Jox was amused to observe their differing personalities. Montgomery was clipped, brusque and condescending. Patton, showy, bombastic and foul-mouthed, whilst Clark was equally fond of the cameras, but more politically astute and cunning, stage-managing the quotes and angles to best effect. In contrast, General Sir Harold Alexander and Lieutenant General Dwight Eisenhower, the respective supreme commanders for their armies and therefore effectively 'sponsors' of the Trout memo deceptions, were far less showy. The former was affable and patrician, the latter folksy and self-effacing.

A few weeks into the visits, the 'King Zog's Circus' descended on airborne troops training for the invasion of Sicily, codenamed Operation Husky, near the ancient city of Kairouan in Tunisia. What was being planned was an ambitious undertaking, where a hundred and seventy thousand troops would hit the island in the largest combined amphibious and airborne operation ever attempted.

The airborne component would see the US 82nd Airborne Division commanded by Major-General Matthew Ridgway, and the British 1st Airborne Division under Major-General George Hopkinson dropped at night by either parachute or glider. Their targets were positions beyond the beaches where the main amphibious assaults would land. They were tasked with neutralising defenders and seizing strategic points like bridges, fortifications and artillery batteries, as well as clearing routes off the beaches.

The glider-borne element was codenamed Operation Ladbroke and would be the first mass glider assault by Allied forces. The British 1st Airlanding Brigade would leave airfields in Tunisia under cover of darkness in almost a hundred and fifty Hadrian Waco and Airspeed Horsa gliders, carrying over two thousand men under the command of Brigadier Philip Hicks CBE DSO MC. Hicks was a distinguished Great War soldier, recently promoted and a champion of this innovative new mode of attack. He reported to a youthful-looking Lieutenant General Frederick Browning, GOC (General Officer Commanding) of the new 1st Airborne Division.

Browning was married to the novelist Daphne du Maurier and was a habitué of high society literary circles. He'd employed his spouse's creative talents to create the Parachute Regiment's new emblem, the mythical Greek hero, Bellerophon, riding on Pegasus the winged horse he'd captured and tamed. In Greek mythology he was known as 'the greatest hero and slayer of monsters', a description which appealed to Browning's taste for the dramatic, his self-confidence and well-known vanity. He and Hicks were both in their forties, moustachioed like most senior British officers, but that's where the similarities ended.

Hicks was tall, puffy-faced and tending towards heavy-set, rather like a placid, paternal farmer. Browning was shorter, slim and dapper, a terrier sort of fellow. He was the product of Eton and the Grenadier Guards and known to be a bit of a martinet. When introduced, Jox was struck by just how much they were chalk and cheese.

Both played great attention to 'King Zog' and were keen to introduce him to their officers. Lined up for presentation, most were large, dangerous-looking men. Amongst them Jox recognised two familiar faces. As the dignitaries passed, the pair's expressions went from stern and serious to creasing into broad smiles.

'Would you look at that,' said Captain Grant MacNeish in his lilting Irish brogue. 'If it isn't a bad penny that's just turned up.'

'Jox McNabb, what a sight for sore eyes,' added Captain Dougal Preston, hawk-nosed and intense, with friendly twinkling eyes. 'It's been a while since we saw you at Bône. I'm thinking, you'll be joining us to make some mischief in Sicily. About time you flyboys got stuck in,' he teased. 'Can't expect the Red Devils to do everything now, can you?'

The three were laughing, leaving Hook and Dundas bemused at the unexpected reunion and outburst of hilarity. They bustled 'King Zog' towards the press pack, with Browning and Hicks glaring at two of their most capable captains roaring with laughter in the presence of a youthful squadron leader.

Jox was grateful for the shuttle flight from Tunis back to Malta but felt the usual pilot's trepidation when someone else was flying.

Perhaps his nervousness was because he was returning to his nascent squadron, and he feared what he might discover. So much had already happened over the past few weeks, tragedies and triumphs, events already tumultuous and unsettling.

He'd enjoyed catching up with Dougal Preston and Grant MacNeish, the brusque, confident pair oozing with deadly competence and an eagerness to get stuck in. *With men like that*, thought Jox, *how can we possibly fail?* For all their talk of Aryan supermen, he didn't think the Nazis stood much of a chance against the likes of big Preston and the mad Irishman. The pair were pleased to hear Jox had recovered from his 'malaise' and enjoyed the tale of the 'rabid' squadron leader 'biting' his commanding officer. The story had made its way around the Red Devils airborne division, something that appealed to the subversive, unconventional nature of paratroopers, that elusive Airborne Initiative.

They were keen to know what he was up to and glad to hear of the 'Black Pigs' night-fighter squadron, as it was likely it would be involved in overwatch when they went in with their gliders. In turn, they shared that their objectives were inland from the cliffs of Cape Murro di Porco in southern Sicily but could give no further details.

Operation Husky would be starting soon, a matter of weeks rather than months, and the burly paratroopers were keen to get going, believing it was better to hit the Germans whilst they were reeling from the defeat in Tunisia. Their biggest concern regarding any delays related to the summer temperatures in Sicily. The mountains and plains got scorching hot, not something 'pongos on the ground' particularly relished. Jox wished them good fortune and hoped their paths would cross again.

Before Jox's departure, Hook had come looking for him. He was excited and carrying an armful of newspapers. He laid them out on a table, papers from England, but also English language editions from North Africa and the Middle East, from Cairo to Jerusalem, Malta to South Africa. He had Canadian, Australian and American ones too, plus some in French from North Africa, Italian from Libya and Spanish from Francoist Spain. Finally, there were a stack of armed forces newspapers catering to soldiery from the British Isles, Dominions, Commonwealth and other Allied forces.

Many of the headlines were in languages Jox was unfamiliar with, but he recognised the three letters of ZOG on most. One said: *Zog Has Troops Agog*, featuring a picture of Monty Falls dressed as an Albanian Field Marshal, festooned with decorations and playing the piano for clearly delighted American troops. Elsewhere, he'd been photographed with a constellation of generals, visiting politicians, personalities and starlets. There were some more sombre photographs standing stiffly beside the post-liberation leaders of Morocco, Algeria and Tunisia.

Hook handed over some telegrams. The first from King Zog's chamberlain read: *His Majesty is delighted to have made such an impact. He wishes you good fortune in this great endeavour, wishing the peace and blessings of Allah upon you all.*

The next was from Commander Fleming on Gibraltar: *The fish is on the hook. Well played. Now we wait before reeling him in.*

A third came from Sandy Bullough: *Marvellous, it's working.*

Of the three, Bullough's missive had the greatest impact on Hook. Whether it was from unspoken things they had in common or simply professional admiration was unclear. Jox recalled how Doc Ridgway was also a great admirer of Bullough, who by all accounts was achieving legendary status within Allied intelligence circles. Who'd have thought the skinny little chap with big ears, bowler-hatted out of flight school, would end up such a big shot amongst the spies?

Takes all kinds to win a war, thought Jox, as the aircraft's engine pitch changed. They were losing altitude, surely it was time to land.

Jox peered through one of the Dakota's portholes. He could see the entirety of the island, shaped vaguely like a pufferfish diving towards Egypt, leaving in its wake the smaller islands of Kemmuna and Gozo. He knew both islands well and had very nearly lost his life over both several times. He knew their familiar outlines would forever be unsettling and yet somehow also exhilarating. He would always view them with equal amounts of affection and trepidation.

It struck him how small Malta really was. Having recently flown and fought over the open vistas and massive mountains of Tunisia and Sicily, it was remarkable that such a tiny landmass had played such a pivotal role in the battle for the Mediterranean. He was proud of the part he'd played but knew more perils were to come. This time he was leading new men, some of whom he hadn't even met yet.

The Dakota transport landed, its fat tyres squealing then rumbling reassuringly along one of RAF Luqa's sun-bleached runways. The pilots taxied her to a parking stand, following a clapped-out vehicle with a sign saying: FOLLOW ME. Once parked with chocks placed, one of the crew swung back the side door letting in a fearsome blast of oven-hot air.

Jox began to sweat. He was wearing his smart new tropical uniform bought from a chic Lebanese tailor in Tunis, paid for by the military intelligence budget. It was deemed a necessary expense when he was part of 'King Zog's' entourage. Jox smiled, recalling how the tailor had lapsed into German as he measured him up, language skills no doubt acquired for his most recent Teutonic clients. The airy shop was elegant, not to mention pricey, but there were missing portraits on the wall, visible as pale rectangles. At the time, Jox wondered who the previous patrons gracing the walls might have been. He was amused there were German officers with whom he could share the classic Englishman's reference, 'We have the same tailor'. Other than, 'We went to school together' and 'We served in the same regiment' there's nothing that quite cuts the mustard better amongst Britain's elite.

Maltese summers were no respecters of sartorial elegance and Jox could feel the damp patches in the middle of his back and under his arms. He'd be a puddled mess if someone didn't pick him up soon. This wasn't the impression he'd wanted to convey.

There were no other passengers and the Dakota's crew had almost finished unloading their cargo. It appeared to be stationery and office supplies, and if anything told Jox that the terrible siege of Malta was over, it was surely that precious air transport was being dedicated to providing the 'ammunition' to feed the administrative supply chain. He wondered if he preferred the 'good old, bad old days' but banished the thought. A tedious, safe peace would always trump fear and chaos.

His heat-stupor revelry was interrupted by the sound of a gunning engine. From around the back of a tired-looking hangar came a jeep. In the driver's seat was a tanned face with a paler one in dark sunglasses beside him. Jimmy Waerea was driving, Jimmy Baraldi, the passenger. *I'm going to need to find a nickname for one of them*, thought Jox. *It's bad enough having two Kilpatricks.* The jeep cut through wobbling thermals rising from the baking tarmac and looked like the mirages he'd seen in the desert. He waved a grateful but sweaty hand at the crew and squelched towards the jeep in damp socks and shoes.

The two Jimmys screeched to a halt, got out and saluted smartly.

'No need for that,' said Jox. 'It's far too bloody hot.'

'You're the skipper,' replied a grinning Baraldi. 'Got to do things right. I'll not have slovenliness in my squadron, thank you very much.'

'All present and correct,' echoed Waerea. 'Welcome back to Malta, sir.'

'Come on, boys, I'm in no mood for that. If you want to impress me, get me a cold drink and a pair of shorts. Then I'll play any game you want.'

They grinned and all three climbed aboard, Jox in the back with his kitbag.

'Right, fill me in, what's new?' Jox asked. 'I'm glad to see you've finally joined us, Jimmy B. No, that won't do. It can't work with a Jimmy W. Listen, how about this? If you don't mind, I'm going to start calling you Don Baraldi. Take it as an homage to your Sicilian background, a sign of my esteem, but also your considerable age. It's either that or being called "Uncle",' he added, a twinkle in his eye.

Baraldi laughed, lowering his specs. 'I'll take "Don", not "Uncle" for heaven's sake.'

'*Grazie Mille*, Don Baraldi,' replied Jox. 'Seriously though, how are your eyes doing? Wearing dark goggles on doctor's orders?'

'Afraid so. Blood sugars are down but the damage is done,' Baraldi replied. 'They're not going to get better, just hopefully not worse. My flying days are over but I'm all right with that. My focus is to help you make these boys as good as they can be. It's a good mission and I want to thank you for that, Jox.'

270

'Come off it, I need you more than you need me. We're in it together.' They drove in silence. 'And in any case, Mister Waerea is doing all the heavy lifting.'

Waerea glanced over, nodded but said nothing.

'How are the men shaping up, Jimmy?'

'I thought I'd wait until you've had that drink,' said the big Kiwi. 'I'll update you later, but to summarise in rugby parlance, it's been a game of two halves. We've seen some fair play, had some injuries and a few disciplinary issues.'

CHAPTER EIGHTEEN

They were in Jox's new office. It was beside the squadron office where Baraldi, Waerea and an airman typist now had desks. The air was stiflingly hot, despite the ceiling fan that was doing its noisy best to swirl the torrid thermals.

The two Jimmies had tried to make things homely, but interior decoration was neither man's forte. Mounted on the wall outside the office was a huge moth-eaten black boar's head. It glared with glassy eyes at visitors, mouth agape, a pink papier-mâché tongue between fearsome yellow tusks that curled up the snout.

'Where did you find that monstrosity?' Jox exclaimed, catching sight of the beast.

'Amazing what you find at bomb sales,' said Baraldi, nonchalantly. 'We've named him Jimmy, so the boys know there's always one of us watching.'

Waerea pointed at the tail flap of an Italian fighter also mounted on the wall. It was covered in black 'spaghetti' camouflage squiggles on a mustard background. 'Bagged by the Kilpatricks last week over Valletta,' he said. 'Those two goons are quite capable when they concentrate. They're also on a charge, so will need to appear before you later. I think they've learnt their lesson.'

'What have they been up to?'

'Don't ask,' said Baraldi. 'Here, get your chops around this.' He handed Jox a stubby glass bottle filled with a dark liquid, pulled out from beneath his desk. It was deliciously cold. He had another for Waerea and one for himself.

'Where on earth did you get an icebox?' asked Jox.

'Remarkable how resourceful you can be when you put your mind to it,' replied Baraldi. He passed the bottle to Waerea, who with a deft click of his artificial left hand flipped the bottle cap off, swapping it for the one Jox was holding. 'Clever that,' he said as the Māori NCO repeated the motion. 'Go on, try it.'

'You two are becoming quite the tag team,' said Jox. 'Bottoms up.' It was fizzy, refreshing and very sweet, rather gassy but thirst-quenching. Jox hiccupped before taking another swig. 'What is it?'

'Courtesy of our Yank friends,' said Baraldi. 'It's a sort of pop called Coca-Cola. Apparently, it's formulated to refresh and invigorate. Like a cup of coffee but nicer.'

'Very nice, but sweet,' replied Jox. 'Should you be drinking this, with your…'

'Probably not,' said Baraldi. 'But doing only dull things makes me a very dull boy.'

'Well, it's just the ticket, thank you,' said Jox. 'Wait a minute, is that the "Leopard of Africa" panel I picked up in the desert?'

'Ah yes, we found it when we moved your stuff into the office. Thought it looked rather dramatic with Jimmy the Pig and the Italian tail fin. "Know thine enemy" and all that. You don't mind, do you?'

'No, not at all, plenty of them around. I just hacked that one off the wreck I sheltered beside, before being rescued. I've got the Jerry pilot's silk scarf somewhere or other.'

'It's on the hat rack,' said Baraldi. 'We unpacked your stuff. Which reminds me, you must meet Corporal Shillington, your new batman. Shifty-looking fellow with terrible spots but efficient in a supercilious sort of way.'

'There really have been some changes around here. Right, less of the idle chit-chat, tell me how the men, new and old, are shaping up.'

'Where to begin?' said Baraldi, peering at a clipboard which he picked up from his desk. 'Right, Ghillie and Axel arrived from Tunisia with Ralph and Kanga before you left. They've been up a few times with our Malta chaps and they're finding their feet together. Half a dozen replacement pilots have arrived to beef up the squadron and they're out right now being taken through their paces by the flight commanders. Jimmy would normally be with them, but we wanted to meet you together, show a unified front and all that. He's met Axel and Ghillie and is rather impressed by both, eh, Jimmy?'

'Yeah, they are very different, but I can tell they are seasoned warriors and good friends,' said Waerea. 'I admire the loyalty they show to each other. That's what we need to build, squadron camaraderie, a sense of belonging to a single tribe. At the moment, I think too many of our pilots fly for themselves, they need to feel like part of something bigger, worthwhile and noble. That is what we need to foster.'

'I couldn't agree more,' replied Jox. 'Now, tell me about the new men.'

'Three pilot officers and four sergeant pilots,' replied Baraldi. 'All straight from flight school except for two of them. Pilot Officer Mike Barson is South African, just out of hospital after catching some flak over Kasserine and is still picking out the pieces. The other is Canadian, Pilot Officer Danny Woodgate, an experienced pilot who has delivered several aircraft along the Takoradi trail before catching malaria that laid him out for the last couple of months. Technically, he's sound and an excellent navigator but hasn't much combat experience.'

'What about the rest?'

'McPherson, Bedford and Lee are English,' said Baraldi. 'Foreman is an Aussie and Smyth another Canuck. Lee and McPherson are from London, Bedford from the Midlands.

Turns out Sergeant Foreman is a school friend of Kanga's, and he's already taken him under his wing. I think he's rather missing his pal Waring who stayed with the Treble Ones.'

Waerea added, 'Sergeant Smyth is from Nova Scotia, a fur trapper and a real crack shot. He reminds me of George Beurling, the deflection shot whizz who did so well during the siege. What was it they called him, the "Knight of Malta"?'

'Something like that,' said Jox. 'Built up quite a tally. Well into the double figures. He was in my flight when I first got here. Nice chap, but quite unpredictable.'

'It got to thirty,' said Waerea.

'Let's hope Smyth is even half as good,' said Jox. 'Right, no more beating around the bush, what have those Irishmen been up to?'

Baraldi smiled. Waerea looked deadly serious.

'We went on an afternoon patrol over the north of the island,' said Waerea. 'Clear day with good visibility. We were vectored onto some raiders harassing shipping in the port. Nothing heavy, just a few fighters and fighter-bombers. Turned out they were Italians and we managed to put holes in some before they ran. The Kilpatricks did well and got one down between them. That's the tail fin over there.' Waerea sighed. 'When we got back, the men were in high spirits. Axel and Ghillie thought we should celebrate, so the boys headed for The Gut.'

'I'm not sure I like where this is going.'

'Well, Axel isn't scared of anything. The rougher the better; I think he saw it as a test. Anyway, the boys held it together, even with The Gut's drunken sailors looking for trouble. Jumbo had been doing a great job keeping the two Kilpatricks apart, but he needed the loo. I should have paid more attention, but before I knew it, those idiots were knocking lumps out of each other, each claiming they'd downed the Italian. By the time we got them apart, the fight turned into a riot, sailors and airmen at each other's throats. We cleared out, but the bar was trashed. We've been saddled with a bill of over a hundred pounds. Jumbo is furious, but it's not his fault. He shouldn't need to be the guard dog over those two morons. I'm afraid I got angry and took things into my own hands, I'm not proud of how. You may want to reconsider my role with the squadron.'

'Don't be daft,' said Baraldi. 'You sorted them out like no one else could.'

Later, there was a commotion outside Jox's office. He knew what was coming but was still startled by how loud Waerea really was.

'Punishment detail, punishment detail, attention! Commanding Officer on parade. March in, quick time. Left, aiht, left, aiht, left!'

The frosted door swung open and two bruised Flight Sergeants marched in at double time. The Kilpatricks had matching black eyes, Pat a swollen nose, Paddy a split lip.

'Punishment detail, right … turn. Left, aiht,' snarled the Māori WO1. 'Detail … halt. Commanding Officer on parade … salute.'

Jox had his fists on the desk, straightening both elbows in response to the salute from the Irishmen. Both had on peaked caps, nervous eyes peeking out from under black brims.

'At ease,' said Jox as brusquely as he could muster. 'Explain yourselves.'

Pat Kilpatrick spoke first. 'Sorry, sir, I've no excuse at all.'

Jox glanced at his companion.

'I regret the incident, sir. I've no excuse,' Paddy Kilpatrick parroted.

'Will you accept my punishment, or do you wish to proceed to court martial?' said Jox, feeling like a fraud, given his own disciplinary record for not dissimilar infractions.

Both replied that they would accept his punishment.

'Two weeks confinement to barracks. Stoppage of pay for twenty-eight days. Monthly docking after that until you've repaid what the squadron had to shell out for your behaviour.' He glared at the pair. 'You are a disappointment to me. Mister Waerea, march them out.'

'Punishment detail. Left … turn. March out, quick time. Left, aiht, left, aiht!' Waerea followed them out, nipping at their heels like a bad-tempered sheepdog.

Baraldi slipped into the office and closed the door.

'Strewth, that man's terrifying when his gander is up,' said Jimmy, slowly exhaling.

'Right, let's put all that behind us,' said Jox. 'What's on the agenda for the morning?'

'Well, you ought to meet the new replacements and after lunch there's a briefing for all Malta-based fighter squadron COs and their flight commanders. I thought I'd tag along for the ride. Cam Glasgow telephoned through the details and Tommy Thompson is giving the briefing. It's regarding the next big Op.'

'What? Sicily already?'

'No, Operation Corkscrew, the invasion of Pantelleria. Rehearsal for the big show.'

'Pantelleria!' said Group Captain Thompson, slamming a swagger sick against the map of the island that he'd just dramatically revealed. 'The Arabs call it the "Daughter of the

Winds" and believe the sweet wine from grapes grown in its volcanic soil are the surest way to a woman's heart. The Italians call it the Black Pearl of the Mediterranean and also *Isola Fumosa*, the smoky isle. Those of you who have flown from Tunisia and Malta will know it as the homebase of the nastiest viper's nest of Axis fighters in the Mediterranean.'

It was unusual to see the tiny island, barely thirty-two square miles, quite so large. For the newcomers, Thompson explained it was a satellite volcanic island to Sicily, that would hardly merit a footnote in history, but for the twelve thousand Axis troops stationed there with a powerful force of fighters. It was arguably the largest fly in the ointment for planners of the forthcoming invasion of Sicily. Every variant of Macchi fighters were present on the island, as part of the 1st and 53rd *Stormo*, with Germans also operating with the latest Bf 109s and FW 190 fighters of JG 27 and JG 53, *Sturmgeschwader* 10 and *Schlachtgeschwader* 26 respectively. In addition, long-range Me 110 fighters and Ju 88 night fighters were known to be present. An estimated three hundred and fifty aircraft were on Pantelleria, with the potential for an Axis air armada of over a thousand if reinforcements from Sicily, Sardinia, Corsica and the Italian mainland were called in. 'However we cut it, gentlemen, this Black Pearl packs a nasty punch.'

Thompson explained that the island was famed for its hot springs and fumaroles, smoking vents from which hot volcanic gases and vapours were emitted. When the wind wasn't blowing in from Africa, the island was wreathed in a sinister nape of swirling smoke, hiding the volcanic Montagna Grande, reaching eight hundred metres above sea level and lying in wait for unwary flyers.

Apart from the forces stationed there, the island was also strategically important as it was just seventy miles from Sicily, one hundred and fifty from Malta, and on a clear day was visible from Tunisia. The airfield and radar installations were currently supporting Axis troops withdrawing from North Africa but represented a significant threat for forces targeting Sicily. Its capture would also provide a new 'unsinkable aircraft carrier' for that operation.

'The AA and artillery defences on the island are formidable,' said Thompson, rubbing a finger through his moustache. 'The Royal Navy and the USAAF have been bombarding and bombing around the clock since the middle of May, so four weeks now. Our planners estimate that half the guns should be out of action, but there's no guarantee.' He waved his hand over the map. 'Recent reconnaissance flights indicate Pantelleria is covered in a swathe of smoke and ash, not just volcanic in origin as it's been given a proper pasting.' He stood hands on hips. 'D-day is tomorrow at first light. There'll be a final naval bombardment, then Operation Corkscrew is on, beginning with the seaborne landing of the British 1st Infantry Division. Our role will be to provide overwatch for the landings, take on any retaliation and pursue any aircraft trying to escape the island. The bombs and shells should take care of a good deal, but don't be fooled, we're still rattling a big stick in a hornet's nest. They'll come out in force and be angry as hell.'

Thompson indicated a lanky man in baggy shorts with knobbly knees. 'Most of you know Wing Commander Dundas. He'll be leading the Malta-based elements of No. 324 Wing, whilst Gilroy handles the rest out of Tunisia. You'll be flying with a contingent of our American friends, so aircraft recognition is important. Most of the bombers should be clear by the time we get there but watch out for the P-38 Lightnings and P-40 Tomahawks. They'll be out in force, as will we, not to

279

mention the Germans and Italians. Should make for crowded skies, like the old Battle of Britain days. After the mission, you'll return with them to stations in Tunisia for refuelling. You know, boys, I rather envy you; this should be quite a party.'

CHAPTER NINETEEN

It was an hour before dawn and the sky was lightening from the east, the opposite direction to Pantelleria, so they would be coming out of the sun. Jox was watching clusters of riggers, fitters and armourers finishing last-minute tasks before take-off.

No. 333 Squadron's pilots filed from the dispersal in twos and threes, eyes puffy from the early rise, some smoking, others chatting about nothing in particular. They knew what was expected of them and that the Jimmys, their veteran flight commanders, and the boss Squadron Leader McNabb were watching. A cool breeze brought the smell of the island and sea, wafting away the harsher odours of petroleum, glycol and soot. The aircraft were wing tip to wing tip on either side of one of RAF Luqa's taxiways. Across the airfield, other resident fighter squadrons were similarly getting ready.

Jox took a moment to admire their jet-black Spitfire Mark IXs, painted as night-fighters, and was surprised to note their wing and fuselage roundels were edged in yellow, rather at odds with the dark camouflage. Each aircraft bore the letter 'J', his with *Marguerite* inscribed below the cockpit, Ghillie de Ghellinck's named for his resistance-fighter sister, *Véronique*, and Axel Fisken for his missing love in Norway, *Tove*.

Jox liked the pugnacious look of the aircraft. Wide sweeping wings and the long nose in the air as if sniffing for trouble. There wasn't a straight line as his hand ran over the smooth, cold surface of the rivetted metal. It was like a racehorse, a thoroughbred, Black Beauty from the novel. He remembered it was one of Alice's favourites and the title had unexpectedly popped into his head. Yes indeed, black beauties to take on the black pearl. He wasn't sure if there was anything poetic about that, but it seemed appropriate.

'You all right there, sir?' asked his rigger, whose name Jox didn't yet know. He'd have to sort that out, but for now too many new names had been thrown at him.

'Fine, thanks,' he replied as nonchalantly as he could muster. 'Everything ready?'

'Tip-top,' the man replied. 'We're all set when you're ready.' He was plugging the leads from the starter trolley into the sockets beneath the nose.

'Right, we better get on with it,' said Jox, pulling on his flight helmet, adjusting the goggles over his forehead and ensuring his radio leads, oxygen mask and air tube weren't tangled. He heaved on his parachute with the rigger's help and allowed him to tighten the straps. He then placed a booted foot into the footplate, lifted himself over the open half-hatch and sank into the narrow cockpit and bucket seat. Not for the first time he wondered how the hell big fellows like Jumbo Johnstone or Moose Grant ever managed to fit.

Moose … he felt a sudden wave of sorrow. *This one's for you*, he thought, but was distracted by the rigger tightening the Sutton harness. Jox plugged in and the same rigger's voice asked, 'All set, sir?' He was speaking through the headset and long lead plugged into the fuselage.

Jox gave the thumbs up, clipped on his mask and took a few deep breaths. A whiff of oxygen always blew away the cobwebs. He began his cockpit checks, identifying his controls automatically: throttle, electric undercarriage retractor, magnetos, canopy release, oil pressure, engine temperature gauges. The rigger standing on the wing gave him the thumbs up and hopped off. Jox waved a gloved hand in response before pressing the starter.

The engine whined then coughed into life, bright flames spouting from sooty exhaust stubs like the angry snort of a wild boar. *How appropriate*, thought Jox, as he dialled up the revs. He waved the chocks away, then checked the ground crew were clear before releasing the brakes and started to roll forward.

As he swung the Mark IX onto the taxiway heading for the runway, he sensed other aircraft in motion. He checked his temperature gauge, seeing it was already climbing, so he needed to get off. Reaching the end of the runway, he waited for the aircraft ahead of him to get going before releasing his own brakes, opening up the throttle and trundling forward into the wind.

Jox glanced left and right at his elliptical wing tips, as the Merlin howled gaining speed down the track. The nose dropped as the tail lifted, clearing the forward view over the aircraft's long nose. He skidded left and right to make sure the path was clear before throttling up further and gaining real speed. The rumbling wheels silenced, then whistled in the airflow until he pressed the electric undercarriage retractor, a luxury he certainly hadn't had in the Hurricanes and Spits he'd flown during the Battle of Britain.

The airfield dropped away, and he was over the blue waters of the Mediterranean. Gaining altitude he flew in a wide circle, waiting for the others to catch up. Orders were for radio silence until in sight of Pantelleria, so they formed up automatically as four sections, each in 'finger-four' formation, with Jox's aircraft adding a 'thumb' onto Red Section led by de Ghellinck.

Approaching the besieged island, the sea appeared to be boiling and bubbling, with smoke bursting out in large bubbles like when depth charges explode deep underwater. There was a good deal of volcanic activity happening just below the surface of the sea. It was such a striking sight that one of the replacements, the Londoner nicknamed 'Suggs', cried out, 'Bloody 'ell, what's going on there? It's like the sea's on fire.'

'*M'enfin*, radio discipline,' growled de Ghellinck, embarrassed Jox had heard.

Up ahead, Pantelleria was a mass of smoke, rising into the air like an old woman's long grey hair blown in the wind. Jox could see the volcano and beyond it the principal airfield on the island at Marghana, amidst flashing explosions and a blanket of smoke at ground level. To the southwest, battleships fired long guns, as dozens of landing craft bounced on choppy waves towards the coastline, leaving feathery wakes.

For Pantelleria, the moment of liberation had finally come.

'Where the hell are they?' said Dundas in the earphones of Jox's flying helmet. 'There should be hundreds of the bastards.'

Through gaps in the smoke and ash billowing up from the island, Jox could only catch momentary glimpses of the squadron flying alongside him.

'This is no damned good,' Dundas continued. 'BLACK wing, this is BLACK Wing Leader. If they won't come to us, we'll have to go down to them. On my mark, I want HOTPANTS Squadron, followed by NELLY then BACON to strafe the airfield at Marghana. It's over there in that parallelogram sort of shape. Focus on the hillock to the southeast, where the two underground hangars discussed in the briefing are dug into the hill. Intelligence say they're huge, capable of holding over eighty aircraft plus a vast store of fuel. The bomber boys have been hitting them for weeks but since we're closer to the ground, we might pick-off something useful. If we can manage to skid one of our pickles into the hangars, we could do some real damage. Big enough target at three hundred metres long, twenty-six wide and eighteen high at the mouth. Even you lot couldn't miss that,' he added with a guffaw.

The squadron callsigns were another of Dundas's attempts at humour. HOTPANTS referred to No. 185 Squadron, 'Malta's Own' whose crest featured a red-legged griffin on a Maltese Cross. NELLY was for the charging elephant of No. 249 (Gold Coast) Squadron and BACON for No. 333's black pig. All three had been equipped with a pair of wing-mounted 250lb bombs with time delay fuses, unfamiliar for most and creating weight distribution challenges. The flight from Malta had consequently been trickier than expected. Fuel consumption was high, and they would definitely need the layover in Tunisia after the sortie.

Approaching the target, features on the ground became clearer. Outside the hangar doors several aircraft appeared to be parked, one hangar dark and open-mouthed, the other sealed shut. From this altitude it was unclear if they were wrecks, but it seemed likely. An intense barrage of anti-aircraft blossomed around them. Bursting like black smudges with dirty red hearts, they were vivid against the lighter grey smoke swirling over the island. They hung, turnip-shaped, like inky thumbprints in the sky, becoming more and more numerous.

Jox felt the jolting thump of an explosion quite near to him, then the rattle as if struck by shotgun pellets. He ducked, but that offered no protection. His fuselage had certainly been perforated, but nothing vital was hit, the shrapnel small enough to have done no real damage.

Jox could see HOTPANTS formatting at near enough ground level. They were following some red-nosed American

Curtiss P-40 Warhawks that had completed a strafing run. No. 185 Squadron went in guns blazing, releasing bombs when at a sufficient speed to provide enough forward momentum. Most detonated immediately, the pilots barely having time to guide their aircraft through the blast, but some did skid before exploding. One skittered between the lines of wrecked aircraft like a ball through pub skittles. It failed to explode but caused havoc through sheer weight and momentum.

At low-level one of the Spitfires was struck by groundfire, seeming to stagger in its horizontal trajectory, thrown off course by the impacts. It tumbled, then violently collided with the top lip of the open hangar with a resounding boom, showering burning debris into its throat. A clearly discernible scar was left on the masonry, a target to aim for.

Damn, thought Jox. *It's getting far too hot down there and of course, we're tail-end Charlies.* 'Right, BACON Squadron, BACON Leader, we're going in. Hold it together. The sooner we're in, the sooner we're out. Tally-ho, tally-ho.'

Echoing over the airwaves came the sound of squealing pigs. Amongst them, Jox recognised Fisken, giving his best impression of a berserking boar. Jox smiled. There was no doubting the growing camaraderie amongst his Black Pigs.

With AA already breaking around his swooping aircraft, Jox became aware of more twinkling fire rising from the ground in long tendrils of white-hot tracer fire. He held his breath, angling towards the dark throat of the huge hangar before him. His targeting ring crept across the expanse of the airfield as he opened fire with guns and cannons, at a little more than a hundred feet. He could see his fire striking targets, and he was dimly aware of a human-shaped figure tossed into the air but without a leg.

The rings crept up the scarred masonry above the arch of the hangar and using his favourite TLAR (That Looks About Right) reckoning, released his ordnance. His bombs fell away and skidded along the dusty tarmac, unseen by him as he was already pulling away. For a brief moment, nothing much happened, and he feared they were duds, but then he heard or rather felt a reassuring boom through his fuselage. For better or worse, he'd hit something.

Curious to see the damage, he banked and spotted something unexpected on the ground. There was a large white cross in the middle of the much-cratered main runway of Marghana airfield. It appeared to be made of sandbags, that had been whitewashed and arranged to be visible from the air. He called de Ghellinck on the radio. 'BACON Black Leader, BACON Leader here. Can you see what's down there?'

'Where?' asked de Ghellinck.

'Right on the main runway,' replied Jox, perplexed. The cross effectively put the runway out of use.

'I see it. What do you think, BACON Leader?'

'Not sure, but the runway is U/S. Might be a sign of surrender. Better report it.'

'Yes, but if they're surrendering, why are they still shooting?' asked de Ghellinck.

'Not unusual, left hand not knowing what the right is doing. The Germans and Italians may well have different points of view too.'

Flying on, gaining altitude, they circled the airfield like wood pigeons casing a farmer's pea field.

'BLACK Wing Leader, this is BACON Squadron Leader,' said Jox, calling for Dundas. 'Something odd is going on down there. Seems to me like they're indicating a willingness to surrender. Are you in touch with ground command?'

There was no answer at first, then his earphones crackled. 'BACON Squadron Leader, this is BLACK Wing Leader,' replied Dundas. 'Have passed on your message. Standby for patch through from seaborne commander.'

Jox's eyebrows raised beneath his goggles as a hesitant voice came over the airwaves, speaking in precise received pronunciation.

'Spitfire pilot, Spitfire pilot … ground command … er … please confirm your sighting.'

Jox was surprised to find himself talking to someone who sounded to be Major General Walter E. Clutterbuck, commander of the British 1st Infantry Division. He was presumably aboard a battleship offshore, overseeing the beach assault by his troops. At the pre-mission briefing, Dundas had pulled Jox aside, joking that apparently the commanding general had little faith in the combined air forces' ability to reduce the enemy on Pantelleria. He expected his division would suffer heavy losses as a result.

Clutterbuck was a traditionally trained Army general who'd served his apprenticeship during the First World War, so was somewhat sceptical regarding air warfare. His division had done well in Tunisia and had even won three Victoria Crosses and captured thousands of Axis soldiers. It had also suffered heavy casualties, so there may have been an element of 'once bitten, twice shy'. In fact, the general's persistent protests to air force generals tasked with delivering the bombing and air cover missions, had earnt him the nickname 'Clusterbottom' given his 'doom and gloom' predictions.

'Roger, ground command, this is BACON Squadron Leader,' replied Jox. 'We are in a holding pattern above Marghana airfield. Visibility is not good and groundfire continues to be heavy. We have observed a large white structure, believed to be constructed of painted sandbags. I estimate it is about three feet high and a hundred feet across in the shape of a cross. It is making the runway unusable. My guess, it's an indication of the wish to surrender.'

'Have you observed this yourself, BACON Leader?' said the sceptical voice.

'Yes, sir, as have several of my squadron pilots.'

'Hold your current pattern, we will get back to you.'

'Sir, holding fast means we're sitting ducks for the gunners on the ground.'

'I ordered you to hold fast!' roared the voice on the radio.

'Right, chaps,' said Jox wearily. 'You heard the man, but let's not make it easy, speed up and start jinking. Make yourself small, fast and hard to hit.'

Moments later, the voice was back on the R/T. 'BACON Squadron Leader, this is ground command. You are ordered to withdraw. I can confirm we are receiving radio communication from belligerent troops indicating they are willing to surrender the island. It's a miracle…'

Ahead and starboard of Jox's Spitfire, there was a sudden bright flash of white, followed by a catastrophic boom and an expanding circle of smoke. Falling debris was radiating from the epicentre of a cataclysmic explosion.

Jox didn't know what had been hit until the severed black tail of an aircraft fell past him, turning end over end as it dropped. From the colour, he knew it was a night fighter, and by the bisected vestiges of the letter J, it was one of his. He watched it fall for too long, before catching himself and saying, 'BACON Leader here, we have our orders. Time to get out. Turn to the pre-set vector for Fordjouna airfield in Tunisia.' This time there was no pig squealing or joshing. 'BLACK Wing Leader,

BACON Leader relaying withdrawal orders. Did you catch that?'

'Roger that, BACON Leader,' replied Dundas. 'Gentlemen, we are out of here. All BLACK wing callsigns to get out of range of ground gunners as soon as possible. Keep a sharp lookout for bandits trying to slip away in the chaos. There ought to be more of them. Maybe they gave us the slip overnight but with any luck some may be penned up in those hangars. We've hit them hard, well-done, now let's find somewhere to roost. Callsign leaders report casualties.'

'NELLY Leader here,' said the Perthshire accent of Ian MacDougall, CO of No. 185 Squadron. 'Aye, I've lost one of mine, young South African laddie called Fox. Got caught by groundfire. Damned shame.'

'BACON Leader here,' replied Jox. 'We've got one aircraft down too. He got caught by something high calibre while we were stooging about like clay pigeons. No confirmation of I.D. yet, but I saw him go down and I'm sure he's one of mine. There won't be much left to identify and there was no chute.'

'Yellow One to BACON Leader,' replied Waerea huskily. 'That was Yellow Four. One of the new boys, Sergeant Smyth, the fur trapper from Canada. God damn it, he showed potential, a great shot and now squashed like a fly.'

'Roger, Yellow One,' replied Jox. 'Sometimes you're lucky, sometimes you're not.'

The 'Black Pigs' made it back to the ground at Fordjouna airfield. They parked their Spitfire Mark IXs and then gathered for an informal debrief.

Some, mainly the replacements, were still high on adrenaline, others quiet and brooding, shocked by what they'd seen and experienced. The veterans were divided into those who appeared detached, having seen worse and taking it in their stride, whilst others circulated amongst the youngsters like coaches after a match. Jox noted that Axel Fisken and Ralph Campbell were amongst the former, Ghillie de Ghellinck, Jimmy Waerea and somewhat surprising the Kilpatricks, the latter.

Across the runway were a squadron of Curtiss P-40 Warhawks, the red-nosed ones they'd seen over Pantelleria. Their pilots were conspicuous by their smart leather blousons, loud volume and the high spirits they were displaying. In the bright sunlight and from a distance, Jox couldn't see them well and paid little attention. He was more interested in getting confirmation of their losses and wanted to be sure no one else was unaccounted for. De Ghellinck and Waerea stood together with a few of the replacements, many of whom Jox was still having trouble putting names to faces. A tall, well-built chap, a Londoner from his voice, was talking.

'Did you see the flippin' water?' He pronounced it wah-ta. 'Right before we got to Pantelleria,' he was saying excitedly. 'Was like a pot of boiling taters, all bubbles. Never seen anything like it.'

Waerea grinned. 'You've just come from battle for the first-time, son, and you seem more excited about volcanic activity than getting shot at. That's impressive.' He placed a hand on the man's shoulder, trying to calm his babbling. 'What you saw was lava below the surface of the sea. New Zealand is very volcanic, and we often see islands appearing and disappearing off the coast. Sounds like the gods were landscaping, just like we were on Pantelleria.'

'Anything on Sergeant Smyth?' asked Jox. 'Never got a chance to meet him properly.'

'The lads called him "Smash", sir,' said McPherson. 'Lovely bloke, best target scores in training…' His face fell, realising it was in the past tense. Tears welled up in his youthful eyes.

'It's all right, son,' said Waerea. 'It's always hard.' He turned to Jox. 'No, nothing further, sir. We just know it's Smyth because he's the only one missing. There's still a chance he may have baled out over the island.'

Jox winced. 'Don't think so. He was above me and his Spit took a hell of a hit. All I saw was debris and his tailpiece falling like a tombstone. Terrible to see.'

De Ghellinck spoke up. 'I've just spoken with Dundas. According to the intelligence officer for the US 33rd Fighter Group whose field this is, at eleven o'clock, Pantelleria's *governeur*, Vice Admiral Pavesi, surrendered the island and the garrison of fourteen thousand to the 1st Infantry Division coming ashore. Apparently, there was only one friendly casualty on the ground.'

'Christ, we've lost more than that in the air,' said Jox.

'Dundas says "their airships" think it was worth it. Reports are that Marghana airfield is heavily cratered. The underground hangars took many direct hits, with over eighty enemy aircraft destroyed or damaged and only two apparently left intact. Those are good kill figures, but there's a feeling the majority of *les canailles* escaped the bag, with Germans pulling out days ago. He says we'll be facing them in Sicily.'

'We live to fight another day,' replied Jox. 'We must be grateful for that, except of course, Sergeant Smyth and that chap from HOTPANTS Squadron, I forget his name.'

'Fox, Pilot Officer Justin Fox,' replied South African Mike Barson, the veteran of the Takoradi trail. '*Ja*, I did a round trip with him, delivering Hurricanes earlier this year. He was from Cape Town, a posh kid from a well-known family. Shame.'

The noise from across the runway grew louder, some sort of celebration was going on amongst the Americans over there. They were laughing and Jox recognised Southern accents, their bonhomie misplaced with the talk of the death of two comrades.

'Will you look at that,' said Barson. 'Those Yank pilots are Black. Look there's even officers amongst them. What's going on?'

Eyes ablaze, Jox turned on him. 'Those men are our allies, and they bleed just as red as your Boer blood. Why should they not be officers?'

'I … meant no offence, sir,' sputtered Barson. 'I'm just surprised. In Africa, we've never seen such a thing.'

'We're fighting to change the world from attitudes like that,' said Jox, still fuming. 'I don't know who those men are, but they've put their lives on the line today and deserve the same respect as our lost comrades. Is that clear, Pilot Officer?'

'Yes, sir,' mumbled Barson.

De Ghellinck looked across at the Americans. 'Those men are from the 99th Fighter Squadron, the "Tuskegee airmen". Pantelleria is their first combat mission, and you have no idea the skill, talent and perseverance it has taken for those men to achieve that. I think we should go congratulate them. I don't think their colleagues in the USAAF will be doing so.'

'An excellent idea, Ghillie,' replied Jox.

CHAPTER TWENTY

'There you are, sir, a nice pot of tea and some toast,' said Shillington, Jox's batman. 'Let me know if I can do anything else. I'll be outside giving your flight boots a polish, they're a bit scuffed. I'll give your jacket a brush up too.'

Jox wasn't used to having a batman. He'd had one before, shared with Pritchard at the beginning of the war. What was the name of that old boy? He'd certainly helped the pair of them, brand new to the squadron, the RAF and the war. Corporal Higgins, that was it. Gosh, whatever happened to him? Jox could almost hear Higgins' supercilious Brummie accent. Corporal Shillington was a bit like that. Perhaps that was the way of batmen. Shillington always seemed on the make though, up to something. He was bright, efficient and thoughtful but rather sneaky. Jox's instincts were rarely wrong.

'That's fine, Corporal,' Jox replied. 'Mind you don't lose the porcelain doll's arm and switchblade in the pockets. They mean a lot to me.'

'Oh, I did see that blade,' cooed Shillington. 'I'm from Sheffield see and know a thing or two about knives. Must have cost you a pretty penny, sir.' There was a covetous gleam in his eye.

'It was a gift from a dear friend, a master craftsman.' Jox stopped and stared at Shillington's sunburnt face. 'You really must be more careful in the sun. It can be ferocious in Malta.'

'I'm told it might help my acne.'

'Doesn't seem to be working. Could make them worse, certainly more painful.'

'Don't mind me, sir. I'm a survivor. Been on Malta for almost two years.'

'Gosh, I'd no idea,' replied Jox. 'Thought with the sunburn, you must be new. Been a batman before?'

'Aye, sir, served six gentlemen, I have.'

'Six? That's quite a lot. Did they make it home?'

'No such luck, sir. All lost in battle, missing in action, not one recovered. If you don't mind me saying, I'm rather hoping you'll be the one to break the jinx. Some of the lads even call me Jonah, but it's not my fault, I weren't even there when they went down. I'm told you're a lucky officer, so I asked to be assigned to you. Hope that's all right.'

There are few people more superstitious than fighter pilots. On hearing this startling news, Jox swallowed hard to keep his swelling panic down. *Don't be daft*, he told himself. *Stuff and nonsense*. But the queasy feeling in his stomach remained. He took an irritated bite from his toast, forcing down his fear with a mouthful of tea. 'No, that's fine,' he spluttered. 'Glad to have you on board.'

'Thank you, sir,' replied Shillington. 'I'd love to meet your craftsman. There's plenty of fellows that would pay handsomely for a blade like that. I could make him a fortune.'

'Maybe one day, Corporal,' said Jox. 'By the way, if our fates are to be linked, you better tell me your first name.'

'Angus, sir, Angus Shillington.'

'That's a very Scottish name for a Yorkshireman.'

'My father's, sir. He was Scottish, but a bit of a scoundrel. Never knew him, ran off when Mum got pregnant. My uncles still want to put a hole in his hide. I've inherited his complexion apparently, more's the pity.'

'We can't choose our fathers,' said Jox, thinking of his own 'missing in action' father, who'd coped with his wife's early

295

demise by dumping a young Jox at boarding school, then disappearing off to India. 'That'll be all, Corporal.'

'Right you are, sir. There's post on your desk and Flight Lieutenant Baraldi asked me to remind you to call Group Captain Bullough. There's a squadron COs' briefing with Wing Commander Dundas at two o'clock. Something about a night mission.'

Right, thought Jox. *Let's get the easiest done first.* There was a large Bakelite telephone on a side table behind his chair. The cord was long enough to use when seated, but he had to turn to dial. He checked the number for Bullough's secret lair within the Lascaris underground complex. He dialled carefully, listening to the clicks as the apparatus counted out the number. Malta wasn't a terribly big island, nor were there many telephones, but it did seem to take an inordinate amount of time to get through to someone. The first respondent was female, followed by more clicks, then a stern-sounding chap, yet more clicks, then a friendlier one and finally the urbane South African accent of Sandy Bullough.

'Jox, darling boy, haven't you done well. I was so sorry to hear of dear Moose and his sweet wife, Stephanie. What a tragedy and utter waste. I suppose we can take some comfort in knowing they died together and serving their country. We who remain must simply carry on.' He sighed. 'Hook tells me your chap Monty Falls has done a capital job, with everyone eating out of his hands. Did you know that rascal even had Patton convinced that he'd get a medal if he's the first to Messina? Then an Albanian knighthood if he liberates Sardinia. "Old Blood and Guts" has a powerful belief in reincarnation, and thinks he's lived many times before. Apparently one of his previous lives was as a general riding with Marshal Murat in Napoleon Bonaparte's army. He claims to have passed through what is now Albania and says he remembers their eagle banners. Falls didn't bat an eyelid and charmed him. Wherever did you find him? He's played an absolute blinder.'

Jox's response was muted. 'I'm glad it worked out, but to me Operation Tinned Fish will always have cost me two of my dearest friends and more besides.'

Bullough was hushed. 'I'm sorry if I sound unfeeling. Moose meant a lot to me too. Remember, I go back as far with him as you do. I was the intelligence officer at RAF Croydon, when you were both there. We've been through some scrapes together. It's a tragedy, but their passing, directly or indirectly, has got the Sardinia deception plan working. Ironically, the Pantelleria operation has provided the cherry on the cake. At the insistence of King Victor Emmanuel and Field Marshal Kesselring, the German forces evacuated from Pantelleria have been directed to Sardinia rather than Sicily. Two whole German divisions have also moved. Operation Tinned Fish appears to be a success.'

'Like I said, I'm glad it worked out, but it was a high price to pay. Personally, I'm looking forward to straightforward combat operations again.'

'I can understand that, but I reserve the right to call on you again. *Ja*, there are just two things to finish up. One concerns our friend Monty Falls. He has served his purpose and can now be returned to normal duties. To ensure no one recognises him, I'm afraid he's going to have to shave off that splendid moustache, at least for a while.'

'He's not going to like that. It's his pride and joy.'

'For the good of the service, I'm afraid. Necessary sacrifices, and all that.'

'I'll have a word. Perhaps if he transferred to my new squadron, the Black Pigs, where he doesn't know too many people… I'm sure he'd die of embarrassment if he were to appear "denuded" before the Treble Ones.'

'I'm sure that can be arranged. Leave it with me.'

'You said two things?' Jox prompted.

'Yes, I've a bone to pick with you. I lent you a perfectly gorgeous and competent fixer, and you return him damaged.'

'I don't know what you mean.'

'Hook! You've ruined him. With that bloody great scar, he's constantly smirking, like the Pirate of Penzance.'

'That's hardly my fault. Take it up with the *Luftwaffe*. Just another sacrifice for the good of the service, eh? It's cost us a friend, Monty his world-famous moustache and now Hook's pretty looks. I wonder what else it's going to cost?'

'We'll know soon enough. Husky is on for tonight.'

'Tonight!' said Jox. 'That explains the briefing. "A simple night mission," they said.'

'Well, it is a night mission.'

'A bit more than that. It's the first step in attacking Churchill's vaunted soft underbelly of Europe. This is a big deal.'

'Yes, it is,' replied Bullough. 'Good luck, my friend. See you on the other side.'

After his call, Jox turned to the correspondence on his desk. One was postmarked from Rabat. He recognised Julianna's handwriting immediately.

The Officers' Mess, Hotel Point de Vue,
11th July 1943

My dear Jox,
This is a hard letter to write. We have wronged you terribly and I hope you can find it in your heart to one day forgive us.

298

William and I never meant to hurt you, we never meant to hurt anyone. You remember I once told you our fates were not in our hands, but in those of fickle gods. I don't know what we did to deserve their ire, perhaps it was falling in love when others were suffering.

When you went away, the siege was terrible, and our poor Elias was cruelly taken from us. It was such a blow when we were already suffering. My family were crushed, and William was kind. I needed you so desperately, but you weren't here. I don't blame you and I was weak, just a wounded, tortured animal needing a haven. My dear Jox, you must know that you had all of my heart until it was smashed to pieces by this war. William was here to pick them up and piece it together. He was a comfort, and something grew from that. He is a good man and never meant you ill. He is deeply troubled by our betrayal and mourns the loss of your friendship, something very precious to him.

My grandfather has told me you know William and I have married. He has been posted away with the fleet, but will soon be assigned to Trincomalee in Ceylon, the home port of the Eastern Fleet. I will join him as soon as he is settled, so we'll be far from sight and mind if it's still painful for you. I would so like to see you before I go, but if that's not possible, I understand and I'm sorry, perhaps once more time has passed.

My grandfather says you have been kind. Thank you for that, he has suffered terribly and is so lonely. He came to see me after visiting you, so I have you to thank for that also. He has not forgiven me, but it's a start.

I am sure the war has brought you back to the island for a reason. I hope you still think kindly of it and remember our time together fondly. I thank Santa Maria she has seen you safely though the travails you have surely endured. We have all suffered most cruelly.

I wish you well always. You will always be in my heart.

With fondest affection,

Julianna

Jox's first instinct was to crumple the letter up and throw it in the bin, but in the end, he put it in his drawer. He would think about a response later.

Jox spoke with his opposite numbers from No. 185 'Malta's Own' Squadron and No. 249 (Gold Coast) Squadron. He and Ian MacDougall, CO of the Red Griffins, exchanged condolences for the men they'd lost over Pantelleria.

'Aye, I think we got away lightly,' said MacDougall. The two had played rugby together at school, he for Morrison's Academy in Crieff, Jox for Dollar. MacDougall was a Cranwell graduate and had a full moustache that made him look older than Jox. 'I expected worse.' MacDougall looked over at Dundas, who was deep in discussion with the wing's Intelligence and Meteorological Officers. 'Dundas is as nervous as an expectant father. Must be the big one.'

'Aye, seems likely,' replied Jox. 'I was chatting to a chap in the know. He pretty much confirmed it. I don't expect any surprises beyond that.'

'Friends in high places, eh?' said Eric 'Timber' Woods, CO of No. 249. He was a tall, dark-haired Canadian, but born in Buenos Aires. Jox had flown with the squadron when first posted to Malta and knew many of the squadron's 'great and good'.

'Order, gentlemen, take your seats,' said Dundas, a little more forcibly than he normally would. Behind him was a large-scale map of Sicily and the waters to the south and west. Coloured tape of various hues was wrapped around pins stuck into the map, starting in Tunisia and Malta, but also, Jox noted, Pantelleria. Someone had obviously worked hard to turn Marghana airfield around, making it serviceable after the pasting it had received.

Three differently coloured tapes led from RAF Hal Far where they currently were. Red was probably for the Griffins, yellow for the Gold Coasts and the black for his Pigs. There were two sets of black lines. The first went from Malta to a position over the sea, south of Pantelleria, where it joined a light blue tape out of Kairouan, Tunisia. Together, they continued towards the curved Bay of Gela in Sicily, separating inland, the blue turning to green then following the black back to Malta.

The second black tape went from Malta but this time to a position over the Strait of Sicily, where it rendezvoused with a dark blue line again from Kairouan airfield. Together, they followed the coast around the southern heel of Sicily, cutting inland near the port city of Syracuse. Here the dark blue ominously disappeared and the black returned to Malta once again.

If this jumble of coloured lines represented what was expected of Jox's squadron, the missions of the other air units in the room made the whole map look like a child had run riot with a set of colouring pencils.

'Settle down,' said Dundas. 'Well, gents, this is it. We're on for tonight.' He turned towards Jox. 'And your boys, my dear McNabb, will be leading the way.' Seeing the confusion on Jox's face, he added, 'Don't worry, I'll explain.' He pointed at the map. 'What you see, rather nicely plotted out by our spies, is what will happen over the next twenty-four hours. After that, the boys will start all over again and will plot the missions for the next day and so forth.' He smiled and passed a nervous hand through his waxed-back hair, conscious of their scrutiny through the fug of smoke in the room.

Jox glanced at Baraldi and his flight commanders, Fisken and de Ghellinck, all three listening intently.

'These are the opening salvoes for the airborne portion of Operation Husky, the invasion of Sicily,' Dundas continued. 'Specifically, the parachute drop and air-landing portion of American and British airborne troops starting from just after midnight tonight, the 9th of July. Two regiments of US Parachute Infantry of the 82nd Airborne Division, plus supporting artillery and engineers will jump over two locations near the town of Gela. They will be followed by Glider Infantry of the British 1st Airborne Division's 1st Airlanding Brigade aiming to seize Ponte Grande, the bridge over the Anape river, south of Syracuse. It's our job to protect them whilst getting there and then keeping the *Luftwaffe* and *Regia Aeronautica* off their backs, once they wake up and realise something big is kicking off. Details are in your packs, but these are the broad strokes.' He turned to Jox again and smiled. 'Pay attention, McNabb, you're on.'

'Yes, sir, of course, sir,' blustered Jox, but the room knew they were mucking about and rumbled with laughter.

'Given your Black Pigs' prowess as night fighters, and the disdain our American fighter friends have for night operations, you'll be representing the Wing straight out of the gate.' Using a pointer, Dundas indicated the black tape emerging from Malta up to where it met the light blue one from Kairouan. 'No. 333 Squadron will rendezvous with Yank transports carrying the paratroopers at around 2200 hours, to escort them to their targets. It'll be key to keep Jerry's night fighters off, whether long-range FW 200 Condors out to sea, or Bf 110 and Ju 88 night fighters known to be on the island. If they get amongst the transports, it'll be a massacre, so you need to be on it.' Jox, Fisken and de Ghellinck were all nodding. 'Once their drop is complete, the transports will make their own way back. You'll hightail it here for refuelling on a quick turnaround to meet with Pip Hick's 1st Airlanding Brigade.' Dundas indicated the second black trace. 'They'll have been in the air since late evening, in Airspeed Horsa and Waco CG-4/Hadrian gliders towed by Handley Page Halifax bombers. They won't be fast or manoeuvrable so are very tempting targets. By all accounts, those gliders have come a long way over the last two weeks, all the way from Blighty and are, shall we say, rather ropey.' Dundas smiled grimly. 'I certainly wouldn't trust my life to those flying boxcars. Those chaps are far braver than me, or perhaps just foolhardy. Airborne initiative, eh? In any case, you'll escort the gliders to Syracuse, where they're to secure the Ponte Grande Bridge, so our seaborne troops make it off the beaches and together they can secure the city and its strategically important docks.'

He went on to explain that No. 185 Squadron would take over just before dawn, providing cover for troops on the ground over Ponte Grande. The relay would then be picked up by No. 249 Squadron, concentrating on interdiction missions called in by the ground troops, focussing on artillery positions, as well as countering any enemy fighters that dawn might reveal.

Dundas stressed that what was on the board covered only his No. 324 Wing's operations. There would be countless other aircraft across the island's air space. 'Expect very crowded skies, so please be careful. I don't want you shooting down any friendlies.' He smiled, relieved his part of the briefing was done. 'Right then, "Storming Norman", it's over to you. What's the weather got in store?'

'Thank you, sir,' said Flight Lieutenant Norman Fowler, the Wing's meteorological officer. 'Nothing too nasty, just a breezy start. By nine it might pick up, with the possibility of stronger gusts. Shouldn't be a problem for your Spits, but I'm a little worried for the gliders on the end of their ropes towed by those Halifax bombers. They're pretty high-sided, so things could get a bit messy if the wind really gets going. Let's hope their weathermen know their business and have factored in the conditions when deciding on the go–no go call. Either way, gentlemen, I wish you God speed.'

CHAPTER TWENTY-ONE

The Merlin engines coughed into life, echoing across the falling dusk at RAF Hal Far. The flaming smoke bursting from the Spits' nose stubs was snatched away by the stiff breeze blowing across the runways. The signature smell only momentarily tainted the air around the ground crews completing last-minute checks and helping their pilots get set for take-off.

'Looks like a lively one,' said Jox's rigger, his hair flapping. He was an older fellow and Jox only knew him as Jake. 'Best of luck, lad, your young fellas look like they might need it.'

Jox glanced at the replacement aircrew, clustered together and nervous at their first major night operation. One of them, Woodgate, stumbled a few feet before vomiting on the wheel of the nearest Spitfire. His companions teased him until one of the Kilpatricks said, 'That's enough, lads. You're all feeling it, not just Woody.'

Baraldi was standing beside Jox, his clipboard under his arm. He checked his wristwatch. Jox did the same with his charred Rolex.

'It's time, better get going,' said Baraldi. 'With this wind, visibility will be poor, so finding those Yank transports will be challenging, but at least there should be plenty of them to spot. Mind you, I'd be no help. With my eyes, I wouldn't stand a chance.' He squinted at the setting sun as Jox absentmindedly checked his pockets for his doll's arm and switchblade, a part of his routine pre-flight drill.

They shook hands and Jox clambered aboard his aircraft, with Jake giving him a leg up. The rigger gave him a paternal pat on the arm. 'Give them hell, lad.'

Within fifteen minutes the squadron were airborne, scattered across the sky in a wide formation, to maximise the eyes on the horizon. They would be on the same heading as for Pantelleria, but without the sunrise at their backs. The moon was already high and bright, illuminating the cloud cover. They would need to drop below it to rendezvous with the transports, since the American C-47 Skytrains and C-53 Skytroopers weren't equipped with oxygen masks for the two thousand-odd paratroopers they were carrying. Once over land, the transports would drop to four hundred feet, the prescribed height for the jumps.

Radio chatter was kept to a minimum and the squadron pilots kept a sharp eye out for night fighters as well as the approaching American armada. The flight progressed westwards without incident, apart from occasional unexpected thumps of air turbulence as the wind picked up. It was unsettling but not dangerous, and they made good time.

It wasn't long before outliers in the Black Pigs' van reported the formations approaching in ragged Vees of nine. The lead aircraft began blinking identification codes, so Jox instructed the Treble Threes to separate into four sections, positioning themselves above, below, in advance and to the rear of the sixteen Vees of some hundred and forty-four C-47s and C-53s. Crowding the night sky, they were like the wild geese that were a familiar autumnal sight in Scotland.

The sheer number of transports before them was daunting. Jox scanned the heavens, worried the Black Pigs were spread too thinly. There were far too few sheepdogs to protect such a big flock from the wolves. The USAAF's doctrine of daylight precision bombing, rather than the British policy of night-time area bombing, meant American night-fighter expertise was in its infancy and practically non-existent. This was exacerbated by most Allied night-fighting capabilities being understandably concentrated on United Kingdom-based operations striking against the Reich. The Black Pigs were one of the few night-fighting trained squadrons in the Mediterranean theatre. The others, mainly twin engine Beaufighters, would no doubt be engaged elsewhere in the pantheon of actions on this first night of Operation Husky.

The squadron and their lumbering charges approached the long, sweeping bay of Gela, where breakers on the pale beach were luminescent in the moonlight. No doubt hearing the formations overhead, neighbourhood lights were extinguished, and probing searchlights switched on. Beginning their descent, the sea shimmered like liquid mercury revealing a vast panorama of ships, the seaborne element of the force heading for Sicily. Wakes of vessels of every conceivable shape and size frothed like scratches on a glass surface.

The C-47s and C-53s flashed I.D. codes as they dropped. These codes were drilled into every naval gun crew providing AA cover for the flotilla. Whether it was due to poor signal recognition amongst the sailors or simply the terror of looming shapes overhead, guns began to fire at the shadows. Their targets, the slow lumbering aircraft lining up for the parachute drops.

The first few Dakotas managed to discharge their paratroopers squarely on target. Those following were not so fortunate. To the growing dismay of Jox and his men, viewing from above so as not to cut across the line of dropping troopers, nervous gunners began firing from offshore and along the length of the beach. Enemy gunners, awakened by the droning armada may have also been startled into action by the gunfire, but the majority were Allied guns. Vast sheets of tracers rose towards the rumbling behemoths, too big and slow to miss.

Jox saw a C-53 disintegrate before his eyes, trailing a long line of flame, illuminating the men leaping from its side door. They fell like burning droplets of plastic until they were extinguished by the sea.

Dozens of transports had been hit. One exploded, lighting up the sky like a firework. Others tried desperately to ditch, some on land, others in the sea, to save their precious human cargo. Any sense of order that may have existed was gone. The mass of straining C-47s and C-53s were separating, trying to re-form, then scattering to the four winds.

Sickened, the Black Pigs could only look on helplessly, the airwaves filled with their cries of horror and frustration. Attempts to contact the flotilla were futile, as the naval frequencies were unknown. Frustrated and utterly dejected, Jox finally made the call. He instructed his desolate men to vector back to Malta. However much the first airborne effort had begun disastrously, they still had a duty towards the gliders and Halifax bombers of the 1st Airborne Division's 1st Airlanding Brigade enroute to Syracuse and the bridge at Ponte Grande.

As the night fighters impotently pulled away, yet another transport was struck by ground fire, slowly catching alight and falling towards the earth. In a final moment of courage, the doomed pilots of the C-47 veered away from the shipping in the bay. In doing so, a wingtip caught the water, sending it careening over itself. The aircraft trailed an orange plume, scattering men like sparks from a falling log in a fireplace. It extinguished immediately, hitting the water amongst the ships which had played such a part in its destruction.

Back at RAF Hal Far, the Black Pigs were shocked and silent. Several fell to their knees and were physically sick, forgetting the earlier ridicule of young Woody. The horror was etched into their faces, deep frustration at their impotence draining confidence and morale.

I've got to get a grip of them, thought Jox. *Otherwise, our next mission will be a disaster.*

Baraldi came running towards him. 'You're all back, everyone's safe, but what the devil's wrong with them? Was it so bad?'

Jox had to control his breathing before he could answer. The doll's arm was in his fist, his thumb frantically rubbing the worn surface. 'It was sheer carnage,' he whispered. 'You can't imagine, Jimmy.' He dry-heaved a few times before straightening up. 'We saw no sign of any enemy fighters and the transports were coming in for their drops. Then the whole world opened up on them. We did this to ourselves. Dozens went down, like during the raids of the Battle of Britain, but this was even worse. All we could do was watch; it was not as if we could fire on our own fleet. That's why the boys are so gutted.'

'I guess that's what the Yanks call a snafu,' Baraldi said bitterly. 'There's going to be hell to pay. But listen, that's not your problem. Yours is to get these boys back in shape to deliver our next mission. There's an entire 1st Airlanding Brigade depending on your cover to get them in. There's less than half an hour to get back in the game. You've got to speak to them, and you've got to do it now.'

Jox scanned the faces of his assembled men. It was obvious they'd been through the wringer. Ghillie de Ghellinck was pinched and pale, Axel Fisken had the 'thousand-yard stare'.

Jimmy Waerea's eyes bulged with barely suppressed rage, whilst the veins in the neck of Jumbo Johnstone pulsed with raised blood pressure. These were the veterans — the less experienced were in an even worse state. Ralph Campbell looked like he needed a blood transfusion, the Kilpatricks rested arm in arm, unexpectedly supporting each other through physical contact. There were tears in the eyes of many and McPherson kept repeating, 'Madness, it was sheer madness.'

'Pack it in, Suggs,' said Spud Inverarity, his face even redder than usual.

Jox took a deep breath. 'That was a rum deal. Something that's going to stick with us for a while. Some of you have seen worse, some haven't, but for me this was as bad as it gets.' He searched their faces, suspecting some might well be on the edge. 'There's nothing we can do. What's done is done.' He tried to catch the eyes of as many as he could. 'As per the briefing, Magliocco Aerodrome, a major Jerry airfield, is between Gela and Comiso. The gliders must fly directly over it on their way to Syracuse. It's been bombed to bits, but I've no doubt the Germans are still active. Many of the worst raids during the siege of Malta came from that field at Comiso. They know their stuff and will be after the gliders if they spot them, otherwise they will certainly have a go at the invasion fleet.'

'To hell with the fleet,' growled Paddy Kilpatrick. 'They're killing their own men.'

'We've got a job to do, Paddy,' replied Jox. 'The pongos on the gliders are depending on us. This is something we can actually do, rather than simply watching the slaughter. I'm not saying what happened earlier won't haunt us, but for now we need to put it to the back of our minds. Dig deep, boys. I won't have it said the Black Pigs let anyone down.'

A few nodded.

Axel Fisken stepped forward and glared at the circle of men through his little round spectacles. 'Come, my brothers. Are we good?' He took off his glasses and his face suddenly transformed into a fearsome snarl. He gave the shrill call of a wild pig.

A few laughed nervously, but stopped when Waerea and de Ghellinck joined in. Before long, they were all at it, even Jox. The grotesque cacophony was oddly thrilling and resolved into brotherly laughter. Jox glanced at Jake the rigger who gave him the thumbs up.

'Right, boys,' Jox said, 'let's get going. This war's not going to wait for us.'

The flight west was hauntingly familiar, with the Black Pigs lost in their own thoughts. Air turbulence had picked up and there were occasional harsh expletives heard over the R/T.

'Shouldn't be long now,' said Jox into his mask. 'Keep it tight. The wind's picking up and might cause problems. Keep your eyes open, everyone.'

At first sighting, it was clear the gliders and their slab-sided tugs, Handley Page Halifax bombers, were in trouble. Earlier in the war, the four-engined heavy bombers were the backbone of Bomber Command, especially for their Canadian crews who affectionately called them 'Halibags'. Specially adapted versions had since been developed for troop transport and paradrop operations. They were already lower than Jox had anticipated, still over the sea and some visibly in distress.

Several of the US-built Waco CG-4s, known as Hadrians by the British, had separated from their tugs and were at discordant angles and altitudes, their Halibag 'parents' long gone. Made of fabric-covered wood and a metal lattice, they were crewed by two pilots and carried thirteen paratroopers, or a Jeep or artillery piece like a 75mm howitzer. But they weren't in any way manoeuvrable or easy to handle in high winds.

The winds buffeting the Black Pigs' sleek Spitfires was causing havoc amongst the snub-nosed CG-4s. Poor visibility at lower heights and the threat of anti-aircraft fire, whether friendly or other, meant that some Halibag pilots had climbed or taken evasive action, abandoning their towed charges and inexperienced glider pilots to their fates. Watching helplessly for the second time that night, Jox stopped counting when over a dozen gliders had ditched into the sea. *What a bloody shambles*, he thought, banking to get a better view of heavily laden men thrashing in the water. A cold chill ran down his back. Many wouldn't survive long, despite Sicily being so tantalisingly close.

Operation Ladbroke, the first-ever massed glider assault by Allied forces, was proving another disaster, before a single shot was even fired. The finest men of the British 1st Airborne Division, fighting men Jox knew well, were being dumped like teabags into the sea, floating just as lifelessly in the flotsam of their crumpled gliders, the wood and fabric instruments of their premature destruction.

Horrified at this second fiasco, Jox instructed his men to head for the coast where he hoped some of the gliders might have made landfall, the paratroopers needing protection. Inland, he could see searchlights probing the early morning sky, still ostensibly dark, but the time when songbirds start to sing. There was no dawn chorus today, any sweet trills swamped by gunfire, the booms of aerial bombardment or the fleet's big guns providing a deep bass cadence to an invasion that had started disastrously.

Over the sea, Jox spotted a formation of aircraft and larger gliders approaching, spaced in tidy elements of four and still in some semblance of order. He recognised larger Airspeed AS.51 Horsas, which he assumed were at the rear of the airlanding deployment because of their size and slower speed. Each carried up to thirty fully loaded troops and again were of mostly wooden construction. Long and pencil-shaped, the Horsas had panelled Plexiglass cockpits where, as he got closer, Jox could see the shadows of the pilots, side-by-side guiding the aircraft through the wind and thermals, a prospect that filled Jox with abject terror. The bravery of men at the mercy of the air currents was sobering, making Jox realise how fortunate he was to be his own master as a solo pilot.

This moment of inattention cost him. Up ahead, a mere hundred yards away, a Halibag and Horsa combination released their umbilical cord. The Horsa began to dip, the bomber pulling away and gaining altitude. In doing so, it released the cable between them.

Freed from the torque applied during the tow, it sprang through the air like a coiling serpent. Before Jox could react, it had wrapped itself around his starboard wing. He heard it screech along the metalled leading edge, gouging deep marks into the black paintwork. He held his breath and prayed it might slip off, but with ripping violence it began to bite. He could feel it through the fuselage.

A yawning V appeared and the outer third of his wingtip fell away like a lopped off limb. The aircraft went into a lateral spin, Jox desperately trying to control the yaw. He was too low to jump, and knew he was doomed. He just had time to tighten his straps and crack open the cockpit hatch.

He cried out, 'PORK Leader going down,' before the aircraft belly-flopped very hard into the milling surface of the sea.

CHAPTER TWENTY-TWO

The breath was knocked from Jox's lungs. He was dizzy from the centrifugal force of the spinning aircraft. He gulped oxygen from the mask as his vision dimmed and pressure built in his ears.

The cockpit was bathed in an eerie blue as seawater poured through the partially opened canopy hatch. It swirled at his feet, as he struggled with the Sutton harness. It gave way with a ping, and he was bodily lifted from the bucket seat by the rising water, his back jammed up against the dome of the canopy, pinning him upside down. He was drowning, head below his rear end, completely disoriented. Stinging salt water seeped into his goggles, and he felt some tugging. His vision lightened. There was definitely something pulling at his waist.

Bursting through the surface he was blinded by the brightness. He ripped away his mask and took a huge gasp of life-giving air. His instincts kicked in and he began to swim, glimpsing a bronzed arm in his peripheral vision. He turned to see a thrashing figure in khaki, who grabbed him by the 'handle' at the back of his Mae West life jacket. Designed for rescue crews to drag survivors from the water with boathooks, he was towed helplessly, as he pulled the toggle of his life jacket. The CO_2 canister fizzed and inflated, propping him higher in the water. Now, all Jox could see were his flight boots trailing in the wake. After about twenty yards, the traction stopped and Jox could turn in the water.

He saw a large man wearing the sodden Denison smock of a British Paratrooper. His nose was bent as if recently struck, with blood leaking from the left nostril. The soldier was treading water, the blood from his nose bubbling as he panted.

'Jox McNabb, you rascal. Of all the places to run into you.'

Jox recognised the glint in the eyes, despite the bent nose and the plastered-down hair. Captain Dougal Preston of the British Parachute Regiment looked like a drowned rat, albeit a very large one.

'What a bloody day,' Preston spluttered. He had a circular life preserver under his arms but was still struggling to keep afloat. He was a strong man but was clearly tiring. 'Look at what they've done to my beautiful boys, Jox. Grant MacNeish is out there somewhere. I've lost them all to the waves before they even got a chance to fight. What a bloody waste.'

Across the effervescent sea, Jox could see the lumpen forms of floating men, all deathly still. Unlike Jox, who had a Mae West, the paratroopers had only rubber inner tubes like Preston's. Many had on backpacks, some were still attached to parachutes. The weight of their packs had pulled their heads under the water. Dozens of up-ended paratroopers, some of the finest in the British Army, had met an undeserved and undignified end. Preston's eyes were haunted.

'I'm so sorry, Dougal. What a bloody mess, but I'm glad we've found each other,' said Jox. 'Thank you for saving my life. I was a goner. Things may look bleak, but we'll get out of this.' The raft of drowned men was slowly dispersing in the swell. 'I'm sorry for your men, no one deserves this. This whole day's been one disaster after the next.' Jox reached for Preston's arm. 'Let's focus on surviving the day, to maybe live to fight again. These chaps are past helping. You're exhausted. Hold on, I'll get my dinghy inflated and you can rest.'

The Spitfire Mark IX was equipped with a K-type dinghy, clipped to the seat of Jox's parachute harness, between that pack and his rear end. That usually meant sitting on a hard, folded dinghy, but for the first time Jox was grateful for the months of discomfort. He released his parachute and tugged at the flat, folded-up dinghy. He was managing quite well to keep afloat in his Mae West, its pockets full of flares, sea marker dye and basic survival rations.

His plan was to let Preston have the one-man rubberised cotton dinghy. It was the least he could do considering the man had just saved his life. It was pale orange, had a lozenge-shaped inflatable loop and a canvas bottom. It also had a hood for shelter and came with a rudimentary sail and oars.

There was room for an average-sized man, but that wasn't Dougal Preston. Easily as large as Moose Grant, he was probably heavier. Trying to get in, the paratrooper capsized the simple craft, but finally managed it, promptly puncturing the membrane where the canvas met the lozenge-ring with his commando knife, strapped to his belt. A thin stream of bubbles was immediately in the water. The pair tried to patch the puncture as best they could. As they worked, they drifted away from the floating corpses.

The dinghy wasn't going to last, but at least it gave Preston some respite to catch his breath and lose some of his bulky clothing. The pair were strapped together. As the sun came up and hit the open water, conditions got hotter, and they were blinded by brightness and reflections. Soon, they were sunburnt and parched.

Sicily was close. They could hear waves on the shoreline, as well as the ominous sound of gunfire and artillery. The invasion was progressing despite the poor start. Occasionally, aircraft wheeled and buzzed overhead, mostly Allied but some Axis. A pair of sinister Ju 87 Stuka dive-bombers were having a go at the shipping beyond the horizon. The gull-winged raiders swooped near-vertically, releasing bombs on unseen targets. Jox had once examined a crashed Stuka in the scrapyard on Malta known as the Boneyard. It was the central repository for the wrecks on the island, a lonely, windswept place with smashed, burnt-up aircraft piled high or lying in bits. He remembered it had smelt of death.

The Stukas delivered ordnance with remarkable accuracy, diving onto targets after sighting them through a window in the cockpit floor. This made the Stuka, not to mention its wailing 'Jericho trumpets', the terror of the skies early in the war. Now, without the same air superiority, Stukas were vulnerable to Allied fighters. Jox had downed a few himself and wondered if these courageous but foolhardy pilots were from Comiso, the airfield the Black Pigs were tasked with interdicting.

'The old girl's going under,' said Preston, sitting in a foot of water in the swamped dinghy. 'I'm too big for this kiddy's bathtub anyway. I'll need to swim again.'

'Might have helped if you hadn't stuck your bloody knife into it.'

'Fair enough,' Preston replied, contrite. 'Not much I can do about that now.'

'We can't be far from shore,' replied Jox, trying to orientate himself by the sun. 'Sicily is north, so we could swim.' He pointed to where most of the noise came from.

'I'll try, Jox, but I'm knackered,' said Preston. 'Not exactly built for swimming either, otherwise I'd have been a bloody Royal Marine, heaven forbid.' He smiled wearily. 'Having my nose in this state isn't helping me breathe either. Wasn't too straight in the first place.'

'Can't say it looks too clever,' replied Jox. 'Rather flat and there's bruising down the sides. I can try to straighten it but won't pretend I know what I'm doing.'

'No chance,' said Preston. 'That'll be sore and right now I don't feel too much. Not ideal for swimming though. Listen, I won't hold you back. If I have to go down with my boys, well, I'm resigned to that. Doesn't need to be both of us. You'll be all right with your life jacket. There's bound to be more traffic as the day progresses and you'll get picked up.'

'I'm not giving up on you yet, you big lummox,' said Jox. 'Come on, where's that airborne initiative you lot are always on about?'

'Running a bit low to be honest,' Preston replied. 'All right, I'll give it a go.' Preston heaved himself off the sinking dinghy, his feet and long legs plunging towards the depths. To his surprise, his drop stopped abruptly when the sea level reached just short of his shoulders. 'Bloody hell, we're in shallows. I can stand up.'

Shorter and propped up high in the water by his vest, Jox couldn't feel the bottom. 'We must have drifted onto a sandbank.'

'Doesn't feel sandy, harder than that,' replied Preston. 'Scratchy, like ridged rock.'

Jox was perplexed by how this was possible, then it came to him. 'My pal Ridgway is always on about the volcanoes around Sicily. He says volcanic islands often pop up in these waters, existing for a while then submerging. Just the other day, east of Pantelleria we saw the sea boiling and bubbling with what looked like lava below the surface. I think that's what this may be.' Jox smiled. 'It seems like Vulcan, the Roman god of fire, is playing with us again.'

'What are you on about?' said Preston. 'All I know is I'm standing on solid ground which means I don't have to bloody swim. Buys us a little time. Can you touch the bottom?'

'Not quite,' replied Jox testily, his stature always a bit of a sore point. 'I'm all right bobbing here. As long as I'm tethered to you, I won't drift off.'

They were there for hours. The sun was now high in the sky, slowly making its way across the azure hemisphere as it had for millennia, whilst war raged around them, but out of sight.

Perhaps the volcanic cays and rocky shallows were indicated on naval charts so maritime traffic kept away. Stranded and steeping like pickles in brine, the pair began suffering from exposure, the chaffing of salt, but worst of all from raging thirst. Jox tracked the hours on his Rolex, still appearing to keep perfect time despite the dunking. He was finding the rocking swell soporific, and he began to drift off, not physically, since he was still attached to Preston, but mentally. In truth, the big fellow was probably the most solid anchor Jox could have hoped for.

Jox was daydreaming about the Black Pigs and whether they'd fulfilled their mission. What were the people of Sicily making of their liberation, their world torn apart by violence brought to these shores by foreign forces? From the early hours, if they survived the initial onslaught, their lives would never be the same. According to Baraldi it wasn't the first time the fate of Sicilians was in the hands of others, and it probably wouldn't be the last.

Jox stirred, awakened by sudden splashing. He opened his salt-encrusted eyes to find his bulky companion chasing something in the water. He looked like a grizzly bear going after salmon, trying to scoop up the four-inch silvery fish darting all around them.

Preston cried, 'Quick, scoop them into the dinghy.'

It was too deflated to carry Preston's weight but still held enough air to provide a useful 'fish pen'. For a frantic few minutes, the pair used their hands to flick wriggling fish from just beneath the surface, through the air to land flapping in the dinghy. They stranded a dozen or so before the shoal moved on, leaving a few floating scales and oily residue on the surface. Preston roared with laughter, the frantic interlude raising his spirits.

'Now what do we do with them?' asked Jox.

'Don't know about you,' replied the paratrooper. 'But I'm starving.' He reached into the dinghy, caught a wriggling fish and despatched it with a quick flick. He removed the gut then popped the whole thing into his mouth, swallowing without chewing. 'Bit fishy, but delicious. Couldn't be fresher, mind. You try one.'

'What are they?'

'No idea,' replied Preston. 'Look like herring.'

'I think they may be sardines. That would make sense.' Jox chuckled at the irony of being swamped by a shoal of sardines whilst stranded off the coast of Sicily. Especially considering all the shenanigans with King Zog, Monty Falls and trying to establish Sardinia as the target for invasion. What a preposterous predicament. 'The gods are definitely playing with us, Dougal. Come on, pass one over,' he said. 'I'll give it a go.'

'Good man, got to keep your strength up,' said Preston. 'A man's got to eat.'

Jox rather liked the sardines, even raw, just wishing he'd had some lemon juice. Ironically, there were probably lemons growing tantalisingly close. They ate and were surprised at how invigorated they felt after the fishy repast. Even their thirst was temporarily quenched. They chatted and dozed, occasionally dunking their heads beneath the water to escape the heat of the sun.

It was past mid-afternoon when they heard the putt of a boat's engine. It woke Jox from his stupor, but he didn't pay much attention as they'd heard noises before, and nothing had materialised. This time things were different. It was a wooden fishing boat, barely large enough to carry a single man let alone three, especially one the size of Preston. It had timber sides and was painted sky-blue with a white stripe around the hull. The name 'Violetta' was scrawled in childish letters on the bow.

The captain was in his early thirties, clean-shaven and had a tanned face, rather thin and boyish. He peered at them from beneath the peak of a bulbous *coppola* cap, sort of like the flat caps Jox had seen Yorkshire miners wearing when in the pub.

He began to wave and called over in what Jox assumed was Sicilian. Baraldi had once explained it was like Italian, but had Greek, Arabic, French, Catalan, and Spanish all mixed in. Jox couldn't understand what he was saying but he seemed friendly enough and concerned for their welfare.

He cut off the engine, spewing diesel exhaust across the surface of the water at the level of their faces. He unshipped a pair of rough oars, cut from single planks, and was remarkably adept with them. The bottom of the boat held a throwing net and crates of silvery sardines.

Jox reached up as the man manoeuvred towards him. The man's eyebrows rose seeing the size of Preston and he opted to help Jox first. The boat rocked as Jox was hauled over the gunnel onto the slimy net. It stank, but it was good to be out of the water.

'Giulio Cesare Dennini.' The man pointed at his chest. 'Giulio,' he repeated, grinning to reveal white teeth and laughter lines around his eyes. He pointed at them. '*Miricanu?*'

Jox didn't speak Italian or Sicilian but had a little French, so he used that to tell Dennini that they were Allied soldiers.

Preston flung up the maroon beret taken from his pocket which the fisherman deftly caught.

'*Paracadutista?*' he said, pointing at the sky, his hand cupped to mimic a parachute descending. He had a star-shaped tattoo between his thumb and forefinger. Jox had seen one like it before but couldn't remember where.

Preston tried to haul himself out of the water, very nearly capsizing this vessel too.

Together, Dennini and Jox pulled Preston's weight into the boat, the gunnels worryingly low in the water. Dennini indicated Jox should bail as water lapped over every now and again, but first he handed Jox a glass demijohn bottle filled with fresh water. As a fisherman he knew all too well how parched they'd be after hours on the water. Jox and Preston drank gratefully.

It took half an hour of steady motoring before they reached a peaceful-looking cove. Dusk was falling after a long day, perhaps the longest of days Jox could remember. The sound of the gunfire heard earlier had diminished. Stepping over the side, leaving a boot print on the wet sand, wrinkled and patterned by the tides, Jox had little idea where he was, but at least he'd finally landed on Sicily.

Dennini pointed east to a hamlet, 'Licata' and then the horizon, 'Gela'.

The last name meant something to Jox. He knew the wide bay of Gela was where the American portion of the amphibious invasion of Sicily was taking place. He could see a good deal of smoke and hear rumbling gunfire through the evening air. On the breeze was the chemical taint of fire and spent explosives. In more peaceful times, the cove would have made an idyllic spot, crystal-clear water filled with dancing light, casting patterns in the shallows.

Dennini beached his little boat and led them to a dilapidated shack on the beach. He evidently spent nights there during his fishing trips. It was basic but comfortable and rather cosy once he got a fire going. To Preston's delight he produced a bottle, unwrapping it like a prized possession. '*Nero d'Avola. Vinu tipicu di Sicilia. Preggo, mi amici.*'

The wine was dark and full-bodied. They passed around the bottle and it didn't last very long, warming their bones and cheering their spirits. With a mishmash of Sicilian and Jox's schoolboy French, Dennini explained that he went on regular fishing trips to catch the sardines that were the basis of a fish paste that was his family's trade. His wife and daughter lived inland near Ragusa, and he was worried and was cutting short his trip. Tomorrow, he planned to walk home, but it was quite far, almost fifty kilometres away. They were very welcome to join him. They might run into friendly troops, but if not, in Ragusa someone could surely help. The town's name was familiar to Jox, recalling that he'd dropped the OSS officers, Paolino and Lomasso, in a meadow above there.

They'd expected simple grilled sardines for supper but instead were treated to a feast. Dennini produced his family's signature pasta dish. Part of the day's catch was quickly fried with fennel, onion, garlic and some wine, to which Dennini added the secret recipe paste. He then served the fish ragout folded through some thin pasta.

Preston complained the servings were too small and that it contained too much garlic, but it was by far the best thing Jox had tasted in a long while. After supper, Dennini handed Jox a jar of aloe vera-based cream for their stinging sunburn. Aloe grew wild on the hills and its cooling effect was very welcome.

Life on Sicily might not be so bad, thought Jox, feeling optimistic for the first time that day. Who knew what tomorrow would bring? He was brought back to reality by ominous rumbling in the night, growing in volume. Preston reminded him that a second night of airborne operations was planned. 'Let's hope things go better than last night's disasters.'

The next morning, they set off early, Dennini carrying a backpack full of jars of sardine paste. He refused any help. Throughout the night, the artillery barrage had clearly been playing on his mind, so he was keen to get underway.

Once clear of the beach, they came across signs of the naval bombardment they'd heard. Raw red earth was gouged up in great holes by heavy calibre guns. Soil, trees, walls, fortifications and other structures were torn apart.

The remains of a man in a tattered Italian uniform was hanging from a tangled nest of barbed wire stretched between two trees. His arms were spread apart, held by sharp barbs, his head lolling, feet above them. Dark, viscous blood dripped from the tips of his boots into the dust. The symbolism was not lost on Dennini who crossed himself repeatedly as they passed silently.

They came to the shattered remains of defences which must have been in good order before the bombardment, as evidenced by a shrapnel-perforated flag of the Kingdom of

Italy flapping listlessly at a mast. Around the remains of the encampment, the hillside had been set alight. As they trudged by, ash and smoking stumps of what must have been fruit orchards or olive groves were everywhere.

Through the clearing smoke, they approached an abandoned artillery battery of several guns, dug in and well protected by sandbags and surrounded by shiny piles of shell casings. After what had evidently been frantic activity, the site was deathly quiet and still. The gunners had withdrawn under the naval bombardment, choosing to destroy their guns before running. They were heavy Cannone da 149/40 guns with a range of some twenty-three kilometres, so could well have done serious damage to the offshore fleet and troops landing on the beaches. Their barrels, six metres long, pointed defiantly at the azure sky, but the end of each was opened like a banana peel, with a second charge having blown out their breeches.

They stopped for water at the crest of a hill. It was getting hot, and they were sweating, feeling the sting on their sunburn. The pause merited a fresh application of aloe paste and as they let it dry, high above their heads, a dogfight unfolded between a pair of P-38 Lightnings mixing it up with a single FW 190. They were too far to see much, but the contest ended with the German despatching one of the distinctive Americans, sending him crashing into the sea, whilst he himself retreated trailing copious smoke. Of the other American, there was no sign. It appeared he chose the path of discretion over valour after the loss of his wingman.

During the contest, when the 'killer Shrike' swept overhead whilst firing, the spectators were forced to run for shelter under some walnut trees, heavy with green fruit but not yet ready for harvest. Bright shell casings clinked all around them, raining down with potentially deadly consequences.

Over the next ridgeline, they came across an abandoned ammunition cache, hidden in a thorny hedgerow. It consisted mainly of ammo but there were also some antiquated Glisenti Model 1910 pistols. They were short-barrelled versions of German Lugers, prized by American troops as souvenirs. Preston told them to arm themselves, as there was no way of knowing whether they'd meet friend or foe. He was the ground warfare expert, so Jox did what he was told.

'They're a little fiddly,' said Preston. 'But can still pack a decent punch with 9mm parabellums. The bullets are designed to tumble so will put quite a hole in you.'

The brutal simplicity of that was terrifying to Jox, but the paratrooper was in his element. The stockpile also included a box of German stick grenades. Preston shoved a couple in his belt and handed one to each of them. 'You unscrew the bottom of the wooden handle,' he explained, 'pull the cord that pops down, then throw the damned thing. How long you've got is stamped on the cylindrical metal head. These say seven seconds.' He pulled the cord on one and flung the grenade a prodigious distance. It exploded harmlessly, the noise shattering the silence and setting scavenging crows to flight.

They continued on, dipping into a deep, shaded ravine where pockets of mist had gathered. It blanketed the rocky ground, covering violent sights under an opaque shroud. Their heads bobbed along the mist line, like fishing floats skittering across the surface of a loch.

Walking a battlefield after the fighting is done is a forlorn, melancholy experience. The mist lent an eerie atmosphere to what lay in front of them. It appeared Allied and Axis tanks had clashed here for a first cataclysmic time. Burnt-out hulls of several were scattered but also clumped together in places. Blackened limbs protruded from hatches like charred bits of wood. The barrels of the menacing behemoths pointed at discordant angles. The whole grisly panorama was deathly silent save for munitions cooking off. Battle-hardened Dougal Preston snorted every time Jox or Dennini flinched, as he began turning corpses over, looking for a weapon more substantial than his Italian pistol.

'These uniforms aren't Italian, they're German,' said Preston. 'These are *Fallschirmjäger*, paratroopers or "parachute hunters" as the Germans call them. They are part of the *Luftwaffe*, Germany's best soldiers actually being airmen.' He pulled a bolt-action Mauser 98 *Karbine* from under a corpse and began searching through its pockets for clips. 'This lot certainly aren't light troops, they've got tanks in support and bloody big ones at that. Over there, that's a Panzer IV. We saw plenty of them in Tunisia, but that bigger one surrounded by burnt-out Sherman M4s is a new one to me.' They walked cautiously towards the tangled wreckage. 'We've had reports of armoured *Fallschirmjäger* from *Panzer-Division Hermann Göring*, the "Fat Man's" pride and joy, being based in the Calabria region of Italy. Looks like they've crossed the Straits of Messina to Sicily. If that's the case, that means big trouble, especially for our lightly armed airborne troops.'

The hull of a Panzer IV was in a mortal embrace with the Sherman it had collided with. The panzer's skin was ridged with *Zimmerit* paste, the anti-magnetic mine coating covering most German armoured fighting vehicles. It was painted sandy yellow to match the hills, the Sherman was olive drab green, the colour of the stunted trees growing by the roadsides. The Sherman's driver remained at his post but without a head.

Surveying the tragic scene was a traditional Sicilian windmill, an ancient sentinel watching over the carnage of modern-age warfare. Several burnt-out Shermans surrounded the largest tank Jox had ever seen. Most had lost their turrets, flipped off like the lids from bottles of Coca-Cola, which Baraldi had become so partial to. The German tank barrel seemed impossibly long, Preston identifying it as the 88mm gun of a Tiger I Mark VI heavy tank. Jox had heard these new tanks had caused havoc in Tunisia, notably at the Kasserine Pass.

Jox recognised the charnel smell of the Boneyard once again. He shuddered as Preston explained, 'This beast has frontal armour almost four inches thick. The gun mantle is protected by eight inches and the sides are three inches thick but welded at angles to increase effective thickness and deflect incoming rounds.' He ran his hand over its pitted skin. 'Look at the hits it took from those Shermans. They simply bounced off, not one penetrating. That's impressive. I'm told their only weakness is that they break down a lot and they're often too heavy for bridges, getting stranded and stuck. Looks like what's happened here. The M4s certainly didn't hurt it. There's half a dozen or so, destroyed by the one Tiger. The only damage I can see on it is a thrown track. That's probably why the crew baled. Don't blame them with all the Yanks around, but the question is, where are they now?'

Jox cast his eyes over the many wrecked AFVs. It seemed catching fire was the greatest hazard the M4 tankers faced. Most hulks showed signs of a penetrating shot, then catastrophic fire. Preston explained their German nickname was 'Tommy cookers' and even the Americans called them 'Ronsons' after the cigarette lighter that 'lights every time'. Should a tanker survive the initial hit, he faced horrendous burns. Jox looked down at his own burn-scarred hands, and feared the nearest facilities would be in Malta, which felt a very long way away.

They decided to bed down for the night amongst the wrecks, for the shelter but also the opportunity to scavenge for rations. Preston proved to be an expert forager and quickly collected an impressive array of foodstuffs. He tasked Jox and Dennini with pulling it all together into a meal. In the meantime, he set up a defensive position with a fifty-calibre gun scrounged from a Sherman and amassed a collection of firearms which he distributed. To Jox he gave a tanker's 'Grease Gun', an M3 submachine gun, the cheaper, lighter, massed-produced alternative to the Thompson of Al Capone fame. For Dennini, a 'Schmeisser' or MP 40 *Maschinenpistole 40*. Neither were terribly accurate but could lay down a decent rate of fire.

He then took it upon himself to extract what remained of the US tankers from the wrecks around them. He laid the bodies out in a forlorn row under a tarpaulin that he'd found, hoping that troops following on would find and bury them.

They had a peaceful night surrounded by the dead, dining on an eclectic menu of dried German paprika sausage, tinned pickled sauerkraut and smoked cheese. To this was added tinned American C-rations variously labelled as 'Meat and Beans', 'Meat and Potato Hash', or 'Meat and Vegetable Stew', plus, of course, the US Army's ubiquitous dry crackers. Jox used his switchblade to open the tins, as Preston's commando dagger was only good for punching holes and Dennini's filleting knife was too weak for the task. He knew he was ruining his precious blade but there was no alternative, and they were hungry.

It was Dennini's turn to be impressed. Calories were at a premium on the island as was evident by how skinny the young fisherman was. This rich bounty was unheard of in hungry

Sicily, and he marvelled at every mouthful, especially the cheese.

They settled down to sleep, as it would be a long day ahead, but artillery rumbled continuously through the night. The only enemy they needed to contend with were the swarms of aggressive mosquitoes, who drew first blood.

Dawn came as a blessed relief from their tormentors. Dennini was the first up, whistling tunelessly as he stoked up the campfire.

A single shot barked through the still morning air, snatching away the stick in his hand. He shrieked and dove for the cover of the nearest hulk. Preston roared, 'Heads down, keep still.' Dennini didn't understand, but the implication was clear. 'Jox, can you see where the shot came from?'

He couldn't but said, 'That windmill looks likely, it dominates the whole gulley.'

'All right, I'm going to throw a grenade and hopefully it'll draw another shot. If not, at least it'll provide a distraction so we can move. Ready? Throwing now.'

Preston threw long and far, and as anticipated the explosion drew fire, but aimed at him. A single round struck the armour of the tank he was beside, the round ricocheting away leaving a silvered dent not two inches above the top of Preston's maroon beret. It was as if the unseen sniper had aimed for the glinting winged badge.

Worried for his friend, Jox cried out and began firing blindly, emptying an entire magazine in the direction of the windmill. Its stalled and tattered wooden sails were above a sloping roof of bright terracotta roof tiles. His rounds splintered several, but amidst the fracas his fighter pilot eyes sensed movement at the base of the sails.

Dennini began firing inexpertly in the same direction as Jox. Preston chose the moment to launch himself towards the mill, making it to the base of the towered structure, despite a shot whining off a boulder at his feet. He was leading a charmed life, and from where he was lying, Jox could see Preston had his fighting dagger in one fist and a stick grenade in the other.

'I think he's on the top of the windmill,' shouted Jox. 'I saw movement.'

'Right, keep his head down. I need covering fire,' cried Preston.

Moving quickly and silently for such a big man, Preston slipped around the back of the windmill. A few moments later there was a sharp cry. A caped figure slid down the sloped roof of the windmill, followed by a roaring Preston, dagger in hand. There was a clatter as a scoped rifle followed them off the edge.

Jox surged forward with Dennini, expecting trouble, but they found Preston wiping his Fairbairn-Sykes dagger on the sniper's camouflaged smock. The dead *Fallschirmjäger* sniper had close-cropped dark hair, very pale eyes and a startled look on his face. The was a bloody patch at his abdomen but it was clear he'd taken a powerful blow to the side of the head.

'What did you hit him with?' asked an incredulous Jox.

Preston raised his hand, holding the German stick grenade. There was blood and hair sticking to the metalled end.

'Why didn't you throw the bloody thing?' said Jox. 'That's what it's for.'

Preston shrugged. 'This worked pretty well.' He grinned. 'To be honest, it never occurred to me.'

CHAPTER TWENTY-THREE

Dennini's hometown was spread over two hills divided by a deep ravine. Whilst on the road with Dorian Hook, Jox had been briefed on the role Ragusa would play in the forthcoming invasion. As early as the 1800s, the city was considered a hotbed of rebellion, providing many of the armed volunteers for Giuseppe Garibaldi's thousand-strong army of Redshirts. Leading those forces, the Italian patriot, revolutionary and republican drove Italian unification and the creation of the Kingdom of Italy. In the twentieth century, socialist ideals had taken hold of the city to such an extent that the Fascists in control of the mainland called it a 'Fiefdom of the Reds'. Repression was severe and sustained, and the regime of Benito Mussolini was deeply unpopular in the city. Consequently, the Allies and the American OSS in particular had high hopes the flames of rebellion could be fanned into life by their contacts in the Sicilian Mafia or *Cosa Nostra*, the criminal society who truly ruled Sicily.

Hook had explained that the term Mafia was the Sicilian word to 'swagger' or to be bold or show bravado. Ambiguously, it also meant that a man was an arrogant bully, but also fearless, enterprising, cunning and proud. When applied to a woman it meant she was beautiful and desirable. For such a simple word, it spoke deeply of the fear and awe, respect and subjugation that the general population felt towards them.

Even at the outskirts of the city it was clear *Il Duce* was unpopular. His portrait was stencilled everywhere on the sand-coloured walls of the streets and piazzas. His helmeted, bulldog face jutted defiantly towards whatever destiny might bring. Elsewhere the Fascist slogan, '*Credere, obbedire, combattere*', believe, obey, fight, told Sicilians what was expected of them. In Ragusa, however, without fail they'd all been defaced, daubed with red paint with a five-pointed star or the crude symbols of the hammer and sickle.

Approaching the centre of the old town, they passed the blue-domed belltower of the church of *Santa Maria dell'Itria*. The baroque ornateness of it reminded Jox of the tiered cake that Moose and Stephanie Grant had at their wedding. That thought sent a wave of melancholy through him which he had to shake off as an unwelcome distraction.

All around him were signs of battle. The ancient façades of Dennini's neighbourhood were pockmarked by shrapnel, with yawning gaps where artillery had devastated local shops, cafes and homes. The streets were deserted, the population cowering from the bombardment. Dennini's footsteps hastened when he saw a baby's knitted bootie lying in the dust outside a neighbour's shattered house. He darted from doorway to doorway, through the empty streets, tailed by Preston who moved tactically, head swivelling, constantly looking for threats. At the rear, a puffed-out Jox was having trouble keeping up.

Dennini finally reached a door identical to many others up a deserted street. He fished out an iron key from a leather thong around his neck, swiftly unlocking it. He indicated they should follow and stepped into a corridor calling out, 'Elisabetta! Violetta!'

Jox and Preston followed, the darkness inside gloomy after the brightness of the street. The corridor led to a kitchen with a large workbench and a wood-fired range to one side. It smelt of cooking and also of the braided shallots and garlic cloves hanging from hooks in the ceiling. An entire wall was shelved with row after row of glass jars of all different sizes filled with what was doubtless the family sardine paste.

'*Patri?*' said a little voice from under the table. It grew into a shriek as a small girl no more than five flew sobbing from the shadows into her father's arms. She had Dennini's dark hair with a purple bow on top. It matched her remarkable violet-coloured eyes, tear-filled and wide with evident alarm. She had on a white cotton dress, grubby from the kitchen floor and it looked like she'd skinned her elbows on the flagstones.

'Violetta,' cooed Dennini, holding his daughter tight. He was down on his knees, when he pulled back to arms' length and asked after her mother.

Jox recognised the word for market in Violetta's reply.

Dennini looked worried. It appeared Elisabetta, Dennini's wife, had been missing since yesterday. The little girl had been left alone overnight and had understandably been terrified by the bombing and worried for her mother. Dennini indicated that Jox and Preston should stay with Violetta, while he went to look for his wife. Preston was unhappy at the role of babysitter, but Jox convinced him he would attract too much attention outside if seen by the wrong people.

Dennini left his submachine gun on the kitchen table but held onto the pistol which he could hide in his pocket. Violetta was reluctant to let go of her father, clearly unhappy at being left with two unknown and rather smelly foreign men. Dennini talked to her intensely for a while, and she nodded, her remarkably coloured eyes trusting. Her father hugged her tight, then gave her little hand to Preston. He then got up and solemnly shook the hands of his two travel companions.

'*Bonne chance,*' said Jox, hoping the sentiment if not the language was clear.

'*Grazzi, amici miu,*' Dennini replied. Jox saw the tattooed star on his right hand again, remembering now that the American OSS officers he'd dropped off near here both had the same. Dennini pulled his *coppola* flat cap low on his head and hastened from the kitchen.

'What are we going to do in the meantime?' asked Preston, towering over the little girl who stared up at him as if he was some kind of mythical giant.

'For a start, try not to look so intimidating,' replied Jox. 'Smile a bit and get down to her level.'

'Then what?'

'I don't know, play with her or something. You must have siblings.'

'Only my older brother Callum and he wasn't exactly cuddly.'

'Wasn't?'

'He was killed at St Valéry with the Gordons in 1940.'

'I'm sorry,' said Jox, remembering his own early days flying over the retreating 51st Highland Division. He had many school friends who served with the "Highway Decorators", so called because of their propensity to paint the divisional insignia, the conjoined letters "HD" anywhere and everywhere they could. He'd last seen them in the desert before El Alamein, but knew they were bound for Sicily.

'Let her have your beret or something. Children always like hats,' said Jox, not terribly helpfully. 'I'll see if I can rustle up something to eat. She must be starving if she's been alone since yesterday. What rations do we have left?'

'Don't know, Giulio's bag is on the table,' replied Preston. 'There's certainly plenty of that fish paste.' One of his big hands was now holding Violetta's. She was fascinated by how large it was compared to hers. He was doing his best to smile and keep her giggling.

'I'm not messing with that,' said Jox. 'There are a couple of eggs here and potatoes on the sideboard. With a tin or two of compo stew it might be all right. I'll pull something together, you keep her calm and distracted. We don't want her upset or worrying about her parents.'

'Righto,' said Preston. 'She seems happy enough now.'

Violetta was poking him with little fingers, his beret low over her eyes. She gave up trying to tickle him and began clambering up onto his broad shoulders. She was chattering away in animated Sicilian, enjoying her human climbing frame.

'What a little pixie,' said Preston. 'I think she's all right, but hurry up, I'm starving.'

'You're always starving.'

'A man's got to eat. It's all right for you wee fellas, us big lads get hungry.'

After their improvised meal, they managed to convince Violetta to take a little nap. Getting her to sleep involved sitting cradled on Jox's knee as he repeatedly sang 'The Bonnie Banks o' Loch Lomond'. Preston joined in on the chorus of 'O ye'll tak' the high road, and I'll tak' the low road, And I'll be in Scotland afore ye,' singing rather too lustily, and waking the slumbering child. Eventually, she settled and fell into a deep sleep. For Jox, it was an unfamiliar sensation caring for such a little thing. She'd been scared and traumatised, and was utterly exhausted, but only now felt secure enough to sleep. It was something that moved him deeply, thinking of how helpless she must have felt waiting anxiously for her mother's return. Who knew if she would? He'd felt that same helplessness just a day ago, floating at the mercy of the sea, desperate for rescue. It was an unexpected connection with the slumbering child.

Preston decided it was an opportune time to field-strip the firearms they'd collected. Soon a bewildering jumble of springs, bolts, sliders and barrels littered the kitchen table, with Preston wiping, oiling, and carefully picking at stubborn bits of corrosion or built-up grime on the gun components. Not for the first time, Jox was impressed by his friend's competence and single-mindedness. As reassembly was completed, there was a sudden clatter at the door. Preston was up, locked and loaded in an instant and heading for the corridor. Jox, with Violetta in his arms, was slower to react, having to lay her on some chairs before following.

She was woken by the commotion, as Dennini staggered into the kitchen struggling with the weight of a slim, dark-haired woman. She had a bloodied bandage around her head and another visible high on her thigh where the hem of her floral sundress had ruched up. '*Matri?*' screeched an alarmed Violetta. Her mother was pale but managed a tired smile reaching for her child's embrace. Both mother and child were bare footed and looked far too thin.

The relief on Dennini's face was palpable. Seeing the pair of foreign soldiers, Elisabetta smoothed her dress with a wince and pushed a lock of curly shoulder-length hair behind her ear. She was dark-eyed, full-lipped and had high cheekbones. Dennini had obviously told her about the last few days.

'Pleased to meet you. I am Elisabetta Anna Dennini. Welcome to my home. I am sorry I was not here to greet you. *Signore*, you must be Jox.' She looked at the big paratrooper. 'And you are surely Preston. I'm sorry if my English is not so good.'

'It's excellent,' replied Jox. 'Better than my Sicilian. How is it you speak English so well?'

'Not so fluent, but before I marry, I work at Florio Winery. We export vintage Marsala to Great Britain. The English like to drink in London clubs.'

Jox nodded, recalling sharing a bottle with Grant and Pritchard at the RAF Club the night before they'd met King Zog. Mind you, they'd drunk an awful lot and there wasn't much else he remembered concerning that night.

'You are hurt,' said Jox. 'Is there anything I can do? What happened?'

'In the market, I was buying onions when the *Tedeschi bombardamenti* came. I never hear a noise like that. Like screaming women. Shoo-shoo-shoo! Explosions everywhere. I hurt my head and my leg, but Don Pietro's men were there to put on the bandage. They no let me come home until Giulio, he come. I was so worried for Violetta, but they would not let me go. Don Pietro, he say a man of honour would come for his wife. And my Giulio, he come.' She reached her hands to either side of her husband's smiling face and kissed him tenderly.

'That sounds like a *Nebelwerfer* multiple rocket launcher,' said Preston. 'They land in volleys, saturating a tight area with devastating fire. Landing on a crowded marketplace would be utter carnage. The boys call them "Screaming Mimis" and "Moaning Minnies" because of the shrill howling of the incoming rockets.'

'*Si*, like screaming women, shoo-shoo-shoo!' said Elisabetta. 'Many people killed. I am lucky, I think. Lucky to have Don Pietro.'

'Who is Don Pietro?' asked Jox, suspecting he probably knew the answer.

Elisabetta gave Dennini an anxious look, but he nodded reassuringly.

'Don Pietro Tramontin is *sottocapo* of Ragusa, second only to Don Cálo Vizzini the *capo* of all Sicilia. He has liberated our city from the *Tedeschi* and the *Fascisti*. He says he has no need for your *soldati*. He make Sicilia free.'

'That may be, but there are still thousands of Allied troops risking their lives to liberate the rest of your island,' said Jox. 'A little gratitude from this Don Pietro may not go amiss.'

Elisabetta's eyes were disturbed by his response and Dennini asked what he'd said. She translated and her husband replied in rapid Sicilian. 'My husband he say you too must be grateful. He saved you and that is a debt of honour. In Sicilia, we live the Sicilian way, *la cosa nostra*. He has been ordered to bring you to Don Pietro.'

'Why does Giulio follow Don Pietro's orders?' asked Jox. 'What hold does he have on you?'

'My husband is how you say a "made man", a man of honour. He is *soldati*. You see *la stidda* on his hand, it has been there since he was fourteen. He must obey Don Pietro.'

Jox and Preston were shown into the courtyard of a large sprawling house, entering through an unassuming door from the street. There was the trickle of a fountain, and the air was scented by the lemon trees growing in large pots on the ancient flagstones of a small square.

It would have been a tranquil setting if not for the armed men in shirtsleeves milling around the periphery of the courtyard, and the four young women huddled on the ground weeping. They'd clearly been manhandled, one with a torn dress hanging off her bare shoulder, another with a cut and swollen lip. They looked terrified, their tear-filled eyes darting anxiously. Preston growled at the sight, and the men raised their weapons.

Don Pietro Tramontin was a heavy-set man in his sixties. He had olive skin, spectacles on the end of his nose and a shock of white hair, carefully combed in a side parting. He was wearing voluminous velour trousers held up with leather braces and an open-collared shirt, white chest hair visible, bringing to mind a bad-tempered polar bear.

Dennini introduced them as *Capu di Squadruni* Jox McNabb and *Capitanu di Paracadutisti* Dougal Preston. Tramontin expected them to kiss the signet ring on his finger, but neither were willing after seeing how the women had been treated, so had simply come to attention instead. This irritated Tramontin, who waved his hand to two of his men, one who ushered the women from the courtyard, the other running off to carry out another allocated task. Tramontin stared at them impassively for a long while. He looked up when a side door clattered open, and two men entered.

'Well, well, if it isn't Jox McNabb,' said the taller of the two. '*In bocca al lupo.*'

Jox replied archly, '*Crepi il lupo.* May the wolf die.'

The shorter of the two men crossed the courtyard and took a position at Don Pietro Tramontin's shoulder. He whispered into the ear of the *sottocapo*, the underboss of the Ragusa chapter of *la cosa nostra*.

Jox immediately recognised the unsmiling face of Major Giuseppe Paolino. He was the senior of the two OSS officers that Jox and Jimmy Waerea had dropped off by Lysander in the hills above the city some weeks ago. He was evidently unhappy at Jox's presence in 'his' city.

'What the hell are you doing here, Squadron Leader McNabb?' asked Paolino. 'What is the nature of your mission in Ragusa?'

'Good to see you too, Major Paolino. I see you're amongst friends,' replied Jox, irritated by being questioned in this manner. 'I'm not on any mission at all. I went down in the Bay of Gela, three nights ago. I'm simply here because our rescuer, Giulio here, brought us to the city as he was worried for his family. He promised to get us to Allied lines and believed a certain Don Pietro might help.'

'You expect me to believe that?' said Paolino. 'You work for Sandy Bullough, which means nothing is ever as it seems. I know of your involvement with Operation Tinned Fish, so don't tell me you're just an innocent bystander. Are you here to undermine the OSS's operations with the *cosa nostra*?'

'Major, I know nothing of your *cosa nostra*, other than it smells rather bad to me,' Jox replied icily. 'I would remind you I expect a degree of courtesy, not to mention gratitude, given we are of the same rank, and I was the one that brought you to Ragusa in the first place.'

'You expect me to believe your presence is a coincidence?'

'Frankly, I don't care what you believe, nor do I care for whatever intrigues you're cooking up with your star-spangled Sicilian friends. What I do want to know is how the invasion is progressing and how Captain Preston and I can get back into the fight, rather than skulking in the shadows like the two of you.'

From behind Jox, Preston added, 'Look, I don't know what you two are on about. I just want to get back to my unit and get stuck in. I've lost too many good men and I'm itching for a fight. I'll take it out on Jerry, the Italians or whoever. Don't know who the hell you lot are, but don't get in my way.'

Tramontin laughed unexpectedly. 'McNabb, your big friend Preston is brave but stupid, like all good soldiers should be. He is honest and a man of honour. You, I think are a tricky one.'

Jox started to reply when Tramontin held up a hand. 'No, now you shut up when I speak. You are like Lomasso here, always talking but not thinking. In *Sicilia*, we think then we talk, not like in America.' He waved his hand as he spoke, on it was the five-pointed *stidda*, the same as on Dennini, Paolino and Lomasso. 'My new American *Consigliere* is suspicious of everything. This is good, but he must remember I have been the wolf of these mountains for a long time. I am not new to *la cosa nostra*.'

Jox saw Lomasso grinning at his superior being taken down a peg.

Tramontin continued, 'I do not know you *Signor* Jox, but I know Giulio from a boy. He is my trusted *soldati*. If he says you can be trusted and that he saved you and the big one from the sea, then I believe him. Your lives are in his debt. One day that debt must be repaid. You don't understand *la cosa nostra*, but you are in its debt. *Capisci*?'

Jox didn't like what he was agreeing to but nodded.

'And the giant?' Tramontin muttered, indicating Preston.

He nodded too. 'I agree, just get me back to my unit. I'm sick of these intrigues.'

'*Bonu*, it is agreed,' said Tramontin. 'Come *Signor* Jox, take my hand on it and then my nephew's, Giulio Cesare Dennini.'

'Your nephew?' said Jox seeing Dennini through fresh eyes.

'*Naturalmente*, in *la cosa nostra* we are all family. He is my sister's boy. A *caporegime* of the family. Even these two *miricani* are my cousins. He's a brave boy, no? He saved your life. You not forget it, I not forget it. One day we will talk again.'

'There you go, fellas, we're all pals again,' said Lomasso. 'We'll get you situated and then back across the battle lines as quick as can be.'

'How's the invasion progressing?' asked Jox. 'We've seen a lot of damage but not a lot of fighting.'

'The British landed south and east of the city along the coast,' replied Lomasso. 'Our forces landed southwest of Ragusa in the Gulf of Gela. The Germans are counterattacking with heavy armour and airborne troops, so the Allies are not having it all their own way. It's a race who gets here first, but as you can see, we've already liberated ourselves. You may not approve of our methods but they're effective, have limited the damage, and saved lives.'

'I'm not sure the women we saw earlier would agree,' replied Jox. 'What did they do? What will happen to them?'

Lomasso looked surprised, as if he'd never considered the question. '*Collaborazioni orizzontali*, sleeping with the enemy. I guess it won't be too long before they're on their backs under American GIs or Tommies, working in our brothels.' He dismissed the thought from his mind. 'To answer your questions more specifically, for you Captain Preston, British Airborne are east of here near Avola. For you Jox, the nearest RAF fighter base has been established at Comiso airfield, west of here.' Jox smiled. 'You know it?'

'It was my squadron's objective to interdict it before I came down.'

'Well then, your boys must be making good progress. My sources tell me there are already RAF fighters and US transports flying out of there, so we'll get you back, okay, buddy?'

'That'll be fine, thank you, Captain.'

CHAPTER TWENTY-FOUR

Just after dawn the following morning Preston, Jox, Dennini and Lomasso were standing at a crossroads in the mountains behind Ragusa. It was time for a parting of ways, to once again be scattered to the winds of war.

Lomasso and a pair of guards would accompany Jox to Comiso, whilst Preston, Dennini and two others would try to pin down exactly where the airborne troops were, somewhere across the south-eastern end of the island.

'Dougal, we've been through a lot together,' said Jox, a lump in his throat and affection thick in his voice. 'I owe you my life.'

'Don't be so daft,' Preston replied. 'I'd be at the bottom of the Med with the rest of the boys if it wasn't for you. I owe you mine just as much.'

'All right, we'll call it a draw, but know this, you can always call on my friendship. We owe it to each other to keep an eye out for one another. Here's my hand on it.'

The big paratrooper seized his hand rather harder than Jox expected. 'Screw that,' Preston said. 'Give me a hug. We both stink like polecats, but our little adventure deserves a hug.'

'I hope you find Grant and at least some of your men,' said Jox. 'They can't all have gone down. My heart goes out to them.'

'Aye, well, we'll see.' Preston seemed embarrassed at getting misty-eyed.

'And take care of that nose,' said Jox. 'If you don't, it may just stay like that.'

'Not sure if it's an improvement or not,' laughed Preston.

They turned to Dennini. There was no debating, he had definitely saved their lives. They embraced him and with Lomasso's help expressed their gratitude.

'I don't have much to give you as a gift,' said Preston. 'I can only offer you this dagger. It means a lot to me as it represents my commando training. I give it to you with my thanks.'

Dennini appeared touched.

'I have no gift to offer,' said Jox. He fumbled in his pocket and pulled out the porcelain doll's arm that was his lucky charm. He showed it to Dennini who looked puzzled. 'This object is precious to me and has seen me through many dangers. You can see that inscribed on it are the names of two children. They are who I fight this war for. One was in France, the other Malta. Marguerite and Elias. I would like to add the name of Violetta too. It would be my honour. Will you permit me to do that?'

Dennini was quiet, clearly moved. He nodded and embraced Jox, kissing him on either cheek. He then pointed to the *stidda* tattoo on his hand. 'You remember us, *amicu miu.*'

'We better get going,' said Lomasso. 'It won't be a piece of cake. There are a lot of guys on the island with itchy trigger fingers. We don't want you getting slotted after everything you've been through. Plus, we don't know any of the passwords, so will need to be real careful, deliberate and non-threatening.'

'Halt! Who goes there?' a nervous sentry asked at the improvised barrier on the periphery of Comiso airfield.

'Take it easy, soldier,' Jox replied. 'British officer returning to our lines. Stand down.'

'Advance and be recognised,' replied the sentry. 'Keep your hands where I can see them.'

'Dinnae worry, I've got them covered, Stan,' said a second gruff voice.

Jox could see the flared muzzle of a Bren light machine gun protruding from the slit of the concrete pillbox behind the guard. Someone had hung up a sign saying, 'Under new management'.

Jox shook hands with Lomasso and the armed *cosa nostra soldati*, then advanced towards the sentry post, his hands raised. The sun was at his back, so it took a while for the sentries to recognise his uniform. It was also pretty grimy after several days' wear including a prolonged dunking in the waters of the Mediterranean.

As soon as the first sentry got a good look at his flight jacket and RAF wings, he called back to his companion. 'It's all right, Hamish, he's an RAF pilot. Name and rank please, sir.'

'Squadron Leader McNabb, CO of No. 333 Squadron, the Black Pigs.'

'He's a senior officer too, Corp.'

'Hold on, it might be a trick. Ask him where he comes from.'

'Just a formality, sir. For security, my corporal wants to know where you're from.'

Jox was impressed by their wariness. 'I'm from Scotland, grew up in Dollar in Clackmannanshire.'

'Ask him what a Sassenach is?' said the voice at the gun.

'You are, Private,' Jox said. 'An Englishman.'

Stan looked confused. 'He says I'm a Sasse-wotsit, Corporal.'

'Aye, that's right, so you are. Let him in then.'

'Aha, the return of the prodigal son,' exclaimed Dundas, as Jox hobbled into the bar. Most recently it had been a German mess and still had trophies of British and American aircraft adorning the walls. Jox recognised the charging elephant crest of No.

249 Squadron presumably hacked off a downed fuselage.

'Dundas, good to see you. What the devil are you doing here?' asked Jox.

'I might well ask you the same question,' smirked the lanky wing commander. 'Looks like you've been through the wringer.'

Jox smiled wearily. 'You could say that, certainly had a good steep and soak beforehand, then a long, very hot spell to dry out.'

'Better tell me what happened. Actually, before you do, get yourself a drink on me, and I'll quickly send word back to your squadron at Hal Far. They've been beside themselves, holding all manner of memorials for you. One of your chaps reported you lost a wing and tipped into the sea. Said it was all over, with no parachute sighted.'

'Well, it was pretty much like that, but thankfully a big paratrooper already in the water pulled me out of the kite before it sank to the bottom. It's a long story, but I did eventually make it to Sicily, then fell in with, I suppose you could call them partisans, who brought me here.'

Jox got his drink while Dundas was making his call, gin with rather flat tonic, jazzed up with a fresh slice of Sicilian lemon. He hadn't tasted anything quite so good in a while.

Dundas returned. 'Well, they're rather pleased to hear you're alive and kicking. Should make for quite the reunion. It occurred to me that I ought to let Group Captain Thompson know you've turned up. He and Glasgow have been like grieving parents. Thompson was really quite moved when I told him.'

'He's a grand old boy,' said Jox raising his glass. 'Here's to him. But listen, never mind all that, how's the invasion going and what are you doing here?'

'Why, I'm leading the No. 324 (Spitfire) Wing's advance fighter force for the USAAF Twelfth on Sicily,' replied Dundas with a smirk. 'We're here protecting outgoing airborne and glider operations. We've a dozen troop carrier C-47 squadrons based here now, plus the 340th Bombardment Group of North American B-25 Mitchell bombers and then three squadrons of RAF Spitfires along with No. 3201 Servicing Commando to support them.'

Jox looked around the crowded room. 'Which squadrons are here?'

'The "Fighting Cocks" of No. 43 Squadron, the "Seahorses" of No. 243 and of course your Treble Ones.'

'The Treble Ones are here?'

'Yes, of course. Gale and Mouland are over there. You know them, don't you?'

'Yes, of course I do. Gosh, it's great to see friendly faces again.'

They joined the Treble Ones at the bar. It felt good to be back amongst them, but oddly, Jox no longer felt like one, hankering instead for his own Black Pigs.

'Gee, Jox, I'm sure glad you turned up,' said Gusty Gale. 'I'd heard you'd bought it. I was really in two minds on how to react to that news.'

Jox frowned. 'What do you mean?'

Gale shook his head with a sad smile. 'Well, if you had bought it, I wouldn't have to tell you the news regarding Monty Falls. I know you two were close and went on that special mission and everything.'

'What the devil's happened to Monty?'

'Yeah, good question. He re-joined the squadron when we transferred to Malta, getting ready for Operation Husky. He went on a couple of missions, in fine blustering form as ever, and then just simply disappeared. We have him posted as missing in action somewhere between Malta and Sicily. I'd assumed you'd gone the same way, but listen, I *am* glad you made it. I'm sorry, I know he was a friend. Hell of a character. The Treble Ones will miss him.'

Jox chewed at his lip, struck dumb by the news. 'Thanks, Gusty. You'll never really know quite the impact he made. I'm not exaggerating when I say he changed the course of the war.' Jox raised his glass, his voice cracking when he said, 'To the glorious memory of the great Monty Falls.'

'Damn it! Where's my new Savile Row uniform, Shillington?' Jox asked his batman.

'I … I packed it all up and disposed of it, sir,' Shillington spluttered, trembling before the fury of his commanding officer.

'What do you mean? What am I supposed to wear? That uniform cost a bloody fortune,' said Jox.

'But … but you were dead. I thought I was doing the right thing, sir. Flight Lieutenant Baraldi told me you were missing in action. I'm sorry, sir, I've been here before and no one's ever come back. I *am* glad you have.' He smiled hesitantly. 'I thought it was my fault, but you've broken the Jonah curse. Thank you, sir.'

It was hard to stay angry in the face of such contrition. 'So, where is my stuff?'

'I sold it to a rag trader down at the Valletta Covered Market. I've used him before, and he gives me a good rate for officer's clothing and accoutrements.'

'I bet he does,' said Jox, bristling again. 'You're probably one of his best suppliers. How much did you get for my worldly possessions?'

Shillington shuffled nervously. 'Seventeen pounds, sir.'

'Seventeen! Hardly thirty pieces of silver,' cried Jox. He took a deep breath, trying to calm himself. 'Look, go back to your chap, and get my stuff back. He hasn't had it long, so hopefully it's not all gone. Tell him, if I don't get redress, I'll report him to the snowdrops for profiteering from the fallen. If that doesn't work, I'll leave him to the boys. I'm sure the Kilpatricks, Jimmy and Jumbo will tear his shop apart. They've had plenty of practice with that bar down in The Gut.' He eyed Shillington. 'I warn you, Corporal, if you don't fix this, I'll send you off with such a flea in your ear that you'll be cleaning toilets for the rest of your life. Is that clear?'

'Yes, sir.'

Jox reached into his pocket and handed Shillington his porcelain doll's arm charm and Maltese switchblade. 'Here, I want you to track down that blade master I told you about, his name is Giovanni Vella. I'll give you the address. The blade needs fixing and sharpening, I rather abused it whilst on the run in Sicily. Ask Mister Vella if he would do that and also add the name of "Violetta" to this arm, below the other two names. Get this done and I may forgive you. God help you if you let me down again.'

CHAPTER TWENTY-FIVE

'Better let me have the butcher's bill while I was away,' Jox said wearily to de Ghellinck, Fisken and Baraldi. They were sharing a pot of tea in his office, the morning after Jox's raucous homecoming.

'Not as bad as might be expected,' replied Baraldi. 'The only major loss was you.'

'Nothing major about me,' Jox replied, rubbing his eyes. 'Give me the bad news.'

'Two casualties but no fatalities,' said Baraldi. 'Spud Inverarity got shot up again, on the same mission as you. Those gunners with the fleet were good shots even though they were shooting at their own men. He managed to nurse his kite back to Malta but crashed short of the airfield. Ended up bellied in an olive grove, which would have been fine if not for one of those blasted stone walls. Spud wasn't strapped in properly and was flung from the wreckage, ending face-first in one of those olive trees. They're small but have a hard wood trunk, which he discovered to his chagrin.' Jox winced at the image conjured. 'He's lost a lot of teeth. Poor chap really doesn't have much luck. Old Spud's going to be eating mashed potatoes for a while.'

'He lives to fight another day,' said Jox. 'Can't ask for more than that. He's a survivor. We can all learn from him. Who's the other casualty?'

'He's in my flight,' said de Ghellinck. '*Jeune Canadien*, his name's Foreman, but *les gars* all call him Chrissy Boy. Flying Blue Four in Kanga's section after a sortie over the beach at Gela. You'll remember *les imbéciles* shooting at everybody, well it wasn't only the first night. It was every time we cross the beachhead. Anyway, Kanga tells me they made it through this "friendly flak", and everyone seemed all right. They come back to Hal Far, but Chrissy Boy was very quiet. The section lands *sans problèmes*, pull into the parking pens and start climbing out. Blue Four stops short with the engine still running and nothing happens. Kanga gets suspicious and runs over with some of the ground crew. Approaching the kite, he sees the portside of the fuselage has been ripped open with jagged holes everywhere and fingers of blood are streaking back from them. The boys jump onto the wings and see that Chrissy Boy is pale and practically unconscious. They pull back the canopy and the cockpit is like an abattoir. He says, "My leg's gone. I heard a bang and it's gone." Kanga said that from mid-thigh there was nothing but gore.' De Ghellinck sighed. 'I don't know how *ce brave garçon* managed it. He flew a hundred miles back to Malta with a leg like that. *C'est formidable.* A miracle.'

'At first, we didn't think he'd make it,' added Baraldi. 'He'd lost so much blood, but he's fit and strong. His flying days are over though.'

'How are the boys taking it?' asked Jox.

'Tell you the truth, not so well when you went down,' said Baraldi. 'We held a wake. Jimmy Waerea did one of his ceremonial dances with that club of his. The boys thought it was fitting but we've had real trouble shaking off the funk that had settled on the squadron.'

'Listen, Jox, we tried our best to get morale up, me and Ghillie,' said Fisken. 'But it was getting the call from Dundas saying you turned up at Comiso that did it. Telling the boys was like a shot of adrenaline. Last night, seeing you alive and kicking was the best medicine. You don't realise how important you are to us.'

'Cut it out, Axel. No man is irreplaceable. Any of us could go down at any time. As fighter pilots we all know that and have to accept it.'

'*Ja*, that's true, but you know, my friend, there's nothing wrong with taking the compliment too.'

Baraldi and de Ghellinck smiled and nodded in agreement.

'All right,' replied Jox, embarrassed but moved by what his often rather gruff Norwegian friend had said. 'Op-wise, what's on the board for the next few days?'

'Fighter sweeps most days,' replied Baraldi. 'Morning and afternoons. Occasionally, some bomber escort duty, but otherwise it's pretty much free hunt as our friend Jerry would say. Mostly taking on ground targets since the *Luftwaffe* don't seem keen on coming out in the daylight unless they're after the bomber streams raiding the mainland.'

'Some of the boys are getting rather good at taking on Jerry's panzers,' added de Ghellinck. 'The Kilpatricks, Jimmy Waerea, and Suggs McPherson are quite the experts with a few kills apiece. The secret is to keep low and slow, aiming for the back of the turret or the ventilation grills over the engine block. Firing from any further away than a couple of hundred yards is useless, and you must keep hammering at the same spot. Most of our 20mm cannon shells bounce off but it only takes a few to penetrate and disable the beasts. We rarely destroy them, but no panzer crew sticks around a stranded battlewagon that becomes a magnet for every gun in range.' He gave a gallic shrug. 'Personally, I am a fighter pilot, hunting for other fighters or bombers. This ground attack business is like gardening to me, a chore like mowing the lawn. Necessary perhaps, *mais pas pour moi*. I'm glad the boys like it though.'

'We need to adapt for the needs of the service,' replied Jox. 'Pritch is retraining on Typhoons, specifically to target armour and artillery on the ground. That's what we'll need when we eventually invade continental Europe. What we're seeing in Sicily is like a dress rehearsal. The role of the fighter is changing, either to a fighter-bomber ground attack role or as high-altitude bomber escorts. Our Spitfires don't have the range for deep penetration raids, so perhaps we'll need other aircraft, but until then we need to be adaptable. I'd certainly like to have a go at a panzer. I saw one of those Tigers close-up in Sicily. What a beast and virtually impenetrable. Right, anything else to report?'

'Yes, one thing,' replied Baraldi. 'You mentioned you saw some chaps from the Treble Ones in Sicily, well there's another joining us. Doc Ridgway has finally been released and he's arriving this afternoon. Actually, that's another reason I'm glad you're back. I really didn't fancy having to tell him you'd bought it.'

'Oh, I'm so sorry,' winked Jox. 'I wouldn't want to inconvenience you by dying at an inopportune moment.' Baraldi pulled a face and they all laughed. 'It'll be good to have Doc back in the fold. He's always got the inside track on what's what.'

'Yes,' said Baraldi. 'As long as he's not banging on about Vulcan and his volcanoes.'

'You know, I've got every reason to be grateful to old Vulcan,' replied Jox. 'It was one of those bubbling-up volcanic islands that saved my bacon when I ditched, well that and a paratrooper called Dougal Preston. Come to think of it, there's a couple of Sicilians I ought to be grateful to as well.' He smiled ruefully. 'Now all I need is for bloody Shillington to get my clobber back, so I can at least start looking like the CO of the squadron again, rather than some damned scarecrow that the wind blew in. The cheek of the man, selling my gear like that.'

'Yes, well, he did come asking if some of the boys would back him up when visiting his rag and bone man. I told Jimmy and Jumbo to pick some burly boys and pay the chap a visit. I'll let you know how they get on,' said Baraldi, ever the efficient adjutant, fingers in every pie of squadron business.

'Welcome to the Black Pigs, Doc,' said Jox when Ridgway had appeared. 'I nearly didn't make it back for your arrival. I'm glad you've finally joined us. You'll find plenty of familiar faces.'

'Good to be here, Jox,' Ridgway said as they shook hands. 'These are interesting times we're living in. Before I forget, I've been asked to pass on the compliments of Bullough and Hook, your friends in the Intelligence community. Sandy's tickled pink on how well "King Zog's" tour went. They filled me in before I left the Treble Ones. That Monty Falls, it's incredible he managed to pull it off.'

'You haven't heard the news then?' Jox asked.

Ridgway frowned. 'No, what?'

'We've lost Monty. Missing in action, over the sea.'

'What happened?'

'I don't have details. He returned to the Treble Ones and then a few days later disappeared somewhere between Malta and Sicily.'

'Bloody hell, that's a blow. You don't meet characters like that every day.'

'The world's a duller place without him, but we can't dwell. Listen, how are things going overall? We don't get much of an overview at squadron level.'

'I only have the Intelligence reports, but there is some big news,' said Ridgway. 'You remember the little King of Italy, Victor Emmanuel III? Zog's arch-rival?'

'Yes, of course. I saw a photo of him, barely five foot tall.'

'That's right, the Italians call him *Sciaboletta*, the little sabre,' replied Ridgway. 'Anyway, by all accounts his been sticking that knife in. On the 25th of July, the King and Count Dino Grandi, President of the Italian government, held a vote of no confidence in Prime Minister Benito Mussolini. So, that means *Il Duce* is out and is apparently under arrest. The whole Italian Fascist state is crumbling, which has to be good news, but it does mean the Germans will become unpredictable. They're furious, are digging in and will take a hard line.'

'What's happening on the ground?'

'Well, after those disastrous airborne drops, the British amphibious landings to the east were comparatively unopposed. They've since run into stiffer opposition inland. Patton and his troops around Gela initially had a tougher time but are now progressing well. In fact, they're moving rather faster than Montgomery, who's always been a bit of a plodder. Last I heard, Patton is racing for Palermo trying to split the Axis forces up against the northern shoreline. Montgomery's troops are spread out and currently suffering on the parched plains of Catania, up against heavy armour and well dug in opposition. The worst of it is fighting in temperatures well above a hundred degrees Fahrenheit. That's warmer than blood. On top of that, the place is infested with mosquitoes and malaria is spreading. I'm told thousands are going down with fevers and heat exhaustion.'

'I certainly got eaten alive during my little excursion to Sicily,' replied Jox, distractedly scratching at the remains of a bite.

'In the meantime, Jerry is pulling back to the high ground around Mount Etna, digging into defences they're calling the Etna Line. We've learnt that Field Marshal Kesselring, "Smiling Albert", the German Commander in Chief and one of Adolf Hitler's best defensive strategists is on the island. He's appointed two of his best generals with the twin tasks of holding the Etna Line and the Straits of Messina. *Generaloberst* Hans-Valentin Hube, known as *Der Mensch*, the good guy, is in charge of holding the Etna Line to enable the Germans to make a progressive retreat of their forces back to the mainland. That task and the defence of the Straits themselves is the responsibility of *Generalleutnant* Ernst-Günther Baade. You'd like him, he's quite an eccentric apparently, wears a kilt, carries a claymore sword and a Luger pistol in a holster worn as a sporran.'

Jox looked at Ridgway, surprised. 'How on earth do you know that?'

Ridgway's eyes twinkled. 'That's my job, to gather intelligence.'

Jox shook his head. 'And do you think they know as much about us?'

'I have little doubt about that.'

'And you say this Baade actually carries a claymore?'

'It's true, he's of Scottish ancestry, is a bit of an odd fish, but is also very competent. He's reportedly installed over two hundred flak and shore batteries on either side of the Straits of Messina, which are twenty miles long but only two wide at the narrowest point. That concentration of fire makes it some of the deadliest airspace and coastal waters we've ever encountered.'

'Sounds like we're in for a hell of a fight,' said Jox, wearily.

'I think there's little doubt. We're unlikely to succeed with a frontal attack on the Etna Line. There are rumours circulating of another night-time airborne operation to get behind it by jumping onto the slopes of the volcano, seizing Messina and holding it until relieved by Patton coming from Palermo or Montgomery from the south. The pongos call it a "*coup de main*" mission, defined as "an offensive operation using surprise and the simultaneous execution of supporting operations to achieve success."' Ridgway pulled a face. 'I'm not sure if I buy that. Airborne have already been through the wringer, the last thing they need is a "Garryowen".'

'Garryowen? What's that?' asked Jox.

'I thought you followed rugby,' replied Ridgway.

'I'm not an expert.'

'Well in rugby, the Garryowen is named after the Irish club which used the tactic to win the Munster Cup several times in the twenties. It's a high kick designed to hang in the air, putting the opposing team under pressure and giving the kicking team time to arrive and compete for the high ball.'

'Ah yes, at school we called it the "up and under",' said Jox. 'I suppose I get the analogy but wouldn't fancy a night jump into combat near a live volcano. Those paratroopers really are nutters.'

The rest of the week was spent on interdiction missions over the plains of Catania and the mountains, following ragged lines of Allied troops advancing like ants along the dusty paths and mule tracks stretching like capillaries across the arid countryside. It was the height of the Sicilian summer, and the sun-bleached plains were more desert than farmland.

The Black Pigs flew in shirtsleeves, canopies left open to catch the airflow and escape the relentless heat. They had to be careful with their bare arms, risking burns on the hot fuselages. With R/T contact established with the advancing troops, they waited to be called in to harass enemy strongpoints, unblock chokepoints and take out artillery or armour bunkered down in the featureless expanse of the arid yellow landscape.

A highlight was when Fisken's B Flight were called to tackle a stubborn trio of entrenched panzers. They were a pair of Panzer IV medium tanks and a huge Panzer VI or Tiger I heavy tank, recognisable by its bulk and 8.8cm KwK 36 gun, the infamous 'eighty-eight' feared by all Allied troops. The medium tanks were already big at nine and a half feet tall, but the Tiger was twice the height of the average man. Hull down in prepared firing positions the German armour was practically invulnerable, calmly taking out Allied vehicles and then the armour sent out against them.

When B Flight's nine aircraft arrived, including Jox in a borrowed Spit, Allied artillery were delivering a stonk on the trio. Hull down, they were perfectly safe with their five-man crews simply having to grin and bear the cacophony. Protected by their dense armoured carapaces they were in no immediate danger and yet when one of the Panzer IVs received a direct strike from what must have been a fairly large calibre shell, the crew panicked. Inexplicably, it pulled out of its prepared position and withdrew. Perhaps the sight of their *kameraden* running away triggered some instinct of self-preservation amongst the other tankers. The remaining two plumed black exhaust smoke and followed suit.

The first tank reversed up the slope, heading away from the Allied ground troops, but keeping its thick frontal armour facing the enemy. This was when Jimmy Waerea, followed by the Fighting Kilpatricks swooped onto its exposed rear. From his open cockpit, Jox could hear the roar of cannon fire, one intense burst following the next. Each only had time on target of no more than a one-second burst, with perhaps a dozen of the four and a half ounce projectiles striking. Waerea's burst shattered the Zimmerit paste coating on the rear bin of the turret, raising a cloud of saffron-coloured dust.

The subsequent bursts from the Kilpatricks sounded different, more like a series of hammer blows on a metal water tank. Some of the 20mm rounds must have penetrated because a moment later an orange secondary explosion blew the main turret cupola into the air like a dustbin lid. A roman candle surged from the gaping hole like the mouth of a volcano, incinerating the *Panzertruppen* within.

'I got you good, boyo,' exclaimed Pat Kilpatrick on the R/T, with undisguised glee.

'Away with ye, he was mine,' answered Paddy Kilpatrick. They were clearly enjoying themselves.

The second Panzer IV met a similar fate, struck by Blue Section's fire but also tellingly by a 6-pounder anti-tank gun, aiming over open sights having caught the tanks' movements. The gun turned its attention to the Tiger, as Jox with Fisken and Johnstone in tow, had a go at it. It was a huge target, but it was hard to angle the attack, so rounds had a chance of penetration.

When Jox came to fire, the tank's ridged Zimmerit coating had already been pulverised. He heard the same roar as before, but this time from his guns, feeling the recoil through the aircraft's structure and deep within his body. Almost immediately, his rounds hammered the Tiger's armour. Earlier, when the others had fired, he hadn't seen the flashing ricochets that now bounced off the slanted armour. Several rose like a deadly curtain, coming dangerously close to striking his delicate wings, the fragile kite wobbling violently in their wake.

The big panzer continued to retreat, unperturbed by the swirling trio harassing it like seagulls chasing chips on a promenade. It seemed invulnerable, continuing to fire its monstrous gun at the six-pounder who had *dared* to engage it. After just two booming reports the presumptuous anti-tank men were taken out, punishment for offending the mighty Tiger. Frustrated by the ineffectiveness of their fire, Blue Section were out of ammo and short on fuel. They had no choice but to leave the ground troops with their Tiger-shaped problem.

It was clear that despite losing its *kameraden*, the giant tank had emerged victorious, withdrawing unscathed from the furious engagement. There was clearly a lot of fight and deadly competence left in Jerry on the beleaguered island of Sicily.

CHAPTER TWENTY-SIX

The first indication that the night mission was on came with the squadron's transfer from Hal Far to Comiso, joining the other No. 324 group fighter squadrons. With no external slipper tanks, their Spitfires simply didn't have the range to reach Mount Etna and still have time to usefully patrol the area. The land mass of the tallest active volcano in Europe covered some four hundred square miles and a height of three thousand metres. Whatever the outcome, it would be a battlefield like no other.

Jox was flying a new aircraft, freshly painted in night-fighter livery with the squadron's letter J, Marguerite's name, his claymore emblem and then something new, the dark silhouette of a Black Pig, proudly worn by all of No. 333 Squadron.

The entire fighter group would be involved in this operation, tasked with protecting the paratroopers and transports from any night-fighters sent against them. As the nocturnal specialists, the Black Pigs would be amongst the massed C-47s, whilst 324's other fighters would be ranged above and to the side of the formations to be called in as required. The biggest threat to both transports and fighters would, however, be the bristling mass of flak guns ranged along the Sicilian shore and mainland Calabria, the most heavily defended spot in Europe.

Ultimately the paratroopers' objective was Messina, the closest city to the Italian mainland, but they needed to survive long enough to get there. All enemy troops and supplies would have to pass through the city to get in or out, and it was the island's largest port. The north-eastern corner of Sicily was dominated by the volcanic mass of Mount Etna, a looming, malevolent presence. As recently as 1908 it had caused an earthquake which destroyed ninety per cent of Messina, with tens of thousands killed, and proving to be the most destructive earthquake to ever strike Europe.

In ancient mythology this was the land of the Cyclops, tricked and blinded by the Greek hero Odysseus. Perhaps the one-eyed mythical creature was a reference to Etna's malevolent eye, which according to the pre-mission weathermen was currently acting up, minor eruptions throwing up smoke and ash. It appeared Vulcan was awakening to the prospect of battle on the pitch-black volcanic slopes.

Approaching Etna's stark silhouette, rivulets of molten lava could be seen slipping from the main crater, like blood from the mouth of a lung-shot man. The night sky had a deep mandarin orange glow, reflecting off a nearly full moon, except when obscured by the plume of ash and smoke rising from the crater itself.

Ranged below the Black Pigs were row after row of C-47 Dakotas ferrying American, Canadian and British airborne troops on their latest foolhardy mission. Jox wondered how else to describe an operation jumping into known hostile territory, which happened to be on the steep slopes of an active volcano, with the very real possibility of landing within the five-hundred-metre-wide fiery mouth.

As elements of the air armada neared Messina, searchlights probed the night sky from across the water in Calabria. Before long, arching tentacles of bright flak fire criss-crossed the heavens like bull whips lashing at targets. A first unfortunate Dakota was caught, dropping paratroopers as it fell, flames illuminating the vast traffic jam of vessels crossing the straits full of evacuating Axis personnel. Orders over the R/T instructed some of the outlying fighter squadrons and the accompanying B-25 Mitchell bombers to have a go at them. In doing so, they would be exposed to the full intensity of the flak, like flying right down the barrel of a loaded shotgun.

The transports protected by the Black Pigs began deploying their human cargo. Several sticks of paratroopers took to their 'silks', the light olive-green of British parachutes interspersed with the darker green of the Americans, both black against the orange-hued night sky. Nearer Messina, Jox spotted lighter-coloured parachutes, glowing almost white. Perhaps they were for equipment or supplies. He watched them descending as a transport crossed beneath him. He recognised immediately that it wasn't an Allied aircraft. It was a twin-engined Ju 52, the workhorse of the *Fallschirmjäger*, the airborne branch of the *Luftwaffe*.

Jox was very familiar with the "Auntie Ju" or "Iron Annie". He'd shot one down during the invasion of France. It was one of his first kills and at the time he'd been tormented by the thought of killing a dozen helpless paratroopers. The aircraft below him was followed by three more, each with the Ju 52's distinctive corrugated fuselage painted in a disruptive camouflage pattern.

Side doors opened and began disgorging scattered sticks of *Fallschirmjäger*. The Germans were clearly deploying a night drop on these very same slopes. Once on Etna's scree, the opposing paratroopers would immediately be locked in the gladiatorial contest that Dougal Preston had predicted weeks ago. The flower of airborne infantry would slog it out on Vulcan's fields of lava and ash. Was Preston down there, he wondered, but Jox knew the answer. There was no way his big friend would miss out on a fight like that. What was less certain was if Grant MacNeish had survived to join him, whirling his claymore 'Maeve' like a shrieking banshee.

Jox activated his rocker trigger to ON, and edged the targeting reticule projected on the forward part of his canopy until it covered the nearest enemy transport. It was an easy shot, with minimum deflection. Jox no longer had the qualms of his younger self. He was simply evening up the odds stacked against the brave Allied paratroopers.

The Ju 52 before him staggered in the night sky, a final few members of the stick managing to escape before his cannon fire took its toll. The aircraft's pilots had no such luck, as it spiralled groundward, striking the liquid lava within Etna's wide crater. Molten rock splashed spectacularly, a sign that neither they nor the aircraft would be seen again.

Jox turned his attention to the next Ju 52 in his eyeline. His wingman, Waerea, opened fire on it. He was about to do the same when he was distracted. The orange-hued darkness was punctured by powerful pulsing white light, above and starboard of him. He raised the Spit's nose to investigate. From the glowing darkness, a primeval-looking creature emerged, nose covered with antennae-like twisted antlers. Below the cockpit was the emblem of a night owl perched on a crescent moon.

In the vivid brightness of its target, an exploding Dakota, the full length of the black night-fighter was briefly illuminated. It fired again, delivering a powerful *coup de grâce*. Jox recognised an old adversary, a *Messerschmitt* Bf 110, a twin-engined *Zerstörer*, an early war heavy fighter converted to a night-fighter role. Jox had tangled with them before and knew they had bigger teeth than the placid Auntie Jus. He'd very nearly been bested by one over France, barely making it back to crash above the chalk cliffs of Kent.

Irrationally, of all the enemies he'd faced, it was the *Zerstörer* Bf 110 in this sinister night-stalking role that Jox loathed most.

He felt a surge of hot anger, driving him to pull over hard to get after it. *This one's mine*, he thought, deadly focussed.

The night-fighter fired again, this time at a slim, silhouetted cruciform shape with elliptical wings. The target was a Spitfire, quite possibly a Black Pig. Further enraged, Jox engaged the raider, firing too high in his fury. The targeted Spit was bowled over by the weight of the *Zerstörer*'s fire, flung off its flight line and began to tumble out of control.

With growing horror, Jox watched the falling aircraft swing into the risers of a hapless paratrooper's parachute. The cords were reeled in by the propellor, acting like a fishing reel. In a matter of seconds, the man in the harness was pulled into the spinning prop and pulped. With the parachute strings now wrapped tightly around its nose, the Merlin engine screamed, then came to a grinding halt, the unidentified Spitfire now falling like a dead weight.

No pilot baled out and Jox was furious at what he'd witnessed. He fired again at the assailant, grunting with satisfaction as he saw hits register. The Bf 110 disengaged immediately, pulling hard for the refuge of the Calabrian coast. Blinking return fire from its rear gunner enticed Jox to follow. 'Oh no, you bloody don't,' he said, chasing after it.

The *Messerschmitt* Bf 110 is fast, but not as fast as a Spitfire Mark IX. The German pilot did have a head start but Jox was soon back in firing range. The racing aircraft were in a desperate escape and pursuit, the land beneath them slipping away to reveal the dark, boiling surface of the ocean.

Away from Etna's glow, Jox discerned teeming numbers of blacked-out sea vessels zigzagging across the narrow strip of water between the land masses. Calabria was visible as a long, pale beach marked by frothing breakers. Distracted from his prey, Jox suddenly became aware of fiery sheets of anti-aircraft fire rising from the ground. With no way of knowing friend from foe, both pursued and pursuer came under a staggering weight of fire. Jox observed the Bf 110 throw off a few sparks, but the fire soon spread, and it became like a comet streaking through the night sky.

Jox's Spit was buffeted and rattled by air bursts, some worryingly close. Inevitably, with a loud bang, one found its mark, striking the leading edge of his starboard wing. He glanced across and it looked like something had taken a big bite out of it. His engine must have been struck too, as it began misfiring, the cockpit filling with the acrid stink of a glycol leak. He pulled back his canopy to clear the air and saw the engine temperature on his control panel was skyrocketing. It wouldn't be long before it seized. *Damn it*, he thought. *I'm not going down in the bloody drink again.*

Desperate to avoid a repeat performance of a few weeks ago, Jox abandoned his chase, straining his eyes in the darkness, desperate for somewhere to get the kite down. Flak was bursting all around, but as he was losing altitude, much of it was overshooting. Spread out in a teaming panorama beneath him, massed enemy sailing vessels of every description churned through the waters of the Straits of Messina in what could only be described as 'Germany's own Dunkirk'.

There was no refuge for him down there, so he banked sharply, trying to turn his descent parallel to the white sand beach of Calabria and the pitch-black lands of Italy that lay beyond.

He'd tried several beach crash landings before, with varying degrees of success, but was less worried about that than what fate had in store once he was down. Sicily had been contested territory, but Italy was still firmly in enemy hands. Surviving the night-time ditching would be one thing, escaping whatever came after was quite another.

Jox felt the cold hand of fear run down his spine. He reached for the comfort of his talisman doll's arm and switchblade, remembering suddenly that he'd left them with Shillington for repair. The realisation filled him with further dread.

He had little time, though, to dwell on his precarious situation. He felt desperately exposed without his lucky charms, but could only brace for impact, fearing what the blacked-out shores of Italy might bring.

Whatever might happen, he was determined, this was not the end of Jox McNabb. He would live to fight another day.

EPILOGUE

London, 1991

'*Château de Beaucastel 1989, Châteauneuf-du-Pape, ça vous plait, monsieur?*' asked the dark suited sommelier of *L'Escargot* restaurant on Greek Street, Soho.

'What do you think?' Luc asked Melanie, who he'd insisted should also try the wine.

'Delicious,' she replied. 'You know how to live well. A man of many talents.'

He smiled at the compliment. 'It should be, it's eye-wateringly expensive, *ma chère*.' He turned to the sommelier and added, '*Incroyable, merci.*'

The man bowed his head and filled their glasses.

The restaurant's low candlelight was presumably designed to create a romantic ambience and also did a good job of disguising the slightly faded grandeur of the ancient French salon. Above them, elegant crystal chandeliers glittered, and the walls were covered with many black and white photographs of notables, most of whom Melanie didn't recognise, despite many wearing military uniform. She did however spot a snap of a youthful-looking Mick Jagger, standing outside the restaurant.

'This wine is produced by *la famille Perrin* in the southern Rhône,' said Luc. 'My father may be a *bon vivant*, but it was actually your grandfather who introduced him to this wine.'

'What? Grandpa didn't know the first thing about wine,' replied Melanie. 'He really wasn't much of a drinker, but if he did, it was usually an old malt.'

'Well, perhaps he didn't know much about this particular wine, but he certainly knew the man who produced it. They met during the war and remained friends afterwards. He would send my father and your grandfather a crate of his finest every Christmas.'

'I think I do remember a crate arriving every year,' said Melanie. 'Was he a friend of your father's too?'

'No, actually they never met, but in a world of "his brother is my brother too", things just happened that way. It was all about friendship and honour back then, which we see so little of these days. *Monsieur* Perrin was a comrade of your grandfather, though. I believe they were actually *Kriegies* together.'

'Prisoners? Where? When? I don't know anything about this.'

'I thought you'd surely know.'

'There is so little of my grandfather's war that I really do know. He never liked to talk about it. I guess perhaps that's what fuels my curiosity about his mysterious life and ultimately kindled my interest in military history. So, where in Germany was he imprisoned? Which of the *Stalags* was it?'

Luc looked a little surprised. 'No, it wasn't at a *Stalag Luft,* it was at a *Campo di Prigione di Guerra.*'

'He was a prisoner in Italy?' Melanie sighed, then began to chuckle at the thought of how her grandfather was still surprising her after all these years. 'I knew he was involved in the Sicilian campaign and had assumed that's why he had the Italy Star. I never realised he'd actually fought in Italy too. I can remember though he would get very angry when people called the troops posted there "The D-Day Dodgers". For some reason, I'd always assumed he'd gone straight from Sicily to prepare for Operation Overlord in France.'

'I think they had quite a tough time of it,' said Luc. 'I know it was a very fraught period for my father too. He was very reluctant to take over command of the Black Pigs, and the squadron was absolutely desolated at the loss of Jox. As my father tells it, the Treble Threes barely survived without him.'

'So, what happened?' asked Melanie.

Before Luc could answer, they were interrupted by the waiter bringing their Entrée course. They'd both opted for the house speciality, *Escargots à la Bourguignonne*, served with a green parsley and shallot sauce and a crusty baguette. It smelt delicious, but it was a good thing they were both having the same dish as there was a lot of garlic involved.

'Did you know the Americans call their main meal Entrées?' said Luc, trying to lighten the conversation. 'That caused me no end of confusion when I was training in the United States.'

Melanie laughed. 'My grandfather always loved working with the Americans but did often say they were "two great nations divided by the same language".' Luc smiled in response. 'So, as I was saying, what happened next?' asked Melanie.

'It's a long story, and I'm not sure I'm best placed to tell it,' said Luc. 'I'm only aware of what my father told me, and he wasn't even there when Jox went through it. All I know is that he was delighted to see Jox return to the squadron after the trials and tribulations he went through to get back. It was like the return of the prodigal son to the bosom of the squadron. My father had been so desolate at the loss of his friend, and the squadron had also been taking heavy losses. He admitted to me that he felt out of his depth, despite having the staunch support of the other veterans clustered around him. He desperately missed Jox's friendship and more importantly his leadership.' Luc raised his glass. 'So, here's to Group Captain Jox McNabb, a fine leader and who, for a most distinguished fighter pilot, certainly did a lot of walking.'

Melanie looked at him quizzically. 'I don't understand.'

'Well, he walked out of Italy. Practically crossed the breadth of the country, through a bitterly contested warzone. My father said it was over two hundred kilometres, including some of the most savage mountains, appalling weather and devastated landscape. I don't know how long it took or what it cost Jox, but my father always said he was never quite the same after that.'

'What do you mean?'

'I'm not exactly sure. My father spoke of a sadness and weariness that Jox carried for the rest of his days. What moved him most, though, was that despite everything, Jox only ever cared about his men, rather than himself.'

Melanie wiped away an escaping tear. 'Yes, my Grandpa Bang-Bang was always a little sad.'

Luc took her hand. 'When I told my father that we were seeing each other, he asked me to give you something, something that means a great deal to him. He told me when the Treble Threes thought they'd lost Jox, as their interim squadron leader, he was given Jox's personal effects. Your grandfather had a batman called Corporal Shillington, who was utterly convinced that Jox would return. He gave my father two precious items, very insistent that they be kept safely until Jox could reclaim them.'

Melanie's eyes widened. 'What were they?'

'One was a switchblade knife, with a signature and a red Maltese Cross. The other, a porcelain doll's arm on which the names of three children had been painted.'

'Yes, I've seen that blade in my grandfather's box of precious things. It fascinated me as a child, but I was never allowed to touch. He kept it with that porcelain doll's arm which I know was his lucky talisman.'

'When he returned, Jox was so touched that my father had kept them safe for him, that he made him a gift.'

'A gift of what?'

'This. My father says it is right that it should return to you.' Luc placed a blue-faced wristwatch on the table between them. 'This is a Rolex Oyster Perpetual, a very fine, if a little fire-damaged, timepiece. Jox inherited it from a fallen comrade. It was very precious to him and was with him throughout his captivity. When he returned to the Black Pigs, he insisted that my father have it to mark his first squadron command.' Luc smiled. 'My father always said he felt like a fraud wearing it, until the day he finally did get command of his own squadron, with Jox's recommendation as his wing leader before D-Day. He has kept it all these years, worn it every day and now wishes for you to have it.'

Luc reached for the watch and turned it over to reveal an engraved silver metal back. It said 'W.I.S.H. III.'

'What does that mean?' asked Melanie.

'I believe the original owner was a young American called William Huntington the Third, known as Billy Three Names. Those were his initials. Apparently, Jox came to see it as standing for his wish to command the Treble Ones. That was never to be.'

Melanie strapped the watch onto her wrist. It was too big, but she turned it and rubbed the hazy glass face with her thumb. It felt good to be wearing something of her grandfather's.

'You must make a wish now, I think,' said Luc.

'It's already been granted,' she replied, and leant across the table to kiss him.

A NOTE TO THE READER

Jox McNabb and many of the characters in his story are the product of my imagination but are often an amalgam of some real historical figures, people I've met and known, and occasionally with an author's conceit, there's a bit of me in there too. I hope they tell a tale that is authentic, compelling, moving and believable.

On occasion, I do embellish the flow of the historical narrative, allowing our Jox to participate in some momentous events, sometimes requiring some creativity with timelines. I hope that I haven't taken too many liberties. Invariably, there will be mistakes, particularly on certain technical aspects, and I take full responsibility and there is never any attempt to deceive.

Some of the events described are entirely fictional, but many did happen or might have happened as described. I hope that readers won't spot the 'joins' between historical fact and fiction but will let you be the judge of that.

In no particular order, here are some historical points that have touched upon this Jox McNabb's most recent adventure.

Operation Torch, the invasion of North Africa in November 1942, did kick off in appalling weather conditions, to the great surprise of Allied servicemen expecting sunnier climes. The offensive was initially 'easier' than expected, but did soon get bogged down because of the weather, the difficult geography and the increasingly dogged resistance from a determined enemy. Logistical challenges, disconnection with the local population, mismatches in the experience between Allies, and the 'lack of grip' or 'SNAFU' mentality were all as described.

Amongst the characters that Jox meets and interacts with, the following are all real, but on occasion, I have 'massaged' the truth.

Squadron Leader Tony 'Bolshie' Bartley, CO of the Treble Ones was a larger than life, gregarious, playboy of a man, a decorated war hero and one of Winston Churchill's 'Few.' He loved a party, mixing with socialites and starlets, but did burn out, eventually leaving North Africa after suffering a mental breakdown. Jox's part in that departure is fictional, but we will see Bolshie again. In real life, he went on to marry the Hollywood actress, Deborah Kerr, and became a film industry executive.

General James 'Jimmy' Doolittle, the leader of the Doolittle raid on the Japanese islands, the United States' first retaliation after the Pearl Harbor attack, is much as described. This 'All American' war hero, a recipient of the Medal of Honor, was tasked with re-invigorating the US Twelfth Air Force in North Africa, going on to command the Fifteenth Air Force over the Mediterranean, and the Eighth Air Force over Western Europe. We will also see him again.

George 'Sheep' Gilroy and Hugh 'Cocky' Dundas, both at some point Jox McNabb's CO as leaders of No. 324 Wing, are also both real, and were remarkable air warriors who I hope I have represented fairly.

It may be hard to believe, but Flying Officer Thomas 'Monty' Falls is also real. One of life's real characters, he was a very talented pianist and was described as the life and soul of the Treble ones. He also did have an extraordinary moustache and was said to look remarkably like King Zog I of Albania. You can judge for yourselves by the portraits I've uploaded onto Instagram. We have of course met Zog and his sisters before, and the rivalry between him and King Victor

Emmanuel III of Italy was also real. I have however contrived to make this, their feelings over the kingdom of Sardinia and the ambitions of British Intelligence's 'Trout' memo into something more than they were. The very real deception plans of Operation Mincemeat and Operation Barclay, have therefore had Operation Tinned Fish added to the mix. The role of Lieutenant Commander Ian Fleming, of later James Bond fame, in the 'Trout' memo and 'Mincemeat' is real, so it is conceivable he would be involved with 'Tinned Fish' too.

Monty Falls involvement is of course also fictional, but he did serve with the Treble Ones in North Africa and Malta, and was tragically lost over the sea between Malta and Sicily. He is commemorated on the Commonwealth Aircrew Malta Memorial, near Floriana. Similarly, Sergeant George 'Longers' Longbottom and Flying Officer Dennis 'Mossy' Moss were both lost in Tunisia, and are buried in the Medjez-El-Bab CWGC cemetery. They were aged 20 and 21 respectively. Monty Falls was just 20. *Per Ardua Ad Astra*, gentlemen.

Whilst describing the harsh conditions in Tunisia, I have also tried to convey the richness of culture and historical heritage of this ancient land. The conflict is only one of the more recent that has tragically blighted the region, a land that has been a battlefield for centuries. As a young man, I visited Tunisia many times and was always struck by the grandeur of the landscape and the vast ancient cities, appearing unexpectedly at a turn in the road, seemingly in the middle of nowhere. Bulla Regia and Carthage are both breathtaking, with history seeping from every stone, column, temple and mosaic.

In marked contrast, and of more modern origin, there are several vast cemeteries, both Allied and Axis, where those who were lost in the conflicts now lie. The North Africa American Cemetery is in Carthage itself, with almost three thousand burials and four thousand missing commemorated here alone. What was particularly humbling for me at the time, was seeing that most were barely older than I was. During the research for this book, one snippet I came across really chilled me. That so many more, here and elsewhere, are missing rather than buried was explained by the vast wildness of the Tunisian battlefields, where many of the lost lay for long periods, becoming carrion for the feral dogs and wildlife living and presumably thriving on the results of man's conflict. Axis forces even dropped propaganda leaflets on Allied lines referring to these packs of wild dogs, warning the long-suffering troops of the fate that awaited them.

In this story, I have also written about the terrible forces of nature that have and still do affect the region. Earthquakes and volcanic eruptions have plagued the Mediterranean for centuries. I'm pleased to report that the magnificent ancient ruins of Bulla Regia were not further devastated by the earthquake that I described, but I was however terribly struck whilst writing of the terrible devastation and loss of life in Morrocco, Syria and Turkey during 2023. Similarly, accounts of the past earthquakes, tsunamis and volcanic eruptions which I detail in Sicily are all real. Vulcan and his cohort of gods have been toying with the lives of the people of this region since the dawn of time.

Nearer to home, Bournemouth, were I now live, is in Dorset, England. The seaside town features significantly in Jox's story. On the 23rd of May 1943 it endured its worst air raid of the war. The attack was on a Sunday lunchtime and was as terrible as I've described. This raid has a major impact on Jox and indeed his granddaughter Melanie. For an author, it is a big decision to have one of his principal characters die, but losing Moose and his nascent family, was I feel important to communicating the devastating impact of war, and how it can strike unexpectedly and seemingly so randomly. The losses and devastation to the town are as described, and I have visited the graves of the lost many times.

Moving on to the storyline in Sicily, one aspect of the island's history I couldn't ignore was the insidious influence of *la Cosa Nostra,* the Mafia. It was, as recounted, exported to the United States through the mass immigrations that followed several natural disasters, but never fully left the island either. Mussolini's regime was arguably the most successful at curbing its sinister impact, but the 'Black Hand' continues to darken the island to this day. During WW2, the Allies, particularly the US intelligence services, did try to harness the *soldati* of this shadowy army, but it is difficult to discern quite how successfully. During the Italian campaign, which Jox will doubtless be engaged in, he is more than likely to cross these dark forces again.

The launch of Operation Husky, the invasion of Sicily was preceded by Operation Corkscrew, the liberation of Pantelleria, much as I've described, where the invading forces were met with much less resistance than expected. I have partially attributed this success to the fictitious 'Operation Tinned Fish', but it is true that perhaps a degree of over-confidence was created prior to the launch of Husky itself. The British and American airborne operations did occur disastrously, as I've described, however I have had to reverse and combine the timings to allow Jox and the Treble Threes to participate in both and describe the tragic events. What they first witnessed was the worst case of 'friendly fire' or combat fratricide between American forces during the whole of the war. Out of a hundred and forty-four transports, twenty-three were lost and a further thirty-seven were badly damaged. Eighty-eight paratroopers and aircrew were killed, with a further sixty-nine missing, presumed dead, and a hundred and sixty-two were wounded. Among the lost was Brigadier General Charles Keerans Jr, the assistant commander of the US 82nd Airborne.

Operation Ladbroke, the first-ever mass glider assault attempted by Allied forces, used gliders to transport the men of the British 1st Airlanding Brigade. In the hours that followed, a combination of strong winds, low visibility, and inexperienced tow and glider pilots meant many gliders were released too early. Sixty-nine failed to reach land, with 252 men drowning. Of the fifty-six gliders that did reach land, the majority were scattered and nowhere near their target. It is said that no battleplan remains intact upon first contact with the enemy, but there was certainly no denying that Operation Husky started disastrously. The tables would turn and the Allies would eventually prevail, but the Sicilian campaign, with its relentless heat, constant mosquitoes and related diseases, the widespread devastation and unsanitary conditions, not to mention the challenging geography and the sheer savagery of combat would remain seared in the memories of many. The 'grande finale' of the campaign did involve a massed airborne drop on the slopes of Mount Etna, near the city of Messina, with paratroopers from both belligerents jumping over the lava fields at the same time. The scene could hardly be more evocative of Dante's inferno.

As is my way, there are a number of names, stories, snippets scattered throughout the story, like the 'Easter eggs' in some movies. They are there to keep me amused whilst writing, but also hopefully are enjoyed by the readers when discovered or realised.

I hope you've enjoyed reading my fourth Jox McNabb novel. Reviews and ratings are very important to authors, so if *The*

Vulcan and the Straits, has touched, entertained or thrilled you, I hope you would be willing to post a review on **Amazon** or **Goodreads**. Readers can also connect with me on **Twitter (@P33ddy)** or **via my website**. Also, for anyone who may be interested, I have loaded some images on **Instagram (jox_mcnabb)** that inspired me to write the story of Jox's remarkable war.

Per Ardua Ad Astra.

Best regards,

Patrick Larsimont

patricklarsimont.com

Sapere Books is an exciting new publisher of brilliant fiction and popular history.

To find out more about our latest releases and our monthly bargain books visit our website:
saperebooks.com

Printed in Great Britain
by Amazon

43148296R00215